Part Three

Invincible

Contact details for the author can be found on

www.the realtomfield.com

On Twitter @therealtomfield

Facebook: The Real Tom Field

For Louis

My best friend

Maggie Davenport had twenty nine minutes left to live.

She put her eighteen month old son, Troy, down in his filthy cot. He had not stopped crying for the past five hours.

Maggie was uneducated and lived in a dirty apartment block in Queens, which social services had provided her with to get her off the street. She had been raped nine months ago by four men, and exactly nine months later Troy had been born. She tried so hard to see him as the one good thing in her life, but with each day that passed, she felt more and more trapped by him because he acted as a constant reminder of how worthless her life was. Troy had now become her prison, and there was no escaping prison for people like Maggie.

Until now.

The Columbian guy who regularly walked the halls of her apartment building had seen her looking exhausted and unkempt.

Approaching her, he asked her if she wanted to escape from her tiredness and destitution for a moment, telling her that he could offer her the feeling of joy and pleasure that everyone who was the target of her envy regularly felt.

He explained to her that he had a pill that would take her to the places where she would be free like them. He said it would make her feel alive and energetic, and she could run to wherever her fantasies wanted to take her. She had immediately invited him into her filthy apartment.

4

She asked what the pill was called. He replied with one word.

"Invincible."

She put the pill in her mouth and within four confusing minutes, her world changed.
Warmth and joy rushed through her frail body. She saw sunshine and was running through open fields, and then a moment later, she was in a big house with a grand swimming pool in the garden. All of her old school friends were lined up .Sitting on a garden wall looking at her with envy.
The one great love of her life, Aaron Wisley, was there, looking at her with such desire that her whole body longed for his touch.
She savoured the way her life could have been; engulfed by the dreams that she had dared not to believe in, but longed for to come true. Right then, she genuinely felt that she was living that life. This vision, this reality, was heaven. It lasted for twenty five minutes.

And then everything changed.

All of a sudden, she couldn't breathe. She felt a searing pain shoot through her chest, and she pulled at the tee shirt covering her breasts, trying to get air to her body and her lungs. Then she collapsed to the floor and her visions changed.
All of her old friends, who had looked at her with such envy a few moments ago, were now laughing at her.

She saw Troy open his arms wide for her to pick him up. And then everything went dark.

The Columbian guy took out his cell phone and called Miami,

"Twenty nine minutes," he said into the phone and then hung up.

He stood up, looked at Troy crying in the cot, walked over to him, and smothered him with a dirty, stained blanket until he stopped crying. He didn't want the cops being called by the neighbours sick of hearing a child screaming.
He walked back across the dirty carpet, stepped over Maggie's lifeless body and walked out of the apartment.

In Miami, the man who had received the phone call looked out over his vast, immaculate grounds and dialled a number on his cell phone. He exchanged no pleasantries with whoever answered, he simply said, "Everything had better be ready. I want them all there by tomorrow evening, all thirty one of them. If you fail me, your whole family will be dead by midnight tomorrow," he then hung up.

He was sure the person on the end of the line would not fail him. Just as sure as he knew that he was going to unlock the secret to running the most powerful drug cartel the world had ever known.

ONE

Denver

Ryan Ward stepped off of the jet at Denver International Airport and squinted in response to the bright afternoon sun. Mike Lawson was still flirting with the pretty stewardess who had waited on them during their four and a half hour flight from New York.

There was a dark blue Ford Taurus waiting for them, the keys left in the ignition, fifty yards away.

Ward headed towards the car and Lawson followed ten feet behind, busy tapping on his cell phone to save the stewardess's cell number. He reached the car and climbed into the front passenger seat and waited for Lawson to climb into the driver's seat.

"I want your focus on this Mike," he said without looking at him.

"I'm switching it on...... now!" Lawson replied.

Ward rolled his eyes and shook his head.

Mike Lawson, ex-SAS soldier, and current MI6 operative, was good, very good, but Ward felt a constant frustration towards him that his need to captivate and sleep with every pretty girl he met was stopping him from being the best.

He continually lectured Lawson on his need to focus, and Lawson continually made light of it. The truth was, in the field, Lawson was among the best that he had ever worked with, but there was more to being a Deniable than being a killing machine.

Being able to analyse events and predict movements during the quieter moments of a mission, was equally as important as the ability to kill a man in the heat of battle. Lawson spent too much of his quiet time thinking about his next female conquest and Ward was sure that one day this would lead to his death.

"Where is this Coal Creek place?" Lawson asked, as he started playing with the cars satellite navigation system.

"It's on the edge of Mount Falcon Park," he replied, and watched as Lawson started to type in the address.

"Forty minute drive," Lawson said as he adjusted his seat to provide more leg room for his impressive six foot four frame and started the engine.

They pulled away and drove up to the perimeter fence where a guard looked at the car plates, and then waved them through straight onto Pena Boulevard without them stopping. No need for checks, The Old Man would have taken care of all necessary checks, or rather, ensured that there was no need for them.

As they drove onto the Boulevard, a bright red Kawasaki motorbike sped past them, the guy riding it, carrying a bag which contained, what Ward assumed, were fishing rods, over his right shoulder.

"I hate fishing," Lawson said.

"Lots of sexy young women go fishing," he replied.
"Really" Lawson enquired an air of excitement and interest rushing through his voice.
"No Mike, not really," Ward said rolling his eyes and shaking his head for at least the tenth time that day.
"This Tom Bass guy," Lawson said, "We are going to kill him and then we are going straight back to New York?"
"That's the idea," he replied, and said no more.
But the more he thought about Tom Bass, the more he decided that killing him was not enough.
Eloisa Hammond was Ward's future, the one sane thing in his crazy world, and she had put him onto Tom Bass. Eloisa worked for the United Nations, in a formal role within child protection, but she was effectively in place to feed information through to him, regarding the evil men who trafficked, abused or hurt children. Ward would simply eliminate them in the downtime that he had.
His main role was as a Deniable. He was part of an elite team of operatives, made up of five operatives from the CIA, and five from the U.K's MI6. They were off the books entirely, non –existent people who had no affiliation to either government. There was no irony in the name they were given, it was a fact. If they were caught doing anything that was illegal, the governments would deny their existence.
 The Old Man, or Centrepoint as he was officially codenamed, could not sanction Ward's operations offline that Eloisa handed to him, but he would ensure that whatever resources he needed were always readily

available. It was his way of pacifying Ward and keeping him on board.

Tom Bass was evil.
Pure evil.

Bass employed teams of people who trawled the deprived inner-city areas of the States, looking for hookers and drug addicts who were desperate for their next fix. His teams would select the more presentable women from these areas, and convince them to become pregnant for him on the promise of unlimited drugs. Ward had discovered that Bass would get his teams to carry out a quick HIV test on the addicts, and anyone found to carry the virus would be dumped back on the street.
Literally dumped.
Their favourite trick; which they boasted about, was to throw those women infected with the virus out of moving vans as they discarded them.
The women that were clear of any virus would be taken to safe houses, impregnated by his team, and kept in squalor for nine months until the baby was born, then they were discarded, back onto the streets and more than likely, thrown out of a moving van also.
The babies were nurtured for a few years and then sold on the dark web to the sickest of paedophiles.
Tom Bass was going to die today; there was no doubt in Ward's mind about that.
He had got Bass's attention by getting his computer experts, Nicole-Louise and Tackler, to steal two million dollars from him.

After a brief discussion, where Ward posed as an interested buyer who wanted to purchase some of the children, a meeting was set up for this afternoon, and Bass's money returned with an additional fee of a half million dollars that Bass demanded as an introduction fee for meeting him.

Thirty five minutes later they were driving towards Mount Falcon Park along I-70 East. They crept out of the suburban areas and into the vast, open expanse of mountains and fields, without really noticing the subtle change in their surroundings before their satellite navigation informed them that they had arrived at their destination.

They first drove past the ranch to assess what they were walking into, but the truth was, there was very little to see. There was a wooden fence that marked out the boundary to the ranch, and an opening that led onto a dirt track which ran as far as the eye could see. There were no buildings visible from the road.

"Not really much point in recon," Lawson said, "Do you know how many men he's likely to have with him?" he asked.

Ward shook his head,

"I'll call The Optician," he replied, "He has been here since this morning."

The Optician.

Wards closest friend in the world.

Yet he had never met him.

He was his protector, the one constant who accompanied him in everything he did.

And he was also the best sniper on the planet, revered throughout the Special Forces world.

He pulled out his cell and pressed speed dial.

"Finally arrived I see?" The Optician asked without any greeting.

"Lawson drives like an old lady," he replied, "How practical does taking Bass out appear from where you are?"

"There are two outbuildings to the right of the main house. From what I can make out, one has women inside; due to me looking at a guy right now walking out, doing his pants up, and the other must be where the babies are. I've seen three women walking in there in the last five minutes carrying blankets," The Optician replied.

"How many men?"

"I've counted five around the buildings, I can't see in the house. The five I can drop whenever you want, they are all in my sights."

"Then we will just have to bring the rest of them out to you," he said and hung up the phone.

"Drive up to the house," he said to Lawson.

"Don't tell me, we are just going to knock on the door as usual?"

"It has worked every other time we have done it."

Lawson put the car in gear and started heading up the dirt track. They drove at least a mile before the buildings came into view about half a mile in the distance. The track was dead straight and narrow. Two cars would struggle to pass each other without one of them moving off the track onto the rough terrain that ran endlessly alongside. As the house came into view, with the outbuildings on the right, his phone vibrated.

"You missing me already?"

"Two shooters have just climbed onto the flat roofs on either side of the house and are crouching behind the walls. You sure this guy wants to negotiate with you?"

"You can take them out quietly?" Ward asked.

"Of course I can. But be careful on this, I don't think this Bass guy plans on talking."

"As soon as me and Lawson step out of the car, take them out," he said and hung up the phone.

He pulled out his silenced Glock from his jacket and tucked it into his waistband at the back of his pants. Lawson did the same while keeping one hand on the wheel.

They eventually reached the buildings, after what seemed like an eternity, and pulled up just fifty feet from the house, where the track turned from dirt into a beautifully laid bright red paved parking area.

The house was a painted brilliant white and reminded him of the old houses the cotton masters used to live in a long time ago.

"Leave the talking to me, you just look tough and dumb," he said to Lawson.

"A different approach this time then?" Lawson asked sarcastically and smiled.

Ward smiled back.

"Whoever he comes out with, shoot them before they get on top of us, I don't think they want to talk," he said.

Lawson nodded.

They stepped out of the car.

Four men walked out of the house in a neat line, five feet behind them, a guy in his early fifties, wearing a Stetson, a checked shirt, jeans and cowboy boots, was peering over their shoulders cautiously.

Out of the corner of his right eye, Ward saw a feint mist of red spray and then two seconds later, caught a glimpse of the same colour in his left eye. The guys on the roof were down. He knew that definitively.

The Optician never missed.

"Mr Ryan," a deep voice came from behind the four guys, Ward's view of Bass was still obstructed, "You are either desperate or dumb to come here, which one is it?" Bass asked.

Before the guys had a chance to step closer, Lawson reached into the back of his pants with lightning speed, pulled out his Glock and shot all four of the lead guys in the chest.

Two seconds.

Four direct hits.

Four dead guys.

"Impressive," Ward said. Lawson smiled at him.

Tom Bass stopped in his tracks. He didn't call for help; his brain was still trying to compute what he had just seen. A few seconds later, he looked over his left shoulder, up to the roof of the house.

"They won't help you," Ward said, "They were dead before these idiots. The other five guys you have here are dying just about now," he added.

Bass just stood there, not saying a word.

"So, can we get down to business?" he asked.

"What do you want?" Bass asked.

"I told you on the phone," he replied.

"You want the merchandise, take them, take them all, there are 10 of them in that building there," Bass said hurriedly, pointing to the nearest of the two outbuildings to their right.

"Free of charge?"

"Yes."

"How many women do you have here?"

"Fourteen," Bass replied.

"How many are pregnant?"

"Fourteen."

"And the mothers of those ten babies have been gotten rid of?" Ward asked.

Bass said nothing in response to the question.

"You throw them out of moving vans at sixty miles per hour," he continued, "There can be no possible reason for that, other than knowing that you will cause them horrendous pain."

Bass still said nothing; he was looking over Ward's shoulder, willing for someone, anyone, to come to his rescue.

"No one's coming," he said, "They are all dead by now."

"I can give you money," Bass said desperately.

"I'm going to take your money anyway, so as of this moment, you are penniless and all alone," he replied.

"What do you want?"

"I want you to take me to those outbuildings there and show me what is inside them," he said, pointing his Glock at Bass, and then towards the outbuildings to indicate to Bass that he was to lead the way.

Bass dropped his shoulders and started walking towards the nearest outbuilding. The building was solid, built of thick pinewood sleepers. There were no windows, just a solid double door that was painted green. There was a metal bar that ran the full length of the doors that connected to a metal hasp, with a hinge on the left hand side, and a padlock on the right. Bass took out a set of keys and after sifting through them for a few seconds, slid a key into the padlock, unlocked it, and swung the bar around to the left. He opened the door and walked in. They followed two feet behind.

The first thing that hit them both was the stench. It smelt like a sewer.

The second thing was the noise. The sound of babies crying, and toddlers coughing, echoed around the room, the noise magnified by the solid pine walls allowing no sound to escape.

The room was dark and Bass moved his arm to the wall and hit a light switch.

There were ten cots in the building, five on each side. The cries of the babies intensified when the light came on, and Ward noticed that in four of the cots with high sides about three feet tall, the children were standing up, holding onto the spindles for support, it looked like they were in a prison cell.

Ward and Lawson just stood there, feeling sick to the core at what they were looking at. Ward wanted to kill Bass right then but simply said, "Take me to the other building," and dug his gun sharply into Bass's ribs.

They walked out of the door and across to the adjacent building, which had bright red doors. Bass went through the same motion of opening the door, by selecting the right key, unlocking the padlock and swinging the metal bar back and pulling the doors open.

He walked in and they both followed him.

There were seven metal beds on each side of the room. On each bed, was a pregnant woman, some much further into their pregnancies than others.

They were all chained to the headrests of the bed by their right wrists. Two of them were eating a porridge like substance out of a bowl with their fingers.

The same stench of a sewer hit Ward, and he noticed the bed pans under the beds that were all full to the brim.

"Unchain them now," he demanded.

Bass moved over to the first bed and started sifting through his keys and started to unlock the first woman.

"I want you to let me kill him," Lawson said.

"I know what we will do," he replied.

The two of them stood there motionless, watching Bass as he continued unchaining the women. Even after they were free, they just sat on the edge of their beds looking at Ward and Lawson. They had no idea that they were there to save them. Ward did not let himself imagine the horror that they had been exposed to.

"Call The Old Man and get police and social services over here immediately," he whispered to Lawson quietly, "But give us a fifteen minute window before they arrive."

Lawson nodded and stepped out of the building.

Ward watched Bass unlock the last of the women .He then stood at the far end of the building, as far away from Ward as he could.

"Come here," he shouted to Bass, "Bring two chains and padlocks with you."

All of the women sat motionless on their beds, looking at Ward with fear on their faces.

Bass picked up two chains and padlocks and walked across to Ward and handed them to him, just as Lawson walked back in,

"He will have them here in fifteen," he said.

"In fifteen minutes," Ward said clearly and loudly to the room, "The police and other agencies will be here to look after you. No more harm will come to you."

To emphasise this point, Lawson unleashed a quick solid right hook that caught Bass on the left side of his jaw and knocked him off of his feet and onto the floor.

"There are ten babies and toddlers in the building next door, I want you all to go next door and look after them until the police arrive, and they all need cleaning and changing. Can you do that?"

To a woman, they all nodded and stood up. They started to walk out of the building, and the third woman that walked past them spat at Bass who was still on the floor holding his jaw. She was young, no older than nineteen, and she looked at least seven months pregnant. And now, she would have a constant reminder of her ordeal. For a brief moment, he wondered if she would keep the baby of hand it over as soon as it was born. Either way, it was not how it should have been.

When the last woman had left the building, he reached down and pulled Bass up to his feet by his hair. He screamed as Ward yanked hard on his hair.

"You are the vilest of the vile," Ward said calmly, "And I deal with a lot of scumbags but you top the pile."

Bass said nothing.

He turned him around and looked into his eyes. He saw the fear, saw the desperation and then noticed a panic spread across his face.

Tom Bass looked into Ward's eyes and saw a monster. Ward suddenly looked about seven feet tall to him. What Bass saw was a hundred dead people, people like him, who had come face to face with this man and died, all swimming in a pool of agony deep within his eyes.

"Just kill me and get it over and done with," Bass pleaded.

Ward looked at him and smiled a knowing smile that frightened Bass even more.

"What goes around comes around," he said, "Mike, how long do you think that drive to the house was?"

"About mile and a half." Lawson replied

"That Taurus outside, how long does it take to get to sixty miles an hour?" he asked, holding up the chains and padlock in his left hand.

Lawson smiled,

"Let's see," he replied as he pushed his Glock into Bass's side and led him out of the building doors. Lawson led Bass out to the rear of the car and as they reached the trunk, he stepped in front of him and unleashed a solid right jab into his stomach, all two hundred and forty pounds of his giant frame transferred into his right fist. Bass doubled over and fell to his knees, hitting his forehead on the car trunk on the way down. Ward tossed Lawson a chain and padlock, and then secured Bass's left wrist to the bumper and padlocked the chain, while Lawson did the same with Bass's right wrist and he tossed Ward the key when he was satisfied Bass was secure.

Tom Bass was on his knees, his arms spread wide, chained to the bumper of the car.

Ward looked down at him, and lightly kicked him in the side of the ribs to get his attention.

Bass looked up at him.

"You have nothing. I've taken all of your money and killed all of your men. You are now going to die," he said calmly, "We are also going to find all of the people who paid you money for the babies and hunt them down and kill them too."

Bass looked up at Ward and tears started to fill his eyes. Tears of fear.

That was all Ward needed to see.

"Let's go Mike," he said and they both climbed into the car.

Lawson started the engine and accelerated quickly. Eight seconds later, they were bouncing along the dirt track at sixty five miles an hour.

The screams of Bass were drowning out the engine as the dry ground ripped his clothes to shreds and then started tearing into his skin. With every bump in the track, Bass's face smashed into the dirt and a mile into the drive, there was no skin left on his face, legs or torso.

They reached the end of the track and stopped at the perimeter fence. They stepped out of the car and walked around to the trunk.

Tom Bass was lying face down. Ward unlocked the padlocks, stepping over his body to reach the left wrist and watched as Bass slumped to the floor.

He rolled him over.

Bass was unrecognisable but to Ward's delight, he was still alive. That confirmed to him that he would have felt the pain right the way through the journey.

Lawson looked down at him and kicked him hard in the ribs.

Bass groaned.

"How did that feel?" Ward asked, as Bass continued to groan, "Shall we do it again?"

Tom Bass turned and looked up at Ward. He begged him to die without speaking, his eyes were pleading for it. Ward obliged.

He lifted his Glock, pointed it at Bass's face and pulled the trigger, blowing what little flesh he had left clean away. Lawson shot him in the back of the head as his body slumped forward.

"Let's go," Ward said, they climbed back into the car. Lawson pulled away and looked at Bass's body lying in the dirt like a dead animal and he smiled to himself.

Ward pulled out his cell phone, and wrote a text message that simply said, 'It's done' and sent it to Eloisa.

He then leant back in his chair and exhaled loudly.

"Now back to New York?" Lawson asked.

"Yes," he replied, "Maybe I will get a few days off."

Ryan Ward could not have been more wrong.

TWO

Miami

Pablo Cardona stepped out into the glorious morning sun onto his patio which looked out over his vast grounds. His loyal foot soldiers were all sitting at their allocated tables, like a football team awaiting their instructions, twenty four of them in total. All eyes were on the coach. He reached his table and one of his lieutenants, who was sitting on a chair on his own, to the left of the table, stood up, pulled out a chair, and once Cardona was seated, he snapped his fingers at the servant who promptly approached the table carrying a pot of coffee. Everyone watched as Cardona slowly and carefully poured his coffee into his cup and took a sip. He nodded his approval to himself and then put his cup down.

"You are all ready to leave?" he said to no one in particular.

His lieutenant was the only one to respond.

"Yes Mr Cardona," he replied.

"Run it past me one more time so I have faith that there will be no mistakes," Cardona said.

"Eight teams of three men," the lieutenant said, "We have spotters on each of the premises and they have all confirmed this morning that everyone is where they should be."

Cardona nodded his approval.

"The eight targets are all in sight, and the men are waiting to move on your command," the lieutenant stated.

"The holding blocks are ready for use?"

"Yes Mr Cardona," The lieutenant replied, "Everything is exactly how you instructed."

"And the lab is ready?" Cardona asked.

"Yes, with everything that you demanded available."

Cardona smiled. He liked the fact that his men understood that he demanded and never asked.

"Give me the numbers again?"

"Twenty three to be held in block one, and the eight specialists in block two. They will be kept apart until you instruct otherwise," the lieutenant replied.

Pablo Cardona stood up.

"Then go now. Make sure you frighten them all so they know how bad we are," he said, he turned and walked back into his sprawling mansion.

Pablo Cardona walked through his grand entrance hall, with its marble floors, and grand open staircase, and stopped in front of a big, solid oak door and took out a set of keys. He unlocked the door and walked in, closing the door behind him and putting the key in the lock.

In the centre of the room was a chair.

Tied to the chair was a man.

Cardona walked over to the man and pulled a chair out from under the table to the right of him, and placed it directly in front him, three feet away.

"Are you comfortable?" Cardona asked.

The man said nothing.

"What I don't understand is that you could have been somewhere safe, away from all of this, and yet you chose to interfere with what I am doing," Cardona said, "Is it a sense of righteousness, or is it because you want a slice of my pie?"

The man said nothing.

"I know torturing you won't help me, you are trained to withstand pain, but I need to know exactly what you know and who you have told."

The man said nothing; he just stared straight into Cardona's eyes, no fear, no emotion and no anger. He could see the man was calculating, analysing and thinking.

"You mean nothing to me," Cardona said, "But I have to keep you alive because the people helping me want you alive. I don't even know who you are or what they want from you, but I will tell you now, when they no longer need you, I will cut your eyes out while you are still alive," he added, and then laughed a loud and long laugh.

Adams Key – Upper Florida Keys

Adams Key is an island north of the upper Florida Keys in Biscayne National Park, and it was the perfect place for Pablo Cardona to do what he had to do. The key is only accessible by boat, and overnight docking is prohibited. Very few people ever visited the island. The majority of the island was covered in trees, and there were very few clearings. Cardona's men had spent the last three months preparing the island for their guests. They had erected five buildings.

There were two for their visitors, one for work, one for his men, and one for Cardona. He would need to be on site at all times until the experiment was completed. His powerful new friends had ensured that there would be no unwelcome visitors to the island, and they had somehow managed to arrange for DEA agents to patrol the area by boat, turning away any unsuspecting college kids who thought they would check the island out.

The first building erected; for their visitors; was almost like a sauna. It was built out of solid wood sleepers; four inches thick, and the flat roof had been laid using three inch plywood and secured with six inch nails. There were no windows in the building, and the only light was a single bulb hanging down from the centre of the room. There were no beds or chairs, and the twenty three people who were going to be imprisoned inside, would have to lie down on a rough, splinter laden floor made of hardwood.

The second building was for the important visitors. It was built exactly the same way as the first building but the inside was luxurious in comparison. There were eight metal beds, four lined up on either side, each one with its own thin mattress and blanket. Air conditioning was fed into the room through two vents, and there was a toilet in the far corner. No privacy would be afforded to those who used the toilet, but they should think themselves lucky that they had it. A small sink with cold running water was to the left of the toilet. They would at least be able to sleep. Keeping them alert, refreshed and focussed was crucial to getting this done quickly.

The third building was the biggest of the three. It was where Cardona's men would rest. It was at least five times bigger than the other buildings, and had a kitchen, showers and fourteen beds. Only fourteen would be allowed to rest at any one time, the rest of the men would be watching the visitors or patrolling the island.

The fourth building was where Cardona would be staying. As expected, it was the grandest of all of the buildings. It had carpet, windows, air conditioning, a large fridge, stocked with the finest foods, and a bathroom that had both a shower and a bath. It had a king size bed with a thick mattress, and a leather three seat sofa against one of the walls.

The fifth building was the most important building. It was where the work would be done, where the answer to the only thing preventing him from total domination would be found. And it would be found, he was sure of that. He was sure thirty one times over that within two days, he would be holding in his hand the key to dictating to every cartel in the Americas who did what, when and who with.

Pablo Cardona was on the verge of greatness.

No one could stop him.

THREE

Pinecrest – Outer Miami

Dr Robert Anderton lived a perfect life. He was married to his college sweetheart Claire, whom he had met when they were both studying chemistry at the University of Florida twenty two years ago. They both achieved masters degrees, and had begun promising careers at the same time, working for a private pharmaceutical company. He had rapidly progressed through the ranks from part of a team, to running his own team, and now, he was the head of product development at Newton Pharmaceutical Limited, one of the biggest pharmaceutical companies in Florida. Nine years ago, Claire had given birth to twin boys, Robert and Adam, three years after that, their daughter Lucy was born. Claire devoted her life to raising their children, and it had been ten years since she had stepped inside a lab. They lived in Pinecrest, an affluent area about thirty minutes outside Miami. Their house on SW 69th CT was beautiful. It had six bedrooms, beautifully manicured lawns, and a large pool in the back garden. Weekends were spent taking the children to soccer, or on camping trips, and they were the perfect All American family. Life was good.

Dr Robert Anderton was thinking how lucky he was as he watched Claire put the freshly baked croissants on the table. Breakfast was always a happy time in the Anderton household; they were all most definitely morning people. His son Adam was explaining to him how babies are born without kneecaps, and they don't appear until the child is two to six years of age, a fact he didn't know, but told himself that he would check later. Robert Junior was desperately trying to hide the fact that he was reading something on his cell phone under the table, by looking around innocently every few seconds, because normally he would be reminded that electrical equipment is not allowed when people were eating, but such were Dr Robert's spirits today, he decided to pretend that he hadn't noticed. Lucy was being Lucy. She was eating her breakfast without fuss or noise and throwing a smile in his direction every time he looked at her.

He knew without doubt that he was the luckiest man in the world.

Life wasn't just good.

Life was perfect.

And then, with one simple ring of the doorbell, his whole world collapsed.

He stood up from his chair with his croissant still in his hand and walked to answer the door. He opened it and froze.

Three men were standing in front of him pointing handguns at him; over their shoulders he could see a dark blue van with the side doors pulled open. Before he could speak, the tallest of the three men stepped through the doorway and jabbed him hard in the face with the butt of the gun. He was momentarily blinded, but was still aware enough to hear the other two men step into the hall and shut the door.

He managed to quickly regain focus, and looked at the three men. They were all South American, he could tell that by their features and their skin colour, and his immediate thought was for his family.

"Please, take what you want," he pleaded, "I have money in a safe upstairs."

The tall guy looked at him and smiled.

"Where are your family?" he asked.

"They aren't here."

"Try the kitchen," he said to the two other guys. He watched as they walked towards the kitchen.

"Please, don't hurt them," Anderton pleaded.

The tall guy smiled at him again.

A few moments later, Claire came walking out of the kitchen, with Robert and Adam in front of her. One of the guys was pushing his handgun into her back.

She looked petrified.

Not because she had a gun in her back but because the other guy was carrying Lucy.

Robert Anderton felt sick.

"What do you want? Please, don't hurt my children," he pleaded.

The tall guy walked over towards Claire and the boys. He raised his handgun and pointed it at the two terrified children.

"Enney, meeny, miney, mo," he said as he moved the gun from one frightened boy to the other, "Which one dies, I don't yet know," he added, and then laughed. Claire moved the boys behind her and stood in front of them, desperately trying to protect her children, like any mother would.

The tall guy looked at her and smiled. And then he unleashed a quick and full force uppercut, his fist caught her in the centre of her stomach, and she doubled over immediately, all the air in her lungs leaving her body at the moment of impact.

Robert Anderton sprung to the defence of his wife and was immediately punched in the side of the face by the tall guy, he staggered back and the guy pointed the gun at Claire,

"One more move and I shoot the bitch," he said, looking at Anderton, a threat that stopped him in his tracks. Claire was still struggling to breathe and the two boys both started crying. Lucy was still being Lucy, no fuss, no panic, just watching everything that was happening.

"What do you want?" Anderton screamed, anger and the need to protect his family far outweighing any fear that he felt.

"We are going on a family vacation," the tall guy said.

"On a vacation. A vacation where?"

"To a place where you can work."

"I will go wherever you want me to go," Anderton said, "Just please leave my family here."

"You need your family to complete your work Anderton," the tall guy replied.

"What do you mean, complete my work?"

"You are the first one of eight Dr Anderton. So walk out of the door, into the van, and if you say one more word to me, I will kill your bitch and then the little bitch next," the tall guy said, pointing at Lucy.

"It will be OK," Anderton said to Claire, as one of the other guys pulled her to her feet by her hair and started pushing her towards the door.

"It will be, only, if you find the answer to the problem," the tall guy said, as he pushed Robert Anderton out of the house, across the drive and into the waiting vehicle.

"What is the problem?" Anderton asked.

"Get in the van," the tall guy said.

Westchester – Outer Miami

The fourth person taken was Dr Sardar Taremi. He was a forty one year old chemist who lived in Westchester. He had lived in the U.S. for the past twenty two years after arriving in America from Iran, and gaining asylum from the tyranny of the Ayatollah's regime on political grounds. He had built an honest and rewarding life in The States, and he considered himself wholly American. He had worked on Dr Anderton's team for the past four years and he was one of his most trusted colleagues. As soon as Robert Anderton had been promoted to running his own research team, Taremi was the first person he had requested to be part of it. He had married a Chinese woman named Liu Peng, whom he had met when she was working as a lab assistant, when Newton was an up and coming company, and not the giant it was today. They lived in a small bungalow on SW 94th Avenue. They didn't need any more than the two bedrooms they had, as they had learned two years ago that Liu Peng was unable to have children. This did not affect their relationship at all, they just accepted it and continued to live a simple life of working, spending evenings watching the sunset over the sea from their favourite spot on the beach, and their greatest passion, cooking. They lived a completely inoffensive existence. They were good people.

Dr Taremi was in the kitchen preparing breakfast while Liu Peng was marinating some beef for the culinary experimenting they were planning on doing when they got home from work that evening, when there was a knock on the door.

"I'll get it," Liu Peng said as she rinsed her hands under the tap, and walked out of the kitchen wiping them on a towel. She reached the front door and opened it. She caught a glimpse of three South American men standing on the doorstep. The next thing she saw was a fist approaching her at lightning speed, and then she felt the impact of the fist on her jaw and she stumbled back, falling onto the floor and landing on her backside.

Dr Taremi heard the sickening sound of fist hitting flesh, and dropped the waffles he was holding in his hand, and quickly moved to the kitchen door, just as a thick set man burst through it.

Before he could protest, the man punched him hard in the stomach, his small five foot five frame lifted off the floor by the impact. He fell to his knees, all of the air knocked out of him.

The man stepped forward, and another man walked into the kitchen, dragging Liu Peng along the floor by her hair. He had not witnessed or been a part of such violence since he had left Tehran, twenty two years ago. He was still struggling to get his breath back when a third man walked into the kitchen and said,
"It's all clear."
"We have no money," Dr Taremi said.
"Shut up," the guy who had punched him in the stomach said.
"What do you want?" Taremi asked.
"This," the guy replied and he turned around and kicked Liu Peng hard in the side of her face. Dr Taremi struggled to his feet and was promptly punched back down by the guy. He had no defence against these men, they were too strong, and he was simply an academic, not a fighter. He started to sob quietly.
"The little man is crying," the guy standing over Liu Peng said, and they all laughed.
"On your feet," the guy standing over him demanded. Dr Taremi stood up slowly, the pain in his stomach now worse than it was a few moments ago.
"That's the problem with you clever men," the guy said, his English clouded by a heavy South American ring, "You are all brains and no strength. You are not a real man. You can't protect your women," he added, and then he turned around and kicked Liu Peng hard in the face with the flat of his right foot.
Dr Taremi started to cry harder. He felt weak and helpless.
"What do you want?" he whimpered.

"I want you to come with me, you can bring your Chinese bitch for company, and if you complain once, I will kill her. Is that clear?"

Dr Taremi nodded.

The guy standing over Liu Peng pulled her up by her hair and she screamed loudly.

Dr Taremi went to say something but decided against it. The guy grabbed his arm and led him out of the kitchen, and he watched as the third guy opened the front door and walked out. They all followed. Liu Peng dragged by her hair. They stepped up to a van that had the side doors already open.

"Where are you taking us?" Dr Taremi asked softly.

"To solve a problem," he replied.

"What problem?"

"Get in the van," the guy said, before punching Dr Taremi hard in the kidneys, as he lifted his foot up to step into the vehicle.

Kendall – Outer Miami

The eighth and last person they needed was less than four miles away from where the van was pulling away from Dr Robert Anderton's house in Pinecrest.

 Catherine Lambourne had just stepped out of the shower in her parent's modest house on SW 82nd CT in Kendall. Catherine was an only child and was the apple of her parent's eyes. She had been a high achiever at school, both academically and in sports, and she had gained her degree in chemistry as easily as she had made the sports teams for every trial that she took part in. The house was on a long road, with a half-moon driveway which stopped just short of the front door at its furthest point. Catherine had worked for Newton Pharmaceutical Limited for fourteen months and had recently been promoted to Dr Robert Anderton's research team as an assistant. She was the youngest of the team, just twenty four years old. She had recently found herself a new boyfriend called David, and everything was on the up for her. Catherine was very pretty and was devoted to exercise, a devotion that was reflected in her stunning, athletic body. She put on her running shorts and top after drying herself down and putting her long, dark hair up into a bun, she walked downstairs.

When she got to the bottom of the stairs, she screamed. Her mother and father were kneeling on the floor with a man standing behind them, holding a gun pointed directly at her father's head.

She turned and pushed quickly up the stairs.

Straight into the arms of a tall, thick set, South American looking man who was holding a gun in his right hand. She turned quickly and there was another guy moving up the stairs towards her. She screamed again.

"One more noise and they will both die whore," the man standing further up the stairs said in a heavily accented voice.

"Please," her father pleaded, "Don't hurt her."

The man holding her smiled at her. She could smell stale cigarettes, and as he smiled, she could see that his front teeth were missing and the teeth he had left were discoloured a dark brown colour.

She pulled back and tried to push his hand away but he was too strong and he maintained a vice-like grip.

"I like a whore who fights," he said.

"Get your hands off of me!"

The toothless man increased his grip even tighter and it started to hurt her arm. He looked down at the other man who was standing on the stairs behind her and he nodded to him. He smiled a big toothless grin at her and then said,

"You look sexy in your running clothes and I bet you look even sexier with them off."

Catherine froze.

"Please, don't," her mother said, "We will give you whatever you want, just please don't hurt her," she begged.

"You want to watch me have fun with your girl?" the toothless guy asked, raising a laugh from the other two men with him.

"Do it," the man holding the gun to her parent's heads said, "Do the whore and make her parents watch," he added excitedly.

The toothless guy raised his right arm and smashed the butt of the gun down on top of Catherine's head. It landed with a loud crack, and her knees gave way, he had to put his arm on her to stop her rolling all the way down to the bottom. She lifted her hands up to her head to try and stem the flow of blood which was now running down the side of her face. As she did so, the guy standing on the stairs behind her pulled at her shorts and removed them; Catherine was frantically trying to stop him with one hand, while the other clutched at the gaping wound on her head.

Her father pushed himself up from his kneeling position and lunged at the guy pawing at his daughter, and as he did so, there was a muffled crack and he fell forward face first, onto the tiled floor.

For a split second, everything went quiet and then her mother screamed, followed by Catherine's desperate howl.

"Shut the whore up," the toothless guy said, and the guy who had shot her father slammed the butt of his gun hard down onto the top of her mother's skull, and her torso collapsed like a house of cards, and she fell forward, her head landing on the heels of her dead husband.

Catherine screamed again and the guy standing behind her put his hand hard over her mouth.

"Why did you shoot him?" the toothless guy spat at his friend, "The boss will not be happy."

Catherine was struggling to breathe as the pressure of the guy's hand covering her mouth intensified.

The three of them stood there looking at each other for almost ten seconds before the toothless guy spoke,

"We will say he had a gun and came at us so we had no choice," he said.

"What about the whore?" the guy holding his hand on Catherine's mouth asked, aware that she had witnessed the whole event and she could easily tell Cardona what had happened at a later date.

"Good point," the toothless guy said, "I will go first while you hold her and then you two can have a go."

They all laughed together, Just as Catherine passed out through lack of oxygen.

FOUR

JFK Airport – New York

No sooner had Ryan Ward and Mike Lawson stepped off of the jet at JFK airport when Ward's cell phone vibrated in his pocket. He took out his phone and looked at the caller I.D. and saw Eloisa's number.

"We've just landed," he answered, without offering a greeting.

"Then my luck is in," Eloisa's soft voice replied. He felt a wave of calm engulf him; she always managed to have that effect on him.

"I've told my boss that I am going to take a few days off," he said, feeling himself smile as the words came out of his mouth.

"Then it is most definitely my lucky day."

"Do you want me to come straight to your place?" he asked.

"I'm at the office at the moment so it would be easier to come to your place. Fancy a race?"

Ward felt an instant surge of anticipation rush through his loins.

"What do you have in mind?" he softly enquired.

"You tell me…." she said, deliberately, passively.

"Get yourself there and if you beat me, I will reward you appropriately," he replied, and then hung up the phone.

Lawson looked at him and he couldn't help but notice the smug grin across his face. It was a look that Lawson had spent virtually his whole adult life wearing, and he knew exactly what it meant.

"Someone looks happy," he said.

Ward ignored him.

So Lawson decided to push the point further.

"Only your woman makes you look like that," he said, "So what has she said to make you look like you have just discovered the joys of sex?"

Ward found the smile disappear from his face. Lawson was one of those men who enjoyed sharing stories of his conquests, but as with every aspect of his own personal life, Ward kept quiet and gave nothing away. He decided to change the subject.

"Has The Old Man said anything to you regarding moving Stateside?" he asked.

"You know he has," Lawson replied, "Because before he formally invited me onto the team he lectured me about my need to focus more on what I was doing and less on the female race," he added.

Ward had championed Lawson to Centrepoint for the last few days. He trusted him explicably, and wanted him by his side more and more frequently. His only reservation about Lawson was that his sexual appetite would distract him, but the truth was, not once had it ever got in the way of something they were focussed on. The problem with Lawson was that he never had to try. He was, without question, the most handsome man that Ward had ever seen, and this was a view shared by pretty much every woman who came into contact with him. Added to his looks was an incredibly athletic six foot four frame and a smile that could melt the heart of even the staunchest Woman's Rights supporter. But it was his eyes that literally everyone, male or female, was drawn to. They were the most stunning, sparkling blue colour and they made you feel that they were drawing you towards him. He had lost count of the number of women who had literally thrown themselves at Lawson. A long time ago Ward had put in a formal request to move Lawson away from MI6, who were officially his employers, onto his team. Because of the trust and confidence that he had in him, it was no longer practical to have him based three thousand miles away in London. Ward wanted him based in New York so he was ready to move, wherever they had to go, immediately.

"What did he say about moving you to The States permanently?" Ward asked.

"He has cleared it with my bosses in London and asked me if I really wanted to work solely with you," Lawson replied.

Ward was surprised at the answer that he had just heard, "What did he mean by that?"

"He told me that he felt I would be better suited working as a Deniable on my own. That I was equally as capable as you, and he felt that I had a lot more to offer than just a support role to you."

Ward was taken aback by the response to his question but after a few seconds of reflection, he could see clearly where The Old Man was coming from.

"And what do you feel about that?" Ward asked.

"What do you feel about it more to the point?"

"He's right to an extent," he replied, "I mean, no one rates you as highly as I do, but you know my reservations about you."

"Seriously Ryan, have I ever let you down?"

"No," Ward replied without a second's hesitation.

"And have you ever thought that my apparent distractions, based on my liking of the opposite sex have stopped me doing my job properly?"

"No," Ward replied, equally as quickly.

"So maybe what I appear to be, what I chose to show people I am is my ruse to appear less focussed. Just like you with your mean and moody persona."

It took Ward by surprise a little that Lawson knew him much better than he thought he did. So he went back to the original subject,

"So what did you say to him when he said that?" he asked.

"I asked him if working alone came with a couple of sexy, young assistants," Lawson replied completely straight faced.

Ward laughed.

"So really," Lawson continued, "There is only one question that you need to answer."

"Which is?"

"What exactly did she say to put that smug grin all over your face?"

"Get the car Mike," Ward replied.

Adams Key – Upper Florida Keys

Pablo Cardona watched from the clearing as the last boat docked on the jetty. He had counted all the people in. He was not overly concerned that at least one person from each boat had blood covering their clothing, or even the fact that the youngest of the chemists appeared to be unconscious as his men carried her onto the Key. What he was concerned about was the fact that there appeared to be one person missing from the last boat that brought the youngest chemist onto the island.

"As soon as they are all in their blocks, go into block one and carry out a head count and then report back to me Emilio," he demanded of the guy who was patiently standing behind him, waiting for any instruction that his boss would give him,

"Yes sir," Emilio replied, as Cardona walked off towards his own building.

Emilio scurried across the clearing and reached the edge where the mass of trees started to form. The blocks had been built mainly under the cover of the trees so that they would not be visible from the air. He walked towards the first building and approached the three men standing outside, all heavily armed with MP7 submachine guns.

"Are they all in there Carlos?" Emilio asked the guy standing directly outside the door to the building.

"Yes, the woman they put in is the last one," Carlos replied.

"Open the door, I need to count them and confirm the numbers back to Mr Cardona," Emilio demanded.

Carlos took out a set of keys and put one into a top lock, which was eighteen inches on the left from the top of the door, and turned it. The lock clanked as the key turned. He then removed the set of keys and then repeated the same movement in the lock that was about eighteen inches off the ground on the same side, the same clanking noise echoing out as the new and freshly oiled locking mechanism did its work, and then finally, he did the same thing with the lock in the middle of the left hand side of the door. He removed the keys and stepped back, allowing enough room for Emilio to step inside, "You will need this," Carlos said to Emilio as he handed him a large, industrial sized flashlight.

Emilio turned the flashlight on and opened the door. He shone the bright light inside.

He smiled to himself. There was a group of people all huddled together at the far end of the building. There was a humming noise of numerous people crying, and he could see by the way that they refused to look directly towards the light that they were all terrified. The majority of the group was made up of women and children. Not one of them spoke or even shouted out in anger or protestation. They looked disorientated and dirty already.

Emilio stepped inside to begin his headcount. He moved to within six feet of the group. He would not dare make a mistake in counting the people in there; his life would depend on it.

"You came in eight groups. I want each group to move to the left, one group at a time so I can count you," he demanded, "Say your surname as you move and the names of all of those in your group. You go first," he added, shining the flashlight into the face of a woman who was holding two young children tight to her body, one under each arm.

"Dunn," the woman said as she shepherded herself to the left hand side of the room, shielding her two daughters behind her, trying to protect them from the bright light as she moved.

"Name?" Emilio demanded.

"I'm Lindsey," she replied.

"The kids?"

"Morgan and Julie."

"Husband?"

"Dr Eric Dunn."

Emilio quickly wrote down all of the information that he was being given onto a scrap of paper. Mr Cardona would be impressed with how thorough he had been, he thought to himself.

"You next," he said, shining the light into Claire Anderton's face"

"Anderton, Claire," she replied, "Robert, Adam and Lucy. Dr Robert Anderton," she added after a pause, and only when her children were safely to the left hand side of the room.

"You," he shouted, the bright light blinding the woman he was pointing it at. She turned her back on Emilio.

"You," he said again, "If I have to come over there I will kill you."

The woman turned around slowly. She had a stream of dried blood down the side of her face and the right side of her neck.

"You killed my husband you sick bastards," she spat at Emilio.

He reached around to the back of his waistband and pulled out a handgun. He pointed it directly at Lindsey Dunn.

"Three seconds to answer and move or this bitch dies too," he screamed at the woman.

"Lambourne, Heather," she said immediately, as she started to move to the left, "Mother of Catherine you animals."

"You next," he said, shining the flashlight in Lin Peng Taremi's face.

"Taremi, Lin Peng. Dr Sardar Tameri," she replied as she moved over to the left and put a consoling arm around Lindsey Dunn.

"You" Emilio said firmly, his light resting on an extremely pretty face.

"Keeley Beasley, wife of Heath Beasley," she replied.

"I'm going to have fun with you later bitch," he said, "No kids?" he asked.

Keeley Beasley shook her head.

"Why not?" he asked, "Is your man not a real man? You want to learn to have fun with a real man like me?" he said, fully aware that she would never live long enough to have kids in the future.

He swung his flashlight around onto the face of the only man in the group.

"You," he said to a man who was standing in front of three small children.

The man moved sideways, like a crab, keeping his children behind him at all times,

"Alexander, Brandon," he said, "Brian, Sam and Carli. Dr Allie Alexander."

"Are you not a real man? You send your bitch out to work while you clean and cook?" Emilio said, and laughed at his own attempt at humour.

Brandon Alexander did not respond, his only concern was to not say anything that would irritate the guy holding the gun that might jeopardise his children's safety.

"Next," Emilio said, his flashlight shining on a large woman, standing in front of two small children with two teenage children to her side.

"Emily Johnston," she said as she started to move, "Becky, Ali, Freddy and Chris. Kyle Johnson."

"Hurry your fat ass over there," Emilio said mockingly, enjoying the power that he felt right now.

There was just one group remaining, he shone the flashlight in a woman's face.

"Quickly," he demanded.

The woman held the hands of the two young boys with her as she started to move to the left hand side of the room,

"Crystal Wynne," she said in a soft, frightened voice, "This is Kyle and Bobby. Dr Justin Wynne is my husband."

Emilio scribbled her details down and then shone the light on the entire group again, and carried out one more headcount to confirm that he was correct. There was no margin for error in anything that Mr Cardona demanded. He satisfied himself that he had counted correctly and then he turned and walked out of the building.

"Secure it," he said to Carlos, as he dropped the flashlight on the floor.

He walked back out into the clearing and turned to the right. Fifty yards later, he was knocking on the door of Pablo Cardona's temporary home. The door opened and Emilio looked straight into the eyes of Dorlan Franco, Pablo Cardona's chief enforcer. He looked immediately down at the floor. He would never give Franco any reason to accuse him of looking at him in a provocative manner.

"I have the information that Mr Cardona requested," he said, suddenly feeling completely irrelevant in the hierarchy of Cardona's operation.

"Come in," Franco said, and turned his back on Emilio which made him feel even more inadequate.

He stepped inside.

He was surprised to see the same guy tied to a chair that he had seen in Cardona's mansion in Miami. He could see no possible reason for Cardona to bring him with him, but he dared not ask any questions. He was not important enough to warrant a reply.

"Have you counted them Emilio?" Cardona asked.

"Yes Mr Cardona. There were twenty two people. One man, seven women and fourteen children," Emilio replied, looking down at the information that he had written but making no attempt to actually read it.

"Who is missing?" Cardona asked.

"The husband of Heather Lambourne and father of Catherine," he replied immediately, having already anticipated the question.

"What happened to him?" Cardona asked.

"The wife said that we killed him," Emilio replied.

"Who collected them?"

Emilio pulled out another scrap of paper and looked for the name of Catherine Lambourne,

"Johan, Stefan and Fabian," Emilio said reluctantly.

"Franco," Cardona said, "Go and collect Johan, Stefan and Fabian and meet me outside of block number two," he added menacingly.

FIVE

DUMBO – New York

Ward's apartment in New York was the one place that really felt like home to him. It was on Washington Street, a neighbourhood in Brooklyn. More specifically, it was in an area that the locals had affectionately named DUMBO which stood for 'Down Under the Manhattan Bridge Overpass'. He lived in a six storey apartment building which looked both old, due to the grime on the brickwork, and new, due to the double glazed windows that adorned the front.

"Do you think that The Old Man could set me up with a place down here?" Lawson asked as he drove slowly down the street.

"I guess that all depends on how well you stick to his rules," Ward replied, a comment which had Lawson raising his eyebrows and rolling his eyes, as he knew full well how much Ward infuriated Centrepoint by never following his rules with regards to updates.

"Where are you staying anyway?" he asked.

"I have a friend who lives down on 5th Avenue who will put me up until I get sorted," Lawson replied.

"You'll find it tough sharing one woman's bed for a while," he said with a smile.

"Don't be stupid, she has two roommates, Chantel and Amy, they have already agreed to take it in turns to have me sleep with them," Lawson replied, a comment which had Ward shaking his head once more, because he knew without a doubt that Lawson was being serious.

He pulled the car to a stop thirty feet up from the apartment.

"Have a few days to get settled Mike. I'm definitely going to have some long overdue downtime and make the most of the quiet," Ward said, "I'll be in touch when I need you."

He watched as Lawson drove off and then walked the thirty feet to his apartment building.

He walked into the foyer and jogged up the stairs, wondering if Eloisa had got there before him, his wonder turning to a desperate hope with each step he climbed, the excitement of feeling her close to him consuming every part of him. He reached his apartment door and put the key into the lock, opened the door and stepped inside.

Eloisa was standing in the middle of the hallway.

She was wearing a long coat which was hanging open. She was completely naked underneath apart from the stiletto heels that she was wearing.

He studied her for a moment, focusing on her perfectly toned stomach, and the cleavage of her full, ample breasts.

Her body was incredible.

She had her head tilted to one side, and the little finger of her left hand was inserted slightly into the left hand corner of her mouth. Her beautiful black hair was shining much more than usual, due to the rays of sun that poured in through the window at the end of the hallway. He took five urgent steps forward and grabbed her by the throat and pushed her hard against the wall. He moved his face to within two inches of hers and whispered, "I want you."

"You can have me," she replied eagerly.

He was struggling to contain his urge to kiss her and get lost in her, but the excitement that he felt rushing through his veins made him want to savour the moment. "I've missed you," he said.

Before Eloisa could speak, he moved his hand down between her legs, while the other hand remained clamped around her throat, and he started to roughly pleasure her. Her whole body started to tense and she began to moan loudly.

"I want you," he said again, increasing the strength of the grip around her throat. Her legs became rigid and so he moved his hand faster, and then her body started to convulse as she began an intense orgasm.

"I need to taste you," he whispered to her, and then he let go of her throat, spun her around, and pushed her face up against the wall by the back of her head. With his other hand, he pulled her coat off and threw it to the side. He studied her perfect back and shoulders for a few seconds and then he stared at her perfect long legs, melting into the pert, tight buttocks at the top. He gripped her hair in his hand and yanked her hair back,

"I need you now," he whispered.

"Please Ryan, take me," she begged.

He said nothing at first. He used his free hand to undo his jeans and let them fall to the floor, his boxers followed immediately, he then forced himself deep into her and she groaned with pleasure as he started to thrust deeply and quickly into her. She didn't last much more than a minute. Her body started to jerk, intense mini-orgasms rippling through her body, one after another, and she started to moan louder and louder. He quickened the pace of his thrusts, their naked skin colliding with each movement. When Eloisa reached full orgasm, she let out a loud scream that he was sure most of the neighbours would have heard, and her body went into convulsion,

"Oh My God!!!" she screamed one more time, and her knees gave way and she fell to the floor.

For the next two hours, Ward continued to bring Eloisa to orgasm. He pushed her, pulled her, demanded she fight back, and called her every derogatory name that he could think of, her excitement levels increasing with each insult. He was impressed by her speed and strength when she did fight back; they were skills that he never knew she possessed. When he finally climaxed, they collapsed on the hallway floor together and both lay there, naked and gasping.

"We should meet up more often," she said breathlessly. Ward laughed.

They showered together and then decided to go out to eat. Nothing grand, just a small pizza place two blocks away.

They found a quiet booth at the back of the restaurant and ordered two king size pizzas. As Ward sipped on his beer and Eloisa on her wine, she said to him,
"Tell me what Tom Bass was like before he died?"
He pondered the question for a moment without speaking. He studied her closely. There was no fear over what she might hear in her eyes, not even a curious tone to her voice, and for the first time since he had known her, he realised that she was as business-like as he was when it came to death and eliminating a target.
"He was petrified, and to be honest, pretty unrecognisable by the time I killed him," he eventually said.
"Did he beg? Like those poor women would have begged?"
"Yes he did."
He felt his phone vibrate in his pocket so he pulled it out and checked the caller I.D. Centrepoint was trying to contact him. He slipped the phone back into his pocket.
"Do you need to take that?" she asked.
"No. I'm having a few days off. Someone else can deal with whatever it is."
"Do you ever have a day off in your line of work?"
"I do now," he replied.
"No, what I mean is, are you ever able to switch off completely? I know that I can't. Even when an issue is resolved definitively, such as with Tom Bass, I spend the next few days thinking about those poor women and children until my focus moves onto the next victim. My mind never seems to be free of bad thoughts."
"There are techniques that you can use," he replied, thinking about how he washes his mind at the end of

each mission, simply by exhaling the thoughts out of his body.

"Does it get easier?" she asked.

His phone vibrated again, he checked who was calling. It was Centrepoint again. Once more, he slipped the phone back into his pocket without answering.

"No," he replied, "It doesn't get any easier,"

Eloisa looked down at the table. She looked almost sad for a minute and alone with her own thoughts.

"But it gets more satisfying," he said quickly.

She looked up from the table, her beautiful green eyes staring deep into his, willing to hear what he had to say.

"What works for me," he began, "Is that I don't think of the pain that the victims of the animals that I hunt have had to endure. I think of the arrogance of the men who I chase."

"What do you mean?"

"Those types of men have an unpleasant arrogance about them. It is made up of a total disregard for other people, and they feel that everyone's life but their own is worthless. Completely irrelevant," he replied.

"So you focus on them alone and not the victims?"

"No. The victims are everything. At the end of the day, we are defending them. We are standing up for those who can't stand up for themselves. I think of myself as the big brother, the strong husband, or the enraged father they don't have."

His phone vibrated in his pocket again. He didn't even bother to check who it was, he knew it would be The Old Man, and so he just let it ring out until the vibration stopped.

"So you just think how they would feel?" she asked.

He didn't feel like he was explaining himself very clearly.

"No. I take it personally. It's always me against them in my mind."

"Doesn't that make you as arrogant as them?" she asked quizzically.

"Yes it does in a way. I believe that I am going to beat them no matter what."

"So are you any different than them?" she asked, genuine curiosity in her voice.

It was a question that stopped him in his tracks. He had never once in his life compared himself to any of the people that he had hunted.

But he knew there was one big difference and that made him smile as soon as he realised it.

"That makes you smile?" she asked him, a confused look on her face.

"There is one big difference between me and them Eloisa," he said.

"Which is?"

"I do what I do because it's the right thing to do, for no other reason than that."

She smiled at him, a big happy, loving smile.

"And I should think exactly the same way, shouldn't I?" she asked.

"Yes you should. What we do is not about personal gain to us, it's about doing the right thing. So don't think of the victims, think of the people you are saving in the future. It's a lot easier to think of faceless or nameless people," he replied.

"Everything is about keeping the children of the world safe, we do make a difference, don't we?"

"We make a very big difference."

"I'm looking forward to the next few days together," she said.

Their waiter came over to the table and stood to the side of them looking awkward.

"Is everything OK?" Eloisa asked him.

"I've just had a phone call for you sir," the waiter said to Ward.

"How do you know it's for me?" he replied, instantly suspicious.

"Because you are the only customer in here sitting with a beautiful Irish woman," he said, his exaggerated Italian ring to his perfect American accent making Eloisa giggle more than feel complimented.

"Tell them I'm busy," he replied.

The waiter shrugged his shoulders and walked off.

"The same person who has been ringing you throughout the meal?" she asked.

"No doubt about that" he replied, "But he will have to wait. I'm on leave for a few days."

"Good."

"How is your promotion at work going?" he asked, genuinely interested to know, in spite of the fact that he was the only one sitting at their table who knew that she had been promoted to pacify him after the events of his last mission.

"It's amazing. They have given me access to files, investigations and records that I didn't even know existed. Officially, I am now leading a risk assessment team on individuals who have been flagged up as committing a list of violations, and crimes, against children," she replied, enthusiasm and excitement rushing through her voice.

There was no way that Ward could ever tell her the real reason why she had been promoted. And from his point of view, she had worked so hard and given so much to the U.N. that she deserved it.

"And unofficially?" he asked her.

She smiled at him,

"Unofficially Ryan, I decide who you test your terrible arrogance against."

Ward laughed.

"So now you are deciding who I hunt?"

She nodded at him

"So I guess that makes me your boss," she said, and poked her tongue out to mock him.

Ward laughed again.

"OK boss, can you do me one favour?"

"Can't it wait for your annual review?" she said seriously.

He laughed yet again.

"Just because you are sleeping with your boss, it doesn't mean I will cut you any slack," she said, clearly on a roll with her quips.

"Please, just one little favour for your star employee?" he asked again.

"Shoot."

"Can you please try and pick some bad guys in New York, so I can deal with them and then be home in time for dinner?"

Eloisa laughed. She gazed into his eyes and then glanced over his shoulder.

"Valentino is coming back over," she said, watching the waiter walking back to their table, flashing his sickeningly smug smile as he approached.

"If he flirts with you again I will shoot him," he said, feigning an angry face.

The waiter reached their table and stood there for a few seconds, saying nothing.

"What?" Ward said to him.

"I have a message from your 'Old Man'" the waiter said, completely forgetting his Italian twang this time, a mistake that had Eloisa laughing out louder than a polite person should.

"What is it?"

"You need to ring him urgently."

"He can wait."

"He said, you need to know it's urgent."

"He can wait."

"He said Lawson is down."

Ward immediately stood up and walked towards the door of the restaurant, pulling his phone out of his pocket on the way out. He hit speed dial for Centrepoint's number with a sick feeling in his stomach.

SIX

Adams Key – Upper Florida Keys

Franco marched Johan, Stefan and Fabian over to block number two. It was the block where they were holding the eight employees of Newton Pharmaceutical Limited. "Stop here," he demand as he stopped six feet away from the solid doors of the building.

Pablo Cardona walked slowly towards them, drawing slowly on his cigarette, staring at them but at the same time looking deep in thought.

The three men that Franco had brought to the building had yet to speak one word between them.

The biggest guy was called Stefan Valencia. He had worked for Cardona for the past fifteen years. He was someone that Cardona trusted because he had proved his Loyalty many times over the years. He was a mean looking guy, he had no teeth at the front of his mouth, and when he spoke he often whistled. The guy standing to his left was Johan Balanta. He was relatively new to the Cardona cartel, but he had already killed nine people in the two years that he had worked for him, mainly small time drug dealers and relatives of people who had dared to get on the wrong side of Cardona. To the Columbians, killing defenceless family members was a better threat than killing an enemy. That threat would just push an individual underground. It was harder to hide an entire family away.

Johan Balanta was the one who had killed Catherine Lambourne's father.

The third guy was called Fabian Martinez. He was the youngest of all of Cardona's men on the island. He was only twenty two years old. He had originally worked as a runner for one of Cardona's drug dealers on the streets of Miami, but after Cardona had killed the dealer for stealing just three hundred dollars from him, Martinez had been promoted. He had increased profits three times over in just six months, and so he was invited to join the top team as a reward for his endeavours.

Cardona reached the group and stopped a few feet away. He continued to pull on his cigarette for a whole minute without speaking. When he reached the end of the cigarette, he put it between his thumb and middle finger and flicked it towards the group. It hit Stefan Valencia on the left hand side of his face. He didn't flinch. He could not show any weakness to Mr Cardona.

"You were in charge of collecting the Lambourne's," he said looking at Valencia, "Is that correct?" he asked.

Valencia nodded,

"Yes Sir Mr Cardona," he replied.

"So can you explain to me how their group was one person short?" Cardona asked calmly.

"We had a problem sir," Valencia replied.

"No. You had a situation," Cardona said, "Now you have a problem," he added.

Valencia shifted uneasily on his feet. He was in a real catch twenty two situation. If he explained what had happened, he might get away with his own life being spared, at the expense of Johan Balanta's, but if he failed to provide a reasonable answer, there would be no reprisal for him at all.

"You need time to think about your answer which tells me already that you are going to lie to me, and that means that you are being disloyal to me and you know the importance that I put on loyalty," Cardona said calmly.

"I would never be disloyal to you Mr Cardona, I swear," Valencia replied.

"So Stefan, explain to me clearly what happened?" Cardona said, "It will be the last time that I ask," he threatened.

"We were doing exactly as you requested Mr Cardona. To frighten the family, as you instructed, we were going to rape the girl on the stairs while her parents watched. To show them that we mean business, as you requested," Valencia replied.

"And then?" Cardona asked.

"Me and Fabian were holding her down and the girl's father went for Fabian and so Johan shot him in the head sir."

Cardona looked to Valencia's left and shook his head.

"Do you know how important it was to get all twenty three people here?" Cardona asked Johan Balanta, "I thought I was very, very clear on that? Was I not?" he asked.

"You were Mr Cardona, but….."

"There is no 'But' Johan," Cardona interrupted, "There is never a 'But' as far as my instructions are given. There is no deviation or alteration to what I demand, ever. Do you not understand that?"

"Yes sir I do," Balanta replied.

"You," Cardona said looking to Valencia's right at Fabian Martinez, "You have been given the opportunity to join us. Do you think that Stefan is a suitable leader? Do you think he did all that he should have done? Do you think you could do better?" he asked.

Martinez felt backed into a corner with the first question, by the time he had processed the third, he knew that his response would dictate his progress through the cartel and both safe his life or end it. In that situation, self-preservation always kicked in.

"In answer to your first question," Martinez began, "I do think that Stefan is a suitable leader Mr Cardona," he said, having weighed up the fact that Valencia had worked with Cardona for the past fifteen years and he would be much more reluctant to get rid of Valencia than a new employee like him.

"I admire your loyalty to Stefan," Cardona said.

Martinez nodded his appreciation at the comment.

"But your loyalty is to me alone, not to him, so now I am thinking that maybe I was wrong to put my trust in you," he added.

The words hit Martinez like a right hook, but like a prize fighter, he quickly saw a way back.

"In response to your second question sir," he started, "I don't think that he did all that he should have done."

"Why?" Cardona asked.

"Because he should have known that Johan is trigger happy and he should have put me on the parents of the whore. I understood clearly how important it was to get everyone back here as you instructed," Martinez replied.

Cardona nodded.

"And my last question. Do you think you could do better?"

This was the question that Martinez didn't want to answer the most. He was sure that if he said yes that Cardona would demand that he killed Valencia, so he compromised his answer in the middle,

"I think in a few years I will be able to sir," he began, "But right now, I have a lot to learn and a lot to do to earn your trust and the opportunity to demonstrate that I am capable. But most of all, I have learnt a very valuable lesson here, so if this type of incident ever happens again, I would never make the same mistake that has been made here," he added.

Cardona nodded.

"I am satisfied with your answer Fabian," he said.

"Thank you Mr Cardona," Martinez replied.

"But I am not satisfied with you Stefan or you Johan," Cardona said menacingly.

"Luckily for you, I need as many good men that I can get on the island until we are done with this and so I will give you the chance to correct your weak leadership," he said to Valencia.

"Thank you Mr Cardona," Valencia whistled, "I will restore your faith in me."

"You better had Stefan."

He then looked at Johan Balanta and shook his head.

"As I am one person short now, it is only right that you take the place of the missing person, don't you agree?"

Balanta felt panic rush through his body.

"But that won't really work, will it? Because you mean nothing to any of them so there is no point in putting you in there with them," he said, "So, you have had a lucky escape."

"Thank you Mr Cardona, I will never let you down again," Balanta replied.

Pablo Cardona nodded at Franco who had been standing to the left of the group for the duration of the entire conversation. Franco pulled out his handgun and shot Balanta directly in the side of his right knee. Balanta fell to the floor, clutching his knee and screamed on the way down.

"As I can't use you to help me, I will use you to strike fear into them," Cardona said as he stepped forward and leant over Balanta who was writhing in agony on the floor.

"Franco," Cardona said calmly, "Get them to open the door. It is time to show the chemists how serious we are."

Franco looked over at the guard who had been standing in silence to the right of the door and said, "Open it."

The guard proceeded to unlock all three locks and pulled the door open.

"Bring him inside," Cardona demanded as he stepped through the doorway and into the building.

Inside, eight people looked up at him with both fear and hate in their eyes at the same time.

"What have you done with my wife and children?" a man shouted and then stood up as Cardona walked into the centre of the room, followed by Franco dragging Johan along the floor by the scruff of his jacket, making light work of the one hundred and eighty pounds that he was pulling. He dropped Johan next to Cardona's feet, stepped past Cardona and walked up to the man and delivered an uppercut into the man's stomach. The man doubled over immediately and fell to the floor.

"None of you dare speak to Mr Cardona. The next one to talk gets a bullet in their brain," Franco shouted as he turned, and looked into the eyes of each of them, one at a time, willing to see a hint of a challenge in someone's, anyone's, eyes.

No one in the room spoke.

Kyle Johnston was not a strong man. He was the guy who had always got bullied at school by the sports jocks. He had done exceptionally well, academically at school, and even though he had fallen short of his doctorate at university, he was still an exceptional researcher held in very high regard by all who had worked with him over the years at Newton Pharmaceutical Limited. The anger that he had displayed a few moments ago was the first time in his life that he had ever confronted a man, and even now, as he struggled to get his breath back, he needed to know where his wife and children were and most of all, that they were safe. So he reverted back to what the kid who was always bullied at school had gotten used to doing.

He put his hand up, asking for permission to speak.

Cardona looked at him and nodded, giving an adult permission to speak in the most condescending and patronising act possible.

"My wife Emily," Kyle started, "And my children, Becky, Ali, Freddy and Chris. Are they all OK?" he asked, with clear desperation in his voice.

"For now, all of your family members are safe. That is all you need to know," Cardona replied, looking at Kyle with utter contempt. This was no man; he thought to himself, it was just another pathetic, weak American, who made everything that he had built over the years easy for him.

Dr Robert Anderton raised his hand.

"No more questions," he shouted and turned his attention to Martinez who was still gripping his right knee, curled up into a ball on the floor.

Dr Robert Anderton lowered his hand.

Cardona looked around the room and then fixed his eyes on Catherine Lambourne. She was still shaking and covering her torso with her arms. She was a very pretty woman he concluded, and he could tell just by looking at her that she had been raped and abused. He had stood and watched his men rape relatives of his enemies on countless occasions, and he knew the look that Catherine was displaying in her eyes well. Her eyes had completely glazed over. She was in the room and she wasn't.

"You," he shouted to her, "Come here!"

Catherine just sat on the bed, still in her trance-like state. Franco decided to take control of the situation and walked over to her and grabbed hold of her hair, and yanked her off the bed and dragged her across the room to Cardona's feet.

He looked down at her with complete disgust.

"Your father trying to be a hero has caused me a problem," he said.

Catherine continued to look at the floor.

"I'm talking to you!" Cardona shouted. Catherine looked up, tears in her eyes and fear etched all over her face, "If you look away from me once more I will drag your mother in here and cut her throat," he spat at her.

She stared defiantly, right into his eyes.

"This man here helped himself to your body?" he asked, pointing at Johan Balanta who was still writhing on the floor next to her.

"They all did," Catherine softly replied, and started to cry harder.

Cardona leant down and slapped her hard in the face, "I don't care about the other two. I asked if this man, this scum who killed your father, raped you?" he shouted.

Catherine nodded.

Kyle Johnston for one moment almost stood up to go over to Catherine and comfort her, but Franco saw the movement out of the corner of his eye and glared at him. He stopped moving immediately.

"When people disobey my instructions, I punish them. Johan has worked for me for a long time, but he did not do what I asked, and so he has to pay a price," Cardona said, "And now you will all watch how I deal with people who fail me."

He bent down and took a handful of Balanta's hair in his left hand and pulled his head upright. At the same time, he leant around to the back of his waistband and pulled out a knife that had an ivory coloured handle and a jagged blade. In one swift movement, he sliced right across the front of Balanta's neck, the jagged edge of the blade cutting deep into his windpipe. Blood immediately started pulsing out of his neck.

"Look at him!" Cardona shouted at the chemists, "Anyone failing to look will suffer the same fate," he added, an air of excitement now rushing through his voice.

Everyone in the room reluctantly looked, with their hands over their mouths and tears in their eyes.

It only took a minute and a half for Balanta to bleed out and die. His body went limp.

The chemists all looked away.

"Look at me," Cardona shouted.

They all looked at him.

"This is the difference between a Columbian and an American," he said.

He then dug the jagged blade into the right eye of the dead Johan Balanta, and started to saw frantically until the eye ball rolled out of his skull and onto the floor.

"Look at me!!" he screamed as the women started to cry, and five of the eight started to retch violently as he started to work on the left eye of Balanta. In less than a minute, the left eye ball was on the floor, two feet away from the right one. Cardona let go of Balanta's hair and his lifeless body fell into a distorted pile on the floor.

He cleaned his knife on the arm of his jacket and returned it to the back of his waistband.

He bent down and picked up the eyeballs, one at a time and put them in his pocket,

"Souvenirs," he said proudly and he turned and walked towards the door and straight out of the building without saying another word.

SEVEN

Washington Street – New York

Ward didn't like the feeling that was whirling around in the pit of his stomach.

"You got my message then?" Centrepoint said as he answered.

"What's happened to Lawson?" he demanded.

"What?" The Old Man replied, clearly attempting to feign surprise in his voice.

"The message, Lawson is down."

"The message that I gave was Lawson is downtown. I've found a place for him to stay."

Ward hung up the phone.

He couldn't believe that he fell for such a lame trick. He turned to head back into the restaurant, just as Eloisa was walking out,

"I've paid the tab," she said, as she reached down and held his hand, "Everything OK?" she asked.

"Everything is fine," he replied, still feeling annoyed that he fell for such a childish attempt by The Old Man to engage in dialogue with him.

He felt the phone vibrate in his pocket and ignored it. Eloisa could clearly hear the feint humming in his pocket.

"Perhaps you should answer it Ryan," she said, "It's obviously important."

"It's always important."

"But maybe, whatever he wants doesn't need to be dealt with right now?"

"I have told him that I am having a few days off. I need to switch off at times too," he replied, annoyance in his voice rather than tiredness.

"We have years to switch off in the future. If it is important and you find out later on that you could have prevented something bad from happening, I know from personal experience, it won't sit well with you," Eloisa said, her soft, calm voice always bringing him back to reality immediately.

He knew she was right.

"Next time he rings, I'll answer," he said.

They walked hand in hand the two blocks back to his apartment, without the phone vibrating once. He turned the corner towards his apartment building and he immediately noticed the Taurus that Lawson had been driving when he dropped him off, parked on the kerb, thirty feet from his apartment building.

They approached the car along the sidewalk and when they get ten feet away, the door opened and Lawson stepped out.

"The Old Man has found you a place to stay then?" he said to Lawson as he stood in the centre of the sidewalk, waiting for them to reach him.

"What?" Lawson replied, completely unaware of what he was talking about.

Ward just shook his head.

"I'm Mike Lawson," he said as he extended his hand to greet Eloisa.

She took his hand and shook it gently.

"I'm Eloisa," she said softly.

Ward waited for Eloisa to do the double-take on the stunningly handsome Lawson.

But it never came. She just simply looked at Ward and smiled,

"I'll go in Ryan," she said, "Nice to meet you Mike," she added as she walked past him without even the most subtle of second glances.

Ward looked at Lawson. He had a disappointed look on his face, equally matched with slight disbelief.

"That can't be good for your ego," he said and then laughed.

"No idea what you mean," Lawson replied, "She's a stunner. How on earth did you pull something like that?" he asked in all seriousness, shaking his head as he said the words.

Ward briefly thought back to the time that he first met Eloisa.

He had been in a bar on 5th Avenue with an old CIA colleague called Amershaw. He came from Seattle and he had been working with Ward on a mission to hunt down a poisoner who was sending anthrax-laced letters to U.S. Senators. Initially, it had been thought that it was a terrorist plot, but in the end, it came down to simple greed, the mission reaching its anti-climax when Ward hunted the poisoner, Rich Daly, to a squalid apartment in New York. Amershaw had assisted Ward competently and he had received the news that his wife had given birth to their first child back in Seattle. Ward thought it only decent that he invited Amershaw to have a drink to celebrate the arrival of his first born.

They had gone into a bar on 5th Avenue where Amershaw had said that he took his wife to once, and he had ordered the drinks at the bar. As he did so, Eloisa gently touched him on the arm, after recognising his English accent, and asked him if he could save her from the American Vultures that were hitting on her. Ward had engaged in deep conversation with her and they had spent the whole evening talking, Eloisa becoming more enchanting to him as their conversation became more personal. The fact that Ward had an Irish mother seemed to be the winning point. He smiled to himself as he remembered that he had suddenly looked around for Amershaw after thirty minutes of forgetting he was there, and had discovered that he was nowhere in the bar.

"I wonder whatever happened to Amershaw?" he said out loud.

Lawson looked at him confused, but didn't bother to ask who Amershaw was.

"So why am I here?" Lawson asked.

"Because The Old Man told you to be no doubt," he replied, now curious himself as to what was happening.

The phone vibrated in his pocket.

He took it out, saw Centrepoint's name on the screen and answered.

"This had better be very good," he answered without any greeting.

"We have a very big problem," The Old Man said.

"I'm having a few days off."

"This can't wait Ryan."

"It will have to. Get one of the other nine to deal with it," he replied, referring to the rest of the Deniable Operatives at Centrepoint's disposal.

"They are all engaged in other things. It needs to be you; this one has the potential to be catastrophic."

"Then disengage them. If I don't have a break, I will start making mistakes," he replied.

Lawson raised an eyebrow.

"Eight employees of a pharmaceutical company have been kidnapped down in Miami," Centrepoint said, ignoring Ward's previous comment, "That in itself, isn't the problem."

"So what is?"

"Their families have all gone missing too. Twenty three people, although one of them has turned up dead two hours ago in Kendall, just outside of Miami."

"That shouldn't concern us, we don't deal with the kidnapping of standard civilians," Ward replied dismissively.

"That isn't the problem," Centrepoint said.

"It sounds like a problem for the FBI to me."

"There's the problem."

"I don't understand."

"I have a feeling that some people within the FBI or DEA are in on this."

"What use would these people be to anyone?" he asked.

"I know exactly what use they would be," Centrepoint replied, "They can create any type of drug they want." Ward pondered this for a moment. He knew that the drug problem in The States was spiralling out of control, spreading out from the run down inner city areas into picture book suburbia, but he failed to see how corrupt government employees were their problem. He knew that there would have to be something else for this problem to end up on The Old Man's desk.

"And the part you aren't telling me?" he asked.

There was silence on the phone for a few moments.

"The drug that they are trying to make came to our attention two years ago. We stopped it ever going into production. We were the only people who knew what it was capable of," Centrepoint replied

"And now we aren't the only people?"

"So it seems."

"So how did whoever has this information in their possession now, get hold of it?"

"That's what you have to find out, and quickly. If this hits the streets, it will make the scourge of Crack seem like kids eating jelly and ice cream."

"And why do you think that the FBI and DEA are behind it?"

"Because they were the only two agencies who had access to the information that I held, so it could only have come from them."

"Have you any idea where we should start looking?"

"Yes," Centrepoint replied, "Miami, the jet is waiting at JFK."

Ward hung up the phone.

"Go and pack a bag Mike, meet me back here in an hour," he said to Lawson.

Lawson nodded and walked back to his car. He continued walking to his apartment building and went inside. He felt flat and dejected; he was looking forward to his time with Eloisa more than anything, now once again, he was going to tell her that he had to leave.

He walked up the stairs and reached his apartment and went inside.

The apartment was empty apart from a note on the kitchen counter that simply said;

'I understand. I will be here when you get back, just take care; we have a future to think of. I love you'.

He smiled to himself. She always knew exactly the right thing to say.

He took himself into the shower and liked the fact that the shower tray was still wet from where he and Eloisa had been entwined together a few hours earlier. He stood upright under the shower thinking about what Centrepoint had told him about the events down in Miami, and he started to piece things together. Twenty five minutes later when he turned the tap off, he was sure that he knew exactly what was going on with the missing employees and their families. There could only be one simple reason for it, but what worried him was that he knew it did not bode well for all of the people who were missing. He was starting to feel exhausted by the corruption that was rife everywhere he went. The FBI and DEA were involved somehow in this The Old Man had said, once again he was finding himself unable to trust the very people who were meant to protect the innocent.

He dried himself off and took his grab bag out of the closet which contained his change of clothes, Glock, ammunition, silencer and cash. He took another Glock from out of the draw in his kitchen and put it on the bed next to his clothes. He changed and put on his jacket. He looked in the mirror. Forty one minutes after ending the call with The Old Man, he was ready to go. He picked up his cell phone and dialled Centrepoint.

"I need the funds for McDermott and the information that you have on these people immediately," he said as The Old Man answered.

"Already in place," he replied, "I have taken the liberty of copying the information to your computer geniuses in New York as I assume you will need them too," he added, referring to Nicole-Louise and Tackler, Ward's technical experts who worked with him on every mission.

"The Optician?"

"He is already on his way. Ring me when you get to Miami and I will hopefully have a bit more Intel on who could be responsible for this," The Old Man said, more in hope than expectance. Ward rarely called in as instructed.

"Who do you have down in Miami that I can trust?" Ward asked, "And preferably someone as solid as Buck, and not like the other two bozo's," he added, referring to two less than effective operatives called Murray and Peacock that The Old Man had provided to offer assistance in California.

"There will be a man called Bruce Harris waiting for you when you land. I can vouch for him. He has his finger on the pulse in Miami, if it's happening, he'll know about it," Centrepoint replied.

"So how come he doesn't know who's behind it already?" he asked flippantly.

"That's your job to find out."

Ward hung up the phone.

He then dialled Martin McDermott's number.

McDermott was his most trusted colleague and Ward had hardly had a day away from him and his team over the past few weeks, and he had only said a fond goodbye to him a few days ago in Washington D.C.

McDermott answered on the third ring.

"Seriously?" McDermott said and then laughed.

"What can I say," he replied, "I'm bored without you and your boys," he added, referring to McDermott's team of six of the most elite and highly trained operatives that the Navy SEAL'S had ever produced.

"You know that the boys are due some downtime?" McDermott said, reminding Ward that he had told him a few days ago that he was planning on taking his team to Vegas to unwind for a few days.

"This can't wait," he replied, "Where are you, Vegas?" he asked.

"No, change of plan, we are down in Miami, where do you want us?" he asked.

Ward smiled to himself. This would be the first time in all the years that he had known McDermott that he would not have to ask him to jump on a plane and fly all over The States to assist him.

"How about....... Miami?" he asked.

He heard McDermott laugh on the end of the line,

"Do you know," he replied, "That is the first time in all the years that I have known you that we have not had to jump on a plane and fly halfway around The States to get your sorry ass out of trouble," he said, much to Ward's amusement.

"I hadn't realised that," Ward replied innocently, "You have a warehouse down there I take it?" he asked.

"Yep. I'm inside it now; the boys have gone out to play."

"Leave them playing, we won't move until the morning anyway, text me the address and when me and Lawson arrive, we will meet you there."

"I look forward to it," McDermott replied and the line went dead again.

He looked at his watch and just as he did so, his cell phone vibrated. He looked at the caller display and saw Lawson's number on it,

"I'm outside," Lawson said.

And then the line went dead again.

He walked out of the apartment and closed the door. Lawson was parked thirty feet away in the Ford Taurus; Ward climbed into the car and said,

"Straight to JFK, usual entrance, referring to the rear entrance that they always used, courtesy of The Old Man, to avoid any checks.

Thirty minutes later they were both climbing out of the car, forty feet away from the Lear jet which Ward seemed to spend most of his time in recently. They climbed the steps and were welcomed by a pretty flight attendant that he did not recognise from their previous flying time on the jet. She nodded at him and then stared at Lawson hard and blushed; his stunning looks making her smile like a lovesick teenager. He smiled his lethal smile, which no woman, apart from Eloisa and Nicole-Louise, it seemed, could resist, and he shook his head.

"I'm Rachel," she said to him coyly.

"I'm interested," Lawson replied, as he stepped past her.

"Try going one flight without hitting on or having sex with the flight attendant," Ward said sarcastically.

"That so isn't going to happen," Lawson replied.

Ward shook his head.

Twenty minutes later they were airborne. Ward leant back into his seat, closed his eyes and visualised what would happen when they got to Miami.

At the same time, Lawson was leading the pretty young attendant into the bathroom to introduce his latest fan to the mile high club.

EIGHT

Park Avenue – New York

Nicole-Louise and Tackler were sitting at their workstations in their Park Avenue apartment, discussing the names that they had come up with,
"You know Ryan would have probably worked out what is going on by now anyway," Tackler said as he stared at his own screen, with his back to her.
"He probably only knows the why, not the who nor the how," she replied, "And that is where our personal race comes into play."
Nicole-Louise and Tackler were Ward's kings of information. They loved the challenge of hunting down the worlds bad guys from the comfort of their scruffy, yet expensive apartment. They particularly enjoyed the part of their job where they stole the ill-gotten gains from the bad guys and redistributed the funds wherever

80

Ward saw fit. Such was their integrity; they had never once been tempted to steal any of it, even though they knew that the money could never be traced back to them. They were good people.

Ward often told them both collectively and individually that they were the most important people on his team and they always believed him.

"I'm so far caught between it being one of three very nasty people behind this kidnapping," Tackler said, "The DEA files are pretty thick on these three guys, and I'm just about to delve into their financial records."

"I'm down to two already," Nicole-Louise replied from the opposite side of the room, her eyes transfixed on her screen, and her fingers tapping on her keyboard furiously.

Tackler was going to respond and then decided that he would not give her the satisfaction. She was the most competitive person that he knew. He sometimes, like right now, believed that her will to win was as great as Ward's himself.

"Who are your two?" he eventually asked after a few minutes, deciding it was the better option to swallow a little pride, than waste the next hour on someone who would have no bearing on what he was looking for.

"Alesandro Begottoli and Pablo Cardona," she replied, "Who was the other one that you had on your list?" she asked.

Tackler looked at his list. He had three names on it, Gino Bettaga, Vincent Suarez and Deliah Simon. He had no idea how she had concluded that it was none of them but he played along regardless,

"Vincent Suarez," he replied.

"Seriously Tackler," Nicole-Louise said sarcastically, "You are looking at the same DEA records as me, surely you could see that Suarez is getting ready to run," she added.

Tackler pulled up the financial records of Suarez. He could see a personal fortune of fourteen million dollars that had been moved to an off shore account in the Bahamas, and that the only outgoings appeared to be small payments to forty individuals of a few hundred dollars a week but he wasn't sure what that meant.

"How so?" he enquired, trying to sound as disinterested as he could.

"It's easy," she replied, "It's a tax dodge. They set up a fictitious company, employ a group of locals, pay them regularly for doing nothing, and then manipulate the local tax rules to first clean their dirty money, and then avoid paying tax on it," she added in a matter of fact tone.

Tackler had just learnt something new.

"So how does that mean that he is getting ready to run?" he enquired, forgetting that this was meant to be a challenge between them, and now genuinely interested to discover what Nicole-Louise could see in those figures that he couldn't.

"If you trace the money back from the accounts in The Bahamas, you can see that he has spent the last six months consolidating all of his cash into one account. There are also records of three properties which are on the market which he no doubt doesn't want anymore, and finally…. Well, surely you can see it?" she asked.

Tackler had no idea what she was on about. He was looking at the same information as her.

"Unless….." she started, "You want to admit that my financial analytical skills are way better than yours, and that you probably narrowed it down to three people such as Gino Bettaga, Deliah Simon and Suarez?" she asked. Tackler conceded defeat immediately.

He spun his chair around and stood up,

"I don't know how you do it," he said as he was walking across the living room towards her, "Every time. I admit it; math was never my strong point."

She smiled at him,

"And that's why I love you Tackler. You make me feel so smart," she said.

He playfully punched her on the arm.

"This transaction here," she said, pointing to a figure that read just short of two million dollars, "Is for a property in Southern Spain. He's running. From what or who I don't know, but at sixty four, he's quitting the game."

"So that leaves?" Tackler asked, forgetting the name of the other two people that Nicole-Louise had said.

"Alesandro Begottoli and Pablo Cardona," she reminded him.

He looked at her quizzically, indicating that he had no idea who either of these men were.

She sighed and rolled her eyes, as if telling Tackler to keep up. He ignored her and waited.

"Alesandro Begottoli," she started, "Is the newest leader of the Begottoli mafia family. They are prominent in both Miami and Chicago. His dad got killed two years ago, and they have branched out into the drug trade in a big way. They used to be mainly reliant upon racketeering, prostitution and gambling," she added, in a matter of fact tone.

To Nicole-Louise and Tackler, they were just names and numbers on their screens, but recent events had brought the human element closer to them and she suddenly changed her tone,

"And he was arrested two years ago for the kidnap and murder of a seventeen year old girl who was the daughter of a rival, but the charges were dropped due to insufficient evidence. He's an animal."

"So why him?" Tackler asked, not seeing anything she had said highlighting that it could be Begottoli.

"He's just purchased two giant warehouses in downtown Miami and three new SUV's. That looks like transport and storage to me," she replied.

Tackler instantly had a feeling that Alesandro Begottoli was the guy that they were looking for.

"The other guy, Cardona?" he asked.

"Looking through his file, I got suspicious that the DEA seemed to have volume after volume of stakeout information on him but never one arrest."

"That isn't enough on its own."

"It is if you read what is in it," she replied.

"What is in it?" Tackler asked.

Nicole-Louise didn't want to read out the information on the screen herself and so she pointed at it. Tackler leant over her shoulder and started to read, scrolling down with the mouse as he reached the end of the page. After the fourth page of reading, he stopped.

"He cuts people's eyeballs out?" he asked, disgust running through his voice.

"And yet the DEA or the FBI have still failed to arrest him," she replied.

"So what else do you have?"

"I'm still looking through his finances now," she replied, "His money is well hidden, I will have to dig deeper." Tackler looked at her, he knew she was lying. Which meant whatever she had found, she was finding hard to say.

"Just pull it up and go and make a drink for yourself while I read," he said to her.

She half smiled and clicked on a few icons on her screen and a page of invoices for a hardware superstore came up. She stood up from her chair.

"Who is the company?" he asked.

"A money laundering Delivery Company that Cardona set up two years ago," she replied as she disappeared through the kitchen door.

Tackler started to read down the list;

5 tonne of timber beams
2 tonne of hardwood sheeting
4 doors
3 skylights
4 toilets
3 basins
2 showers
Assorted boxes of nails

And then at the bottom, he saw what Nicole-Louise had seen. It simply said,

8 single metal beds
8 single mattresses
1 king-size bed
1 king-size mattress

Tackler instantly had a feeling that Pablo Cardona was the guy that they were looking for. That was now two guys who he was sure were behind it.

Nicole-Louise walked back into the living room and sat back at her desk.

"See what I mean?" she asked as she adjusted herself back into her chair.

"What if it isn't one?" he asked, "What if it is two groups behind it?"

"I thought that," she replied, "But that's down to Ryan to work out. Do you want to call him or shall I?"

"You found it, you can have the honour."

"You are so gracious in defeat Tackler," she said with a smile.

She picked up her cell phone and called Ward.

Ward was still reclined back in his seat mapping out the sequence of events that could be happening in Miami with his eyes closed when his phone vibrated in his pocket. He looked at the time and anticipated that they would be flying somewhere over Jacksonville right then. He pulled out his cell phone and looked at the caller I.D. He saw Nicole-Louise's name appear and smiled to himself,

"You've worked this out quickly," he answered

"We are a long way from working it out, that's your job but we are awaiting your instructions," she replied.

Nicole-Louise was one of Ward's most favourite people, as was Tackler, but he felt very protective of her, and he viewed her as his little sister more than the stunning technological genius she was. If he wanted it found, she would find it, and any information that evaded her, Tackler would find instead.

They had different skill sets; she was without doubt the financial and numerical expert of the two but Tackler was the guy who could get into anything, anywhere. No firewall or security system was in existence that could not be breached by one of them, and he had never once had a request for specific electronic information end in failure. They were the most important part of his team and right then, he knew that Nicole-Louise was going to point him in the right direction.

"So what have you managed to work out so far?" Ward asked.

"I think that the likelihood of it being anyone else other than the two people that we have identified is pretty slim," she replied.

"Knowing you, I would say it's impossible," he said, "So who are they and what do we know about them?"

Nicole-Louise spent the next few minutes explaining all that she had found on Begottoli and Cardona. He didn't interrupt, he had learned a long time ago that Nicole-Louise liked to go into great detail on how she had found the information that she was presenting to him. It always reminded him of a chef explaining how he had created a culinary masterpiece. When she reached the end of her explanation, she finished by saying,

"So what do you want us to do now?"

He pondered the question for a few seconds. He was trying to feel if he had a gut reaction to which one it could be, but he could see that it was feasible that it could be either or indeed, as Tackler had said, both of them working together, but his intuition didn't seem to be working.

"These warehouses that Begottoli has, how do they lay in relation to where the people were taken from?" he asked.

"I can get on that and have that by the time you land."

"And this Cardona guy," he started, "I can see why the purchase of beds might indicate he is involved but there could be a simple explanation and so you need to try and find where he would be able to hold such a large number of people."

"I'll get on it straight away."

"But the first thing we need to do is pay a visit to Newton Pharmaceutical Limited," he said, "I want you to get in touch with The Old Man and get it arranged for as soon as we land."

"OK. I'll get that sorted immediately," Nicole-Louise replied.

"Thanks Nicole-Louise," he said, "How did Tackler take you beating him on this one?" he asked with a laugh.

"How did you know that?" she enquired.

"Easy. The one that calls is always the one that finds it," he replied and he hung up the phone.

He leant back into his seat and looked at Lawson who had been listening to his end of the conversation with interest. He then looked over at the pretty flight attendant who was looking flushed, warm and slightly haggard. He shook his head.

"As soon as we land, you are on a sex ban until we have finished this Mike. I need your focus on this," he said.

"I'm always focussed," Lawson replied, completely failing to comprehend why Ward would think his sexual appetite would distract him, "So what have we got?" he asked.

"When we land we are going to be met by a guy called Harris. He will take us to the Newton headquarters and then we will find out exactly who has gone missing and why."

Lawson nodded.

"So this sex ban I am on," Lawson said, "It starts as soon as we land?"

Ward nodded.

"Rachel!" Lawson called out to the pretty flight attendant.

Ward shook his head and closed his eyes once again.

NINE

Adams Key – Upper Florida Keys

"It is time to speak to our esteemed guests," Pablo Cardona said to Franco, "Go and collect them and bring them all to block number three."
Franco walked out of Cardona's building, into the clearing for a brief moment, and then back under the cover of the trees, until he got to block number two, where the employees of Newton Pharmaceutical limited were being held.
"Open the door," he demanded to the short, wiry guy who was standing guard with his machine gun hanging by a strap from his right shoulder. The guy unlocked the three locks, pushed the door open and stepped to the side to allow Franco to walk inside.

The eight chemists all looked up at the giant Franco standing in the doorway looking down at them all with contempt.

"On your feet," he said in a threatening tone.

They all stood up, Dr Robert Anderton moving to the front of the group without thinking, the correct order of the group hierarchy naturally falling into place.

"Where are our families?" he asked, caution and nervousness running through his voice.

Franco took three giant steps forward and stopped two feet away from Dr Anderton.

"Did you say something?" he asked menacingly.

Anderton looked at the floor and shook his head.

"All of you follow me," he demanded, and he turned his back and started to move towards the door, "If I have to stop once and wait for any of you, then I will let my men loose on the women," he added at the top of his voice without looking back.

The chemists were on their feet immediately, the women scurrying frantically to keep up with the front of the group. Franco led them in silence to block number three. There were three guys standing outside, machine guns hanging from their shoulders, one of the other guys pointed his gun towards the group as they approached. Anderton could see that this building was by far the biggest of the four blocks, and he was sure that his family would be inside. For a moment, he felt a wave of relief rush over him, but as he glanced at the men holding the machine guns, he realised that they were all in the worst situation imaginable, and the sick feeling in the pit of his stomach returned.

Franco stopped at the doorway when he reached the building and turned around,

"All of you, inside quickly," he demanded.

Anderton led the group through the open door and stopped in his tracks. It took him a few moments to compute what he was seeing. Once it had registered, for the first time, he had a good idea of why they were all there.

He was looking at a fully equipped lab.

There were eight desks spaced around the room, all with computers and screens sitting neatly in the centre of them. There were balance scales, Bunsen burners, beakers, mixers, ovens and dryers, laid out neatly on workbenches that ran all the way along the sides of the building. There was a room at the far end of the building with walls of clear glass that ran from the floor to the ceiling, and in the middle of the glass room, on a platform that was raised about five inches off the floor, was a brown leather sofa. It was the only thing that looked out of place in the whole building.

"Move to the centre of the room," Franco demanded, and the group all stepped forward.

"I want to see my husband and children," Dr Allie Alexander said as she turned to face Franco.

Franco walked the twelve feet towards Alexander and looked down at her with contempt,

"Your husband is the stay at home mum, isn't he?" he asked with a smile.

Alexander said nothing in reply.

"So you are the man and your husband is a pussy, isn't he?" he asked as he prodded a finger into Alexander's chest, "So I will have no problem in beating you to death with my bare hands if you say one more word to me bitch."

She did not respond. Her shoulders dropped and she bowed her head. Anderton could see that she was petrified and he moved over towards Franco,

"We will do what you say, just please don't hurt our families," he said quietly.

"No doctor," Franco replied, "You will do what we say because you don't want to kill them yourselves," he added.

There was movement at the door and Franco looked around. He saw Pablo Cardona entering the building and he stepped away from the group and moved six feet to the side. Cardona approached them.

Eight sets of eyes started at him. Anderton was looking at this man who was in his mid-forties, about six feet tall and of South American origin. He had short dark hair and there was nothing spectacular about him until you looked in his eyes and then you could see the evil that existed in him. He briefly made eye contact with Anderton and smiled. Anderton shuddered and looked down at the floor.

"I have a problem," Cardona said as he stopped in front of them and looked each one of them up and down with contempt, "Or rather, you have a problem," he added. They all looked at him with confusion on their faces.

"You are clever people, the best that Newton has. Some of the smartest chemists in the country by all accounts," Cardona continued, "Are you smart whore?" he asked, addressing Catherine Lambourne, who immediately looked down at the floor.

"Your father wasn't very smart. He didn't do what he was told so that made him dumb. Are you as dumb as him? Does it run in the family?" he asked mockingly.

Catherine continued to look down at the floor.

"If you ignore me whore, I'll let my men have you to do what they want with you again, because you must be dumb not to answer," he said, "Are you dumb?"

"No, I'm not," Catherine replied without looking up.

"Good," Cardona said, and then laughed, "Because I'm going to tell you a story, and if you are all smart, you will listen carefully to it, and then you are going to find the solution to your problem."

The chemists all shuffled on their feet as they waited for Cardona to make sense of what was happening to them.

"Fifteen months ago I acquired a recipe for something very important. Actually, not a recipe, I think you call it a composition. Am I right Dr Anderton?" he asked, "Is that what you call it?"

Dr Anderton nodded.

"I can't hear you," Cardona said, "When I ask you a question, you speak. Am I right Dr Anderton?" he asked menacingly.

"Yes you are," Anderton replied, "Everything has a chemical composition."

"Thank you," he said, "I make my living in the manufacturing and distribution of narcotics. It has made me very rich and very powerful. This composition that I was given is the holy grail of narcotics. It is instantly addictive, impossible to break free from, and is simple to mass produce. And most importantly, it costs very little and can all be done in a lab," he added, before stopping

94

and looking at the group as if he was waiting for a round of applause or acknowledgement to continue.

No one said anything.

"We have had a lot of people working on this drug but they are mainly university kids who need the money, and they haven't got the skill base of a working team such as you people combined. I understand that you are a very good team. Is that right Dr Anderton?"

"Our team is very good," Anderton replied, trying his hardest to say it with conviction so that the rest of the chemists would have confidence in whatever it was they were going to be asked to do.

"But it's not 'Our' team, is it?" Cardona asked, "It is your team, and so that means that you are responsible for them all. Am I right Dr Anderton?"

"Yes you are sir."

"This narcotic, this holy grail of drugs has a name. It is called Invincible. Because that is how it makes you feel. I'm invincible without taking anything to make me believe it. I'm untouchable, and the U.S. government don't mess with me, so you can see how that makes me invincible?"

"Yes I can," Anderton replied, completely unsure of where Cardona was going.

"But there is a problem with Invincible. A problem that is now yours to solve."

None of the chemists responded and so Cardona continued.

"It gives an immediate high, which takes about four minutes to kick in, but for some reason it induces a heart attack and kills people stone dead. The longest survivor we have had is twenty five minutes after the rush starts. Some whore in New York."

"And you want us to try and stop the heart attack inducing component of the drug?" Anderton asked, in spite of knowing the answer.

"No," Cardona replied.

All of the chemists lifted their eyes from the floor and looked at him with confusion.

"So what do you want?"

"I want you to save the lives of your families."

"I don't understand what you are saying," Anderton said.

"It's simple. Starting in three hours' time, one of your family members will be randomly picked to try Invincible. If you stop the heart attack inducing part of it, they live. If you don't they die. It's very simple, because if you are as good as you say, everybody will be fine," he said, a beaming smile accompanying his words.

The mood in the building instantly changed.

And then the noise followed.

Catherine Lambourne and Dr Allie Alexander instantly burst into tears and started sobbing loudly.

"I want to see my family now!" Kyle Johnston screamed, desperate to know that his four children were safe and alive.

"You are an animal!" Dr Sardar Taremi screamed at Cardona.

The last comment made Cardona's smile vanish immediately and he looked at Anderton.

"You have a disrespectful team Dr Anderton," he said, fixing his stare deep into Anderton's eyes, "And because of that, you are the one who is going to be held accountable."

"What do you mean?" Anderton asked.

"The composition is written down there," Cardona said, pointing to a whiteboard with a complex looking chemical equation on it. I'm sure it makes sense to you." Anderton looked at the whiteboard and the rest of the chemists turned their heads at the same time.

"If you look on the workbenches there are a number of dishes that hold the chemicals that make up Invincible in their separate parts. The inadequate chemists we have had working on this have given you a head start, so you are at the point of drying now," Cardona said, clearly impressed with the way he articulated the process required to make the drug.

"It's not that simple," Anderton replied, "It requires analysis, calculation and focus," he protested.

"Well Dr Anderton, you had better get your team focussed because in exactly three hours from now, your wife Claire will be the first one to try your work," he said, and then he promptly turned around walked out of the room followed by Franco.

The door slammed shut and the chemists heard the three locks click into place.

"We can't do this in such a short period of time; you know that, don't you Robert?" Dr Justin Wynne said to Anderton.

"Yes I do, so we will have to work on first removing the component that is inducing the heart attacks. I have an idea," he replied, "Claire's life depends on it, and all of our families' lives depend on it. Kyle, you and Catherine do an equipment check, Sardar and Eric, you see what they have in the trays so far, Heath; you need to get the computers up and running. Allie and Justin, we will

97

break this down, component by component and find out what we can do," he said assertively before turning away from the group and silently bursting into tears.

Outside the building, Cardona and Franco were heading towards their living quarters,
"Do you think they will do it in three hours Mr Cardona?" Franco asked.
"I doubt very much they will do it in twelve hours Franco," Cardona replied.
Franco looked at his boss,
"So why only give them three hours?" he asked.
"Because I want to see if Dr Robert Anderton is going to do what I think he is going to do."
He reached his block and walked inside, closing the door and leaving Franco outside. He took out his cell phone and called the number.
"They are all here and starting work now," he said
"And the hostage, he is secure?" the voice on the end of the phone asked.
"I'm looking at him right now," Cardona replied, staring at the badly beaten guy who was still strapped to the chair, "Shall I dispose of him?" he asked.
"No," The voice replied, "Keep him secure for now, he has the composition in his head, and we need to keep him alive until you have solved the puzzle. Be quick, I can only have the patrols in place for three days before people start asking questions," he added and the line went dead.

TEN

Miami International Airport – Florida

Ward stepped off the plane first at Miami International Airport and descended the stairs. He immediately saw Bruce Harris leaning against the hood of a Ford Sedan waiting for him. He knew it was Harris because he had the look about him. The same look that he and McDermott, and all of McDermott's team had about them, it was the same wiry, alert look that the people who moved in his world generally possessed. Lawson was the exception to the general rule, but Lawson was the exception to a lot of things.

Harris stood just over six feet tall and Ward estimated that he was in his mid-thirties. He had short, neat brown hair, and he wore a crisp, white tee-shirt which showed off his muscular arms. He had a pair of sunglasses, which were turned up from his ears and rested just above his hairline

"I like the look of him," Lawson said as he reached the bottom of the stairs behind Ward.

Harris saw them both looking at him and he pushed himself up from the hood and walked towards them.

"Harris?" Ward asked as he extended his right hand when Harris got to within three feet of him. Harris took his hand and shook it firmly,

"Yes," he replied and then swung his hand around to shake Lawson's hand, "I've had my instructions and have arranged two visits for us," he added, as he took a second look at Lawson's mesmerising eyes.

"Who are we visiting?" Ward enquired.

"Firstly we will drive across to the headquarters of Newton Pharmaceuticals and then we have a meet with Dr Pepper," Harris replied.

Lawson laughed at the unfortunate name that, he assumed, belonged to an employee of Newton Pharmaceuticals.

"What's the worst that could happen?" Lawson asked, a comment that left a frown and a confused look running across Harris' face.

"Who's Dr Pepper?" Ward asked as he started to walk towards the car that Harris had been leaning against.

"He's probably the biggest street dealer of narcotics in Miami," Harris replied.

They got into the car, Lawson climbed into the rear and Ward into the front passenger seat.

"Who are we seeing at Newton's?" Lawson asked.

"Hillary Whelan, the operations and research director and Simon Newton the third, CEO."

"And then hopefully they can tell us more about the chemists," Lawson replied, "And then we can get refreshed with Dr Pepper."

Ward rolled his eyes.

As much as he liked Lawson, at times, he would wear the worst joke out, and then recycle it to wear it out again.

"Excuse my friend," Ward said to Harris, "He's on a sex ban and can't think straight."

"Sounds like my wife," Harris replied, and all three of them laughed together.

Newton Pharmaceutical Limited - Miami

The drive to Newton Pharmaceuticals took just fifteen minutes. The site was situated on an area of land that was surrounded by a lake of water called Blue Lagoon. Harris pulled the car to a stop as they reached the security gates at the front of the site. Ward noticed that there were CCTV cameras every thirty feet that ran along the top of the perimeter fence, which was at least ten feet high, and had coils of razor wire wrapped around the top. It looked a very secure place. He doubted very much that whoever had taken the chemists had done so from their place of work.

Harris lowered the window and a large, black guy walked out of the security house and over to the car. He eyed Ward and Harris up almost with contempt, and then glanced into the back seat at Lawson, looked away and then glanced back in again. Lawson flashed him his biggest smile.

"You boys have an appointment?" the guy asked, using the word 'Boys' to show he was a tough guy who saw most men as inferior to himself.

"We are here to see Hilary Whelan and Simon Newton," Harris replied.

The guy seemed instantly impressed by the mention of their names and went through the routine of pretending to read down his clipboard to look for an appointment time when it was obvious to them all that he knew they were expected.

"You guys FBI?" he asked, trying to sound as disinterested as he possibly could.

No one in the car responded, every one of them aware that no response would unnerve the guy.

"Pull into the car park on the left when you reach the end of the drive," he said, and then he turned to walk towards the security house.

A minute later, the large electronic gates were being opened automatically, and Harris drove the car through. He drove up a long drive, which had neat mowed lawns on either side, and a giant building came into view. It wasn't what Ward expected. There were no large chimneys omitting smoke or anything that resembled the pharmaceutical company that he had once visited in the U.K. when investigating the theft of bomb making equipment, this building just looked like any normal office that a financial institution would use. It was a clean white building, an attempt had been made to replicate a Georgian style, an attempt that had failed miserably, and there were flower beds that ran neatly along the front, full of a variety of bright colours.

Harris turned to the left and pulled the car to a stop in a small car park.

They stepped out of the car and walked towards the main entrance. The entrance doors were made from clear glass and they stepped through them, and once inside, they approached a large reception desk with three young women seated in a row, about three feet apart from each other.

"Don't even think about talking to them," Ward said to Lawson, who by now had his eyes firmly fixed on all three of them, already calculating which one he would enjoy flirting with the most.

Ward noticed that there were three guys to the left huddled in a group deep in conversation, wearing blue jackets with the letters 'FBI' emblazoned across the back in bright yellow letters.

"We are here to see Whelan and Newton," Harris said to the middle woman of the three receptionists. He noticed immediately that all three women were looking over his shoulder behind him, clearly transfixed by something.

He turned his head and saw Lawson beaming at the three of them.

"Hello?" Harris repeated.

"I'm sorry sir, your name please?" she asked.

"Hardy," Harris replied.

She scrolled down the list and stopped her finger halfway down.

"If you take a seat over there," she said pointing to some plush leather chairs which were just behind the three FBI agents, "And someone will come down for you."

The three of them turned and walked over to the chairs and sat down.

The three FBI agents stopped talking and watched them take their seats. One of them, a tall thin guy, said something to the other two and walked over towards them.

"Who are you gentlemen?" he asked politely.

None of them spoke, Harris glanced at Ward and Lawson was still looking at the three receptionists.

"I asked you a question?" the guy said.

"We are no one," Ward replied.

The guy studied Ward for a moment, his English accent intriguing the guy rather than making him suspicious.

"Can I ask what you are doing here?" he asked with a polite tone to his questioning once more.

"It's a private matter," Ward replied, equally politely.

The guys' whole demeanour changed.

"Do you see the three letters on my back?" he asked, spacing the words out as he said them, like you would to a child, an act that immediately irritated Ward.

He was always respectful of the job that all law enforcement people carried out, generally they were all good people who just wanted to keep others safe, but he had seen many, many times over the years how to a minority, a little bit of power went to their head. Just like ninety nine per cent of the people he had met who did normal jobs hated their boss. Or the text book managers as he always referred to them, the kind of boss most people have, the one who has no character or charisma, but has read a few management books and thinks they understand people when they are in fact clueless. He always called these people, 'The Stupid's' and right now, this guy was coming across as both stupid and irritating.

"I see them," Ward replied, "And they say two things to me," he added, and then stopped talking.

"What are they then hot shot?" the guy asked, just as he turned and beckoned his two colleagues over to join him.

"Firstly that you were bullied at school and you only did averagely at Quantico, which is why you are put on guard duty with your buddies here, because the real work is being done a long way away from here," he replied. The comment took the guy by surprise and his shoulders dropped slightly indicating that he knew what Ward was saying was pretty accurate.

"And what is the other thing?"

"Your top, top, top director, doesn't even get close to getting an appointment with our boss, so take your attitude elsewhere and leave the real bad stuff to the real bad guys," he said as he fixed a cold stare deep into the guys' eyes.

"Mr Hardy?" a voice said. They turned around and saw a middle age guy walking towards them. Harris stood up and extended his hand. The man took it and shook it vigorously, "Follow me please," he added as he turned and headed off towards the staircase which was behind the reception desk.

Lawson stood up and smiled at the FBI agents as he brushed past them, Ward rose to his feet and headed after Harris and Lawson,

"Keep up the good work Gentlemen," he said as he walked past them, and smiled to himself as the tall guy just stood still, his eyes following him as he passed.

They walked up to the stairs to the first floor and walked a long a heavily carpeted hallway with a number of glass doors that led into offices. He could see people working at their desks, head down, as he passed each room. They reached the end of the hall and saw two large oak doors which were open and they followed the man inside.

There was a large mahogany table in the middle of the room with ten chairs on each side and one each at the end.

Sitting at the head of the table was a guy who looked in his late fifties and to his left, a very attractive woman with long brown hair, tied up in a bun, who was dressed in a very expensive looking jacket and skirt, with a white blouse underneath, with the top three buttons undone to reveal the smallest glimpse of her cleavage. She stood up as the man waved them all into the room and then closed the door behind them as he walked out.

"Hello," she said assertively, "I'm Hilary Whelan, operations and research director," she proclaimed, as she first held out her hand and then took a double, and then triple look at Lawson. Ward could swear that she started to blush.

"I'm Simon Newton," the guy at the head of the table said without standing up. He looked tired and like he hadn't slept for days, which he probably hadn't. Ward knew instantly that this guy felt like he was carrying the weight of the world on his shoulders. The kidnapping of his team and their families was clearly draining the life out of him.

"Sit down please," Whelan said to them. Harris and Lawson pulled out a chair and sat down; Ward decided to stay standing so he used the back of the chair next to Lawson to lean his arms against to support him.

"Whatever you need from us to help to find them, we will do all we can" Simon Newton said, "Just please, find them quickly," he pleaded, genuine distress running through his voice. He looked on the brink of bursting into tears.

"What were they working on?" Ward asked Newton.

"Hilary?" Newton said to Whelan, clearly having no clue about the things that actually happened in laboratories.

"I can't say," Whelan said.

"You can say, there are thirty one people who are missing, the smallest thing might help," he said to her, already taking an instant dislike to Whelan.

"I can't say because I don't know," she replied.

"Some research director you are," he said sarcastically, "Let me ask another question then. The team that are missing, what are they capable of creating?" he asked.

"I don't know. Our industry is not as simple as you think, what might work in theory does not necessarily work in practice, the human body is only designed to accept certain things, we don't know what they are until we try them," Whelan replied, sounding factual and efficient rather than concerned over her missing employees.

"So you have no idea what they were working on or what they can create?" he asked.

"I'm sorry, but what we do is very complex, there is no definitive answer to either of your questions," Whelan replied.

"OK. Thank you for your time, you have been very helpful," he said, much to the surprise of Harris who turned and stared at him. Lawson had seen this from Ward hundreds of time, he was sure that Ward now had exactly what he had come here for, even though Lawson had no idea what it was he had been looking for.

"That's it?" Newton asked.

"That's it," Ward replied, "Let's go," he said to Lawson and Harris. They stood up and both nodded at Newton. Whelan was gazing at Lawson like a teenager, and her cheeks were by now turning a crimson red.

"We'll be in touch if we need anything else," he said with his back to them as he opened the oak doors and stepped through them and headed back along the corridor, down the stairs, past the FBI agents who were glaring at them, and outside into the hot sun.

"What did you learn?" Lawson asked as they headed towards Harris' car.

"Whelan is lying and Newton is under duress," Ward replied, "I need to make a couple of calls," he added as he veered to the left of the car and walked ten feet past it.

ELEVEN

Park Avenue – New York

"It is definitely Cardona," Nicole-Louise said, "I am so smart," she added, and threw her arms up in the air in mock celebration.

Tackler put his head in his hands in genuine annoyance that she had beaten him to finding out who was behind the kidnapping. It frustrated him that every time financial digging was involved, she always got there first. In terms of analytical skills, he was head and shoulders above her, but as soon as finding the answer involved digging through financial records, he never stood a chance.

"Go on then, gloat," he said to her without turning from his screen to look at her, "What makes you so sure?" he asked.

"Two hundred thousand dollars, that's how," she declared.

"Two hundred thousand dollars?" he gasped.

"One payment of two hundred thousand dollars left one of Cardona's hidden accounts, and it bounced around six different accounts and ended up being paid to a guy called Michael Vermont."

"Who is Michael Vermont?"

"He is a senior executive for the National Park Service," she replied.

"So what does that mean?

"He is also the person who makes all of the decisions regarding the Biscayne National Park."

"Which means?" Tackler asked, having no idea what she was talking about.

"Seriously Tackler, don't you know anything about our heritage?" she asked, leaving him unsure if she was being serious or not.

"Clearly not," he replied sarcastically.

"The Biscayne National Park is made up of a group of Florida Keys," she began, "There are fourteen keys which make up the park, it covers one hundred and seventy three thousand acres, and it also includes the water that surrounds the keys."

"Why include the water?" Tackler asked, genuinely interested now.

"Because the fishing is the main attraction of the area," she said, "As I was saying, there are fourteen keys. They are; Soldier, Ragged, Boca Chita, Sands, Elliot, Adams, Caesars Rock, Meigs, Rubicon, Reid, Porgy, Totten, Old Rhodes and Islandia," she proclaimed, feeling really pleased with herself that she knew something that Tackler had no idea about.

"Maybe he is on a fishing jaunt?" Tackler asked, failing to see how a payment to a government employee would confirm it was Cardona, "Or maybe the payment was for making sure a drug route was clear?" he asked, suddenly energised by the fact that he could see a weak link in her assumption.

"You didn't read the DEA file properly," she replied, shaking her head in disappointment as she said it, "The boats can't get that close to the keys, and the area is full of tourists who are fishing. What's wrong with you today? It's like you are losing concentration because yet again, I am whipping your ass."

Tackler turned and threw his pencil towards her; it landed just short of her feet.

"So you are going to ring Ryan again and brag I take it?" he asked.

"Not yet," she replied.

"Why?"

"Because we now have to work out what key they could be holding them on."

Tackler smiled, he now understood.

"And as that requires a super-hack to get into the NSA satellite system, and I am better at doing that than you, the only way that you can find it is if I help you?" he asked, and then let out a long laugh.

Nicole-Louise bent over, picked up the pencil and threw it back at him, the thin, lead filled missile catching him on the side of the face.

He let out another long laugh,

"Temper temper!"

"Just find it Tackler," Nicole-Louise said, her moment of victory now passed, "I'm going to dig deeper into the finances of Newton Pharmaceuticals now," she added, turning she started to tap furiously on her keyboard once again.

Newton Pharmaceutical Limited - Miami

Ward dialled Centrepoint's number on his cell phone.
"Have you made any progress?" The Old Man said as he answered.
"I've only been here forty five minutes," he replied.
"So what have you got?
"The people at Newton know more than they are letting on. I know that for sure."
"So get it out of them."
"Not yet, that can wait a while," he replied, "But I need you to tell me a little bit more about what is going on."
"Relating to what?"
"Your suspicions that some agencies are involved in this?"
"There is a concept of a Superdrug that has been kicking around for some time. A once taken, lifetime addictive drug, that is cheap and easy to mass produce. It is worth billions to the right people."
"And how close is it to being produced?"
"Very," Centrepoint said with a sigh, "The composition has nearly been perfected, and if it gets out on the streets, the devastation that it will cause will spiral out of control like an unstoppable virus. Before we know it, inner cities will collapse, and crime and murders will hit

new heights across the States. So not only is it crucial that you find the people who were kidnapped, it's vital that before you go killing everyone who crosses your path, that you get your hands on the composition too," he added. Clear order a++nd instruction in his voice.

"So why do you think that agencies are involved?" Ward asked, thinking back to the three FBI guys inside the building that he now stood outside.

"Because whoever is behind it is paying a lot of money not to get caught, and it is impossible to do that without help. The DEA have huge resources down there in Florida, they know who all the main players are, and yet they are completely silent on this. Both the FBI and CIA are aware of the damage that this drug could cause and yet the DEA, the people with their fingers on the pulse are playing dumb."

This made perfect sense to Ward. Recent experiences had taught him that it was impossible to trust anyone who worked for government agencies completely.

"OK," he said, "If you find anything else that might help me, let me know straight away."

"Just move quickly on this Ryan," The Old Man said, "Finding the composition and the people who are missing is the only way that this operation will be deemed a success."

Ward hung up the phone.

He turned and walked back towards the car. Harris already had the engine running and Lawson was sitting in the rear seat. He climbed in.

"Is everything OK Mr Secretive?" Lawson asked.

"Let's go and see Dr Pepper then," he said to Harris who was already moving the car out of the car park as Ward finished the sentence.

"Good idea," Lawson said, "What's the worst that could happen?"

Ward rolled his eyes.

He had a bad feeling that things weren't right somehow. In fact, he had a feeling that he was missing something big and obvious, something that was staring him right in the face.

Overtown NW 12th Street – Miami

Fifteen minutes later, Harris was pulling up around the corner of a drab looking, beige coloured building that had an awful blue band of paint that ran around the first floor. The building was in what can only be described as one of the less affluent areas of Miami. At first glance, it appeared to be a block of four apartments but Harris explained that Dr Pepper owned the whole building and the downstairs apartments were where the parties were and the girls hung around all day, and upstairs was where Dr Pepper's business was run with the professionalism that you would expect from a big, legitimate organisation.

"He is suspicious of new people so is it OK if I do the talking?" Harris asked Ward, appearing uncomfortable as he said so.

"He knows what you are?"

Harris nodded.

"Then that's fine. He's your contact, you lead the way."

They stepped out of the car and walked towards the mesh fence that ran across the front yard of the building. There were two muscular black guys standing just inside the gate that opened onto the front path, and two scantily clad girls just behind them who seemed to be doing nothing but trying to look sexy. Ward smiled to himself. The whole 'Gangsta' image that these people tried so hard to portray amused him. He didn't like them. In his eyes, people who peddled drugs and treated women like objects were scum. These type of people heaped misery on the vulnerable with their drugs and their violence, and while he sympathised with the poverty that they had to live and grow up in, he despised what they represented. He despised the fact that they were going to one of these people for help, more than what they were.

They reached the gate and one of the guys seemed to recognise Harris, but still stood in front of the gate so it could not be opened.

"Who are your homeboys?" the guy said to Harris as the other guy stepped forward and stood shoulder to shoulder with him, completely blocking the path. The two women behind were still standing just off the path, staring at the three of them on the other side of the gate, and doing weird, gyrating movements at the same time. Ward wondered if this was their job and they were paid to semi-dance in the front garden all day.

"They are good to go," Harris replied.

"I'll be the judge of that boss," the guy replied, "Are you good to go pretty boy?" he then asked, shouting over Harris' shoulder and looking at Lawson.

"I'm on a sex ban at the moment homeboy," Lawson replied, "So less of the flirting,"

115

Ward laughed out loud.

"Are you good to go homeboy? You laughing at me?" the guy said to Ward.

"I'm good to punch you in the face if you don't stop wasting my time," Ward said as he stepped forward, pushed past Harris and shoved hard on the gate, knocking both of the guys backwards as he forced it open, "And if you pull a firearm I will shoot you both in the face," he warned.

"OK, Cuz, we were just having fun," the guy with all the talk said, suddenly feeling very intimidated by the English guy walking through them and heading up the path.

Bizarrely, the two women continued gyrating, much to Lawson's amusement as he passed them.

They walked up the stairs to the first floor landing, and when they reached the top of the stairs, Ward moved to the side to let Harris step in front of him.

"Try not to antagonise them too much when we get inside please," Harris said, "They don't take to being threatened in their own neighbourhood."

Ward ignored him.

Harris rapped on the door four times and it was opened by a huge, fat guy, who must have weighed over three hundred pounds. He had at least six solid gold chains hanging from his neck, and he was wearing a Miami Dolphins shirt. Ward was impressed that they made the tops in those sizes, the ability of sports teams to milk their loyal fans knows no limit, he thought to himself.

"Hey Beast, how are you?" Harris asked the guy.

"I'm good man," the huge guy replied.

"The Doc is expecting me, is he ready?" Harris asked, sounding more like a 'Gangsta' with every word he spoke, a fact not lost on Lawson who started to smirk.
"Come on in," the fat guy said.
They stepped inside and the first thing that Ward noticed was three scantily clad girls who could not have been more than twenty, standing at the far side of the room in just their underwear, semi gyrating, even though no music was being played. The ridiculousness of the situation was more than compensated for by the fact that all three of them had the most stunning bodies. Ward smiled to himself when he wondered what Lawson would be thinking right then.
There was a guy sitting on a sofa in just a pair of shorts. He was a very muscular guy, with tattoos covering his right arm in a sleeve. This was obviously the Doc. Elsewhere in the room, there were four other guys sitting in armchairs, two of them with handguns on the arms of their seats.
"My man, who are these boys," The guy on the sofa said, pointing at Ward and Lawson.
"We are the shit storm," Ward said, not enjoying being in the same room as these idiots one bit.
"What accent is that?" the Doc asked, "You a Brit?"
"We need a few questions answered," Ward said, "Then we will be on our way," he added.
"No need for the hostility man," The Doc replied, "He's told me what you want already. You are clearly some big, bad boy mother, so I'll tell you what you want to know but please show respect in my humble abode," he added, trying to imitate an English accent and failing miserably.

117

"Fair enough," he replied, "What have you got?"

"Someone is cutting off all of the supply chains man," the Doc started, "That can only mean one of two things."

"What two things are they?"

"The government boys are increasing their interception rate to hike the price of products up."

"Why would they want to do that?"

"And that leads me to the second point," the Doc said, "Because the word on the street is that the Columbians are in bed with the D.E.A, and together they are creating some kind of drug that is cheap and more addictive than even crack."

"So how do they fit together?"

"It's simple economics man. The ones who stand to benefit are those with the ability and resources to supply. When the price of goods goes up because the D.E.A are intercepting everything, less people can afford it and supplies are sparse. Imagine offering something at a fifth of the normal price. Do people buy one or do the buy ten?" the Doc asked

"How accurate is this information you have?" Ward asked.

"The D.E.A have to be in on it man, and the Columbians were talking this up months ago, so one and one makes two."

"What do you know about the people who were kidnapped from the pharmaceutical company?"

"It says to me that the Columbians are having problems with their finished product and they need help," the Doc said, and then laughed a short but satisfied laughed.

"Do you know where they could be holding them?"

"If I knew that, I would be there taking them down myself. I have everyone on the street looking, but they literally seemed to have vanished into thin air man. Gone like a puff of smoke."

"Why would you be hunting for them?"

"Because I want what they have," the Doc replied.

As much as Ward disliked this guy, he at least appreciated his honesty.

"If you help us to find the missing people, you won't get your hands on the new drug, you understand that right?" Ward asked.

"I'll take my chances man. Surely a mean mother like you can respect that I have an obligation to try?"

Strangely, Ward could see it, and it sat OK with him.

"OK. You keep your people looking, and the moment you hear anything, you let him know," Ward said, pointing at Harris.

"We have a deal man. Anything else?" the Doc asked.

Ward was about to say no and then he remembered that there was one thing that he couldn't make any sense of, "Just one thing," he started, "These girls doing this semi dance outside and in here, do you pay them for doing that?" he asked.

"We don't pay the bitches," the Doc replied, "They are just grateful to be here."

Ward smiled, and the Doc's other guys in the room laughed loudly and started to make swiping gestures with their hands which resulted in a clicking noise echoing around the room. He extended his left hand to the Doc and as he reached to shake it, Ward unleashed a lightning quick uppercut that caught the Doc full on the throat and before anyone else could move, Lawson and Harris had their guns pulled.

"Learn to respect women," he said to the Doc, who was now on his knees on the floor desperately trying to get his breath back, "Thank you for your help, and make sure that you call us as soon as you hear anything," he added, and then he turned for the door and the fat guy opened it without saying anything at all, he walked out, back past the girls who were, incredibly, still gyrating, and up the path towards the gate.

"Jesus," Harris said, "Are you crazy? You can't go into their neighbourhood and do that. What was all that about?"

"Simple," Ward replied, "They thought something big was happening before, now, after my little performance, they will be thinking that something massive is happening and they will try much harder to find the missing people. They won't share anything they find with us, and so you need to be all over them Harris. Can you do that?" he asked.

Harris nodded, "It's a dangerous game to play with them, they are very unpredictable," he said.

"With Lawson watching my back, I was never in danger, was I?" he said, looking at Lawson for confirmation.

"I didn't see what happened; did you see how fit those girls were?" Lawson replied and then smiled.

For once, Ward laughed at Lawson's sexual desperation.

TWELVE

Adams Key – Upper Florida Keys

Pablo Cardona approached the chemist's lab, with added vigour, Franco by his side, matching him stride for stride, and Fabian Martinez scurrying behind, revelling in his unofficial promotion. Cardona gained an intense, almost physical pleasure in striking fear into people. The power and heightened sense of control he felt when he looked at the fear in people's eyes that his very presence created, was akin to a sexual orgasm to him, probably a little more satisfying. The ability to strike fear into people had first surfaced on the streets of Bosa, a large locality of Columbia's capital city, Bogota. He had been raised in poverty by his mother, Liana, and once he had reached the age of eight, she made it clear that it was no longer her responsibility to feed him or his younger sister, Catalina, and that it would be his duty to go out into the streets of Bosa to steal food or anything else that he could get his hands on for her to barter with. He had started out, as all street criminals do, stealing fruit or pan de queso, a cheese bread, from the markets, and for every loaf or item of fruit that he managed to acquire, he sacrificed two severe slaps or strikes by a stick as a result of the stall holders getting wise to him. He eventually became indifferent to the pain that he felt, and saw it as a means to an end. There was one particular stall holder called Dayro Mina, who would beat him every time he saw him anywhere near the market. As the years passed and he got to ten, the open palm slaps turned to clenched fists. By the age of twelve, he was running errands for a street dealer called Gustavo Moreno; a guy who the young Cardona thought was a big time drug lord but in truth, was halfway down the food chain in a very small cartel. Cardona would collect pure cocaine from a butchers shop, and move it across the locality to a large house in the plush part of Bosa. Cardona swore that one day he would be rich enough to buy a house there.

He killed for the first time at thirteen.

He had been travelling back into the slums where he lived, when he saw Dayro Mina sitting at the bus stop waiting with his wife. He didn't notice him at first as Moreno was looking straight ahead; it was only when he passed the bench and heard his wife cussing him that he glanced sideways and saw him. For the first time ever, he didn't feel the need to run from Moreno. Instantly, he remembered the slaps that turned to punches and the vile comments that Moreno would scream about his mother and that he was a rat who deserved to die in the sewer. Cardona stopped walking immediately, pulled out his six inch flick knife, walked quietly up behind him, and with all of his force, plunged the knife deep into Gustavo Moreno's neck. As his wife turned to look at him and she opened her mouth to scream, he pulled the knife from Moreno's back, and in one movement, he swung to the right and planted the knife deep into the side of her neck, severing the artery immediately. She slumped forward clutching her throat and Moreno struggled to his feet to face his small attacker and then the young Cardona planted the knife deep into Moreno's stomach. And he kept plunging the knife, again and again and again until Moreno collapsed backwards and crashed onto the floor, facing up to the clear blue sky. In total, he stabbed him forty four times, his wife dead by the time the knife entered Moreno's punctured torso on the twentieth occasion. He looked down at his hands, which were soaked in blood, and he shifted his weight onto his front foot ready to run when he saw something that mesmerised him. Gustavo Moreno was dead but his eyes were wide open, staring up at the sky, and Cardona noticed a fear in them. It was like his eyes had captured the moment when he knew his life was ending and he was begging him to let him live. He felt a pleasure, a sensation run through his whole body like an electrical surge, and for a few moments, he was transfixed by the eyes of the dead man staring at him, and he wanted them, he was desperate for them, so that he could take them home and stare at them for hours. He was transfixed. He was shaken from the moment by a man screaming at him running across the road towards him.

He ran, and he was out of sight by the time the stranger had reached the dead Morenos. But he vowed that if he ever killed again, he would remove the eyes of the people he killed or had killed for a souvenir.

In a cooler in his Miami mansion, he now had over three hundred sets of eyes, belonging to men, women and children, all bagged and all labelled.

The three guys guarding the lab were undoing the last of the locks as he reached the building.

"Tell Fabian to get ready," he said to Franco as he walked through the door into the lab, just as the guard swung it open. He stopped three feet inside the lab and took in the sight before him.

Dr Robert Anderton and his team were all working away frantically at their desks, weighing, checking, calculating and everyone in the room was doing so in complete silence.

This pleased him.

What didn't please him was the fact that Dr Allie Alexander was the only one who looked up at him and looked afraid. They clearly weren't frightened enough of him he thought to himself.

They need to understand that they need to work quicker or the consequences will be something much worse than they ever could imagine.

He walked over to Anderton's desk Anderton only looked up when he stopped two feet away.

"Progress?" he asked calmly.

"You need to give us more time," Anderton replied.

"No," Cardona replied, "You need to work quicker," he said with a smile.

"We are doing the best that we can," Anderton said, an air of desperation now creeping into his voice.

"Your best isn't good enough."

"This is a lot more complex than just turning pure cocaine into crack. The composition you have for this won't work as it is. It's not a question of just putting in more baking soda like the addicts do. You are trying to dilute the purity and volume of the cocaine used massively, if it was that simple, people would have done it a long time ago," Anderton, said, almost in a condescending voice, for a split second, forgetting the severity of the situation and becoming engrossed in his lab work, "I'm sorry sir,", he quickly added, "It's a complex problem we have here."

"I understand," Cardona replied.

"Thank you sir for understanding."

"I understand that I gave you three hours to trial the first sample and your three hours are up."

"We're not ready!"

"Then we will try one of our existing samples," Cardona said as he pulled a small brown envelope out of his trouser pocket.

Robert Anderton looked terrified. Cardona saw the fear in his eyes, and he immediately started to feel the pleasure and electricity build inside of him. He was looking forward to the day that he could add Dr Robert Anderton's eyes to his collection.

"We have one sample that will be ready in a few minutes," Anderton quickly said, "We can try that one."

Cardona smiled, "See Doctor, you can do it if you want."

A scream echoed out in the lab and everyone turned to face the door apart from Cardona. He knew who was screaming.

Franco was blocking the doorway, and when he moved to the side, everyone could see Fabian behind him with his hands firmly gripping the hair of Crystal Wynne, the wife of Dr Justin Wynne, who was on her knees, crying hysterically.

Crystal Wynne was your typical soccer mom. She was in her early forties and attractive in an elegant way. She had long blonde hair, a slim body and a perfect set of teeth that were so white they almost radiated light when she smiled.

But she wasn't smiling now.

She had been holding her two sons, Kyle and Bobby, when the guy holding her hair had walked into the building that was holding them all a few minutes ago. The man had yanked her boys away from her clutches and thrown them to the side, as he pulled her up from the floor by her hair. There had been very few protests of her treatment after Lindsey Dunn, wife of Dr Eric Dunn, had gone to her aide and been punched viciously in the face by the young man who had come to take her.

"Help me!" she screamed, prompting Fabian to yank on her hair harder.

Justin Wynne left his desk immediately to run to her aid. Cardona shouted, "Stop!"

He stopped in his tracks immediately.

"If you take one more step I will have ten of my men come in here and rape her, and after that, I will cut her eyes out and feed them to you." he shouted.

The whole room fell quiet. Even Crystal Wynne stifled her cries.

"Bring her over here," he demanded of Fabian.

Fabian pulled Crystal to her feet by her hair, and pushed her forward until they reached the glass room with the platform ten feet away from Cardona and Anderton.

"Get in there whore," Franco sneered.

"Do you need to be so rough with her?" Anderton pleaded.

Cardona just laughed.

"You are hurting her."

"You have no idea what pain is yet," Cardona replied, "Where is the drug?"

Anderton walked to his right and lifted up the door to a small oven which looked more like a microwave. He pulled out a small tray, and inside the tray; there were eight brown coloured pills. He carried the tray over to a small set of scales and weighed them, jotting the numbers on the digital display of the scales down on a piece of paper.

He carefully and deliberately walked back towards Cardona and put the tray down on his desk.

Cardona inspected the pills and smiled.

"It seems that we have made some progress doctor," he said.

"It's OK Crystal, everything will be fine, I promise," Anderton said.

Cardona smiled again.

Crystal Wynne stood rigid with fear. She had always been anti-drugs, and now she knew that she was going to be used as a guinea pig. She rarely drunk and the thought of falling into a drug induced state petrified her.

"Give her the pill," Cardona demanded.

The whole of the lab held their breath while Anderton reached into the tray and picked up one of the pills. He walked over to the glass room and carefully handed it to her; she stood with her hands firmly down by her side.

"Take it Crystal, everything will be OK," he reiterated again.

He was using his eyes to tell her that it was safe, that it would not kill her, and that she needed to trust him unconditionally.

She lifted her right hand, opened her palm and took the pill from him. Her hands were shaking violently as she placed the pill between her thumb and forefinger and started to raise it to her mouth. Everyone was staring at her. Tears were streaming down her face and she started to gently rock backwards and forwards.

"It will be OK. Trust me; I know what I am doing," Anderton said softly.

She put the pill into her mouth.

"Swallow it," Cardona said firmly, "Pick up that water and swallow it whore," he demanded as he pointed to the beaker of water on Anderton's desk.

She picked up the beaker, raised it to her mouth and took a small sip. She then did an exaggerated gulp to show that she had swallowed it.

"Open your mouth," Cardona demanded, grabbing her jaw with his hand as he said it.

Crystal Wynne opened her mouth. The pill was gone. Cardona smiled to himself.

"How confident are you that she will live more than twenty nine minutes Dr Anderton?" Cardona asked.

Anderton didn't respond at first, his eyes were fixed firmly on Crystal's gaze. The whole room seemed to be waiting for something to happen, anything, the smallest of drug induced reactions.

"Well?" Cardona said, "How confident that she will live more than twenty nine minutes?" he repeated.

"Reasonably," Anderton replied, still gazing at Crystal's eyes.

Chemistry is a science. It is combining the art of calculation and knowledge to give you a predicted result. To Dr Robert Anderton, he was sure that what he had calculated was not going to kill Crystal Wynne. In fact he was positive about it.

"I'm not!" Cardona spat.

And then events turned in a totally different direction to what Dr Robert Anderton had calculated.

Cardona pulled out the same jagged knife that he had used earlier to kill Johan Balanta, and jabbed it hard into the side of Crystal Wynne. Her legs buckled as she grasped the point of entry with both hands, and she immediately lost her balance and fell to the floor.

Dr Justin Wynne ran forward and was intercepted by Franco who delivered a crushing right hook to his face. The force of the punch knocked his feet off the ground and sent him crashing against the desk where Dr Sadar Taremi was standing, rigid with shock, and his hands clasped firmly over his mouth. He was unconscious by the time he hit the floor.

Dr Allie Alexander and Catherine Lambourne started screaming, and Franco stepped forward and slapped Catherine hard around the face, instantly silencing Allie as well.

Heath Beasley leant over and started to throw up on the floor, and the remaining men, Dr Eric Dunn, Kyle Johnson and Anderton, stood in complete silence.

A psychotic smile spread across Cardona's face as he leant over Crystal Wynne and pulled her hair back so he could look at her face.

She was still breathing.

Her pupils were dilating and she was sweating where her body temperature had increased.

"Watch or your families die," he demanded to everyone in the room without looking up.

He raised the knife and plunged it into Crystal Wynne's right eye and with the movement of his wrist that he had used a hundred times, he forced the eye out of the socket and then severed the chord behind it.

Heath Beasley passed out, everyone else looked away, but Cardona did not notice, he was so engrossed in the pleasure that the moment was giving him that he would not have noticed if everyone had left the building. He repeated the act on the left eye and then stood up, his hands covered in blood and holding Crystal Wynne's two eyeballs in his open palm.

"We did what you said, why have you done that you animal?" Anderton screamed, forgetting his own fear of Cardona for a few moments.

Crystal Wynne's body started convulsing. She was still alive. Anderton felt his knees becoming weak and he leant on the desk for support.

"Please, don't leave her like that," he pleaded to Cardona.

"You see what happens when you try and outsmart me doctor? You think that by removing all the components and just leaving pure cocaine in the pills that you could bluff me into thinking you have got somewhere? Maybe I should kill your wife for the disrespect and contempt you have shown towards me?" Cardona asked.

"I'm sorry," Anderton whimpered.

"You have three hours until the next one. Use your time well," Cardona said as he turned and walked away, clutching Crystal Wynne's eyeballs firmly in his hand, another set for his prize collection.

"Pick her up and take her out Fabian," he said as he passed the newly promoted guy, "And if she is still breathing, take her to the men so they can enjoy her body until she dies," he added, loud enough to ensure that every person in the room could hear him.

THIRTEEN

Overtown NW 12th Street – Miami

"Wouldn't you be fit if you danced on the spot for twelve hours a day?" Ward asked Lawson as they walked out of Dr Pepper's front garden.

"Was that dancing?" Harris asked with genuine bemusement in his voice.

They turned right, heading back to Harris's car, when Ward heard a noise that he instantly recognised and he dived to the floor and rolled behind a vehicle in a split second, just as Harris let out a dull yell. Lawson immediately hit the sidewalk and rolled over to Ward, taking cover behind the same vehicle, just as Harris fell down clutching his left arm.

"I've been shot," he groaned.

"How bad?" Ward enquired

"Not bad, it's just a wound, I'm not losing too much blood, it just stings," Harris replied, as he yanked his tee shirt up to take a look, "I'll live," he added.

"Can you see anyone?" Ward asked Lawson as he pulled his Glock from his waistband.

"It came from across the street judging by the way it hit him," Lawson replied as he pulled his own gun out, "It must have come from that car park. The shooter must be at ground level or the bullet would have hit me."

"Could have done the female race a favour just by climbing one flight of stairs then," Ward replied, and they both laughed.

"Glad you find it funny guys," Harris said sarcastically.

"Stop moaning," Lawson said, "It's only a scratch."

"Have you got a feel for where he is Mike?" Ward asked Lawson, who was by now peering around the side of their cover.

"There is a wall behind that row of vans to the left, there is some movement there. Whoever it is, they are not a very good shot."

Two kids on push bikes rode down the road, right past the vehicle they were crouched behind and nothing happened.

Ward turned around as he heard Harris mumbling into his cell phone. He couldn't make out what he was saying. Harris hung up the call.

"Who was that?" Ward asked.

"That was the doc. He said sit tight and he will get some of his boys to find out who it is taking pot shots at me," Harris replied.

"Whoever it is, the fact he watched those kids go by means he has no interest in anyone but us," Lawson said,

They crouched in silence, each taking turns to peer through the vehicles windows across the street, "I don't think he's a very confident shot either. If it was me, I would be shooting our brains out every time we peer through the window," he added.

Ward inwardly agreed with this. He knew without any question that The Optician would have killed all three of them by now, and so they certainly weren't faced with someone of his quality.

"I want you to fire a few shots in his direction Mike," Ward said after another thirty seconds of peering through the windows.

"What for? My handgun isn't going to reach him from here," he added.

"Because I'm not waiting anymore," he replied, "On my count of three, send over four shots," he added, as he moved along to the rear of the vehicle and crouched onto one knee, putting his weight onto his right foot, like an Olympic sprinter waiting to tear out of the blocks.

Lawson positioned himself to the right of the vehicle, ducking low beneath the hood and glanced to his left at Ward.

"Ready?" he asked.

"One; Two; Three."

Lawson raised his head and fired four shots in the direction of where he believed the shooter to be hiding. The first shot shattered the window of a BMW that was parked in the car park. The next three shots, which were fired half a second apart, sailed over the BMW and made no impact with anything.

But the few seconds was all that Ward had needed.

He sprinted across the road while Lawson was firing his shots, and was now tight against a building wall which was adjacent to the car park. No return fire had been returned by the shooter, and everything had gone quiet again.

He heard a door open to his right, spun around with his Glock raised, ready to fire, and came face to face with one of the dancing girls from Dr Pepper's front yard. He was pleased to see that she was, for once, standing still, although she was still scantily dressed and not looking at all phased by the gunfire ringing out.

"This way," she said, and beckoned to him. Her voice was clear and precise, not at all what he had expected. He followed her through the door, along a hallway and out of a back door which led into a small, paved back yard.

"If you go through the gate," she said, pointing directly in front of her at a battered looking wooden gate, "Turn right along the alleyway, it will come out at the rear of the car park and you should have a clear view of what's in front of you," she added, and then turned and walked back into the building.

Just like that, she was gone.

He walked forward to the gate, had to use more force than anticipated to prise it open, and he stepped into the alleyway. He turned right and walked along a narrow path for twenty feet, and reached the end of the building where the alleyway stopped.

He peered around the corner and saw the shooter instantly.

There was a guy with his back to him, crouched on one knee, with a rifle resting on top of a Porsche hood. He was wearing a black top with the hood up and he gauged his height as being tall, judging by the way he was hunching his shoulders to try and keep out of view, and as low as possible.

He knew instantly that he was not a professional sniper. He looked too uncomfortable. The first rule of shooting as a sniper was to get yourself comfortable before you got your breathing right.

He stepped out of the alleyway slowly and crept quietly up behind the guy. By the time he was ten feet away, he was starting to become amused by how dumb the guy was. What sort of sniper pulls their hood up and restricts what they can hear coming from behind them he thought to himself.

A poor one he concluded.

He got three feet away from the guy and even from where he was standing; he could see Lawson peering through the windows of the vehicle across the road.

He turned his Glock around to the side so that the gun was resting ninety degrees in his hand, and brought the butt of the gun crashing down, with full force, into the right temple of the shooter. As the butt connected, the shooter's grip released on the rifle, and he slid down the hood, the rifle following him a second later and landing on top of him.

He leant down, picked the rifle up, and tossed it behind him, and used the sole of his shoe to roll the guy over. The guy was semi-conscious, so no immediate threat was going to be offered, so he bent down and patted the guy down, and then rolled him over onto his front and patted his torso, and found a small handgun tucked into the front of his waistband in the process. He removed the handgun and rolled the guy back over onto his back.

The guy's eyes were starting to clear a little, and he slowly appeared to be coming back to full consciousness, like a boxer recovering from a punch that puts him down.

So he acted on impulse.

He pointed his Glock at the guys left kneecap and pulled the trigger, the bullet shattering the knee into a hundred pieces as soon as it hit.

He shot at me, he thought to himself in self-justification for shooting an unarmed man lying semi-conscious on the floor.

He looked up and saw Lawson and Harris scurrying across the road towards the car park. He heard voices behind him and he spun around and saw Dr Pepper and the two guys who were guarding the front gate, followed by the scantily clad girl, walking towards him.

"Bad shit man," the doc said as he reached him

"You have somewhere that I can take him to question him?" he asked.

"No need my man." the Doc replied, "No one sees anything around here unless I tell them they have seen it."

Ward shrugged his shoulders in acceptance of the fact.

"Take a walk Doc, I need to talk to this guy alone," he said.

The Doc shrugged his shoulders, mimicking Ward, and said,

"You need to share what you know man, this is a two way street."

He ignored him and turned to look at the guy, who was starting to groan in agony, coming back to full consciousness but bringing the pain of his shattered kneecap with it.

Lawson and Harris reached him and both looked down at the guy on the floor who was starting to whimper and writhe around from side to side in agony.

"OK Doc," Harris said, "We'll take it from here."

The Doc nodded and turned around and his boys followed eagerly.

Ward looked up and watched them walk off.

The scantily clad girl started to semi-dance as she followed them. A moment Ward found completely bemusing once more.

Harris walked over to the guy and kicked him hard in the ribs. The guy let out a scream and Harris said, "That's for shooting me."

Lawson leant down and pulled the guy up by the collar of his hoodie and rested him against the side of the Porsche, so he was looking up at all three of them.

"Who are you?" Ward asked.

The guy continued to groan in agony, both of his hands grasping at his knee, his jeans now soaked through with blood, as if he had been kneeling in red paint.

"Last time," he said as he raised his Glock and pointed it at the guys face.

"I'm a government agent," the guy replied through gritted teeth and short breaths, the pain in his knee now escalating to a new height.

"No government agent is that bad a shot," Lawson interrupted.

"I am, my badge is here," the guy replied, pulling up his hoodie and revealing a gold badge with the letters DEA emblazoned across it in blue and the words, 'Special Agent', underneath.

"Name?" Ward demanded.

"Simmons."

"Why did you shoot at us?"

Simmons gritted his teeth again and started to breathe quick, short, sharp breaths, getting louder and louder, "This is killing me, I need an ambulance, help me," he begged.

"Why did you shoot at us?" he asked again.

"I had no choice."

"Why?"

"Call me an ambulance."

"Tell me why you shot at us?"

"I had orders to frighten you."

"Who are we?" Ward asked.

"Someone investigating us," Simmons replied.

"Who is 'Us'?"

"The DEA."

"How did you know that we were here?"

"We have a video link set up in Toby Farriers place."

Ward looked at Harris,

"Farrier is Pepper?" he asked.

Harris nodded.

"You were told to frighten not kill us?" Ward enquired.

"Please, call me an ambulance," Simmons begged, desperation running through his voice.

"Answer my question," he demanded.

"That's all I was told, I was told clearly not to kill you."

"Do you know who we are?"

"You are internal investigators."

"What do you have to hide?"

"I need an ambulance and a lawyer."

Ward raised his gun once more,

"Do internal investigators shoot people in the knees and watch them bleed to death you idiot?" he asked, once again, dismayed at how stupid some of these government employees were.

He could see the logic of the statement hit home with Simmons, and so he asked again,

"What do you have to hide?"

"We are taking a cut of the profits by allowing cargo to go unchecked and not investigate too heavily," Simmons replied as he looked at the floor.

"Whose cargo is it?"

"Alesandro Begottoli."

Ward looked at Harris, Harris nodded back confirmation that he knew who Begottoli was.

"Now please get me an ambulance," Simmons begged.

"One more question," Ward said calmly.

Simmons looked up at him and nodded.

"Who gave you the order to frighten us off?"

"My boss," Simmons replied.

"What is his name?"

"Larry Stanyard"

Ward pulled the trigger on his Glock and shot Simmons twice in the centre of the chest.

"It saves calling an ambulance I guess," Lawson said.

"Why did you do that?" Harris asked, "He told us what we needed to know."

"Go and ask the mother of some fourteen year old kid who has died of an overdose, because corrupt scum like him turn a blind eye, for their own greed and gain," Ward said without once taking his eyes off Simmons's dead body.

"You have much to learn," Lawson said to Harris and shook his head.

"I need to make a call. Either get the Doc to sort this, or call in the cleaners Harris," Ward said as he walked away from them both and stopped thirty feet away so that his next conversation would not be overheard.

FOURTEEN

Park Avenue – New York

Nicole-Louise and Tackler both went for the phone at the same time, Tackler got there first.

"Hello Ryan."

"How much progress have you two made?" Ward asked

"We have made lots. What do you want to know first?" Tackler replied, as he looked at Nicole-Louise and poked his tongue out.

"What do you know about Alesandro Begottoli?"

"We know that it is not him that you are looking for," Tackler replied.

There was silence on the line for a moment.

"So who are we looking for?" he asked.

"Pablo Cardona."

"Are you sure?"

"Yes we are," Tackler said, feeling insulted that Ward would doubt his analytical skills, even for a brief moment.

"Tell me why?"

"Because he has made a payment of two hundred thousand dollars to a guy called Michael Vermont."

"Who is Michael Vermont?"

"He's the guy responsible for the Biscayne National Park."

"Where is that?"

Tackler started to explain about the Keys that make up the park, and how it would be the perfect place to hide people, and that even as he spoke he was hacking into the NSA satellite to search for any sign of where the hostages might be being held.

"That makes perfect sense. Well done but remember, you need to be quick with this. Can you put me on loud speaker?"

Tackler looked across the room at Nicole-Louise with distain, for a brief moment, he felt he had earned all of the kudos. He pressed the speaker button on the phone, placed it on the coffee table near the centre of the room and said,

"You're on."

"How is my favourite hacker in the world?" Ward's voice floated out.

"I'm very well Ryan, apart from the fact my boyfriend keeps stealing credit for my work," she replied, as she looked at Tackler and stuck her tongue out.

"I need you to do something for me immediately," he said,

"Shoot."

"Tell me about the financial state of Newton Pharmaceutical Limited."

"You want me to get back to you?" Nicole-Louise asked.

"No, I'll hold."

"OK" she replied, and started tapping away on her keyboard.

"Tackler, I need you to get some addresses for me right now," Ward said.

"Names?"

"Hilary Whelan, and Simon Newton the third."

"Who are they?"

"They are the people in charge at Newton Pharmaceuticals dummy," Nicole-Louise said over her shoulder to him, as she was looking at their names on her screen.

Tackler picked up his pencil and threw it at her over his shoulder.

It was the same pencil that spent more time in the air flying between the two of them than it ever did being used to write with.

"That's not good," Nicole-Louise said after a minute of digging into the finances of Newton Pharmaceuticals, "You are obviously onto something Ryan," she added.

"What is it?" Ward asked.

"The government are calling in a grant that they gave three years ago for development purposes," Nicole-Louise said.

"How much is the grant for?"

"Twenty one million dollars."

"That must be loose change to a company like Newton's?" Ward said.

"It should be, but it looks like they put all of their eggs in one basket, banking on a pandemic of both Ebola and Bird Flu, and neither escalated into even an epidemic," she replied.

"But they have the cash to pay it back?"

"Just. But if they pay it back now, they will only be left with a few million dollars of hard cash, and the operational costs of a company that size will mean that by the end of this month, they will start falling into debt which would be an unprecedented position for the company," she replied with a factual tone in her voice.

"So we are looking at mismanagement?"

"On an incompetent scale."

"OK. Well done Nicole-Louise. As usual, you've given me what I need."

She raised her arms above her head in mock celebration.

"I have the addresses," Tackler said loudly, almost too loudly, like a demonstration of his own worth.

"I could have got that from the phone book," Nicole-Louise said sarcastically.

"Send the addresses to me now Tackler, and find those hostages, I'm counting on you," Ward said and then the line went dead.

Washington D.C.

Centrepoint picked up his phone on the second ring.

"Where are you?" he asked Ward as he answered.

"I'm thirty feet away from a dead DEA agent."

"How did that happen?" The Old Man asked, sounding completely un-phased, but lowering his forehead into the palm of his hand as he spoke.

"He shot Harris."

"Is Harris dead?" he asked, lifting his head up abruptly.

"No, he's fine but you were right about the DEA. What I want to know is how they knew we were here?"

"I don't know, I will need to dig around. They definitely knew it was us?"

"Well, they have a house under surveillance and they might have got lucky. The guy we killed was under the impression that we were investigators and that we were looking for them?"

"Who is the 'Them' you are referring to?"

"A guy called Larry Stanyard; he's some top man in the DEA. I need you to find out what you can about him and where I can find him," Ward demanded rather than asked.

"OK. What about the hostages? Have you any idea where they are?"

"We are closing in on them quickly. Tackler is looking for them. We know roughly where they are, but it is too big an area to even try to look for them."

"Keep me informed, and I want to know immediately if you have any more trouble with the DEA or you find the hostages. Is that clear?" The Old Man said, trying to sound assertive rather than hopeful.

"Yes," Ward replied.

"And keep The Optician close to you. If people are shooting at you then you need him by your side. I don't want to lose you."

"You are so caring," Ward replied sarcastically.

"Ryan?" Centrepoint quickly said before Ward could end the call.

"Yes?"

"I have to reiterate that you need to get the chemical composition of this drug before you go killing everyone. You have to retrieve it, keep it safe and pass it to no one but me. Is that crystal clear?"

"Yes, you've told me that already" he replied, and the line went dead.

Overtown NW 12th Street – Miami

He put his cell phone back in his pocket and walked over to Lawson and Harris.

"What are you doing with the body?" he asked Harris.

"A clean-up crew will be here in two minutes. As soon as they get here, they will take care of it," he replied.

He felt his phone vibrate in his pocket. He took it out and saw the message from Tackler which contained the two addresses.

The first address was for Hilary Whelan. She lived on Pinetree drive, which was on Miami Beach, and Simon Newton lived in Coral Gables. Both houses were about twenty minutes away from Overtown.

"Get them to bring another car," Ward said to Harris.

"What for?" he asked.

"Because me and Lawson are taking yours," Ward replied, "You can drive over to Miami Beach to talk to Hilary Whelan, see if you can get anything out of her," he added, turning his cell phone to give Harris the address for Whelan which was displayed neatly on his screen.

"I know where that is," Harris said, making a mental note of the address, "And where are you going?"

"We are going to see Mr Newton. There are a number of things that don't stack up here."

"Is there anything specific that you want me to learn from her?" Harris asked.

"We need to know what she is hiding and why. She knows more than she is telling us. Either the chemists were working on something unethical, or they were doing trials that weren't going as planned. Either way, whatever it is, you have to get it out of her," he replied, as he nodded to Lawson and they walked towards Harris' car.

"You should have sent me to see Whelan," Lawson said as he climbed into the driver's seat.

"You're on a ban," he replied as he settled into the passenger seat.

"I'm serious Ryan," Lawson said with a sigh, "You know I can get anything out of any woman, she's more likely to tell me things than Harris."

"I need you with me."

"Why?"

"Because I'm pretty sure that we are going to run into some nasty people at Newton's house and I want you covering my back."

"Perfect," Lawson replied, "Us against the bad guys. Just as I like it."

"Not just me and you," Ward replied as he took out his cell phone and dialled The Opticians number.

Pinetree Drive – Miami Beach

Harris had to wait in Overtown for almost thirty minutes for his replacement car. A young mechanic had dropped it off, clearly new to the agency, because he thought part of his role was to explain the workings and performance levels of the Ford Taurus, the model that Harris had driven a thousand times. After the third round of vehicle specification feedback, Harris had climbed into the car and driven off without saying another word.

The journey over to Pinetree Drive actually took less than twenty minutes, for some unexplained reason, the roads appeared almost empty, which was unusual considering it was approaching midday.

He drove past Whelan's house to see if anything looked out of place, but unfortunately, it wasn't possible to see very much at all from the road.

The front lawn of the house was covered in trees and shrubs, leaving only a small part of the house exposed to prying eyes from the road. From what he could see, the house looked large. It was painted an off green colour, with bright white frames, and a large window above the elegant entrance. There were four white pillars, with stone spindles on top, which formed an open porch below, and patio area on top, but he could see no access door to the patio area, so he assumed it was for show. The pathway was laid in old stone slabs, forming four steps, which led up to the brilliant white double doors that were the entrance to the house.

He parked fifty yards up the road and got out of his car and strolled back towards the house casually. He turned onto the stone path and approached the door.

Everything seemed quiet, and as he could see no vehicles parked on the road directly outside the house, and no driveway, he was pretty convinced that this was a wasted journey. He walked up to the white doors and knocked firmly, three times, even more convinced now that no one was home.

Hilary Whelan opened the door five seconds later.

"Oh, it's you again," she said to him, remembering him from their earlier meeting.

She looked much prettier than she had earlier that morning in her formal work suit. She was wearing a tight vest top, her large breasts displaying an impressive cleavage, her hair was swept back, and it looked wet. She had on a tight pair of denim shorts which complimented her slim, tanned legs perfectly. How attractive she looked took him by surprise for a moment, and he just stared, stopping quickly when he saw the frown cross her face.

"There are a few more things I need to ask you," he said quickly.

"Can't we do it at the office?" Whelan replied, a cross tone to her voice.

"Not really. Time is of the essence here, and so we need to learn as much as we can, as quickly as we can."

Whelan stepped out of the doorway and onto the porch, "I've told you all I know," she said.

He noticed a desperate, urgent tone in her voice, and this instantly confirmed Ward's suspicion that she was keeping something from him.

"Can I come in?" he asked, moving forward one step as he spoke, to demonstrate that he was in charge.

Whelan stepped forward one step herself. It was an action that surprised him and made him feel immediately tense. She stopped about eighteen inches away from him.

"No. I'm busy," Whelan said, "Meet me at the office at 3:00pm and we can talk then," she added firmly.

"You don't seem very concerned about your colleagues," he said.

"You stupid man," Whelan replied.

And before he could say another word, the large white double doors flew open and two South Americans appeared with handguns raised, pointing them at his head. One had a shaved head and the other was no taller than five feet, but was so incredibly stocky that he almost looked square.

"Make one move and you are dead," the stocky guy said as he stepped out of the doorway, walked behind him, lifted his tee shirt and removed his gun.

"Inside," the stocky guy demanded, as he nudged Harris in the back with his gun to make him step forward. Whelan turned and walked back inside, the shaven headed guy moved his arm, keeping his gun aimed at Harris' head with each step he took forward. Harris walked through the doorway and into the hall, and the stocky guy closed the door behind him.

"Give me your cell phone and unlock it," Whelan said. Harris dug into his trouser pocket and pulled out his cell, typed a four digit code into the screen and handed it to Whelan.

"The English guy, your boss," She started, "What is he in your phone as?" she asked calmly.

"One," Harris replied.

"What's his name?"

"I don't know."

"You don't know his name?" Whelan asked curiously.

"We never exchange names."

"Who do you work for?"

"We work separately from the others."

"Who controls you?"

"I don't know his name either," Harris replied, an honest answer as no one knew Centrepoint's name.

"What do you know so far about the missing people?" Whelan asked.

"Nothing at all."

"What does the English guy know?"

"He doesn't know anything either. He sent me here to see if you knew anything that could help us," Harris replied.

"You are lying," Whelan spat at him.

Before Harris could reply, he felt a searing pain in the centre of his back. It was a pain that ran so deep that he could not even let out a scream. It consumed every part of his body. He fell forward, his whole body now locked in a paralysed state, and unable to move. He was starting to struggle for breath. He looked around and the stocky guy was holding an eight inch jagged knife in his hand which was dripping with his blood.

Lots of blood.

"You are going to be dead in a few minutes pig. I've cut you five times," he said.

Harris was confused for a moment; he had only felt one bout of searing pain. But he knew the stocky guy was telling the truth, he was starting to gargle and he felt like he was drowning. Everything was starting to blur and then everything went black.

"I don't like the English Guy," Whelan said, "There is something bad about him. I saw it in his eyes in the way he looked at me when I met him earlier," she added, the vision of Ward's stare etched firmly in her memory. "Then we will scare him off once and for all," the shaven headed guy said, "Frank, remove the eyes."

FIFTEEN

Old Cutler Road – Coral Gables - Miami

"How much do you think you pay for a place like that?"
Lawson asked as they drove up Old Cutler Road and
towards Simon Newton's mansion for the third time.
"A lot of colds and headaches," Ward replied, making
clear reference to how the Newton family had made their
money.
He pulled out his cell phone and called The Optician,
"Took your time," The Optician said as he answered.
"Lawson still thinks he is driving in London."
"Do we have anything to be worried about here?"
"There are three armed guys outside, one at the front and
two patrolling the sides of the house. From what I can
see, there are another two inside. You think you can
manage two of them?"
"I'm sure we can," he replied, and then hung up the
phone.
"How well do you know him?" Lawson asked.

"It's weird. I know him very well, but at the same time, I don't know him at all" Ward replied and then paused, "Pull over here, we'll jump over the wall," he added, as they got to within fifty feet of the brightly painted wrought iron gate which opened onto Newton's driveway.

There was a small, stone wall, about three feet high which acted as a boundary marker for the property, and behind the wall, rows of tall trees which obscured most of the building from the road. He could see that the house was big, very big, and was clearly built to replicate the old plantation houses of America two hundred years ago. It was built of bright red brick, and there were large sash window frames painted a brilliant white. There was some decking that ran along the front of the building. But no matter how hard he tried, Ward could not imagine Simon Newton sitting in a rocking chair sipping ice cold lemonade.

Lawson pulled the car to a stop and Ward pulled out his Glock and screwed on the silencer.

"Are we expecting trouble?" Lawson asked.

"There are two guys inside and three outside. All armed. The Optician will take care of the guys outside; the rest is down to us. But let's keep them alive, we need to question them first."

They got out of the car without talking and climbed over the small wall, taking cover behind the trees in the garden. They could see one guy, who looked of South American origin, holding a machine gun, standing to the left of the front door, and he didn't seem to be paying too much attention.

He felt his cell phone vibrate in his pocket.

He pulled it out and opened the screen and saw it was a message from Harris.

"Seriously, now?" Lawson asked, bemused that Ward was looking at his phone.

Ward opened the message.

It was a picture message.

It was a picture of Harris' dead body lying on the floor and a hand, a strong, small hand, holding two eyeballs in its palm. He could see Harris' face behind the hand, both of his eyeballs had been cut out.

Below were two words.

'KEEP AWAY!'

He stared at it for a few seconds. He didn't know Harris well, today was the first time he had ever met him, but he liked him.

He passed the cell phone to Lawson who studied it for a few seconds and then handed it back.

"I liked him," Lawson whispered.

Ward nodded. It was a nod that said let's avenge him.

They both looked forward again, just in time to see the guy to the left of the front door hit the deck, a cloud of red mist still flowing through the air as his body hit the decking with a thud which could be heard from their hiding place.

Immediately another guy armed with a machine gun appeared from the far left hand side of the house, and before he could register what he was seeing, a 7.62mm bullet hit him in the dead centre of the forehead, throwing his head back while his knees buckled below him. He was dead before he had time to scream.

Ten seconds later, Ward's phone vibrated in his pocket. He pulled it out, The Optician's name was flashing on the screen. He answered.

"The three outside are all down. Now you can do whatever you have to do," he said, and the line went dead.

Ward put his phone back in his pocket and nodded to Lawson.

"How are we going to get in?" Lawson asked.

"The same way as usual."

Lawson sighed and shook his head. He knew that Ward meant they would be knocking on the door like a couple of salesmen, and just wait to see how it played out. It was Ward's favourite play. He had done it so many times before and Lawson had to admit to himself, it was the most effective access manoeuvre he had ever seen. The bad guys never, ever expected the good guys to just knock on the door.

Ward stood up and moved to the right onto the neat, winding driveway and headed towards the front door. Lawson kept a few paces behind, and smiled to himself as he watched how casually Ward was approaching the building, like a regular guy, out for a regular walk, on a regular Sunday.

They reached the steps to the decking and stepped onto the porch, the dead guy laying no more than five feet away to their left.

Ward knocked on the door four times.

Lawson smiled again. He remembered how Ward had once told him that four knocks was a lot less threatening than three knocks. When he had enquired why, Ward had told him that four knocks means familiarity, like the person knocking knew whoever was inside, and therefore would not be bothered about offending them. He had actually tried this himself many times back in the U.K., and was staggered to find that it worked. He knew that whoever was inside would not open the door expecting a threat.

The door was opened by a South American guy who looked extremely overweight, and extremely hot. Sweat was running down his forehead onto his chin. He was holding a handgun down by his side, completely unprepared for any confrontation, after all, he was expecting someone he knew, the four knocks on the door had told him that without him realising.

Ward raised his gun and shot him directly in the centre of the face before he could speak or react.

The bullet smashed through his nose, bone shattering immediately, and ripped his flesh apart. He dropped his gun and fell backwards, his head crunching hard on the tiled floor as they came together.

Ward stepped through the door and put another two bullets into the fat guy's chest, even though he was sure he was already dead.

Lawson quietly closed the door and they listened. They could hear whimpering coming from a room to their right, a room that had a large, oak door firmly closed, and so they headed towards it.

As they reached the door, Ward put his ear to it and heard young voices, children's voices, and a woman's voice whimpering. He then heard a heavily accented voice say, "Shut up whore."

He pulled on the door handle and pushed open the door, and then quickly stepped inside with his Glock raised, Lawson followed, two steps behind.

Inside the room, directly in front of them, there was an attractive woman in her late thirties with one hand tied to a radiator. She was only wearing her underwear and she looked badly beaten and bruised. There was a muscular guy of South American origin standing over her, doing his belt up. The woman was sobbing loudly. Opposite them, were two boys, both under ten, tied to the legs of a grand piano.

The South American guy looked around startled, and turned to look at his machine gun, which was ten feet away on the sofa behind him.

Before the guy could move, Lawson strode past Ward towards him, and as the guy turned square onto Lawson to confront him, Lawson unleashed a thunderous right hook that connected flush on the guys' nose, and his legs buckled and he was unconscious before he hit the floor. For no other reason, than he felt the guy deserved it, Lawson then raised his right leg and stamped down hard on the guys ribs, the sound of his ribs breaking echoed around the room as the heel of Lawson's shoe, combined with his two hundred and forty pounds of solid and toned muscle, connected.

"Is there anyone else in the house?" Ward softly asked the woman, picking up a throw from the sofa as he said it and handing it to her to enable her to cover her violated body.

"There are four others. One in the house, three outside." she said, glancing at her boys as she said it.

"It's OK." Ward replied, "They are gone, they won't hurt you anymore," he added.

Lawson had pulled a knife from his pocket and was leaning down to the radiator and cutting the woman free. Once she was free, she stood up and ran over to the boys. As Lawson cut them free, she was hugging them frantically, moving from one to the other. It hindered Lawson's task of freeing them, but he said nothing. The boys were both crying, and when they were free, she wrapped her arms around both of them and held them so tightly; one of the boys had to slide his hand between her forearm and his neck to allow him to breathe.

"Are you OK?" he asked softly, "Do you have any injuries?"

"No. That bastard raped me in front of my children, they all did, what sick animals can do that?" she asked. She was shaking violently and her voice was breaking up.

"Dead ones," he replied.

She looked up at Ward, she saw a seven foot giant who was there to protect her. She finally felt free from her ordeal.

"All of them?" she asked softly.

"All but this one here," he replied, pointing to the unconscious guy on the floor, "And as soon as you are all out of sight, and we have what we need from him, he will be dead too."

She looked up at him. He could see the hope in her eyes that what he was saying was true,

"But you are the police, you don't do things like that," she said.

"We aren't the police" Lawson said, "We are the good guys, who have the same set of rules as the bad guys."

"I need to take you and the boys to another room," he said, "They can't witness this."

"They have had to watch as those animals raped me and did vile things to me. They will be scarred by that forever. Probably frightened and traumatised. Seeing you take the life from that animal is probably the best therapy that they could ever have," she replied, the anger rising in her voice with each word.

One of the boys stopped sobbing long enough to say, "I want to go mom," and she turned her attention back to her boys.

Lawson looked at Ward and shrugged, as if to say it was Ward's decision. They stood there in silence for a few seconds and then the guy on the floor started groaning, the groans getting louder and louder with each second of consciousness that returned.

"What's your name?" Ward asked.

"Monica," she replied.

"Stand up Monica," he said and extended his hand for her. She took it and he pulled her gently to her feet.

"You want this gun?" he said, turning his hand slightly, so he wasn't gripping the gun in a threatening way.

"Yes I do," she said firmly.

"If you take it and pull the trigger, it will haunt you, trust me on that. Once you do that, there is no going back. It will take part of your soul," he said softly.

"But what they did to me has already taken my soul."

"I know you don't think so now but you will recover. I promise."

"Will the boys?" she asked, with an air of desperation in her voice.

"Yes they will. You survived together, that makes you stronger."

He could see Monica Newton considering this, and weighing up the damage that stepping over a line and taking another human beings life would do, so he reminded her one more time,

"They've taken enough Monica, is it worth letting them take a little more of your soul?" he asked.

She started to shake her head gently.

"I lost mine a long time ago," Lawson suddenly said, and pointed his gun down and pumped three bullets into the guy on the floor, "That was one for each of you. Now he can never hurt you again," he added.

Monica Newton looked up at Lawson and then did a double take at his eyes. Ward could have sworn that for a brief moment, she blushed. At a time like that, he could still have that effect on a woman. He shook his head and rolled his eyes, almost in disbelief.

The moment was broken by a desperate voice,

"Monica, Monica, where are you?" the voice shouted,

"Jacob, Matthew, where are you?" it continued, sounding more and more desperate.

Everyone in the room turned around and Simon Newton the third came in through the door. He stopped in his tracks when he saw what was in front of him and he stepped over to his boys, bent down and hugged them, his wife joined them. He looked up at Ward and mouthed, "Thank you."

"We need to talk," Ward said.

SIXTEEN

Adams Key – Upper Florida Keys

Pablo Cardona was becoming frustrated. Not so much with the lack of progress by the chemists, but more by the call he had received from his men that were keeping a close eye on Hilary Whelan. He was irritated that his men had killed the guy who had visited them without gaining any decent information from him. He walked out into the clearing and across to the chemists block. There were only a few more hours of daylight left, and he couldn't see any progress being made at all today, but he needed to remind them once again what was at risk if they failed him.

"Open the door Franco," he demanded, when he reached the building. Franco nodded at the two guys and they both watched as they started to undo the three locks. "Get Stefan to bring me….," he seemed to ponder for a moment, like he was deciding what burger to pick from the menu at a fast food joint, "The man, Brandon Alexander," he said after a few seconds.

163

Franco nodded and called out Stefan Valencia's name. Ten seconds later, Valencia came jogging across the clearing and stopped three feet short of them.

"The boss wants the Alexander man, go and fetch him," Franco demanded.

Valencia turned and sprinted back across the clearing to the block that was holding all of the family members, "Open it up now," he demanded to the two guys standing outside, "Don't keep me or the boss waiting," he added, revelling in his elevated position in the order of Cardona's army.

The door was opened thirty seconds later, and he stepped into the building, picking up a flashlight from the ledge on the outside of the door on the way through. He shone the light.

Everyone cowered at the back of the building; all of the adults were at the front, forming a screen to protect the children.

He felt a rush of power run through his body, they were all petrified of him, and of what he was going to say. If the boss wasn't waiting, he thought to himself, I would help myself to the women in here, especially the whore whose father Johan had killed.

"You," he said, shining the flashlight into Brandon Alexander's face, "Come here."

Brandon Alexander froze. A number of children started crying behind him, and Alexander stood still, his arms outstretched behind him, protecting his children.

"Come here now or I will shoot your kids right in front of you," Valencia said, "And then I will rape your wife and cut her eyes out while you watch before killing you."

Brandon Alexander stepped forward slowly; he could feel his children pulling at his shirt and his trouser belt, trying to cling onto their father, their last connection to safety walking away from them. The women tried to hush the children, Claire Anderton and Catherine Lambourne reached out to hold the children, and then by instinct, they hid them behind them. They watched as Brandon Alexander walked towards the door and stepped outside, and the door was slammed shut.
They were back into darkness once again.

Cardona stepped into the lab with Franco no more than two steps behind him. Everyone looked up and stopped working.
They were all acutely aware that three hours had just passed.
"I hope you have made some progress?" he shouted to the whole room.
No one responded.
"Dr Anderton," he said, waiting for Robert Anderton to make eye contact with him before he continued, "Do you have some good news for me?"
Robert Anderton had no good news. In fact he had spent the first hour of the last three hours cursing his actions, blaming his foolishness for the death of Crystal Wynne, and then trying to regain composure to concentrate again.
All he had managed to achieve was to establish what was causing the heart failure. But he was also pretty sure that removing that part from the composition would dramatically weaken the hallucinatory effect of the drug.

"We are making some progress but we are struggling to work under this pressure," Anderton said, "Can we at least have a break for an hour and see our families?"

"Do you know what makes up the drug yet?"

"Almost, we know that it is a combination of…"

"Dr Anderton," Cardona interrupted, raising his right hand to indicate that now was a good time to stop speaking, "I am not a clever man like you. Apart from cocaine, I understand nothing about drugs or chemistry. So when I ask you a question, I want a yes or no answer," he added calmly.

"We are almost there. We probably would have got there if we knew our families were safe, and you hadn't of traumatised us by doing what you did to Crystal."

"Do you want to see your family?" Cardona asked, looking directly at Dr Allie Alexander.

"Yes please Sir," she replied quietly.

Right on cue, Brandon Alexander came stumbling through the door of the lab with Stefan Valencia right behind him,

"Here he is, as demanded Mr Cardona," Valencia said, desperate to impress.

"Thank you Stefan," he replied, "I do like someone who does what I ask without complication," he added, and then turned back to face Anderton.

Allie Alexander ran towards her husband and they met in a solid embrace,

"Are the children alright?" she asked, "Please tell me they are?"

"They are fine, I promise, they are fine," Brandon Alexander replied.

"Enough of this," Cardona said, and Franco immediately stepped in and separated the Alexander's, pushing Allie Alexander hard in the chest as he pulled them apart, so hard in fact, that she stumbled back and fell onto the floor. Franco laughed out loudly.

"Pathetic whore," he sneered.

"So Dr Anderton, Mr Alexander here is really, really hoping that you have made progress, and I hope for the sake of his wife and children that you have."

Anderton looked across at Allie Alexander who was now picking herself off of the floor. She was glancing at him with desperation in her eyes, she knew that he had not made any progress, and tears started to fill her eyes.

But then he had a thought.

It was a long shot but it might just buy them more time. He walked over to the impressively filled drug cabinet and started scrolling through the many containers.

"What are you doing Dr Anderton?" Cardona asked.

"I'm looking for something to act as an emetic," Anderton replied, in a tone that sounded way too condescending to Cardona.

"I've told you once before doctor, I am not a clever man and if you don't speak in a manner that I can understand, then your wife will become the play thing for all of my men."

"I'm sorry," Anderton replied, suddenly remembering the gravity of what was happening again, "An emetic is an ingestible substance that induces vomiting. If I can time it right, and administer it at the correct time, after the hallucination part of the drug has kicked in, then that should give us a platform to start from," he added assertively.

Cardona noted that both Catherine Lambourne and Heath Beasley were nodding their approval at the suggestion.

This gave him hope that they were actually making progress.

"So what exactly is it you are looking for?" he asked.

"This," Anderton replied, holding up a small pill bottle.

"What is it?"

"It's called ipecac."

"I think you are trying your hardest to insult me doctor. This is your last warning. Tell me in words that I understand," Cardona spat at him.

"It's a drug that comes from the roots of a plant found in South America," Anderton replied.

"Columbia?"

"Yes."

"What do they call it?"

"Tupi."

"That kills birds of prey," Cardona said, pleased that he knew what Anderton was talking about.

"I didn't know that," Anderton replied.

"Then maybe you aren't so smart after all," he said and followed it with a long laugh, and Franco immediately joined in as a good lieutenant would.

"How long did you say that the longest victim lived after taking the drug?" Anderton asked.

"Twenty nine minutes."

"OK. If I can calculate or as best as I can, the speed that the drug enters the bloodstream, and then induce vomiting to remove the other chemicals from the digestive system, if it works, we have found our foundation stone."

"Then do your calculations doctor. You have ten minutes, and only ten," he said and then turned and walked out of the building.

"Everyone, now, put your heads together," Anderton shouted to the rest of the room, and everyone scurried over to his work station.

Pablo Cardona reached his building and walked inside. The guy was still tied to the chair, the blood that had been running out of his nose and mouth had now dried and he looked like he was wearing war paint. He pulled up a chair, and sat down opposite him and smiled.

"It appears that we have made a breakthrough, so I don't need to keep you alive much longer. I'm going to cut you up slowly. I'm going to watch while you bleed to death, and then I am going to remove your eyes for my collection," he whispered to the guy, moving his head closer to him as the violent threat intensified. He looked into the guys eyes for a hint of fear.

He could not see any fear.

He looked harder; it wasn't resistance or determination that he could see either.

He couldn't make out what it was, but whatever it was, it unnerved him.

"You think that you can find a way out of this, don't you?"

The guy did not say anything.

"Once the good doctor works out what these pills are made of and gets them to work, your time is up."

The guy still did not say anything.

"Tell me why these people in Washington want you kept alive until they know for sure that we can make the drugs to perfection? What do you know? Do you already know the answer? What are you, a chemist?" Cardona fired question after question at the guy.

The guy still did not speak; he just stared into Cardona's eyes.

"No, not a chemist," Cardona said, answering his own question, "No chemist is as tough as you, and no chemist would kill five of my men trying to get to me," he added.

"It was eight. You just haven't found the other three yet," the guy replied and then smiled.

Cardona smiled back at him and then stood up.

"What are you, some kind of superhero?"

"No, I'm no superhero," the guy replied.

Cardona turned and walked back towards the door. When he got to the doorway, he stopped and turned around,

"So what are you?" he asked with a heavy hint of sarcasm in his voice.

"I'm a deniable," the guy whispered, just loud enough for Cardona not to hear as he walked out of the building.

"Your ten minutes are up doctor," Cardona announced as he walked back into the chemists lab, "do this now."

Robert Anderton sighed; it was a long sigh, trying to relieve the pressure that he could feel building inside,

"I think we are ready," he said.

Cardona nodded to Franco who gripped Brandon Alexander's arm tightly and marched him over to the glass room,

"Get in there," Franco demanded, and Brandon Alexander stepped in.

Dr Allie Alexander burst into tears as her husband looked across the room at her, fear spread across his face. She then looked at Anderton who smiled a weak smile. Because he knew, that it was only fifty-fifty that this was going to work.

"I'm waiting doctor," Cardona said, as he pulled his knife out and ran the tip of his finger along the serrated edge.

Anderton walked the few feet to the glass room and stood at the doorway,

"You need to take this pill and then sit down Brandon," he said, raising his right hand, palm open, so that the brown pill was clear to see, "After four minutes, you need to take this liquid," he added, raising his left hand which was holding a thumb sized beaker.

Alexander nodded a less than convincing nod.

"You will feel sick almost immediately but it should take about three minutes for the vomiting to start," he continued, "After that, you should be left with just the effects of the hallucination."

"I love you," Alexander shouted across to his wife, "I'll be fine. Tell the kids I love them more than anything, I always will," he added, and everyone in the room was caught up in the desperation and sadness of the moment. Everyone that is, except Pablo Cardona and Franco.

"Get on with it doctor," Cardona demanded.

Anderton handed Alexander the pill and a small glass of water. Alexander put the pill in his mouth, took a gulp of water and swallowed hard.

The whole room held its breath.

For the first three minutes, Brandon Alexander seemed completely unfazed; he just sat there, waiting for something to happen.

After three minutes and thirty seconds his body started to relax and he slumped back into the sofa, like any guy, in any office around the world would, after completing a ten thousand word report.

Anderton stepped into the glass room and handed Alexander the fluid to drink. He put the beaker to his lips, tilted his head back and poured.

The first drop of liquid ran down his throat exactly as the clock hit four minutes.

Now it was just a question of waiting.

And of Allie Alexander having the silent prayers that she was saying answered.

After seven minutes and four seconds, Brandon Alexander started vomiting violently, he still retained the relaxed manner, slumped back on his chair, and the majority of the vomit landed down the front of his shirt and on his shoes.

Then the vomiting stopped and a smile appeared over his face and he closed his eyes.

"Is he breathing?" Allie screamed as she rushed forward, only to be struck across the chest once again by the strong forearm of Franco.

Anderton stepped inside and checked his pulse.

Brandon Alexander was breathing.

He was in a total state of ecstasy, the wide smile etched across his face and occasional, muffled groans of pleasure escaping from his mouth.

"He's hallucinating," Anderton said to no one in particular.

"Then let's hope it lasts more than twenty nine minutes," Cardona said, as he moved closer to the glass room and then pushed his face up to the glass to get a better view. Almost immediately, everyone stepped up to the glass and peered inside, faces pressed against the glass, holding their breath, waiting to see what would happen. Ten minutes passed.

Alexander started to lightly thrust his groin up and down off the sofa and began moaning louder.

Twenty minutes passed.

Alexander was now mumbling, it was inaudible, but it was making him smile.

Thirty minutes passed.

Alexander was now the longest surviving recipient of Invincible.

An hour passed.

He was still alive and still in a perfect state of chemically induced bliss.

Three hours later, Alexander was starting to regain a sense of where he was once more. He looked at the faces peering through the glass at him and he smiled at his wife.

"How do you feel?" Cardona asked.

"I feel great, I have never known anything like that," he replied, "But I want more, I want it now," he added aggressively.

"How much do you want it?" Cardona asked.

"If you have it, I want it now," he said, as he got to his feet and walked to the doorway, oblivious to the vomit that was running down his clothing. Allie Alexander started crying frantically. Her husband looked out of control, he looked crazed and desperate.

Cardona smiled.

"Come here and get some," he said, beckoning to Alexander, inviting him to approach him.

Alexander stepped out of the glass room and walked the few steps towards him.

When he reached him, Cardona lifted up his knife and rammed the blade deep into the side of Alexander's neck, severing the jugular vein immediately.

Allie Alexander screamed hysterically as she watched her husband collapse to the floor, clutching his neck.

Franco stepped across to her and unleashed a solid right jab into her face and knocked her unconscious immediately.

"What are you doing?!" Anderton screamed.

Cardona's face changed and a crazed look spread across it,

"I told you that you had three hours to make it work doctor. You failed me," he spat at him.

Anderton felt sick to the stomach, and had to put his hand to his mouth to try and stop himself from throwing up. Cardona bent down to Alexander's convulsing body, pulled his head back by the hair and slit his throat. He then rolled him over and went through his sickening ritual of cutting his victims eyes out. By the time he had finished, he was completely covered in Alexander's blood.

The whole room had fallen into silence; no one could dare look at the vile act that Cardona was carrying out. He stood up, clutching his knife in his right hand and Alexander's eyeballs in his left hand.

"You had better work through the night doctor," he said, looking at Anderton, "You are close; I can see that, so work harder."

"How can you expect us to work when you have done things like that? Allie will not be able to think straight and there was no need for that barbaric act," Anderton replied, his own tone now hostile.

"How can I expect it?" Cardona replied, "Easily. Because at 7:00am tomorrow morning, one of your children will be the next one to try the drug," he added, and he turned and walked towards the door, "Clean that up," he demanded of Stefan as he walked through the door.

Dr Robert Anderton put his hands up to his face and started to cry.

SEVENTEEN

Old Cutler Road – Coral Gables - Miami

"I've lost a colleague today, a good man, and it is all because of you and your company. So this is your one chance to stop me from killing you, and the only way that will happen is if you tell me everything you know. Is that clear?" Ward asked Newton, who was now visibly shaking with fear, after he had dragged him away from his wife and children, and roughly pushed him into an armchair.

"Yes. I promise, I will tell you everything," Newton replied.

"I've saved your whole family, so you owe me, are you clear on that too?" he asked calmly, despite knowing that Newton was so afraid of him that he would not lie, no matter what.

"Firstly who is behind the kidnapping of your people?"

"A man called Cardona," Newton replied immediately. Nicole-Louise and Tackler were right as usual, he thought to himself. He could see how willing Newton was to talk, and offload whatever guilt he was carrying, and so he decided to just let him explain things in his own words.

"Tell me what happened. Exactly what happened, right from the beginning and don't miss anything out," he said softly, "Your family are now safe, I will guarantee that, but the more you tell me now, the greater chance I will have of finding your people."

Newton paused for a few moments; he could see he was trying to get things in order in his head before speaking. And then the verbal floodgates opened.

"It all happened so quickly," Newton began, "Four weeks ago, five men were waiting here for me when I got home," he said, looking down at the floor and shuddering at the memory of that day.

"Was this Cardona guy one of them?"

"No, he wasn't. But there was a man that they called Franco, and he seemed important, he did all the talking."

"What did these guys say to you?"

"I walked into the house and they were sitting in my lounge, making themselves very much at home, Monica and the boys were sitting on the couch looking petrified," Newton replied, tears filling his eyes as he spoke.

"They can't hurt you anymore" he said, "The guys out there are dead, and the rest of them will be when I find them," he added, trying his best to make Newton feel safe.

"I couldn't even protect my family, what sort of weak, pathetic man does that make me?" Newton asked, the tears now starting to roll down his cheeks.

Ward really didn't have the time to concentrate on balancing out Newton's emotions, but he knew that if Newton was going to remember everything that had happened, then he needed him feeling in a secure state of mind. So he played along.

"There are very few men who could have endured what you have Mr Newton," he began, "The incredible stress and fear you have been carrying around would have crippled most men. Yet you are here, your family are safe, and no one can hurt them now, there are teams of the finest bodyguards around on their way as we speak," he lied, "You should be proud of yourself, you protected your family and that makes you a real man. I just need you to be brave a little longer, and to tell me everything you know, time really is of the essence here," he added, trying to offer a sympathetic smile as he spoke.

It worked. A look of determination washed over Newton's face.

"We made a mistake," Newton started and then paused, "We took a grant from the government and our analysts were sure that if we mass produced a certain remedy for specific illnesses, when they escalated, we would make a fortune. Unfortunately, we got it wrong," he added, a sad look now spreading across his face.

Ward already knew this as Nicole-Louise and Tackler had already told him about the grant, and the lack of hard cash in the company's accounts, so he decided to speed things up,

"I know about the grant and the small change that you have in the company's accounts, and how your running costs are going to eat that money up quickly," he interrupted, "But what I really need to know is how

Cardona got his claws into you?" he asked, trying to keep the urgency out of his voice so Newton would not feel under too much under pressure.

"I was in the office when four men just walked in. There was a man called Franco, who said that he worked for Mr Cardona, and that he knew about our financial state, and that I could earn five million dollars just by handing over some personnel files," he replied.

Ward was now starting to feel pretty sure that he knew what had happened,

"Then?" he asked.

"Naturally, I refused," Newton said, "My integrity and honour is solid, and I told them to leave immediately or I would call the police."

"And what did they do then?"

"They left."

Ward studied him for a moment. He could see he was telling the truth.

"So what happened next?"

"Nothing."

Now Ward was confused.

"What do you mean nothing?"

"Nothing happened for two whole weeks, and then within three hours, everything changed into this mess," Newton replied with a sigh.

"How did it change?"

"Hilary came into work one morning in floods of tears. She told me that they had taken her sister, and if they did not have the files on all of our research teams within an hour, then they would kill her and cut her eyes out."

"So you handed over the files?"

"No. I said we should call the police and let them deal with it."

Ward knew exactly where this was going, so to save time, he thought he would fill in the gaps for Newton, "So Whelan told you to give her an hour before you phoned the police, and then you get a call from your wife shortly after saying that some men had her and your kids, and you had to do what they said or they would kill them?" he said, trying to sound as sympathetic as he could, but not appearing very convincing as it was now becoming clear to Newton that he was becoming impatient.

"They told me they would rape her and the children and cut their eyes out if I didn't do what they said, what choice did I have?" Newton asked.

"Everyone has a choice," he answered, "So you handed the files to Whelan and you get home and these men are here. And they have been here ever since?"

Newton nodded. He didn't want to say out loud about the violation and abuse that his wife had endured and worse still, what his children had been forced to witness.

"How long has Whelan worked for you?"

"Three years"

"Have you ever met her sister?"

"No. But she has mentioned her quite frequently over the past six months."

No doubt she has, he thought to himself, no doubt she spoke about how close they were and how she was the most important person in her world. He did not need Newton to verify that fact for him.

"The team of researchers," he said, "Tell me about them?"

"Dr Robert Anderton runs the team. He is a brilliant man and most of all, a good man. He has devoted his life to helping people, to finding cures and vaccine's to make people's lives better. I can't imagine what he and Claire are going through right now," Newton replied, looking genuinely devastated.

"And who are the others?"

"They are, Eric Dunn, Catherine Lambourne, Sadar Taremi, Kyle Johnston, Allie Alexander, Justin Wynee and Heath Beasley. All good people, good family people, who don't deserve any of this."

"Do you know what Cardona wants the team for?"

"Yes."

"Tell me?"

"They are trying to manufacture a narcotic to end all narcotics," Newton began, "A once taken, lifetime addictive drug that is chemically impossible to dissect by composition so it cannot be copied."

"They told you that?"

"Franco did. He took great pleasure in telling me, he was almost bragging about the fact."

"Bragging how?"

"Saying that whoever owns and distributes it, will become the richest drug baron in the world within a year."

"Are they producing it already?" he enquired, starting to feel apprehensive that it was already out on the streets.

"No, there is a fundamental problem with it?"

"Which is?"

"It kills anyone who takes it."

"And the researchers have been taken to fine tune the drug?"

"Yes, for exactly that purpose."

He was satisfied with everything that Newton had told him. He knew most of it anyway, but Newton had confirmed everything, and he didn't anticipate any surprises going forward.

There was just one more thing he needed to know, "Tell me, the five million dollars that this Franco guy offered you? I want to know, and I want the truth. I am going to make a call in a minute and I will know within two minutes if you are lying to me. Did you take it after handing over the files?" he asked.

"No. Of course I didn't," Newton replied.

Ward knew that he was telling the truth.

"You've just saved your life by making the right choice," he said as he walked towards the door, "Go and be with your family."

In the hallway, there were now people moving around, Lawson had called the clean-up crew, and they were already disposing of any trace of Cardona's men. Even these expert sanitisers would not be able to remove the effects of the ordeal that Newton's family had endured. But at least they are alive; Ward thought to himself, Harris isn't.

"There will be four guys here within a few minutes to guard the family," Lawson said, "It's crap that those kids had to witness that stuff."

"I need to make a couple of calls," he said and he walked out of the house and into the fresh air.

He felt sympathy for the Newton's, all of them, and it was plain to see that he Simon Newton was a good man and he really didn't have a lot of choice but to do what they had told him to do. He decided there and then that when this is over, he would make sure that Newton would be kept out of any reprisals. He would have to live with what his family had been exposed to, and also any fall out that his employee's would be exposed to. That was punishment enough for any man.

He pulled out his phone and dialled Tackler. Nicole-Louise answered,

"Beat you!" he heard her say. He smiled to himself, he could imagine her and Tackler both lunging for the phone,

"How can I help you Ryan?" she asked in an overly polite tone, purely for Tackler's benefit.

"I need some information right now on Hilary Whelan," he said, "You ready?"

Three seconds later, he heard tapping on a keyboard through his earpiece and then Nicole-Louise said, "Shoot!"

"I want to know about her family and where she has come from?" he said, "And then every cent that she has in the world."

He could hear her tapping on the keyboard,

"I'll ring back in a minute or so," she said and hung up the phone.

He then pressed eight on his phone, speed dial for the leader of what he was sure, were the most efficient, lethal, and best group of mercenaries on earth.

"I've been waiting for your call," Martin McDermott said as he answered, "The boys are getting bored."

They certainly weren't boys he thought to himself. Martin McDermott's was an Ex-Seal commander of legendary status. Everyone in elite teams had heard of him. Ward had once spoken to an SAS captain in

London who had asked him if he had ever met Martin McDermott. He had said that he had not, even though he considered him to be one of the best friends that he had. Secrecy was everything in their world. His team was made up of his son Paul who was probably his father's equal in every way, Lloyd Walsh who was the teams' explosive expert, Danny Wallace who was a telecoms genius, Wired, Adam Fuller and Fringe, who were the assassins of the team. The one thing that they all had in common was the ability to analyse, make the right decisions, and kill without question. McDermott had a warehouse in pretty much every State in the country, and this was funded by the half a million dollars that The Old Man paid them for every day's service that they did. But it was never about the money; Ward knew that, McDermott and his team wanted to bring down the establishment, and with the same sense of justice, as much as he did.

"Are you set up?"

"Yes, I'll text you the address, you coming to meet us?" McDermott replied.

"No. I want you to meet me somewhere first."

"Problem?"

He went on to explain about Harris, the researchers, Cardona, the DEA agent, the agencies assisting Cardona, Newton and Hilary Whelan.

"So you are anticipating a welcoming committee at her house?" McDermott asked.

"Yes I am."

"The Optician?"

"He's my next call."

"Text me the address, we will head over there now and check it out."

"See you shortly," he replied and hung up the phone and then immediately forwarded Hilary Whelan's address to McDermott.

He then pressed two on his speed dial.

"You look tired."

It always unnerved him slightly when he knew he was in The Optician's crosshairs.

"We need to go and pay a visit to Hilary Whelan," he started, "McDermott and his team will meet me there, can you go ahead and check it out?"

"Are you all done here?"

"Yes. I'll text you the address."

"It's OK," The Optician replied, "I already have it, The Old Man copies all the texts you send and receive," and the line went dead.

Next, he called Nicole-Louise back.

"You said one minute," she said as she answered.

"What do you have?"

"Hilary Whelan topped her class in business and finance at Florida International University College of Business, she seems like a smart girl," Nicole-Louise replied, "But nowhere near as smart as me, because what she tried ever so hard to hide was easy to find," she added, without a hint of arrogance in her voice.

"What did you find?"

"Firstly, she has one brother. A guy called Gary, and he is locked up firmly in jail. He got ten years for drug running."

"For Cardona?"

"No one knows. He refused to say who he was running it for, and so he took the hit himself."

"No sister?" he asked, just seeking confirmation for what he had already worked out.

"No sister," she replied, "But she changed her name from Wheelan with two 'E's' to Whelan with one, just two weeks after he got out of jail," she added.

"What else?"

"She's got five million dollars stored in an off-shore account in the Cayman Islands. It was deposited just two weeks ago.

"Where has the money come from?"

"Long story short. Pablo Cardona," she confirmed.

"OK," he said, "I need you to search, and search hard, for where these people can be. Break into any surveillance system you have to, but you both need to get on this and quickly."

"We already are. Any pointers?"

He thought about this for a moment and then had an idea,

"Look at areas that the DEA are keeping secure, we might get lucky."

"OK. We will hack into their system and find where every single agent, boat and car they have is."

He hung up the phone.

Lawson came walking out of the house,

"Shall we go and pay Hilary Whelan a visit?" Ward asked him.

"And issue justice for Harris?"

"Not just for him, but for everyone they have threatened too."

EIGHTEEN

Pinetree Drive – Miami Beach

"It's good to see you," McDermott said as Ward and Lawson stepped out of the car, two hundred yards down from Whelan's house.

"How are you Mike?" McDermott asked, extending his hand for Lawson to shake.

"I'm on a sex ban," Lawson replied, pointing at Ward and rolling his eyes.

All three of them laughed.

"What have you got?" Ward asked McDermott.

"Fringe and Wired have checked the whole house and gardens, and it looks like three guys inside, and three outside. Looking at how alert they are, they think that they have literally just turned up. They are pacing and checking too frequently to have been here very long," McDermott replied.

This made perfect sense to Ward. After the visit from Harris, they would have known that sending the picture of his eyeless, dead body would invite a visit.

They had just seriously underestimated the type of men that were going to come calling.

"Is The Optician here?" McDermott asked.

Ward nodded.

"Well perhaps you could ask him to clear the way for us and look after the guys outside?"

He pulled out his cell and called The Optician.

"I think you might have turned up a little heavy handed," he said as he answered, "Say hello to McDermott for me."

"He says hello," Ward said to McDermott, who then nodded his own hello in return.

"There are three guys outside, just give me the word," The Optician said.

"You have it," he replied, "We are a few hundred yards away and we are walking up now."

"I know," The Optician said, "I'm looking at you."

The line went dead.

"Can you get the team to take out any guys inside so we can just walk in and deal with Whelan; we've had a long day?" Ward asked McDermott.

McDermott lifted up his microphone and said,

"Paul, take the boys in, take out the Columbians and secure the woman," he ordered, dropping the mouthpiece back into the left breast of his jacket without waiting for a reply.

He knew it would be done.

The three of them walked casually down the road, past all the plush houses, the majority of them obscured from view by the thick shrubbery and trees in the gardens, and they looked just like three guys out for a walk in the late evening sun.

Paul was crouching behind a thick shrub at the rear of Whelan's back yard, with Wallace beside him. They watched as the short, stocky guy holding an AK47 collapsed into a heap on the floor, a spray of blood lightly covering the wall of the house behind him. Yet another shot from The Optician that hit the dead centre of his targets forehead.

"Jesus," Wallace said, "That guys aim doesn't even vary by a millimetre, how can he do that?"

"I don't know, but I would never want to be on the opposing team to him," Paul replied.

They continued to watch as another guy turned the far corner of the house. He didn't look any older than twenty, and he was holding his AK47 out like it was an extension to his arm. Three steps after he had turned the corner, his head exploded and his forward momentum took him another step forward and he collapsed face down onto a plant pot, the pot breaking with a large crack.

Ten seconds later, another guy came running around the same corner, and as he stopped to register what he was seeing, another 7.62mm bullet from the rifle of the deadliest sniper in the world, smashed into the dead centre of his forehead, sending blood and bone spraying to the left side of his head, and he was dead on the floor a second after turning the corner.

"Do you think he actually shot that second guy so that he would fall onto the pot and bring the other guy running around?" Wallace asked.

"I doubt even he is that good," Paul replied.

In an elevated position, just two hundred feet away from them, The Optician smiled, feeling pleased with his second kill, a shot which had resulted in the guy falling forward onto the large plant pot and breaking it as intended.

"Damn, I'm good," he whispered to himself.

"Let's go," Paul said to Wallace, "Wired and Fringe, take the front now," he said into his microphone as he stood up. Crouching down, with their silenced machine guns held out in front of them, they both approached the back door of Whelan's house.

They reached the back door and Wallace tried the door handle.

The door opened slightly.

They stepped through into the kitchen and stood still for a few moments, getting a feel for the house, rather than listening for voices.

Paul nodded towards the kitchen door which led into the house, and Wallace walked over to it, stood to the side and eased the handle down to the bottom. Paul positioned himself in the dead centre of the door, three feet back, so that he would not be hit by the door opening, and then nodded at Wallace.

Wallace pulled the door open ninety degrees sharply and as the hall came into view, Paul saw a tall South American looking guy open his mouth to scream. Before any sound could come out of the guys mouth, Paul had fired three shots into the centre of his chest. Before the guy had hit the floor, they had both stepped through it, Paul pointing his gun to the left, facing the front entrance to the house, and Wallace to the right, waiting for anyone to appear behind them.

It was a good move by Wallace because almost immediately, a guy stepped out into the hallway with a handgun raised. Before he could register what was happening, Wallace had fired three shots, the first two hitting the guy in the upper chest and the last one ripping his throat apart.

Paul turned and nodded at Wallace. They started to make their way towards the entrance hall that was in the centre of the house, when they heard a short burst of gunfire.

By the time they had got to the end of the hallway, Wired and Fringe were standing over a dead body at the foot of the staircase.

He pointed upstairs to indicate that Wired and Fringe were to clear the first floor of the house, and he crossed the hallway with Wallace right behind him. There were three doors; painted in a shiny white gloss and all closed, and so Paul selected the second one by nodding at it. Wallace assumed the same position, standing to the left of the door, and pulling down on the handle until it reached its limit. He yanked the door firmly as Paul stepped in.

Hilary Whelan was sitting on a sofa right in front of him, looking terrified.

"Please don't hurt me," she said, with a desperate tone to her voice.

"I'm really not the guy you have to worry about," he replied, "The house is secure and the woman is waiting for you," he said into his microphone.

The whole process of entering the house and securing Whelan had taken no more than forty five seconds.

"Damn we are good," Paul said to Wallace.

Ward, Lawson and McDermott reached Whelan's house and strolled casually up the garden path. To anyone seeing them, they were meant to be there. Fringe was waiting just inside the door and Ward nodded to him, Wallace and Wired as they walked in,

"Where is she?" he asked Wallace.

Wallace pointed to the middle door and they headed straight for it.

He walked into the room.

"Good to see you Ryan," Paul said.

"You too Paul," he replied as he extended his hand to shake.

"How come no one is so pleased to see me?" Lawson quipped.

"Trust you to be here when a woman is the focus of our attention," Paul replied.

Ward looked at Hilary Whelan sitting on the sofa, walked over to her and stood, looking down at her.

She saw the devil. She saw a seven foot giant standing over her, with eyes that were burning right through her. She knew right then that telling the truth would be the only chance that she had of survival. A fact that was confirmed when he pulled out his Glock and slowly screwed the silencer on, his stare not leaving her for one second. When the silencer clicked fully into place, he smiled at her.

"I can see how afraid you are of me," he said softly, "And you are right to be, because what happens in the next few minutes will help me to decide if you live or you die."

Lawson and McDermott casually sat down on the sofa opposite Whelan, like they were just a couple of guys sitting down in a bar. Their casual approach was deliberate so that she felt even more unsettled by the fact that this was clearly no big deal to them at all.

"Tell me about your sister?" he asked.

Whelan paused for a moment, clearly debating whether lying might be a better option right now, but in the end, she decide against it,

"I don't have a sister," she replied, her voice shaking with fear.

"Do you have any siblings?"

There was a pause for a few moments while she weighed up her options again,

"I have a brother."

"Yes you do. His name is Gary and he worked for Cardona. Am I correct?"

Whelan nodded.

"Tell me how Cardona came to contact you?"

"After Gary got sent to jail, a guy approached me and said that as a reward for his silence, they were clearing all of the debts that I had accumulated through my education," she replied.

"Was that Cardona?"

"No. It was a guy called Franco."

"And so you took the money and then what?

"I heard nothing for six months and then six months ago, he came to see me again."

"Wanting what?"

"He asked for the personnel files for the key researchers at Newton's."

"But you didn't give them to them?"

"No."

"Why?"

"Because I can't access them," she replied, "Mr Newton keeps them secured electronically off site, and I didn't know where they were," she added.

"So they gave you six months to get them, so you made up the story about having a sister?" he asked, "So why did it suddenly happen when it did?"

"Because apparently some other government guy has the same composition for the drug and he knew what Cardona was planning," she replied.

"What government guy? D.E.A?"

"No. This was something different. I heard them talking about him. He was like a lone operator who was trying to get the drug for himself to market."

"So you told Newton about your sister and he gave you the personnel files?"

"I had no choice. They told me if I didn't, that Gary would never live long enough to leave jail."

"And you had to protect your brother? I understand that," he said, "So I guess that you are as much a victim as Newton?" he added, adding extra sympathy to his tone of voice.

"Yes I am. We are all victims," she replied urgently, clearly thinking that she had found an angle to escape with her life.

"They raped his wife, over and over in front of his kids," he said, "What do you think of that?"

"It's wrong on every level."

"Did they rape you?"

"Yes," Whelan replied.

Ward could see that was the first lie that she had told because she scratched her nose as she replied.

"There was a guy who came to see you. It was the same guy who was with me when I met you at Newton's offices. Who killed him?"

"One of the men you have killed outside. Marvin."

"Why did they cut his eyes out?"

"It's what Cardona does. Like his calling card."

He nodded.

"Do you know where he is holding the people that he has taken?"

"No. But I did hear them mention The Keys."

He was sure that was a truth. It tied in with the D.E.A. involvement.

"Do you know specifically what Key? There are a lot of them"

"No I don't," she replied.

He felt his phone vibrate in his pocket. He pulled it out and saw Nicole-Louise's name on the screen.

"I forgot to ask you, what would you like me to do with the five million dollars that the woman has in her account?" she asked.

"Steal it," he said, and hung up the phone.

He studied Whelan for a moment. He didn't like her.

"Anything else I need to know or anything you haven't told me?" he asked.

"No," she said eagerly, "I've told you everything."

195

"Not quite."

She looked at him quizzically.

"You didn't tell me about the money Cardona paid you. Money which I have just instructed someone to steal from you."

"I forgot about that," she quickly said.

"You hadn't. You sacrificed how many lives, we don't yet know, for your greed and your own benefit. Worse than that, a colleague of mine got killed because of you," he said, his voice now deliberately stepping up a few decibels, "Want to know what I think?"

Her eyes widened, the fear on her face intensified, and she couldn't look at his eyes.

"I think from the first time you saw me you knew that I was going to kill you," he said calmly.

And with that, he raised his arm, and shot her three times in the face. Her face exploded, and blood sprayed forward and covered his extended arm and hand.

He watched her body slump to the side of the sofa.

"I bet that hurt to see didn't it?" McDermott said to Lawson, making reference to Lawson's desire for pretty women.

"Not at all," Lawson replied, "I'm on a sex ban."

NINETEEN

NW 60th Street – Doral – Miami

They had all made their way back to McDermott's warehouse, which was NW 60th Street in Doral, not far from Miami International Airport, nestled among lots of other units in an industrial park. As always, this warehouse was displaying a sign saying 'A & B Auto's', and a local number stamped underneath. Anyone dialling the number, in any State, would be re-routed to a phone manned by Wallace; who would promptly say they were too busy to take on any new customers. All of the warehouses were identical in every way. Entry into the warehouse would be through a main door into what appeared to be a small reception area, and through the reception and into the warehouse itself, sat two black Range Rovers with tinted windows, always ready to go, facing the roller shutter doors. Two long work benches, one for weapons and one for communication equipment, ran along either side of the warehouse and there was a dry wall at the rear of the building with another workbench against it, the bottom of which was hinged, and once removed, gave entry into a secret room where every single type of weapon and explosive was stored. In the left hand corner there was a table, six chairs and an old battered armchair, and behind the armchair was a sink, an old refrigerator and a microwave.

"This place looks different," Lawson said sarcastically, as he walked into the main warehouse and got a distinct feeling that he had been here before.

"We won't be doing anything else tonight so everyone get some rest and we will go again at 07:00am tomorrow morning," Ward said to McDermott, as his team were moving orderly in different directions throughout the warehouse setting up, without speaking.

"Me and Mike will grab a motel for the night," he continued, "Can you organise some boats in case we need them, because Nicole-Louise and Tackler are tracking the Keys trying to find the hostages, and we both know they will, so we need to be ready to move immediately."

"It's already in hand," McDermott replied, "I thought of that when you first called me."

Of course he had, he thought to himself, he always thought of every single eventuality.

"Give me a couple of minutes Mike," he said to Lawson as he headed towards the door that led out of the main warehouse and into the reception area, "I need to make a couple of phone calls."

He stepped outside and pulled out his cell phone, he pushed Eloisa's speed dial.

Three rings later, she answered.

"Hello Ryan," she said, "I've missed you."

"Likewise," he said softly, "I want you to do something for me."

"Of course."

"I want you to see what you can find out about a guy called Pablo Cardona."

"Who is he?"

"He's a Columbian drug runner. We have the basics but I want to know if there is anything else on him that the agencies don't know."

"OK," she replied, "I'm working on something at the moment but in the meantime, I'll ask our analysts what they can find," she replied flatly.

"Is everything OK?" he asked, "You sound down?"

"It's just this case I am working on, it's not nice."

"Want to share?"

"You have enough on your plate by the sound of it," she replied, trying hard to sound upbeat but failing miserably.

"There's always enough room for your problems. And anyway, it helps me to switch off and think about something else for a few minutes, so you'll be helping me out too."

"There's this man called the Reverend Solomon Tower," she started, "He runs an obscure religious cult in Oregon, and he is just using it as a front for abusing children," she added, her voice trailing off as she finished the sentence.

"Abusing them in what way?" he asked carefully; fully aware that Eloisa struggled to talk in graphic terms about any abuse that was directed towards children.

"He basically uses all of the women for his sexual pleasure, all under the banner of carrying out God's commands of course," she replied, a sigh echoing down the line at the same time, "And also their children."

"He's abusing them too?"

"Worse," she replied, "He's receiving a lot of donations through wealthy contributors to keep his compound and church in the grand manner that he has become used to."

He pondered this reply for a moment, and then he understood exactly what was happening,

"He's charging paedophile's large sums of money to abuse the children?"

"Yes."

"So why haven't the F.B.I. gone in and stopped it?"

"You know what the politicians are like on Capitol Hill," she replied, "Particularly under the watch of this current liberal President and his ridiculous liberal values. Offending any race or religion is totally off of their agenda. Even more so after Waco," she added, making reference to past events when the F.B.I. stormed a compound.

"It's about neither of those things. It's about protecting innocent children, which should come before anything," he protested, realising that his voice was now carrying a threatening tone.

"Tell that to their advisors who tell them to sympathise with all races and religions," she replied, sounding equally as angry.

200

He knew better than most how dishonest and lacking in true moral beliefs the majority of people in politics were. He had seen it up close, through recent events, and at times, like now, he despaired at how out of touch they were with those that weren't privileged enough to be wealthy, actually felt. But he could see the tide turning. Not only in The States but also in Europe, and he knew the era of putting sympathy and tolerance of others, before protecting your own, was fast coming to an end. Globalisation was ending.

And he hoped people like him were speeding up the process.

"Then I guess you need someone who does put the children first to deal with it?" he asked.

"You have enough on your plate, and I'm starting to worry about you. If you don't take a break soon and switch off, you will burn out," she replied, genuine concern running through her voice.

"I'm fine. We have years to switch off when we walk away from this mess. You are always saying that to me. This thing I am on in Miami, I'm hoping it won't be much more than a few days, and so by the time I am back in New York, can you have everything on this Reverend guy ready for me?" he asked, like he was asking her to run to the grocery store for him.

"I can't keep putting on you Ryan," she protested.

"You aren't. Get everything together and we will deal with him as soon as we are done. Agreed?"

"Yes Master!"

"And if you find anything out about Cardona, let me know immediately. OK?" he reminded her.

"I'll look into it shortly. I love you Ryan. I love you so much. You always have a way of making everything better for me. One day, you are going to make an amazing father."

He felt a rush run through his body. It was a rush of contentment and pride. She always made him feel so good about himself, and that was the exact balance that he needed to survive in the evil and dangerous world that he lived in. He knew that she really was the woman that he was meant to spend the rest of his life with.

"I love you too Eloisa," he said softly and then the line went dead.

He walked back into the warehouse and Lawson was in the reception area talking to Paul.

"Let's go and grab a motel Mike," he said without fully stepping through the door, "See you tomorrow Paul," he added as he turned his back and headed towards Lawson's car.

Twenty five minutes later, they were heading up the wooden stairs to the first floor of a cheap motel just two miles away from McDermott's warehouse. There was no point in being any further away, it was just a room to grab some sleep and shower in. Lawson had paid cash for the two adjacent rooms that he had chosen, and the young woman behind the cashier was still drooling over Lawson as they walked out of the reception block.

They reached their rooms, Lawson taking the first one that they got to and Ward next door.

"Be ready at 06:00am," he said, "We will grab a bite to eat and then be at the warehouse for seven," he added, as he stepped into his room, closed the door behind him and left Lawson standing on the landing, debating whether to go back down to the reception area to chat to the woman or walk into his room. In the end, he decided to honour his agreement to the sex ban that Ward had imposed on him. Following orders and making the right choice was what Lawson was good at.

He always had been.

He had grown up in a beautiful house in Southern England with his two brothers, in a village at the foot of what was called the South Downs, The word 'Downs' being an English term for the sprawling hills and countryside.

His father had been a General in the British army, and the army had funded the best private education that money could for his three boys.

They had all excelled academically, and were exceptional sportsman. What they all also had in common was that they were warriors. They had been fascinated by their father's tales of valour and adventure, and each of them was desperate to join the army to emulate what he had done.

He was the youngest of three.

They were three quite remarkable boys too.

His eldest brother John had joined the Paratroopers straight from school and was climbing the ranks rapidly when he applied to join the S.A.S., The elite and world renowned British Special Forces unit that has laid down the training template for most of the world's other Special Forces units to follow. He had walked through their gruelling training, and was currently the captain of their most revered team. They were the team known simply as 'The Assassins', and the British Government were using them constantly to assist other governments of the world, and bank another diplomatic favour owed in the process. Most of the political assassination's that had been carried out throughout the world over the past five years were at the hand of John Lawson's team.

His middle brother was called Dominic and he had taken a slightly different direction in that he had joined MI6 after his early army career, and was now working for Interpol, a job which he had initially enjoyed but now through the liberal governance of the European Union, he was losing faith in, and he was currently in the process of moving back to MI6.

Then there was Mike Lawson.

Aside from his stunning looks and incredible physique, Lawson was one of those people who did everything exceptionally well. At school, he had been known as 'Davie Watts', a reference to a song sung by a British band called 'The Kinks' in the sixties. It was about a boy who was envious of another boy called Davie Watts because he was good at everything.

That summed Lawson up.

He had left school and followed the exact same path as his brother John. Lawson had been every bit as good as his older brother and the instructors had been even harder on him than they usually would be on recruits simply because of who he was. He had earned their respect by facing every obstacle put in front of him head on and beating it.

He had been exceptional on operations, and one day there had been an incident in Hungary where John had taken a non-fatal bullet but it had shaken the younger Lawson to the extent that he decided to move across to

MI6, at the suggestion of Dominic, as he did not want to risk being witness to his brother being killed.

Two years after joining MI6 he had been approached about assisting a joint U.K and U.S. team that was off the books and that had been when he had first come into contact with Ward.

Recent events, and the suggestion of The Old Man to be based in The States, had convinced him that he was within touching distance of becoming one of the fully fledged Deniables.

Exciting times laid ahead for him. He found working with Ward exciting, relentless and rewarding. He admired him a great deal for his sense of right and wrong, and for his determination to protect the world's children.

As much as he joined in and laughed about Ward's perception of him being a sex crazed guy who was easily distracted by the female race irritated him, he played along with it, but he knew, and he hoped that Ward knew too, that he was equally as focussed and capable as he was.

He didn't really know Ryan Ward. No one really knew Ryan Ward, but he felt that there was an unspoken respect and bond between them that was hard to explain, but it felt good to him whenever they were together. Maybe one day Ward would tell him what he really thought of him he would often say to himself, when Ward appeared to be dismissive or under appreciative of him.

But then again, he would say to himself, maybe he wouldn't.

He showered, lay down on the bed and closed his eyes. He thought about the woman in reception. She was cute, like all of the women in his life so far had been cute, but she wasn't Lucy Corrigan, the only woman he had ever loved.

TWENTY

NW 60th Street – Doral – Miami

They were back at McDermott's warehouse by 06:30am.
Ward had a habit of always arriving somewhere early
after he had agreed a set time. He always preferred
leaving a window of opportunity in case something went
wrong. But he was never late. In fact, he was proud of
the fact that he had never been late for anything in his
life. He was also fully aware that if McDermott needed
to be ready for 07:00am, that he would have had the
team up and about, and everything packed and
organised, by 06:00am. As they stepped out of the car,
one of the black Range Rovers approached the roller
shutter doors of the warehouse and then sped inside.
Wired was driving.
"Looks like Wired drew the breakfast run," Lawson said.

"So it seems," Ward replied, "I hope that they included us in their order too."

As it turned out, Wired had indeed included the two of them in the breakfast collection.

As they all tucked into Bacon and Egg bagels, and hot takeout coffees, McDermott asked the question that was waiting to be asked.

"So who else are we fighting as well as Cardona?"

Ward had thought a lot about this overnight.

He knew the D.E.A. was definitely involved, after all, they had tried scaring them off, but there had to be others involved too. Then there was Michael Vermont, the senior executive of the National Park Service, who was responsible for the Biscayne National Park, and the two hundred thousand dollars that Cardona had paid him, he was also involved, and probably the quickest route to find out where the researchers were being held.

"I need to make a phone call," he said, and he walked out of the warehouse and into the bright, morning sun.

He pressed speed dial for The Old Man.

"How was your breakfast?" Centrepoint answered.

He knew that The Optician would be watching, and he would be giving The Old Man a minute by minute update on his movements and so he simply ignored the question.

"Who else are we against?"

"Something this big has to involve a number of agencies," Centrepoint replied, "The D.E.A you have already confirmed, but I have a bad feeling that one of our C.I.A colleagues might be involved too. Plus, the F.B.I don't seem to be making any progress, which is highly unusual, so it appears they are deliberately dragging their feet on this one, almost buying time."

He felt that The Old Man was holding something back. "Now tell me the important thing that you are reluctant to tell me?" he demanded.

Centrepoint paused for a few seconds. He knew what Ward's reaction was going to be and so he braced himself before saying,

"Cardona has built up the biggest operation down there for years. He's growing at a rapid rate too. That in itself is unusual because of the excessive resources that the government are putting in down there, so I dug around and I discovered that he is a government informant."

"He is an informant?"

"Yes."

"An informant of what?"

"He has tipped off the D.E.A on all the routes and players that are running things down there."

"And then they get taken out, and the D.E.A publishes their successes, so it looks like they are winning the war?" Ward asked.

"That's what it looks like."

"And in the process, wiping out all of his competition and giving him a free run?"

"It looks like that too."

He still felt that The Old Man was holding something back, but he figured that he would tell him when he needed to know. Centrepoint often left things for him to discover himself, just to confirm that his information was correct. So he did not push the point.

"How can anyone make a decision that concludes that would be a good idea?"

"They take the view that it is better to know the key players, and the where and how, rather than chasing shadows."

"But all they have done is grow his empire."

"With the belief that they could control him I suspect," Centrepoint replied.

"He cuts out people's eyes. What do you think of that?"

"I think I wouldn't want to be in his shoes when you find him."

That echoed his own thoughts.

"But you have to get the composition before you kill him Ryan. That is so important, and you are to give it to no one but me," Centrepoint reminded him.

He understood that. It was vital that no one knew how to mass produce this drug, and by having the composition, purchases of ingredients could be monitored, and so the agencies would know who to look for.

"Who do you have available that I can trust?"

"I've already sorted that out for you," he replied.

"Well?"

"There is a seal team led by a man called Captain Geoff Dawes."

"I already have McDermott," he said flippantly, "He's the one I trust with my life."

"Captain Dawes used to serve under McDermott. That's why I chose him. As good as McDermott and his team are, and I know they are the best, this is about numbers of men and you need the help. He has a team of seven with him. I'm sure McDermott will vouch for him."

"Well if he doesn't, forget it," he said and hung up the phone.

He then called Nicole-Louise and Tackler.

Tackler answered.

"Do you ever sleep?" he asked, yawning as he finished the sentence.

"I need you to find someone for me and quickly."

"Everything is always quickly," Tackler replied.

"This Michael Vermont guy who is in charge of The Keys," he said, "The guy that Nicole-Louise discovered," he quickly added, knowing that by saying Nicole-Louise had found him first, it would motivate him to get what he needed quickly, "I need his address."

Tackler snorted down the line but didn't comment. Ward could hear him tapping on his keyboard immediately and he smiled.

"How are you getting on with the satellite images?"

"Why don't you ask her?" Tackler said, a sarcastic tone to his voice, "Oh no, you can't because she isn't as good at me at breaking into the feeds."

He smiled again.

"I'm locked onto them all and I've been scanning them for change and movement. If they are on one of the islands, I will find it within a couple of hours maximum."

"Michael Vermont?" he said again.

After a few more seconds of frantically tapping on his keyboard, Tackler said,

"He lives on SW 207th Street in Cutler Bay. Number 8936."

"Does he have a family?"

"Two kids, both away at college."

"So, he lives alone with his wife?"

"Looking at his bank account, I'd say he used to."

"What do you mean?"

"He's paid out fifteen thousand dollars in the past four months to a company of lawyers who specialise in divorce settlements."

Now he understood why a government employee of good standing would take a bribe.

"Well done Tackler. As soon as you get a hit on the Satellite, let me know immediately," he said and hung up the phone. He walked back into the warehouse. Lawson caught sight of him first.

"Any news?"

"What do you know about Captain Geoff Dawes?" he asked McDermott, completely ignoring Lawson's question.

"Exactly what I told The Old Man last night," McDermott replied, "I trust him with my life. He's good, very good."

He shook his head. Centrepoint could have made it easier by telling him that he had already spoken to McDermott, and he felt a little frustrated that The Old Man felt the need to claim a little victory over him. But then he thought about the number of times that he simply ignored whatever he said to him and he smiled to himself.

"I guess I had that coming," he said to no one in particular.

He turned and looked at Lawson.

"Yes Mike, I have some news."

"Fancy sharing it or do we guess?" Lawson asked.

"Michael Vermont. He is in charge of The Keys. He has taken a two hundred thousand dollar payment from Cardona and I'm sure he will be able to tell us where he has the researchers."

McDermott raised his eyebrows,

"Where is he?" he asked.

"He's in Cutler Bay."

"About thirty minutes away," Wallace shouted out from the table where he was sitting with the rest of the team.

"You and Wired come with me and Lawson," he said to McDermott.

"Take Paul," McDermott said.

"Why?"

"Because Geoff Dawes will be here with his team in an hour and I want to brief him."

8936 SW 207th St, Cutler Bay – Miami

Paul McDermott pulled the Range Rover to a stop opposite Michael Vermont's house. It was a well presented house, not overly grand, but elegant enough to indicate that the owner had a better than average job. It had a sloping drive which led to a double garage, and the walls were painted beige with white paint around all the windows with tall, white double entrance doors. The front lawn was small but immaculately well kept.

A silver Lexus was parked on the drive.

"It looks quiet," Lawson said.

"You and Wired take the back, just to make sure," he said to Paul, and he watched them step out of the car and walk down the side of the garage to the backyard.

"If this guy knows where they are, I doubt Cardona would leave him all alone if they are that organised," Lawson said.

"My thoughts exactly."

Three minutes later, Paul and Wired came back down the drive, crossed the road and got into the car.

"There are two guys in there," Paul said, "One old guy and one South American looking guy. They are both in the kitchen."

"Are you sure there is no one else in the house?" Ward asked.

"Positive," Wired replied.

"How?"

"Because I went in through the lounge window and checked every room upstairs," Wired replied as he screwed the silencer onto his handgun.

"If you two take the back, me and Lawson will take the front. If Vermont comes to answer the door, take out Cardona's guy," Ward said as he opened the car door and stepped out onto the road.

Paul and Wired sprinted past him and ran up the side of the house again, as he waited for Lawson to join him from the other side of the car.

"I take it we are just going to knock on the door again," Lawson asked.

"Of course," he replied as the started to climb the drive. He pulled out his silenced Glock and walked towards the door. Lawson drew his own gun and held it down by his side.

Ward knocked four times on the door and waited.

No one answered.

And so he knocked four times again.

A few seconds later he could hear movement behind the door and then the door started to open.

As the gap between the door and the doorframe increased, he could start to see a South American looking guy with his left hand hidden by the door, clearly hiding a weapon.

As the gap got to eighteen inches, he raised his gun and shot the guy twice in the centre of his face.

The guy's head jerked and he fell backwards, his momentum pulling the door open as he did so, and the spray of his blood covering the door. As he hit the ground, there was a loud crack as the back of his head smashed against the ceramic floor tiles in the hall.

Ward stepped in and fired another shot into the guy's chest as he stepped over him.

Lawson followed into the hallway and kicked the guys' leg to one side so he could close the door.

Ward walked towards an open door at the far end of the hallway and stepped into the kitchen.

Michael Vermont was sitting at the kitchen table with Paul and Wired sitting opposite him with their guns on the table in front of them.

Vermont looked terrified.

"You are right to look frightened Mr Vermont," Ward said, "Do you want to go and have a look at the mess of Mr Cardona's bodyguard outside? He has no face left."

Michael Vermont shook his head quickly but didn't speak.

"You know why we are here," he started, "I'm not going to play games. I know most of what you can tell me anyway, I just need you to confirm a few things. If you lie to me once, I will kill you. Do you understand that?" he asked as he pulled out a chair from the table and sat down next to Vermont.

Vermont nodded his head eagerly.

"Good. We have a clear understanding then."

"OK," Vermont said, "I will tell you everything."

"How much money did Cardona pay you?" he asked, testing the water to see how honest Vermont intended to be.

He paused for a few moments, clearly not wanting to lie, but knowing that the moment he said how much, he would be admitting his involvement.

"I do already know the answer," Ward said quickly, trying to prompt him along.

"Two hundred thousand dollars," he said so quietly that he could only just make it out.

"Speak clearly," Lawson said, and he promptly slapped Vermont around the back of the head with his open palm.

Vermont's shoulders hunched and he instantly started to rub the back of his head.

"Two hundred thousand dollars," he said more clearly.

"Why did he pay you the money?"

"To refuse to issue any permits for people to access some of the islands that I am responsible for."

"Do you know why he wanted you to do that?" Ward asked.

"No."

He could see that he was telling the truth and he decided then that he was not going to kill him.

He raised his gun and pointed it at Vermont's head.

"Your next answer dictates if you live or die Mr Vermont," he said, "Do you understand that?"

Vermont went white and just managed to say, "Yes."

"There is one specific island that Cardona has paid you to ensure that it is out of bounds. I want you to tell me what island that is?" he said calmly, and closed one eye

216

and lined the gun up with Vermont's head for added effect.

Michael Vermont knew that this was his moment of truth. His defining moment in life, he either told the truth and put himself at the mercy of Pablo Cardona, or he lied and risked this man shooting him.

He looked into Ward's eyes and saw death.

He saw a threat that was real, that would be delivered if he did not tell the truth.

He saw a seven foot giant sitting next to him.

He saw someone who scared him a lot more than Pablo Cardona.

"It was Adams Key," he said, looking down at the table.

"Thank you Mr Vermont," he replied, and lowered his gun, "Do you have somewhere a long way from Miami that you can go for a few days?"

"I have a sister in Chicago," Vermont replied after a few moments thinking about it.

"Why did you take the money?"

Vermont huffed,

"I took it because I am going through a costly divorce. My wife has found someone younger and less boring than me. Those were her exact words. She wants to take everything. She wants the house, our savings, all of it. I needed the money to employ a legal team good enough to fight her," he said sadly.

Ward felt sorry for him. Vermont clearly had no idea what he had become involved in, and he knew at that moment that if he thought it would have put anyone at risk, he would never have taken the money.

"Keep the money," he said.

"I can't. Cardona and his men will find me and hunt me down. They told me that."

"He will be dead, and all of his men will be too, in a couple of days, so go to Chicago and then come back in a week and try and sort things out with your wife," he said and stood up, "We are done here."

They were on their way down the drive when Ward's phone vibrated in his pocket. He pulled it out and saw Tackler's name on the screen.

"It's Adam's Key," he said as he answered.

"How on earth do you know that?" Tackler asked.

"Nicole-Louise told me," he replied, and he hung up the phone and smiled to himself.

TWENTY ONE

Adams Key – Upper Florida Keys

Inside the building that was holding the researchers families, desperation had taken a firm hold. They had been without food for two days, and the only water available to them was from the rusty tap in the corner of the building. It stank of sweat, and the toilet next to the sink was not properly vented and so that added to the vile conditions inside. The majority of the prisoners were children, and they were finding it hard to breathe in the heat and darkness.

Heather Lambourne leant in towards Lindsey Dunn, who was trying her hardest to keep her daughters, Morgan and Julie calm,

"This can't continue," she said, a stern tone to her voice, "They can't keep the children locked up like animals with no food or water, I'm going to talk to them."

"I'm not sure that's a good idea," Lindsey replied, "We have the children to think of."

"That's why I am going to talk to them; they must understand that the children will become ill very quickly."

"I think you should just leave it Heather. We don't want to antagonise them."

Heather Lambourne stood to her feet.

"Sit down," Lindsey said.

"One of us has to stand up to them."

"The children need food and clean water."

"I mean it Heather, sit down," Lindsey said again, now raising her own voice.

Heather Lambourne started walking towards the door.

"Don't you dare do anything," Lindsey shouted.

By now, everyone in the room, parents and children alike were listening to the conversation.

"What is wrong with you?" Heather demanded.

Lindsey Dunn didn't respond, she just glared at Heather Lambourne.

"Well? Are you afraid to stand up for the children?" Heather asked, as she turned and walked the few strides back to Lindsey in a direct act of confrontation.

"I can't see your children anywhere in here," Lindsey replied, as she stood up and moved closer to Heather, "You can't speak for our children, we can't risk upsetting them," she added.

"I had to kneel and watch as my husband was murdered and my daughter was raped. Do not dare talk to me about loss. Because I don't know if my daughter is even still alive," Heather spat back.

Lindsey looked down at the floor. She was a smart woman and knew that it was not uncommon for members of a group to argue in a pressure situation, particularly when people's lives were at stake, and so she tried a different approach.

"I know how hard this must be for you," she said, "But we have to stay strong and stand together."

"That's easy for you to say, holding your two daughters close to you," Heather replied, "Let me calmly ask them for food and clean water and that is all I will do."

Lindsey nodded at her,

"But no more than that?"

"I promise."

She walked over to the door and banged on it three times, solid, clear bangs.

She waited a minute and nothing happened, and so she banged her fist against it again, this time six thumps of her fist, one straight after the other.

Another minute passed and still they did not hear the keys turning in the locks.

And then, almost like someone had flicked a switch inside of her, she lost control.

She started hammering on the door harder and harder.

She started screaming, a wild scream that you would expect to hear coming from the mouth of someone in agony.

She started screaming obscenities, one after the other and started shouting out the word 'Animals', over and over again.

She kept this up for three whole minutes.

The children in the room started to cower behind the adults, and you could almost feel the fear sweep through them all.

And then the keys could be heard turning the locks.

Heather Lambourne stepped back three feet and waited for the door to open.

After the third lock could be heard opening, the door swept wide open.

Franco was standing there, his hands resting on his hips, his large frame filling up the whole doorway.

"Are you making that noise whore?" he spat at Heather Lambourne.

She looked up at this frightening man and immediately regretted upsetting him.

"I just wanted to ask you a quick question," she said, "If it's OK. Please?"

"No it's not OK bitch. If you make one more noise I will come in here and slit your throat, and then force the men to rape you as you bleed to death."

Lindsey Dunn started to sob quietly and clutched Morgan and Julie even tighter to her body.

"I just want some food and water for the children. They will become ill very soon, and then what use are we to you?" she said very softly, so as not to annoy Franco further.

Franco looked at her and started to laugh.

"You are a pathetic whore. You aren't worth anything anyway. Just like your whore daughter couldn't please my men, and your weak pathetic husband couldn't defend you both. You are worth nothing," he said, stepping into the room as he spoke.

"Just some food and water, that's all," she whispered again, tears filling her eyes as the visions of what Franco had said came back to haunt her.

And then she changed.

Franco was right. They were worth nothing to him. She believed at that point that Catherine was probably dead already, or was being submitted to the vilest abuse imaginable by his men. She felt the anger rising in her, until it exploded out of her mouth, like a volcano erupting.

"You are going to die, you know that?" she spat at Franco, "You think by bullying women and children that you are a big man. There are going to be people coming for us. Real men, men who will kill you and show you up for the weak, pathetic, sad little men you really are," she added, now screaming at him.

Franco stepped into the room and walked towards her. Heather stood her ground. She was no longer afraid, what is there to be afraid of after you have lost everything she asked herself as Franco approached.

"Who is going to come and save you whore?" Franco asked, remaining surprisingly calm after the insult that Heather had directed at him.

"The F.B.I. and others, maybe the D.E.A. and they will find us," she shouted, staring into his eyes as she said it.

"They won't find you and they won't come for you whore," Franco said, with a smile on his face.

"Yes they will. They are probably getting close to finding us now and you know it," she replied, adding her own smile to show she was no longer afraid of him.

"They won't find you and they won't come for you whore."

"And what makes you so sure of that?" she asked, trying to bait Franco.

"Because they already know where you are," he replied, and then took one giant step forward and unleashed a lightning quick right handed punch that carried all of his weight behind it and caught Heather right on the tip of her nose. The weight of the punch shattered her nose with such force that it pushed the bone through her skull and into her brain, lifted her feet six inches off the ground, and she was dead before she even hit the floor. Everyone in the room screamed.

Franco looked at them all and laughed loudly.

"Next one who bangs on that door gets the same punishment," he said.

And then he turned and walked out of the building and the door closed with a loud clunk, and everything went dark again.

NW 60th Street – Doral – Miami

Paul McDermott drove the Range Rover back into the warehouse and the roller shutter doors closed quickly behind him.

"This is Dawes," McDermott said as Ward climbed out of the car and headed towards the new group of seven guys that had arrived.

"Good to meet you Dawes" he said as he extended his hand, "Has he fully briefed you?" he asked, nodding at McDermott as he spoke.

"Yes he has. But there is a lot of ground to cover in those Keys," Dawes replied.

He liked this response, and also liked Dawes immediately for it. He was a realist, a practical and efficient killing machine but still a realist. Just like McDermott.

He knew for sure now that they were going to win.

"They are holed up on Adams Key," he said.

McDermott smiled and shook his head.

"See? Just like I told you, I don't know how he does it, but he does," he said to Dawes.

"Let me introduce you to my team," Dawes said, and Ward nodded his agreement. They walked over towards the new guys. He noticed that Wallace and Fringe were talking and laughing with the group and the familiarity that there seemed to be between them made him smile again. He was sure that they knew each other when McDermott's team were operating as Seals, and he knew without any doubt that these guys could be trusted.

"Mosley, Atkins, Rope, Delaney, Vic and Case," Dawes said clearly, pointing at each guy as he said their name.

Ward nodded at them all and they all nodded back.

"You know for sure that they are on Adams Key?" McDermott asked.

"Is he ever wrong?" Lawson quipped.

He ignored the praise. He was fully aware that time was of the essence right now.

"Can you get Wallace to set up, and I will make a call and get Tackler to reroute the satellite feed to us here," he said.

"I've already done it. I'm waiting on you," Wallace said, without turning his head from the bank of screens that were set up on his workbench.

"Ask him yourself," he replied as he pulled out his cell phone and pressed Tacklers speed dial number, handing the phone to Wallace without bothering to listen if it was ringing at the other end or not.

"We need a plan of attack and quickly," he said to McDermott, "I'm assuming you have everything ready?"

"The boats are ten minutes away, and as soon as we know what we are facing we will be good to go in an hour."

"We are live," Wallace said, and Ward and Lawson followed McDermott and Dawes over to Wallace's screens.

"This screen here is the live satellite feed, and these two here are the recordings of the last forty eight hours. Tackler wanted you to look at this," Wallace said, pointing at a screen showing one of the recordings. They watched as what looked like a small pleasure boat approached Adams Key, and two smaller speed boats appeared and directed the pleasure boat away from the Key in the opposite direction.

"That's the D.E.A," Lawson said, "So reassuring to know they are helping," he added flippantly.

"Now this one," Wallace said, pointing to the next screen showing a recording, "This was forty three hours ago."

They watched the screen and saw a number of people arriving in boats and being marched onto the island, and then they disappeared under the cover of the thick treetops which were acting as a shield. They counted thirty one people in total who looked like they were being held prisoner.

"That's them," Ward said.

"Now Tackler said you need to see this one too," Wallace said, scrolling along a time bar at the bottom of the screen and moving the images forward.

They watched as a group of eight people were marched out of a thick woodland area, into a clearing for a few seconds, and then back under the cover of the trees.

"That's the researcher's, they are keeping them separate," Lawson said.

"And Finally…" Wallace said, as he tapped on his keyboard, "He wants you to see this."

They looked at the screen and it had switched to heat detection mode. There were five buildings, clearly outlined.

They could see in the first one that there was a large group of people huddled at the far end of the building.

"The hostages," McDermott said.

They could see the second building was empty but in the third building, the heat maps of eight people could be seen clearly, dotted around the building.

"There's the researcher's," Lawson said.

In the fourth building there was the heat signature of one person, not moving in the middle of the room.

"Do you think that is Cardona?" McDermott asked.

"Maybe," Ward replied.

The fifth building showed five people lying flat, like they were sleeping.

"Staff quarters," Lawson said.

"And now the answer to the question that you have all been waiting for," Wallace said, sounding like he was playing a game, which to Ward, Lawson and McDermott's team, it was. A game was there to be won. And everything was about winning.

227

"There are thirty of Cardona's men on the island. I assume one of them is the man himself," Wallace said, pointing at the heat map again and touching his screen with his pencil to count out loud the heat signatures that were wondering around outside of the buildings.

McDermott smiled.

"Thirty of them against fourteen of the best Seals and you two," he said to Ward, "We will be home by dinner time."

"Plus an Optician," Lawson added.

The mention of The Optician's name forced all of Dawes' men to look around at Lawson.

"Yes, he's real," Lawson said to them all.

Ward kept studying the screens and not speaking. He could see clearly how the island was laid out but there was something missing or not missing. He had the feeling that something shouldn't be there, and it made him feel uncomfortable.

He knew that he was missing something and he didn't like it.

"One hour to prepare between yourselves?" he asked McDermott.

"We will be ready."

"Good," he said and started to walk towards the reception area.

"Where are you going?" Lawson asked.

"I need to make a call."

TWENTY TWO

Washington D.C.

The call came through exactly as Centrepoint expected, ten minutes after he was aware that Tackler had fixed Ward up with access to the satellite images. He also expected him to see what no one else could see, and he knew that now was going to have to be the time to bring him up to speed with what else was happening.

He saw Ward's name on his caller display and answered. "Gilligan has been released today. He is now recovering at home," he said quickly.

"That's good," Ward replied, genuine delight rushing through his words, "But that isn't why I have called," he added, getting his focus back immediately.

"So I gather that you have found where the Newton people are being held?"

"That isn't why I have called either."

"So what's wrong?"

"Firstly, I need you to use all of your influence to get the D.E.A. boats moved from within ten miles of Adams Key immediately. Then I want you to get me everything on Larry Stanyard, the big fish in this D.E.A. involvement."

"That will be done within half an hour," The Old Man replied.

"And there is something else."

"Which is?"

"I want to know what you haven't been telling me." Centrepoint paused for a moment. He could not avoid telling Ward what was happening, because he was going to be the key player in putting the whole mess right.

"Gill Whymark," he said.

"He was Fulken's handler, the same agent who disappeared?" Ward asked.

"Yes. The very same one."

"What about him?"

"Cardona has him and we need him taken out."

"Why would Cardona have him?"

"That's a complicated story."

"Then give me the simple version," he said sarcastically.

"Whymark went rogue a long time before he disappeared. I had a suspicion that one of the Deniables was putting more effort into building their own empire than putting things in order."

"What do you mean by that?"

"Money was going missing, and so were people who could give vital information regarding the people who were in control of certain events," Centrepoint replied.

"Well I've stolen money," he said, "So does that make me a suspect?"

"I know you have stolen money to buy houses, and you know that I know, and that is completely different."

"Is that why he had pictures of The Deniables on his wall?" Ward asked, thinking back to a previous conversation that he had with The Old Man regarding something Fulken had said.

"Perhaps," he replied, "But this thing with Cardona, it first came to my attention eighteen months ago."

"You knew he planned to kidnap the researchers?" Ward asked in disbelief.

"No. Not that part. But we knew that he was trying to create and distribute a super drug that would cause chaos throughout America."

"So why not take him out then?"

"Because he was too big an asset for the D.E.A," Centrepoint replied, "My job, as you know, is all about balancing things out, it's about the bigger picture."

"And we all know that your bigger picture sometimes becomes very hazy." he said flippantly, "So how does Whymark fit into this?"

"I asked him to look into it and try and find out what he could, and then this thing with Fulken happened and I never heard from him again."

"So how do you know he is on the island with Cardona?"

"Because he called me and said that I was to keep everyone away from the island or the hostages would die."

"But there is something else, what is it?" Ward asked.

Centrepoint was quiet for a few moments and then said, "I don't think he is there under duress. I think that he is behind the whole thing and is using Cardona. He's good Ryan, the best I have had, and he's capable of anything."

"You think he is behind the whole plot?"

"I think he is trying to establish the make-up of the drug so that he can go into mass production himself and make billions of dollars."

"So we will kill him too when we get there."

"The Optician is there with you and will hunt Whymark once you are on the island. Your only job is to find Dr Robert Anderton, and get the information on the drug from him, and then keep it safe and give it to me alone. We cannot risk this getting out, it will cause chaos."

"And what about Cardona?"

"I'm sure you will administer the appropriate punishment as you see fit. I will pull the D.E.A. apart and get you the information that you requested on Larry Stanyard. But get Anderton and the composition of that drug before anyone else. Is that clear?" Centrepoint said, an unusually stern tone to his voice emphasising the seriousness of what was at stake.

"Yes. I'll get the doctor and the composition, I promise."

"And kill anyone else who has the information on the drug, you are authorised to do so."

Not that Ward needed any authorisation to make his own decisions at any time, but he appreciated the support from The Old Man.

"Thanks."

"One more thing Ryan," Centrepoint said before he had the chance to hang up.

"Yes?"

"Be careful of Whymark. Do not underestimate him. He will have a plan B, C, D and E already mapped out and ready to go. Do not drop your guard for a second."

"Do I ever?" he replied and hung up the phone.

Centrepoint leant back in his chair. The conversation had gone better than expected. He had avoided a lecture from Ward about losing control of Whymark, and now he knew that he would end this definitively, and that Whymark would no longer be a problem. And Cardona would never get this drug onto the streets. He was sure about that. Cardona's empire was about to crumble and Ryan Ward was going to bring it down.

NW 60th Street – Doral – Miami

He walked back into the warehouse and across to Wallace's screens where Lawson, McDermott and Dawes were still standing. He looked at the heat screen where the one guy was still in the centre of the room and said,

"That guy there is Gill Whymark. We have to take him out too."

"He's reappeared then?" Lawson said, "How can you be so sure?"

"The Old Man just told me."

McDermott and Dawes looked at him blankly, and so he quickly explained how Whymark had first come to his

attention, and how The Old Man wanted this operation to go, and the specific tasks that each person had,
"Me and Lawson will head for the room where Whymark is, McDermott can take the room with the hostages, and Dawes, you can take out Cardona's men throughout the island," Ward said, "Oh, and you will have a little help from The Optician, but his main target is Whymark."
All of Dawes' men turned around at the mention of his name, and so Ward walked over to them.
"He's very real," he said, "All of the stories and legends about him are all true and a hundred that you don't know. He's been my babysitter for the past two years, and I have never even got close to seeing him. You will be in the presence of one of the biggest living legends gentlemen, don't mess this up, he's likely to shoot you if you do," He said, and then he turned around and winked at Dawes who was looking at him in a way that indicated that he was unsure if he was joking or being serious. The truth was that Ward didn't know if he was being one or the other either.
"We have four boats available, Dawes will take two with three of his men in each, and he will jump into one of those, Paul will take another with Wired, Fringe and Walsh and you two," McDermott said pointing at Ward and Lawson, "Will be in the other boat with me and Fuller. Wallace will stay here and operate the communication systems and keep us informed of who is where and when."
"Sounds like a good plan to me," Lawson said as he started to put on his flak jacket.
"You might want to look at this," Wallace said.

The three of them looked down at the screen and saw a lone figure creeping in from the far side of the island, a good half a mile away from the buildings.

Ward smiled to himself.

"The Optician is there already," he said.

Dawes' men all scurried over to the screens and stood behind Wallace and watched. Ward, McDermott and Lawson moved away from the screens to allow a better view.

There were a hundred stories of The Optician's adventures that got spoken about by the Seals, some were true, some were too far-fetched to possibly be true and this made McDermott smile.

"Something amuses you?" he asked him.

"I'm just thinking of the effect that The Optician and his stories have on people."

"We watch him work, regularly, we know they are not stories," Lawson said.

"I know but some of them are so out of this world that they can't be true," McDermott replied.

"Give me an example?" Lawson asked

"OK. The one where he had supposedly gone over to London to hunt down three agents who were selling information to the North Koreans, and he ended up chasing them across to North Korea, and not only killing the agents but retrieving all of the information and apparently wiping out an army of thirty assassins too," McDermott replied.

Lawson smiled at Ward who smiled back.

"What?" McDermott asked.

"Nothing," Ward replied, "That's way too out of this world".

"My point exactly," McDermott said and headed towards the Range Rovers to carry out one last equipment check, the fifth one that he had done that morning.

"So out of this world," Lawson said and Ward smiled again.

They both knew that what McDermott had just described had actually happened. They both knew for sure, because it was the third time that they had ever worked together and they were witness to everything The Optician had done in North Korea via an MI6 satellite system.

"What's wrong Ryan?" Lawson asked.

"What do you mean?"

"I mean you have that look again."

"What look?"

"The look you always have when you know something isn't right. You had it the first time that we looked at the satellite pictures and it is still on your face now," Lawson replied.

"Does that whole set up look right to you?"

"Right in what way?"

"The way it is laid out?"

Lawson hadn't really given it any thought so he went through it out loud,

"One building for the hostages, one for the Researcher's to rest in I assume, one to work in, the fifth for his men and the fourth one for….." Lawson tailed off.

"There is no need for the fourth building, is there?" Ward asked, "Unless someone wants us to think that it is there for a reason. If it's to hold Whymark, why would you build something just for him?" Ward asked.

"Maybe he is that dangerous that they keep him well secured out of harm's way?" Lawson asked.

"Or maybe someone is trying to lead us there to set us up?" Ward replied.

"Now you have me worried," Lawson said, "You're right, there is no point to that building at all."

"You stay close to me when we get on the island, we will secure the researchers, and then we will take a look inside that building and see why they have really built it."

Lawson nodded his understanding. He noticed that Ward was looking a little more tense than normal, and he had the feeling that he wasn't telling him everything that he knew, but he had learned over the years not to push him, he would tell him when he needed to tell him, so he decided to lighten the mood,

"This sex ban, am I still………."

"The D.E.A. boats are pulling out," Wallace interrupted over his shoulder.

"Then it's time to go gentlemen, are we all clear on what we are doing?" Ward asked the room as opposed to one person.

Everyone to a man nodded their understanding of their individual roles.

"Radio's on now," he said as he switched on his earpiece, "Wallace, you are now the conductor of the orchestra."

TWENTY THREE

Adams Key – Upper Florida Keys

Dr Robert Anderton and his team had worked through the night. In fact, they had not stopped working over the past sixty hours. He called his team over to where he was leant on his bench,

"We've done it. All of you have worked under the most awful circumstances but we have done it," he said, without a hint of celebration or achievement in his voice.

"You believe that you have cracked it?" Catherine Lambourne asked.

He looked at her sympathetically. She had been through hell. Her father had been killed before her eyes, and she had been violated by the sick animals keeping them prisoner, but she had somehow managed to retain her focus in the lab. He was so proud of her,

"Yes I have Catherine, one hundred per cent it will now work exactly as they want."

"So how did you do it?" she asked.

"I'm not telling you Catherine. I'm not telling any of you" he replied, looking at each of them as he spoke.

"But why not?" Kyle Johnston asked.

"Because once they have what they want, they don't need us anymore."

They heard the keys start to turn in the locks and Anderton snapped,

"Back to your work stations!"

By the time the mechanism on the third lock had clicked and the door started to open, they were all looking busy. None of them looked up as Cardona strolled into the room with Franco no more than three steps behind him.

"Good morning Dr Anderton. I hope you have some good news for me?" Cardona asked.

Robert Anderton ignored him, an act that annoyed Cardona immediately.

"Maybe you didn't hear me," he said as he stopped two feet from him, "I hope you have some good news for me?"

"That all depends if you have some good news for me Mr Cardona?" he replied, an air of confidence ringing through his voice that Cardona had not heard before.

Cardona smiled, a wide, toothy smile ran across his face, "You have. You've done it, haven't you?" he asked, "I hope for your sake that you have. Franco, go and get the next guinea pig for us to see if Dr Anderton's new found confidence is justified," he added without even looking behind.

"Now we will see if a child's heart will be able to cope with what you have created, and if I see one hint of vomit, the child will die," Cardona said.

Franco watched as the third key was turned in the bottom lock. He stepped forward and pulled the door hard, and as it opened, he saw Heather Lambourne's body still in the same place that she had landed. He smiled to himself, it was an impressive punch, he knew that, and it would have put most men down. There was something much more rewarding about beating a person to death rather than stabbing them or shooting them. He knew that Heather Lambourne was the eighth person that he had beaten to death, unfortunately as they were all women, he still craved the ultimate satisfaction of beating a man to death. He would do it one day he said to himself.

He stepped over her small, lifeless body and walked towards the throng of people huddled at the back of the room, stopping about three feet away. All of the children were being shielded by the few remaining adults, and it was hard to see who was who.

"Bobby Wynne, come out, come out, wherever you are," he said in a menacing tone. Lin Peng Taremi adjusted her body slightly to the left.

Stupid woman, Franco thought to himself, she may as well have shouted, 'He's behind me,' a thought that made him smile at his own fantastic humour.

"Move out of the way whore or five men will be raping you within two minutes," he spat at Lin Peng.

She reluctantly moved to the side and Franco saw a tall boy with tears in his eyes, crouching on his knees, glancing between the floor and him, with fear etched into his eyes.

Bobby Wynne was a typical all American teenager. He was popular, good at sports, and academically, as you would expect with his parents genetics, a very high achiever. He was tall for a fourteen year old, he was a couple of inches short of six feet, but his thin body gave away his real age. He was the sort of kid that any parent would be proud of. But he was scared, very scared. They had taken his mom and she had not returned. He had played out all sorts of scenarios in his head about what could have happened to her, but as each one concluded, it led him to believe that she wasn't coming back.

"On your feet Bobby Wynne," Franco said, "It's time to party," he added, and then laughed at his own fantastic humour once again.
Bobby knelt, frozen to the floor, too scared to move.
"On your feet or I will slit your throat now you little shit," Franco said, pulling the jagged knife out from its sheath on his waistband as he spoke, "And only after I have killed your little brother first," he added, pointing at Kyle Wynne.
They had not let go of each other's hands since their mother had been taken from the room, and Kyle started to sob loudly.
"You are all pathetic, weak American pigs. A Columbian boy would have stood up to me. You are all weak, and that is why we come here and rule your country. You are cowards, and there are no American men to match our brutality," he said to the group, rather than just Kyle, "I will count to three. If you are not on your feet by then, I will kill your brother."

Bobby Wynne slowly stood from his crouching position. He was consumed by fear, but he summoned up the strength to protect his younger brother. Strength that people like Franco could never understand because they did not understand love. Bobby Wynne was braver than Franco could ever be. He stood straight, extended his tall frame, and looked Franco in the eyes, but he didn't speak. He tried his hardest to look defiant.

"Follow me," Franco said as he turned and walked over to the door.

Bobby followed him and when he reached the body of Heather Lambourne and stepped over her, he shuddered to the core, and tried his hardest not to be sick. He stepped out into the morning sunlight, the brightness of the hot morning hurting his eyes, and it took him a good thirty seconds to adjust to daylight again.

"Hurry up Bobby Wynne, it's time to party," Franco said.

Franco stepped into the lab and Cardona turned and looked at Bobby Wynne,

"Here he is," he said to Cardona.

"He looks like a beanpole. Perfect, if his flimsy body can take it, we are there Dr Anderton," Cardona said.

Dr Justin Wynne rushed from his work area and wrapped his arms around his son. Franco immediately stepped in and separated them and Dr Wynne, stepped back. He had already lost his wife; he was not going to risk losing his son to these animals.

"It will be OK," he mouthed to his son, and Bobby tried his hardest to force a smile.

"Hurry up Dr Anderton," Cardona impatiently said, "I am becoming angry."

Anderton beckoned Bobby Wynne towards him, glancing at Justin Wynne and then nodding reassuringly. "Remember, one sign of vomit and I will slit his throat and cut his eyes out, and it will be your fault that he dies" Cardona said calmly, like Bobby Wynne's life meant nothing.

"I'm going to give you this pill," Anderton said to Bobby, "It won't hurt you, and you will experience new sensations, but mainly you will feel relaxed and happy," he added in a calm voice.

"I'm scared," Bobby replied, tears starting to roll down his cheeks with increasing frequency.

"I promise you Bobby, it will be fine. Step into the room there and sit down," Anderton said, pointing to the glass walled room.

Bobby moved forward, stepped up the elevated platform, and sat down on the sofa.

Anderton stepped into the room and handed Bobby the pill and a small beaker of water.

"Take it now, I promise it will be OK," he said reassuringly.

Cardona felt himself getting excited. He could see how confident Anderton was, and he knew that the next thirty minutes would determine just how rich and powerful he was going to become.

"Hurry up and take it," he shouted at Bobby Wynne.

Bobby put the pill to his mouth and took a sip of water.

"Get out of the room doctor," Cardona demanded of Anderton, "And shut the door."

The whole room held its breath.

For the first three minutes, Bobby Wynne seemed no different. He was glancing nervously side to side through the glass walls.

Cardona started to shift on his feet impatiently.

After three minutes and thirty seconds, his body suddenly relaxed and he slumped back into the sofa and started smiling.

After seven minutes and four seconds, the same time that Brandon Alexander had started violently vomiting, Bobby started to move his hand in figure of eight movements.

Ten minutes passed and he started to sing a totally out of tune song which no one watching through the glass knew.

Thirty minutes passed, all without anyone speaking, just staring at Bobby Wynne and his induced state of pleasure.

"I think you have done it doctor," Cardona eventually said after forty minutes, "You really are a genius," he added, and then patted Anderton on the back, like two college buddies would do after meeting up again after a few years.

"How long do you anticipate that this will last?" Cardona asked a few minutes later, after walking around the glass room and taking in the view of Bobby from every angle.

"Two hours in the awake state, and then he should sleep for another two hours, and still be in his induced state where he will continue to hallucinate and feel the chemically induced responses from his body," Anderton replied.

244

"He really will be OK?" Dr Wynne asked Anderton.

"Yes Justin, I guarantee it. I have worked everything out. It is as chemically safe as taking a paracetamol," he replied with a smile.

"Thank you," Dr Wynne said.

"Stop this bullshit," Cardona interrupted, "Now, all you have to do is give me the ingredients, sorry composition, and then I can arrange for you all to be returned home safely," he added, a huge smile stuck permanently on his face.

"No," Anderton said.

The whole room stopped breathing almost as one.

"What did you say?" Cardona asked.

"I said no," Robert Anderton repeated.

"Bring that whore here," he said to Franco, pointing at Catherine Lambourne.

"That won't work either," Anderton said.

Franco had hold of Catherine's arm and he stopped in his tracks. All eyes in the room were staring at Dr Robert Anderton.

"You have no intention of letting any of us go. You are going to kill us all anyway, so there is only one way this will work Mr Cardona," Anderton said assertively.

Cardona studied him.

He knew that a new resilience had swept through Anderton, and he was so close to greatness that he was not going to mess it up now.

"What way?" Cardona asked him.

"I'm the only person in this room who knows how to make this. That means I am the only person in the world who can make it so that means two things," Anderton said.

"Which are?" Cardona asked, the smile now gone from his face.

"I also mastered in neuroscience. Do you know what that is?" he asked Cardona

"I advise you not to insult me doctor," Cardona spat back.

Anderton ignored him and continued.

"It means that I understand the brain, and I even know how to shut parts of my brain down while I am conscious. The amazing thing about that is that I can shut down the part that makes me think I am feeling pain, so you won't be able to torture me to get the information from me either," he said, becoming more confident with every word that he spoke.

"And we both know that you intend to kill us all after you have what you want, so I will tell you now, if one more person from our group dies, you will never get what you want."

Cardona felt the anger rising and his initial instinct was to slit the throats of all of Anderton's team and cut their eyes out in front of him, but right then, he was unsure how to take the doctors claim that he can shut down his body not to feel pain, so he resisted the urge to kill for the first time in many years.

"You seem to have all of the cards in your hand doctor," he said calmly, "But your idea and my idea of pain and what you can resist are two different things entirely."

"I wouldn't underestimate me Mr Cardona."

"I think it is you who is underestimating me," Cardona spat back at him, "Franco, take Dr Anderton to my block, he can keep our other friend company, and we can see just how helpful his major is in the real world," he added as he turned and walked out of the room.

TWENTY FOUR

Adams Key – Upper Florida Keys

Through his scope, The Optician watched as two men marched an academic looking guy into the clearing for a few seconds, and then back into the wooded area. From his low level, he watched them walk into a building. He knew from the information that The Old Man had given him, that the smaller South American guy was called Pablo Cardona and the academic was Dr Robert Anderton. Simple logic told him that the big guy that was following them would be Franco, Cardona's right hand man.

He also knew that inside the wooden building that they had just entered, Gill Whymark was there.

He had known Gill Whymark a long time. Much longer than he had known Ryan Ward, and he had always admired and liked Whymark. They had never had the same relationship that he and Ward shared, a fact that was down to the age gap between them, rather than any difference in character, and he was feeling a touch of remorse that he knew today was the day that Gill Whymark would die.

They had first worked together six years ago. He had been Whymark's protector for three whole years, and he knew that he was good, in fact, more than good.
He was the best that The Optician had ever seen.
Their first mission together was in Kosovo where Centrepoint had sent Whymark to infiltrate a gang that was trying to sell discarded nuclear material that the Russian's had allegedly disposed of during the most recent arms reduction agreements. He had been impressed with how Whymark had made contact after contact until he got to the top of the food chain, and between them, they had taken out a whole cartel of Kosovan mafia, and the material had been appropriately annulled and then disposed of in the Kosovan countryside.
He had watched how easily Gill Whymark killed men, either with a weapon or unarmed, and he respected him for his dedication to their cause.
He had never understood why Whymark had turned or how he had turned.
He knew that most of The Deniables had taken money at some point, and he knew that The Old Man knew about it, Centrepoint would often tell him what they had taken.

He always believed that The Old Man told him this to see if he would ever be tempted to steal any money but the truth was, he never had.

He had no interest in money.

He believed that his sole purpose in life was to protect the United States of America and to follow Centrepoint's orders.

He didn't see The Old Man as his boss, more like his father, and if he wanted Gill Whymark dead, there had to be a good reason for it.

He just felt disappointed in Whymark for turning his back on his beloved country.

His relationship with Ward was different because Ward had no reason to love America, yet he defended them like the proudest of patriots. He was English by birth, but The Optician knew that England was just an accent and a place to him. He loved the fact that Ward believed that he had a right to defend both sides of the Atlantic, and he did so with equal passion.

As much as he hated admitting it to himself, he felt that Ward was his brother, his colleague and his best friend all rolled into one. Ward understood him.

No one else ever had.

Ward had subtly pulled The Optician's family back together, and never made a point of mentioning it after they had spoken of it once.

He had told Ward things that he had never told anyone else, and he knew that he would never judge him or mention what they had discussed to a living soul.

He wondered for a moment how he would feel if The Old Man ever ordered him to take Ward out. He concluded that he had a switch in him that made disobeying orders impossible, and so reluctantly, he would do whatever Centrepoint asked.

But he also knew that killing Gill Whymark would be much easier, and that was what he was there to guarantee happened.

He pulled out his cell phone and called Ward.

"Are you bored on the island already?" Ward said as he answered.

"You always seem to be half an hour behind me. Where are you?"

"We are ten minutes away, coming in on the far side of the island," he replied, a breathless tone to his voice.

"Are you on a boat?"

"Yes. And for an ex Seal, McDermott has to be the worst handler of a boat that I have seen in my life."

The Optician laughed.

"I will start taking Cardona's men out one by one in ten minutes time."

"How many men does he have?"

"Thirty counting him and his bodyguard."

"Have you had eyes on any of the researcher's yet?" Ward asked.

"Just the one Anderton."

"And have you seen Cardona?"

"He was with him. They are holed up in the hut nearest to the mainland."

"You mean in the same building as Whymark?"

"Yes"

"Have you seen him?"

"No"

"You know that I have to question him before we take him out?" Ward asked.

"The Old Man has filled me in. You have to question him, get what you need and then I have to confirm beyond doubt that he is dead."

"What if I kill him first?"

"Then I will still put four bullets in him to make sure."

"You looked after him for a long time. Don't you feel the slightest bit uncomfortable that we are now going to kill him?" Ward enquired, his voice bouncing as he spoke, due to what The Optician assumed was McDermott's less than smooth operation of the boat.

"He turned. Therefore he becomes the enemy. He made his choice and he will have to live with that when one of us kills him."

"I agree. So maybe I will just incapacitate him and give you the pleasure of finishing him off?"

"You are so generous," The Optician replied and hung up the phone.

He went back to looking through his scope and getting his breathing right. He watched as two men walked to the right of the clearing and along the line of the trees. They lit up cigarettes, and were paying no attention to anything else but each other. They were a good three hundred yards away from the clearing when they stopped and sat down, side by side, on some logs that were piled neatly at the foot of the trees. They were facing him.

He smiled to himself.

It was time for some target practice.

He lined up the guy on the left and then gently moved his scope to the right, getting a feel for the distance that he would have to move his rifle. Then he moved it back again and repeated the movement three times. He now had the perfect feel for it, so much in fact that he knew he could make the shot with his eyes shut.

He lined up the guy on the left, with the crosshairs resting firmly on the centre of his forehead.

And he closed his eyes.

He took one last deep breath, and squeezed the trigger, and then moved his rifle the distance he had felt and rehearsed, and squeezed again.

He kept his eyes shut for a further five seconds.

He then opened them and checked through his scope. He could see clearly the soles of four shoes facing towards him, the force of the 7.62mm bullet had knocked them both off of the logs and flat onto their backs, as he knew it would. He also knew without a doubt that the bullets would have hit the dead centre of their foreheads.

Two down, twenty eight to go he said to himself.

The boats carrying them to the Key docked at a jetty on the far side of the island. Dawes and his team had been told to hold off about quarter of a mile out, with the intention of intercepting anyone trying to escape, until instructed otherwise by Ward.

They sprinted up the Jetty and settled about twenty feet inside the forest. Once Paul and the rest of McDermott's team had arrived, Ward huddled everyone together.

"The hostages are the immediate priority. Paul, you and your team secure them, McDermott, you the researchers, and we will go for Cardona and Whymark. Wallace, are you there?"

"Loud and clear," Wallace said in Ward's ear.

"Did everyone hear that?"

They all nodded.

"Dawes?"

"Affirmative," Dawes replied.

Ward pulled out his cell phone and pressed The Opticians number.

"We are two minutes away from the site," he said as The Optician answered, "Paul will hit the hostages, McDermott the lab, and me and Lawson are going for Cardona and Whymark. So try not to shoot any of us."

"Hurry up, I'm falling asleep with all this hanging around," The Optician replied and hung up.

With Ward leading on the right hand side, and McDermott on the left, they slowly started making their way through the trees and towards the target site. Every fifty yards they covered, they stopped and scanned before moving the next fifty yards. Approaching a site with thirty armed men was not like the movies where guys just stormed in, it required patience, calmness and accepting that every yard in distance gained was a prize. The closer they got without being detected, the greater their percentage of saving all of the hostages increased. Once they were at the target site, they could prevent anyone from entering the buildings, and therefore, subsequently keeping all of the hostages alive. Ward knew that if they got spotted a long way from the site, Cardona's men would be inside the buildings within seconds killing everyone. So patience was everything.

A further fifty yards and they had still not got close to seeing any of Cardona's men.

"We should have seen someone by now," Lawson whispered to him.

"No we shouldn't," Ward replied, "He has the D.E.A. stopping anyone from coming onto the island. He's confident in them. My only worry is that whoever he has in his pocket might tip him off, so stay focussed."

Another fifty yards and they could see the buildings in the distance about three hundred yards away. They could also see movement for the first time. There were three guys standing on the corner of the first building, and two guys standing next to a solid door, one on either side, all South American looking.

Ward spoke into his microphone,

"You see them Mac?"

"Yes," McDermott replied.

"That is where the hostages are, best way to approach it?"

"Come around from the other side, and then we can secure it, because there is no one but you behind us, so we can fight them off easily."

"I'll ask our friend to see what he can do with the five at the front. If you make your way around the back, on his first shot, you secure the building," Ward said quietly.

"Understood."

He pulled out his cell phone and called The Optician.

"Finally!"

"There are five guys by the first building. Two by the door, three on the corner, can you see them?" Ward asked.

"Yes very clearly actually."

"McDermott is coming around the other side of the building. When you see them, can you take out the five guys, if you're up to it that is?"

"Eyes open or closed?" The Optician asked.

Ward smiled and hung up the phone.

"He's good to go," he whispered into his microphone, "As soon as he sees you, he will take the five guys out" he added.

"Understood," McDermott replied.

Another fifty yards was gained without incident. Now they could see all four buildings clearly. It looked like the same set up on each one, two guys guarding the door and three on one corner of each building. That made twenty, Cardona and his bodyguard twenty two. That meant that there were only eight other guys to take out. Ward felt a calm rush over him. He knew without any doubt that they were going to win this battle, and then Cardona and Whymark were going to die.

He settled down and waited.

He knew that they were only about fifteen minutes away from winning.

And winning was everything.

TWENTY FIVE

Adams Key – Upper Florida Keys

Franco shoved Robert Anderton firmly in the back as he reached the doorway of the building, and he stumbled forwards and fell to the floor, landing on the palm of his outstretched hands.

"Your problem is doctor that whatever you think you can tell your brain to do, you won't be prepared for what I am going to do to you because it is unimaginable," Cardona said calmly.

Franco grabbed a handful of Anderton's hair and pulled him to his feet. The first thing that he noticed in the room was the man tied to the chair. His hands and feet were tied by cable ties, and the chair was positioned almost in the middle of the room. The man was just staring at him. He looked to be in his early forties, and he had dried blood covering a large proportion of his face. What unsettled Anderton the most was the look of total calm on his face, like this sort of thing happened to him all the time.

Cardona noticed Anderton looking at the man and smiled,

"This guy is a tough guy doctor, a real tough guy," he said, still with the big smile fixed on his face, "In fact, he is so tough that he has killed a number of my men and we couldn't get close to him. Do you think that you are as tough as him with your mind tricks doctor?"

All of a sudden, Robert Anderton had a lot less confidence in his ability to think past pain than he had one minute ago.

The man in the chair studied Anderton. There was no emotion in his face, just a look of calculation and assessment, like he was measuring just how much pain Anderton could take. He then gently shook his head which indicated to Anderton that he wasn't going to be able to take a lot.

This frightened him immediately.

Franco pulled another chair into the middle of the room and stood it down next to the other man.

"Sit!" he demanded, and like a child being scolded, Anderton sat down.

Franco secured his feet firmly to the chair by using two thick, eight inch cable ties joined together on each leg, just above the ankle, and as he pulled them tight, Anderton felt a sharp pain, and instantly felt his circulation become less effective. He then did the same to his wrists, securing each arm to the metal uprights of the chairs, the plastic instantly cutting into his skin, causing deep abrasions.

"If you get everyone off the island now, I will give you the composition and not only that; I will oversee the mass production of the drug for you. I just want this to end for the others," Anderton said before Cardona had a chance to start speaking.

Cardona studied him for a moment. He could see quite clearly that Anderton was telling the truth, and he knew that having a willing member on his team was worth a hundred times more than having someone who was being forced to perform their duties.

He liked the sound of Anderton's proposal.

"Now we are getting somewhere doctor. I much prefer the route of civilised negotiation rather than forcing you to help me or indeed hurt you. You have achieved what no other chemist could do, and so I have respect for you for doing that," Cardona replied, "Franco, are the boats ready?" he asked.

"Yes Mr Cardona," Franco replied.

"Good. Take them all back to the mainland then."

Franco feigned surprise and said,

"Are you sure Mr Cardona? They will go straight to the police."

"Drop them down the coast, miles from anywhere. By the time they have alerted the authorities, we will be long gone," Cardona replied, "Move them now, the good doctor and me have much to talk about."

"I want to see them leave safely and get a call from my wife when they are safe," Anderton quickly interrupted.

Cardona studied Anderton for a moment.

For a clever man, he was incredibly stupid.

259

"Very well doctor. I need you to be able to perform at your optimum for me and I understand that to do that, you need to know your family are safe," Cardona replied, "But listen very carefully. If you fail me or try to deceive me at any point, not only will your direct family and every one of your team die the most painful death, all of your extended families will too. Do you understand that? I will find them and they will all die."

"Don't listen to that crap," the man tied to the chair next to Anderton said, "They will never make it to the mainland, he will kill them all."

Robert Anderton recoiled in his chair in horror.

"Shut your mouth!" Franco screamed, and stepped towards the guy in the chair and unleashed a thunderous right uppercut that caught the guy fully under his chin. His head jerked back, forcing his body weight to shift to the right, and the chair tipped over, and the guy landed on the floor with a sickening thud, the right side of his face taking the full impact of the floor.

Anderton felt a sick feeling rushing through his whole body as he looked at the man who was by now, unconscious on the floor.

"I want to see them leave safely," he quickly said.

"I need you and you need me doctor," Cardona replied, "I'm a businessman first and foremost, and I know you need to know that your family are safe to perform properly for me, and so I will keep my word in getting them safely onto the mainland."

"Then set them free," Anderton begged.

"Franco, get them all together. I want them off the island within the next ten minutes," Cardona demanded sternly, and then watched as Franco walked out of the building.

"Good choice doctor, you have just saved the lives of everyone you love."

"I want to see them leave," Anderton said.

"Then I shall cut you free."

Ward watched as a big, thick set South American looking guy walked out into the clearing and then headed towards the first building.

"How far are you away Mac?" he whispered into his microphone.

"Ten minutes, we've taken a wide berth so we don't get spotted."

"I don't like the look of this," Lawson said.

"Just be ready to go," Ward replied.

They both watched as the big South American guy waited for the door to be unlocked. He counted three keys being put into the door, for three separate locks, by the heavily armed guys guarding the front of the building. The door was pulled open and the big guy walked inside.

"I don't like the look of this," Lawson said again.

"Mac," Ward said urgently into his mouthpiece, "You need to speed your arrival up."

A minute later, a stream of women, one guy, and a number of children started filing out of the building, the guards who were standing at the front of the building were now pointing their weapons at them and telling them to hurry.

Two guys were carrying four heavy looking crates down to the boats.

"You think that is drugs?" Lawson asked.

He ignored him.

"Hold back Mac," Ward suddenly said into his mouthpiece.

"Make your mind up," McDermott replied into Ward's ear.

They watched as the heavily armed guys led the group down to the jetty where there were six boats moored. The big guy started to point at the boats and the group started to file onto them. He counted as seven women and children climbed into each of the boats, the one guy with them climbed into the last boat, and two heavily armed guys got in each boat with them.

"There are people missing," Lawson whispered to Ward after he had done a quick head count.

He didn't respond. He had a bad feeling about this.

"Come in Dawes," he said into his mouthpiece.

"Here," came the reply.

"It looks like they are moving the hostages in three boats. You have to intercept them," he said.

"Understood."

The big guy then went to the third building and stood back as a guard went through the same process of opening the door, the three separate locks being unlocked one at a time.

He then walked in and a minute later, marched out a line of people in lab coats down to the jetty and shepherded them into another boat.

"Make that four boats," he said into his mouthpiece.

"Understood."

"They are taking everyone but Anderton away. My guess is that they don't plan on dropping them safely back to the mainland. There are two guys on each boat apart from one, can you deal with them?" he asked.

"Seven of us Seals against seven regular guys? Was that a serious question?" Dawes replied.

Ward smiled to himself. He had no doubt that the hostages would be safe.

He watched as the engines started on the boats and they spun around, cutting through the water like a knife through butter.

"They are heading north, they are all yours," he whispered.

"Understood," Dawes replied again.

"That's Anderton over there," Lawson said, pointing to the end building, "And that must be Cardona with him."

Ward looked across to the far building. It was Anderton, and it was definitely Cardona with him.

They were watching the boats pull away and head out into the open sea.

They both watched as the big guy who had been organising the boats slowly walked back towards them.

"That must be his tough guy," Lawson said as they both watched Franco walk towards Cardona and Anderton.

Ward noticed that every guy that Franco passed looked down at the floor to avoid making eye contact.

"He's their tough guy," Lawson said, "I liked Harris, let me take him out."

"As you wish," he replied, and then whispered into his mouthpiece,

"Hold your position, the hostages are off the island. Wallace, you are the eyes for Dawes and his team, focus on them until they are safe."

"Understood," Wallace's voice said into his ear.

"Affirmative," Dawes confirmed.

"We can't move until we know that the hostages are safe," he said, "And we can't risk anything happening to Dr Anderton either, what he knows is probably the most valuable piece of information in the world right now, and we have to get it off of him."

"Understood," McDermott's voice said.

He was now happy the whole team understood what they had to do.

They watched as the big guy approached Cardona and Anderton and then they all turned and walked into the building.

Everything was quiet and calm once again.

The guys who were supposed to be guarding the buildings leant against the walls and lit up cigarette's, once again hanging around aimlessly waiting for their next instruction.

"This doesn't look right to me," Lawson said to Ward.

"It's not."

"Dawes?" Ward said into his mouthpiece.

"Here," Dawes replied.

"You have to intercept those boats urgently; they are going to kill every single civilian on them."

"On it now," Dawes replied.

"How do you know?" Lawson asked.

Ward ignored the question.

But he was right.

As Franco had walked down to the jetty and spoke to his men who would be transporting the civilians, he had told them that they were to take them eight miles out into sea from the island, kill every man, woman and child, and then drop them overboard with the weights that were loaded onto each boat firmly secured around their ankles so that the sharks could feed on them at the bottom of the ocean.

The exception was to be Anderton's wife and kids. They were needed to call him once they had arrived safely on dry land, and after that, they would be killed and disposed of in exactly the same way.

"I've kept my end of the bargain doctor," Cardona said, "Now it is time to keep yours."

"As soon as my wife contacts me from the mainland saying that everyone is safe, and I speak to my children, I will give you what you want."

"That is a reasonable request," Cardona replied, "They should be safely on dry land within twenty minutes," he added and then turned and walked back into the building.

"Follow the boss," Franco said as he pushed Robert Anderton firmly in the back, causing him to stumble forward yet again.

TWENTY SIX

Just Off of Adams Key – Upper Florida Keys

The four boats carrying the researchers and their families sped between Elliot Key and Old Rhodes Key, and as the land disappeared, they headed speedily out to the open sea.
Franco had instructed them to take the passengers eight miles away from the Keys, in an easterly direction towards the tip of The Bahamas.
When they were eight miles out, Franco had instructed everyone be killed with a single shot to the head, men, women and children alike, and then their stomachs sliced open so that no trapped air could bring the bodies back to the surface. The weights that they had loaded on board

would weigh the bodies down to the ocean floor and the sharks would do the rest.

Franco had disposed of well over fifty bodies this way in the past. Getting rid of a body in the sea was easy; it was only when people failed to cut the stomach and the lungs to release all of the air that the bodies would float to the top. Without air, the bodies would be stripped by the sharks.

"Wallace," Ward heard Dawes' voice come over the radio,

"Here."

"Where are they now?" Dawes asked.

Wallace scanned the screens and zoomed in, it took a few seconds longer than he would have liked,

"They have just passed the tip of Old Rhodes Key," he replied.

Ward looked at Lawson, they didn't speak, but they were listening to every word so intensely that it felt as though they were out on the boats with Dawes.

"We are about two minutes behind them, do not let them leave your sight," Dawes replied.

Emilio was trying his best to steer the lead boat in a straight line, but the force of the hull bouncing off of the water was making it difficult. Easing off on the throttle would have made it easier, but so determined was he to demonstrate that he could be a great leader, that urgency took over common sense. Franco had told him that he would take charge of the lead boat and gave him very clear instructions to take the hostages exactly eight miles off of the coast of Elliot Key, and he wasn't going to fail him. This was his opportunity to shine.

267

The three boats behind him struggled to keep up. They were being steered by Pascal, Fabian and Stefan Valencia who was eager not to make one more mistake after the shambles at Catherine Lambourne's house. Catherine was sitting at the back of the boat, glaring at the back of Emilio's head, the animal who had been involved in the death of her father, and the violation of her body. As the boat bounced over the waves, the cable tie that they had secured to the wrists of all of the hostages, including the children, cut deeper into them. With their hands all firmly secured behind their backs, the children were sliding off of the seats and onto the floor, the adults unable to help them back up without their hands being free. The children were screaming and crying.

"The children are in pain, slow down you animal," she screamed at Emilio.

The grimy looking guy who was sitting with his back to Emilio and pointing a gun at the group said,

"Sit down whore or I will throw you off here."

Catherine Lambourne sat down and started to cry again.

The second boat in the convoy was being manned by a guy called Pascal and his twin brother Georges. Heath Beasley was more concerned with what was inside the crate that Georges was sitting on, while his brother struggled to control the boat, than the bouncing and slipping that he had to endure. His calf's were aching where he had his feet planted firmly on the floor, eighteen inches apart, using his weight to try and keep him upright.

"Where are you taking us?" he shouted over the roar of the engine.

"Back to the mainland," Georges shouted back.

Beasley looked out over the vast open sea and knew that they were going in the opposite direction.

"We are going the wrong way," he shouted, a comment that made Sam and Carli Alexander, Dr Allie Alexander's two daughters burst into tears. If two innocent girls knew something very bad was about to happen, that meant every single person on every one of the four boats knew.

Heath Beasley started to quietly sob.

The third boat was manned by Stefan Valencia and the new guy on the team who he only knew as Paco. He had not spoken to him at all from the moment that he had turned up on the island, and he knew nothing about him. Paco was gripping his machine gun in one hand and holding onto the crate that he was sitting on with his other, so that he could retain his balance.

"Where are you from Paco?" he screamed above the noise of the straining engine.

"I'm from Bucaramanga," Paco called back, turning his head as he spoke.

"What a shithole," Valencia said, and they both laughed.

Eric Dunn was sitting just by Paco's feet, his daughters Morgan and Julie just about managing to keep seated by leaning in hard against his body.

"Where are you taking us?" he screamed at Paco.

"Back to the mainland," Paco replied.

"We are going the wrong way," Dunn shouted back.

"Shut your mouth you American pig. One more word and your girls are going over the side," Paco said, waving his gun between Dunn and his daughters.
Eric Dunn started to quietly sob.

The boat bringing up the rear was being steered by Fabian Martinez, and the hostages guarded by a guy well into his fifties by the name of Pablo. He had been with Cardona for the past twenty years, despite offering very little to the cartel, and all of the men were convinced that Pablo was only involved with them because he reminded Cardona of just how far he had come. He was struggling to maintain his balance, even sitting on the crate, and his machine gun was hanging on his neck, swinging from side to side by the strap because his ageing bones were not enjoying the battering they were taken with each crash onto the water. His knuckles were white where he was holding onto the crates so tightly.
Claire Anderton was smart.
She had already worked out what was in the crates, but she was also smart enough to know that she, along with Robert Jr, Adam and Lucy Anderton were important.
She knew that Robert would have wanted a guarantee that they were safe before divulging whatever it was that Cardona wanted to know. She was so sure in fact that at that moment in time, her only concern was for the ordeal that Emily Johnston was going through.
When they had loaded them onto the boats, they had separated the Johnston family. Kyle had been shepherded onto one boat with their sons Freddy and Chris, and Emily had been forced onto the same boat as her, with their daughters Becky and Ali.

She looked at Emily and shuddered when she noticed the fear and despair that was etched firmly on her face.

"It will be alright Emily," she said, trying her best to reassure her.

"What's happening Claire? Where are they taking us?" she asked

Claire looked at her own beautiful daughter. There was an innocence about her, a total ignorance to what was happening and worse, to what was about to happen.

"Where are they taking us?" Emily asked again.

"Back to the mainland," Claire replied, and then looked down at the floor and started to quietly sob.

"You are now exactly three hundred yards in front of them," Wallace's voice echoed in Dawes' ear.

"How far out are we?" Dawe's shouted to Delaney, who was making the task of gliding the boat over the water look simple,

"Six miles," Delaney replied.

"OK," Dawes shouted, "Push it to seven and then start the swing around."

"Is that giving us enough time to head them off?" Case asked.

"Easily," he replied, "These guys haven't got a clue how to handle a boat. Lock and load gentlemen, let's go and be hero's once again," he added, without a hint of drama in his voice.

Clair Anderton looked up from the floor and blinked hard to clear the tears from her eyes.

"You are making a mistake," she said loudly to Fabian Martinez.

"I can't hear you whore," Martinez shouted back.

"I said you are making a big mistake," she repeated, even louder.

"I doubt that. The only mistake is that I haven't raped you yet whore," he replied, and then laughed loudly.

"You don't understand," Claire said, and laughed herself.

Martinez studied her for a moment. After the events at Catherine Lambourne's place, he knew that if he made one more mistake that Cardona would kill him.

"Come up here and steer," he said to Pablo.

Pablo immediately jumped to his feet and slid into the chair, overjoyed to ease the pressure on his frail bones. Martinez stepped down and went and slid onto the seat next to Claire Anderton.

"What don't I understand whore?" Martinez asked.

Claire studied him for a few moments, forcing herself to hold a smile on her face while she did so.

"Tell me?" he demanded.

"Why do you demean women by calling them whores?" she asked, "Is it to mask your own intellectual and masculine inadequacies?" she asked him.

Martinez looked at her confused.

"Shut up whore!" was the best and most intellectual response that he could muster up, which in effect, answered the question that Claire had asked, "What don't I understand?" he asked again.

"What you are trying to get my husband to achieve won't work," she said, and forced a smile again.

"It does work whore, so who's the smart one now?" Martinez replied, genuinely feeling pleased with his response and suddenly feeling pretty smart.

"No. You don't understand," she said again.

He looked at her confused.

"If you know your way around the periodic table, you can make anything work once. My husband is very clever, and he would have made sure it worked," she said, "And we always anticipated something like this happening, so we devised a plan years ago to make sure if it ever did happen, then we would hold the trump card."

"What do you mean?" Martinez asked, seeing a path opening to gain him more yardage up the pecking order in the cartel.

"There is an element that will be missing from the composition, an element that only myself and my husband will know. A symbolic element for us, but one that is crucial for the completion of your creation" she said calmly, fully aware that Martinez would have no idea what she was talking about, "And when your boss finds out and he tells my husband to get back to work, he won't be able to complete the trials without his team to assist him, so you will never achieve what you have set out to achieve, and everything will come crashing down around your ears."

"You're lying to me whore."

"I'm sure your boss will be pleased to know that you had the opportunity to put everything right and you chose to ignore it," she said, "This is probably the biggest mistake you will ever make in your life," she added, as she shook her head, aware that Martinez would subconsciously pick up on her body language and actually believe her. He pulled out his cell phone and called Emilio who was still struggling to steer the boat effectively.

"What?" he answered in a breathless tone, struggling even more to maintain control of the boat one handed.

"This whore back here says that her husband has tricked us. That the drug won't work without a missing consolation," Martinez said.

"What does that mean?" Emilio asked.

"I'm not sure, but its shambolic elements or something," Martinez replied, "Maybe you should call the boss and tell him before we get rid of them all?"

Emilio thought about this for a few seconds. What Martinez said didn't make any sense, but he was sure that the doctors whore wife was bluffing, trying to buy a little bit of time.

"Slap her whore face and tell her to shut up. We are almost there," Emilio shouted and then dropped his cell phone to the floor and planted both hands firmly on the steering wheel once again.

He didn't need to listen to Martinez. Franco had faith in him and that meant more than anything.

He focussed straight ahead, half a mile to go and they should be far enough out.

Focus was important if he was going to climb the cartel and get to where he had always dreamed of being.

And Emilio was focussed. He stared straight ahead and picked a point on the horizon that he decided would be far enough out, and told himself that he would not take his focus off of the point in the water that he had selected until he was there.

That was his mistake.

Because if he had just focussed half a mile to the right, he would have seen two boats with seven deadly Navy

Seals on board, swinging around and heading directly towards them.

TWENTY SEVEN

Adams Key – Upper Florida Keys

Franco pulled up the guy who was tied to the chair by his
left arm, until the four legs of the chair were firmly
planted back on the floor. He had by now regained
consciousness.
"Sit!" Franco shouted at Anderton, pointing to the empty
chair next to the guy as he said it.
Robert Anderton quickly sat down.
He looked at the guy tied to the chair. The man had been
dealt a sickening blow to the head, been knocked
unconscious, and now that he was back in an upright
position, he looked completely unfazed, like it was the
sort of thing that happened to him all the time.
Who was this man? He thought to himself.

He was about to find out.

Cardona pulled a chair up and sat it down a few feet from the guy once again.

"I've enjoyed your company my friend but your time is running out," Cardona said, as he adjusted himself in the chair and crossed his legs.

He took a cigar out of the breast pocket on his shirt and Franco made a big scene of rushing over to his boss and striking the gold Zippo lighter down his leg until a warm, orange flame was glowing, before moving his hand slowly to the tip of Cardona's cigar.

Cardona slowly pulled on the cigar until the end was glowing red, looking over the top of the cigar into the guys' eyes as he did so.

When Franco moved his hand and snapped shut the lighter in another over the top gesture, Cardona exhaled a thick plume of smoke and blew it towards the face of the guy.

The guy laughed,

"The types of villain you are trying to portray are so last century," he said and laughed again, "You're pretty comical."

"I think the only funny thing is that you are trying to be a wise guy while tied to a chair, don't you?" Cardona calmly replied.

"What happens now?" the guy asked, "Do you tie me to a workbench with a giant circular saw in the middle, and then set the timer for five minutes, and all leave the building so that I can escape?" he added, and then laughed again, this time for a good thirty seconds.

"If only it that were that simple," Cardona replied, "It would probably be a lot less painful for you than what I have in store for you."

The guy looked at him, just studying him. It made Cardona feel uneasy. He was used to seeing total fear in people's eyes and hearing them beg for mercy, but this guy intrigued him. He definitely had no fear, and it was obvious to him that no matter what he did to him, he would never give him the satisfaction of hearing him beg.

"You do know that your time is nearly up, don't you?" Cardona asked him.

The guy smiled,

"How many times do you think I have heard that?" he asked, "And in the scale of the scary people that I have dealt with over the years, you don't even make the top twenty. Maybe you should get a white cat to try and give you some credibility. You know, sit there stroking it while you try and scare me. Two pussies might have more impact than you are having on your own," he added, and laughed again.

Franco stepped forward and started to raise his right arm in preparation of delivering another thunderous right hook, but Cardona raised his right hand, indicating to Franco that he was to stop.

Franco stopped in his tracks.

"Not only are you going to die, everything is going to come back on you. That's why you are still alive. You know that, right?" Cardona asked, smiling himself now as he spoke.

"Is that your plan?" the guy replied, "Seems a bit predictable to me. Can't you be any more creative than that?"

He then turned and looked at Anderton who was sat next to him in complete silence, stunned at how calm this man seemed to be in the light of Cardona's threats.

"You know that you signed the death warrant for all of those people that have left on the boats, don't you?" the guy said to him, "And that's not forgetting the millions of people whose lives are going to descend into squalor and misery through what you have created. That's a lot to live with doc; you didn't think any of this through properly."

"I had no choice," Anderton replied, "They have my family."

"Your family? They will kill them as soon as they get them on the mainland. You played this all wrong doc, a smart guy would have known what to do," he replied and looked at Anderton with contempt, a look that made him shrink down into his chair.

"And are you a smart guy?" Cardona asked.

The guy looked at Cardona and smiled,

"Do you think I'm smart?" he asked.

"No. Not one tiny, little bit" Cardona replied, "In fact, you are probably one of the dumbest men that I have ever met."

"That was hurtful."

"Shall I tell you why you are so dumb?" Cardona spat at him, clearly starting to become irritated, much to the guys amusement.

"No thanks."

Cardona ignored him.

"When you people die, don't they put a star on the wall at Langley?" Cardona asked, fully knowing the answer already.

"Not if they are killed by a pussy like you. They have their name put on the wall of shame," he replied and smiled again.

Anderton studied the man again. Langley? That was C.I.A. headquarters he thought to himself. This man must be C.I.A. No wonder he is so calm. Anderton felt three things instantly.

Fear that the man was antagonising Cardona to such an extent that he would soon snap, and he was becoming anxious that he would take the brunt of Cardona's rage.

Curiosity because Cardona had said that everything was going to come back to the man and he wanted to know what that meant.

And hope. Hope that somehow, this C.I.A. man, this man who seemed to be incapable of feeling any fear, might be able to find a way out of this mess for them both.

"And there is no greater shame than what you will be remembered for doing," Cardona said.

"Enlighten me Cardona, share your criminal master plan with me before I am meant to die, and then when I escape and hunt you down, I will take great delight in cutting your eyeballs out and shoving them up your ass. You know, like in the movies," the guy replied.

"When we leave here, you will be found dead and of course, your eyeballs will be missing. Removed by my hand while you scream and beg for mercy," Cardona said threateningly, leaning forward in his chair as he spoke.

"He's so charming, isn't he?" the guy said, turning to Anderton and smiling.

Cardona ignored him.

"The paper trail and all of the records of your greed and deceit will be discovered by the D.E.A, F.B.I. and the C.I.A. It has been made relatively hard to find the evidence that ties you and you alone to all of this, but not impossible. We don't want to make it too easy for them now, do we?" Cardona asked, a calm tone to his voice now, "I am waiting for a call. The call will tell me that there is no more use for you as soon as the doctor has delivered on his promise and after that? Well you know."

"You think it will end there?" the guy asked, "Are you that stupid too that you can't see how this is going to end?"

Cardona raised his eyebrows in mock surprise, the guy smiled,

"You really are dumb Cardona. Do you think that for one minute the people who have assisted you in setting this all up are going to let you run and control it?"

You've been used, like we all have," he said, his eyes fixed in a cold stare deep into Cardona's eyes.

"We have a beneficial agreement to all parties and there will be enough of the pie to go around."

"But none for you. You should never have got greedy and tried to double cross people."

Cardona started at him.

"Unbelievably dumb," the guy said, and sighed.

"You are the one tied to the chair and probably an hour away from death. So who is the dumb one really?" Cardona asked.

"Definitely you," the guy replied, "You've missed the obvious."

"Would you like to indulge me, in the spirit of my liking for the villains of the last century?" Cardona asked and laughed.

"I thought you would never ask!"

Franco was becoming increasingly frustrated with the patronising manner in which this guy was talking to Cardona, and he pulled out his eight inch jagged knife and stepped closer to the guy.

"No Franco. We have to wait. Let's try and be civilised."

"Yes Franco, calm down," the guy said with yet another smile.

"As we are being civilised, at least tell me your name so that we can talk in a nice manner," Cardona said.

"You can call me Mr Whymark."

"Thank you Mr Whymark," Cardona said, "Now, can you give me the benefit of your wisdom?"

"How do you think the government agencies got to hear about your plans in the first place?" Whymark asked.

"There are a lot of people who live in our world who are on the payroll of the government, you know that."

"Let me put the question another way," Whymark replied, "How did you hear about the progress in creating the drug in the first place?" he asked.

Cardona thought back to the first time it had been suggested to him over eighteen months ago. A D.E.A. agent had told him that someone in Philadelphia was getting close to creating a cheap and simple super drug. Whymark saw the first sign of doubt cross Cardona's face and so he continued.

"As I thought, a government agent started you on this path," he said, "But as I said, you are dumber than that."

"So you keep saying," Cardona said, leaning forward in his chair even further so that he was just about sitting on the edge of the chair now.

"And here's why. They are using you."

"And you were sent to steal the key from me?"

"No dummy," Whymark replied, "I was here to stop it from ever being discovered."

"I don't understand," Cardona replied.

"Some people within the D.E.A. are corrupt, we both know that. We know you have been their informant for years, and how they let you do pretty much whatever you want because your information justifies their existence. Just like we know that a lot of agents are on the take."

"Go on?" Cardona said.

"The F.B.I. then got wind of it and tried investigating but hit a dead end every time, so then they pass it on to the C.I.A. to see if you can be of any use to them," Whymark said, "But you know all of this. Because you know the scale to which each agency has become involved. Now they are all fighting each other. Not for a slice of your pie, but for the whole thing."

"And you know this how? Your C.I.A bosses told you?" Whymark ignored the question and continued.

"They won't want the money to leave the U.S. Have you any idea at all how much money is seized and stolen by the government? The whole C.I.A. is funded by taking money gained illegally from people like you. They want control of the money, not have to rely on an untrustworthy scumbag like you."

Cardona was weighing up the likelihood of how much Whymark was saying could be true.

"But that isn't what makes you dumb" Whymark said.

"So what makes me dumb Mr Whymark?" Cardona replied.

"You are dumb because you never asked yourself once why they would get into bed with a small cartel like yours, and totally ignore the big guys who spread all over the country. Have you worked it out now?" Whymark asked.

Cardona looked at him quizzically.

Whymark shook his head and then said,

"It's because you are the smallest of the big boys, and the smallest by a long way. That makes you very, very, very easy to crush."

Cardona looked like the penny was well and truly dropping. Even Franco looked like he believed what Whymark was saying.

"And that's not even the worst part," Whymark said.

Cardona looked at Whymark; his smile had long disappeared,

"You were too dumb to even see it until now."

TWENTY EIGHT

Eight Miles off of Adams Key – Upper Florida Keys

"The boats are now stationary," Wallace said into everyone's ear.

"Here we go," Lawson whispered to Ward, both of them still holding their position undercover on the island, waiting patiently for Dawes to secure all of the hostages.

"We are thirty five seconds away from contact," Dawes said into his microphone, "Mosley, you work from the front, and we will shoot through, and then come up from the back. Use extreme caution, there are a number of civilians, do not take chances. Shoot quick and shoot accurately, eliminate all hostiles immediately."

"I have eyes on you and there are no other boats within a four mile radius," Wallace said.

Emilio raised his hand in the air and finally shut down the engine of the lead boat and then turned to see the others slowing down behind him, a forty foot gap between each of the four boats.
He looked down at Catherine Lambourne,
"I'm going to kill you last whore so that you can watch me gut the others first," he spat at her.
She looked over his shoulder and in the distance, she could see two boats racing towards them, and after straining her eyes she could make out small figures dressed all in black.
"And before I kill you I am going to rape you again and this time you are…."
He never finished his sentence, because his head exploded, bone fragment and blood sprayed forward and covered the front of her tee shirt, and she screamed.
Emilio fell forward and landed face first onto the chest, his head bounced up a good eight inches before slamming down again. Ten seconds later, the boat was speeding past her on her left hand side, the sound of the throttle decelerating ringing in her ears.
She saw three men on the boat, all holding long guns in their hands, kitted out in black combat clothing. She made eye contact with the man who was steering the boat and clearly heard him shout,
"Boat one secure."
The second boat that she had seen had splayed off to the right, and she counted four heavily armed men on board, two looking through the scopes of their long rifles. As

286

the first boat passed her slowly, the man kneeling down at the back winked at her and smiled, and then lifted his scope up to his eye again.

Catherine Lambourne burst into tears once again. This time, tears of relief, and finally of grief, for the ordeal she had been put through.

As Delaney spun the boat around in a perfect one hundred and eighty degree turn to within twenty feet of the boat bringing up the rear, Pablo raised his gun and pointed it towards the Seals, but before he had a chance to fire of a round, two bullets smashed into his chest with such ferocity that it knocked him clean off the boat and into the water. Fabian immediately raised his hands and as Delaney passed them, Dawes fired three shots into his upper torso and his whole body collapsed as if he had been hit on the head by a four hundred pound hammer. Claire Anderton didn't scream, she just stared at Fabian's dead body.

"Look away," she softly said to her three children.

"Can we go and get Daddy now," Lucy asked.

"Yes we can sweetheart," she replied.

"Boat four secure," Dawes said.

Delaney was alongside the third boat from the front four seconds later. Paco managed to fire off a round which missed by a long way because he was struggling to retain his balance on the rocking boat, the movement made even worse by the waves that Delaney had deliberately created when passing them on the way to the tail boat. In response, Vic fired an excessive six shots into Paco's midriff, and the bullets violently ripped his stomach apart as soon as they struck. Stefan attempted to return fire, but before he got off a shot, Dawes had fired a bullet which hit him on the side of his head, just below the temple, and it blew his head apart and his legs collapsed.

Eric Dunn screamed as Stefan fell forward and his head connected with his right knee with such force, that for a moment, he thought that the impact had shattered his knee cap.

The pain soon subsided when he heard an American voice say,

"Boat three secure."

By the time that Mosley had pulled alongside the second boat, Pascal and Georges had clearly computed what had just happened. They scanned both boats and could see that they had no chance against seven heavily armed guys who by now, they were convinced were Navy Seals and so they dropped their weapons and raised their hands in the air.

"We surrender!" Georges shouted out as Atkins and Rope pointed their guns at him.

"We give in!" Pascal shouted even louder.

Atkins looked at Rope and nodded.

They instantaneously fired three shots into the chests of the twin brothers, the force of the bullets that Georges took sending him overboard behind him, and the bullets that hit Pascal ripped his chest wide open, and he fell forward and into the six foot gap of water that was between the two boats.

Heath Beasley shouted,

"Yes!"

"Boat two secure. All enemies eliminated," Dawes said into the radio, "We will secure the civilians on the mainland now," he added.

"McDermott, continue your approach as planned," Ward said into the microphone, "Well done Dawes, very impressive. Notify us when everyone is secure and receiving medical treatment on the mainland."

"Understood," Dawes replied.

Adams Key – Upper Florida Keys

Ward pulled out his cell phone and dialled The Optician. "The hostages are now all secured by The Seal team and so all we have to do now is wipe out everyone on the island apart from Dr Anderton," he said without waiting for a greeting as soon as the ringing tone stopped in his ear.

"Be careful," The Optician replied, "Do not underestimate Gil Whymark."

"I never underestimate anyone," he replied, "We are going to start getting in position, are you going to make your way to the building with Whymark in?"

"I'll be watching you and covering you as soon as you make a move. I've already taken a couple of Cardona's guys out."

"As soon as McDermott is in position I want your shot to be the signal to go," he said, "It's basically a gunfight now."

"Just be careful," The Optician repeated.

Ward pondered on this comment for a few moments.

"Why do you think Whymark turned?" he asked.

"It's like The Old Man says, money. Everything always comes down to money and greed."

Ward didn't quite believe that. He had no doubt, that like him, Whymark would have had access to millions of dollars over the course of his involvement with The Deniables, and that he even could have helped himself to as much as he wanted, like he had, and The Old Man would have ignored it.

"I'm not asking what The Old Man says," he replied, "I'm asking what you think?"

"I'm not paid to think," The Optician said.

He believed that The Optician was not actually paid at all, he had his own reasons for doing what he did, and Ryan Ward was the only man on earth who knew what those reasons were, having recently been told The Optician's biggest secret.

"Let me ask it another way," he said, "Having looked after him for years, knowing better than anyone else how he thought, moved and lived, were you surprised that he turned?"

There was silence on the line for five long seconds and then The Optician said,

"As surprised as I would be if you turned."

"You never found it strange that all of a sudden he went from being loyal to becoming the enemy overnight?"

"In the world we live in, I don't find anything strange. You never really know people, do you?"

"We have access to as much money as we want. I've stolen millions, some I used for personal reasons, like buying my houses, some I used for compensation to families of people who have lost someone, and some just because I believe that someone deserves it," he said, referring to a recent deposit that he had made to The Optician's newly reunited family, "So how much could he possibly have taken?"

He believed that The Optician knew much more than he was letting on. He knew everything; therefore he was sure that The Old Man had confided in him about Whymark at some point in the past.

"I don't think it was what he has taken; I think it is more about what he intends to take. Whether it was what he has taken or what he intends to take is irrelevant. He has turned; he would kill either of us without a moment's hesitation. We have a duty to follow through The Old Man's instructions. My only advice is that you are very careful, I'll remind you again, he is good, very good; better than you are at the moment. If he gets you one on one Ryan, you will die. Whymark shows no mercy, to anyone, ever," The Optician said.

Ward felt on edge. He liked that feeling. It made him super alert, and he always found that he could see things with greater clarity when he felt this way.

"I will be careful," he replied, "And it so nice to know that you worry about me so much too," he added, trying to bring back the usual humour that they shared between each other.

"Let me know when you want me to take the shot," The Optician replied in a serious tone, and he hung up the phone.

"That sounded serious," Lawson said to Ward as he watched him put his cell phone back into his pocket, "Is this Whymark guy Superman or something?" he asked with a smile.

"What would make you turn Mike?" Ward asked him.

"Being put on a sex ban," Lawson replied with a smile.

Ward laughed quietly and then said,

"I'm serious. Just think about it for a minute. What would make you turn? Money, power, what?"

Lawson thought for a few seconds and then said exactly what Ward had been thinking when he asked himself the same question,

"If anyone hurt someone close to me, like my family, friends, or even you, I would forget orders and procedures and make it my mission in life to hunt down and destroy the people responsible for it. That is the only thing that could ever make me turn," Lawson replied.

"Maybe that's what happened to Whymark?" he said.

"Or maybe he isn't like us. Maybe it is simple greed?" Lawson replied.

Ward knew that he was right. He was over analysing it too much. He trusted The Old Man completely, and if he said that Whymark was intending to get the information regarding the creation of this new super drug and use it for his own financial gain, then Centrepoint was probably right too.

"But Whymark isn't my main concern right now," Lawson suddenly said.

"What does that mean?" Ward asked.

"That big guy, the one who thinks he is a tough guy," Lawson said, "I want him. I want to beat him to death with my bare hands."

Ward didn't ask why.

He didn't say anything in response.

He was just waiting for everyone to be in place and then he would make the call to The Optician to take the first shot.

He was focussing on getting Dr Anderton safely out of harm's way and then dealing with Whymark. He decided that he would take The Optician's advice on board and be very careful. He would make no grand speech when he came face to face with Whymark, the moment he set eyes on him he would shoot him in the face three times. As much as he wanted to understand why Whymark had turned, he wanted to make sure that he lived another day much more.

"How long Mac?"

"Four minutes and we will all be ready to go. We will attack from the east of the clearing; you make your way up to Cardona and the other two from the west. I'll confirm when we are all in position."

He was four minutes away from events that were going to change everything.

TWENTY NINE

Adams Key – Upper Florida Keys

Cardona's cell phone rang and he answered it on the third ring.

"How did that happen? Listen to me; I will retain it until we are back in Miami. I have some interesting questions to put to you," he said after a ten seconds of listening to whoever was on the end of the line, looking at Whymark as he spoke, "There is some information that has come to light which I want clarification on."

Cardona listened again for a few more seconds and then said,

"He's still alive. Once the doctor gives me what I need I will cut his eyes out while he begs for his life," he said. Whymark smiled, Cardona instantly looked away from him.

He hung up the phone and slowly and deliberately made a big show of shaking his head and putting it back into his pocket.

"We are out of time Dr Anderton," he said, "Franco, get me a pen and paper".

Franco moved across to a table and picked up the notepad and pen that was sitting neatly in the centre, and handed it to Anderton.

"Now, you will write down the ingredients for the drug, and you will not miss anything out," Cardona demanded.

"Not until I hear from my wife and children," Anderton replied.

"They are safe," Cardona said, "Unfortunately, too safe."

"What do you mean?"

"They will be in the custody of the U.S. Coastguard, F.B.I. and God knows who else within the next twenty minutes, so you are out of time Dr Anderton," Cardona replied, "Not only that, but I have lost seven of my best men, and so my patience in you has now run out," he added menacingly.

"It looks like everything is going to shit," Whymark said and laughed, "And you can't kill me yet because your friend on the phone is not sure if I already have the composition tucked away somewhere safely or not."

Anderton looked at him,

"You knew the composition already? And you let all of those poor people endure the hell that they have had to go through?" he asked, an air of disbelief in his voice.

"Get over yourself doc," Whymark replied, "Your family are safe."

"How can you be so sure?" Anderton asked.

"You've only got to look at how pissed he looks," he said, nodding his head in the direction of Cardona, "And now he's panicking because he knows that he has only got about twenty minutes to get what he needs from you before this place is invaded by agents and the cops."

Anderton looked at Cardona, who was now shifting uneasily on his feet. He felt a wave of relief wash over him. Claire and the children were safe, so were all of the others, and for the first time since he had arrived on the Key, he felt that he could breathe properly.

Franco stepped forward with his knife drawn and prodded the blade firmly into Whymark's left shoulder, the blade cutting about two inches into the muscle. Whymark tensed, and his upper torso went rigid, but he did not make any sound at all.

"Enough Franco," Cardona shouted, "Dr Anderton is our priority now."

Anderton looked at Whymark, who by now was turning his head and looking down at the wound on his shoulder, still without making a noise or even showing the slightest sign of pain or fear.

"You will write the ingredient's down right now doctor. If you don't I will cut you apart, piece by piece until you do. And you will. You are not tough like our friend here," he said pointing at Whymark, "And when I start to cut into your testicles you will give me exactly what I want. Everyone always does."

"Don't do it," Whymark said to Anderton, "If you do, he'll kill you immediately."

"Yes your family is safe. Your only chance of ever seeing them again is to give me the ingredients right now. You have my promise that I will leave you here to be found alive if you do what I want," Cardona said.

"Does that kind offer extend to me?" Whymark asked in a cheerful tone.

Franco stepped forward with his knife raised again, preparing to jab the blade into the same area as before.

"Last time I tell you Franco. No more!" Cardona shouted. Franco immediately stepped back two steps.

"Good dog Franco," Whymark said, "Do what your owner tells you." he added, and laughed again.

"Write!" Cardona shouted at Anderton.

Anderton sat on the chair holding the notepad in one hand and the pen in the other, unsure what to do. He was torn between his need and desire to see his wonderful family again, and his obligation to ensure that the drug never got out into the street.

In the end, the decision was made for him.

Cardona drew his knife, the blade that had removed countless eyeballs glistening, and stepped in towards Whymark.

He knelt on the floor and rested his left elbow on Whymark's right knee. With the knife firmly held in his right hand, he balanced the tip of the blade in the centre of Whymark's left thigh.

"Are you going to start writing Dr Anderton?" he asked calmly.

Anderton did not respond.

He pushed down hard on the blade. The sharp tip of the blade easily sliced through Whymark's pants and pierced the skin, slicing into the muscle about half an inch.

Whymark winced and his whole body went rigid. He then rested his right elbow on Whymark's left knee, so he had leverage for the next push. He pushed down hard and the blade went in a further half an inch. Whymark exhaled sharply and gritted his teeth.

Still he made no sound.

"The further I go in doctor," he said, looking at Anderton, "The greater the chance that I am going to sever an artery. But you know that, don't you? We all know you are a clever man. A clever man would start writing," he added with a smile.

Anderton's eyes jumped from Cardona to Whymark and back again. He sat still, with the notepad in one hand and the pen in the other and made no attempt to start writing.

"As you wish," Cardona said, and he gripped the knife tightly in his right hand and with an open palm, brought his left hand crashing down onto the top of the handle and the blade immediately sliced through Whymark's muscle, and lodged itself firmly three inches into the flesh.

Whymark let out a scream. It was a sickening, high pitched scream that made Anderton jump. He then repeated another scream, and then another and the gap between them was closing to about two seconds.

"You are killing him doctor," Cardona said, "Write now!"

Anderton sat still, frozen. He couldn't stand the deafening scream that Whymark was making. He moved the notepad onto his lap and the pen in his right hand, a hand which was now shaking violently with fear. He started to slowly move the pen towards the notepad.

"Don't you dare!" Whymark screamed, in between his short, deep, desperate breath's, which were now becoming louder and louder.

"I must be very close to the main artery doctor," Cardona said as he used his right hand to slowly twist the knife clockwise.

Whymark let out another scream that shot through to the core of Anderton. He was now panicking and he felt faint.

"Last time doctor, his death will be on your hands," Cardona said, and laughed loudly, a hysterical laugh that indicated how much he was enjoying cutting into the flesh. He looked at Whymark, his eyes were watering over, and the blood coming from his thigh had now soaked through his pants and was staining a bigger area with each passing second.

Dr Robert Anderton started to write.

Cardona stopped twisting the knife in Whymark's thigh immediately.

"Do not miss one thing doctor. I want the weights, quantities, mixing times, everything. And be quick," Cardona shouted, now with an air of excitement firmly in his voice.

Anderton knew every component down to each microgram, and he knew that the slightest change to any measurements would affect how the drug performed. So he considered making the most subtle of changes that it would be possible to hide.

That was until Cardona spoke again.

"Your daughter Lucy, she is a pretty little thing. Is she your princess?" he asked.

Anderton froze, he stopped writing.

"The thing is doctor, I have insurance so that you will not try and trick me," Cardona said.

Anderton stared at him; he felt an anger rising inside of him.

"Lucy has friends called Caiti, Jenny and Chelsea. How do I know this?"

Anderton stared at him.

"I know this because right now, they are being held, at their homes, along with their parents and siblings, by my men. One call from me and the parents are going to have to watch their little whores be abused and violated by my men before they cut their eyeballs out. I will let the parents live and they will have to carry around those images forever," Cardona said, answering his own question in the most vile and sickening manner.

Robert Anderton thought about Caiti, Jenny and Chelsea and how Lucy had told him that they were her B.F.F. He then thought about Chelsea's father, Ian. An upstanding man, he was a senior accountant for an international courier. Ian had recently encouraged him to start to play golf. He was slowly getting the hang of it, and that was mainly due to the patience that Ian showed towards him.

"And that isn't the best part," Cardona said, "Shall I tell you the best part doctor?"

Anderton looked at him, waiting for Cardona's revelation.

"The best part is," he started, in a slow and deliberate tone, "That right now the parents are being told that their daughters living or dying depends on your actions," he added, as though he was revealing the secrets of the universe.

Anderton imagined Ian having to endure the hell that he had witnessed in the lab. But the people killed in the lab were adults, and the way they had been cut and discarded like bad meat had been sickening enough. How would he have felt if Cardona had killed Lucy in front of him? He pictured Ian and all the other parents willing him to do the right thing by their precious children.

He had no choice.

"I'm sorry," he said to Whymark, who was by now concentrating too hard on managing the pain that was ripping through his body to register what he was saying to him.

Anderton started to write.

Precisely.

Accurately.

Exactly.

And honestly.

Cardona watched as each component was written on the left hand side of the page, and a weight written following a dash next to it. His eyes followed every stroke of the pen Anderton did.

In less than forty five seconds, Dr Robert Anderton had written down the components and weights required to create the most devastating illegal drug that would ever be unleashed across America. He knew as soon as he finished writing that it would wreck millions of lives, and for a moment, he understood how those involved in The Manhattan Project, the team who invented the atomic bomb that destroyed Hiroshima and Nagasaki, felt.

They had done it for the right reasons.

And so had he.

He raised the notepad and handed it to Cardona and then hung his head in shame.

Cardona quickly scanned down the component list, not that he could understand it, but more because he was excited at the power he was holding in his hands at that very moment.

He pulled his cell phone from his pocket and pressed redial.

"I have it," he said excitedly down the phone, "You were right, they were planning on double crossing me, and the prisoner confirmed it."

Anderton watched as Cardona was listening to whoever was on the end of the line, and then he started to read out the composition list. He then looked across at Whymark who by now had his eyes closed and appeared to be slipping into unconsciousness. He then noticed that Cardona's knife was still lodged firmly in Whymark's thigh, and he felt sick once again.

Cardona hung up the phone and slipped it back into his pocket.

"Kill them both now Franco," he said as he stepped back towards Whymark and pulled the knife from his thigh, deliberately twisting it anti-clockwise on the way out to inflict more pain.

Whymark didn't move.

Franco stepped forward, yanked Whymark's head back to expose his throat fully and just as he was moving the knife to give an unobstructed path to Whymark's throat, all hell broke loose.

THIRTY

Adams Key – Upper Florida Keys

McDermott had told Ward that he was in position thirty seconds earlier. Paul had confirmed the same three seconds after, and then Ward had called The Optician and told him to take his shot.

The Optician had decided that the first shot he would take would be the furthest one away, which was about six hundred yards. Outside of block number four where Cardona was holding Anderton and Whymark, there was a South American guy, standing in front of the closed door, with his machine gun raised and ready to fire. He seemed to be the only one of Cardona's men who looked remotely alert and on his game, the rest of the guys that he had peered at through his scope seemed to be preparing to clear out, wandering around carrying things in their hands, like a group of people would at the end of a camping trip. He also figured that if he took out Cardona's guard and then fired a shot into the solid door of the building, that he would grab the attention of those inside. You never know, he thought to himself; Gill Whymark might even make an appearance.

He lined up the centre of the guys' head in his scope and relaxed, balanced his breathing to perfection, and squeezed the trigger gently.

The 7.62mm bullet glided through the air, almost with grace, and it smashed into the dead centre of the guys' forehead just over a second after leaving the barrel. The impact of the bullet jerked the guy's head back with such force that the back of his skull smashed against the solid door with the impact of a sledgehammer. The Optician then fired another shot into the solid oak door.

Then the sound of machine gun fire filled the air.

Block One

As soon as McDermott, from his position in the thick bushes that had grown under the dense trees, had seen Cardona's guard take the bullet, he unleashed a short burst from his machine gun, and the two guys loitering outside the building went down instantly. As soon as the bullets had ripped open their stomachs, two other guys sprinted around the corner and unleashed a volley of gunfire in their general direction, and the bullets smashed into the trunks of two thick trees at least twenty feet away from them.

"Amateurs," Wired said to Fringe, who was knelt down next to him to McDermott's left, and almost in autopilot, Wired fired a semi-automatic burst into the chest of the guy standing on the right, the bullets smashing into the guy's head and literally blowing his brains out, and

Fringe then unleashed an equal semi-automatic burst which smashed directly into the other guys' groin and abdomen, and the blood sprayed out of him like someone opening up a can of soda which had been violently shaken.

Even before their bodies had settled on the ground, the three of them were on their feet and sprinting towards the back of the building. They now had perfect cover. With the trees to their right, and the clearing the other side, McDermott and Fringe faced towards the front of the building while Wired covered the rear.

"Block one secure, your turn Paul," McDermott said. From The Optician's opening shot, five of Cardona's men had been eliminated in eight lethal seconds.

Block Five

Paul McDermott, Fuller and Walsh had taken a route deep inside the forest to position themselves ready to attack the fifth building, which they believed was the sleeping quarters for Cardona's men. As soon as they had heard the semi-automatic bursts of gunfire, they had sprinted from the cover of the greenery straight to the door to the building. Before the gunfire had stopped, Paul was bursting through the door with Fuller and Walsh two steps behind.

The first guy they saw was standing in another doorway to their right, with a towel wrapped around his waist and he was dripping wet.

He was unarmed and looked at Paul with complete surprise.

There were eight beds in the room, four on each side.

Paul raised his gun and shot the guy four times in the centre of the chest before he even had time to scream or reach for a gun.

There were three other guys in the room.

All three of them were laying on thin mattresses, on flimsy looking metal bed frames, smoking cigarettes, and in the process of trying to swing their bodies up to go for their guns.

Fuller instinctively moved around to Paul's right and Walsh to his left, and all three of them selected their own target without any form of communication, and opened fire.

Fuller's burst of gunfire smashed into his target, who by now was in the process of putting his feet firmly on the floor, and the bullets ripped through the side of the his rib cage and formed a hole the size of a baseball, and the guy slumped sideways, smashing his head on the metal frame.

Paul took the guy on the bed furthest away from them on the right. The guy had just about managed to get his hands on his gun when Paul opened fire, and the bullets smashed into the left hand side of the guys back and pierced his heart immediately, and he slid from the bed to the floor almost in slow motion.

The last guy, who was in Walsh's sights, quickly raised his hands above his head.

All three of them slowly stepped forward with their guns raised to their shoulders, lining up the guy in their sights.

"Where are Cardona and Anderton?" Paul screamed at the guy.

The guy said nothing but pointed to the door.

"Where are they?" he shouted again.

306

"In the next building," the guy replied in poor English.
"Are they alone?" Paul asked, lowering his tone, as
Fuller and Walsh turned their backs to him and aimed
their guns at the door, prepared for anyone who would
be dumb enough to come rushing in.
"Franco and the Fed too," the guy replied.
As soon as the guy had finished speaking, Paul
unleashed a burst of gunfire which ripped the guys'
stomach completely apart.
"Block five secure," he said into his microphone.

Block Two

McDermott was sure that the second building had been
empty from the moment that they had got into position to
launch the attack. He was sure because the doors to
blocks one and two were wide open. But he still needed
confirmation with his own eyes.
He raised his hand and pointed towards the building and
Fringe started moving slowly, his back still pressed hard
against the wall of block one until they reached the
corner. Block two was about twenty five feet away from
where they were standing.
"You move forward around the back," he said to Fringe,
"And you come with me," he said to Wired, who by
now, had turned to face in the same direction as
McDermott.
They both nodded their understanding without speaking.
McDermott sprinted towards the opposite corner of
block two.

He was expecting some gunfire to come his way but it never did, a fact that initially confused him until Fringe's voice came through his ear piece,

"They are running into the cover of the trees," he whispered, "Five guys armed with machine guns have literally just run off, and they are heading away from the buildings."

"Hold your position for now," McDermott replied.

He moved from the far corner of block two to the front, with Wired two steps behind him, once more with his back to him, covering the rear.

He peered around the corner of the building and looked out into the clearing.

No one was there.

He edged himself along the front until he reached the open doors.

He ducked his head quickly inside the doorway and then back out again. It was a split second movement but enough for him to be able to scan the inside and to see that it was completely empty, and so he stepped through the doorway while Wired stayed tight to the building, his gun pointing out towards the clearing.

The inside of the building smelt of human sweat and damp. He pictured the poor hostages, petrified and forced to live in squalor, and he felt an anger surge through him.

"Block two secure," he said into his microphone, "One more to go and then it is your show Ryan," he added.

"Understood," Ward's voice said clearly into his ear.

"And once we have secured it, it's time to go hunting in the forest boys, five girls have run away," McDermott said without a hint of sarcasm in his voice

Block Three

McDermott and Wired moved along the front of block two until they got to the corner of the building, which meant they were standing about the same distance away as the previous gap in the buildings was.

He nodded at Wired and then sprinted across the clearing to the corner of the building with Wired one stride behind.

They reached the corner, and with their backs hard against the wooden frame of the building, started to slide along the wall slowly towards the door.

They were both concentrating on reaching the door when they heard someone scream from their left hand side, "Morir," the voice echoed across the clearing. It was a word which McDermott knew to be Spanish for 'Die'.

As he turned his head to his left, he saw a stocky South American guy rising up from behind two oil drums with his machine gun held firmly against his waist.

In that split second, they were completely exposed like sitting ducks.

A split second is a funny thing.

There is a saying that your life flashes before your eyes in the split second before you die. They say that you think of a person or a moment in your life that has had a fundamental impact upon you.

That saying is wrong, because all that went through McDermott's mind when he computed what was happening in that split second, was that the oil drums must have been for the diesel that ran the generators on the island.

A split second to most men is nothing. It's a fraction of time that most people can't even register properly.

To The Optician, a split second seems like three seconds when he is in his zone.

And he was in his zone.

He was peering through his scope, watching McDermott's progress, while he kept one eye firmly focussed on block four, with his breathing slow and his finger pressed lightly against his trigger, he caught a glimpse of a guys' head appearing from behind two oil drums, and in one swift and fluent movement, the guy was fixed firmly in his scope.

All in a split second.

Just as McDermott had stopped turning, two 7.62mm bullets smashed into the guys' head, and it exploded like a ripe melon would if you smashed it with a spade. McDermott simply turned his head back and continued moving towards the door of block three.

He reached the door and even though it was closed, he could see that there had been three padlocks fitted to hasps that had been removed and left swung back. He used the palm of his right hand to push against the middle of the door and it immediately opened a few inches and so he stopped pushing.

He stepped across the doorway to the other side, and Wired moved forward to the other side. For a moment, they stood either side of the doorway, like a couple of sentry's looking out into the clearing.

McDermott then nodded at Wired and rested the palm of his left hand against the door, and Wired shuffled on his feet and put his left foot against the bottom of the door so that when the door opened, he could come in behind it using it as a shield. He raised his machine gun and nodded back. McDermott raised one finger, then two and when he raised his third finger, he pushed the door hard and it swung open. Wired followed the swing of the door in perfect tandem, and McDermott followed him in one step behind.

They both stopped as soon as they stepped in.

They were inside what looked like a very modern laboratory and it was empty.

"Take the boys and hunt the runners in the woods Paul," McDermott said into his microphone.

"We're on it," Paul replied.

"Next time you are meant to be covering me, do it properly," McDermott said to Wired, "That was a schoolboy mistake. Learn from it and never, ever, let that happen again. Is that clear?"

"Yes," Wired replied.

McDermott lifted his microphone to his mouth and said clearly and loudly,

"Block three secure. You are good to go, we will deal with the five runners."

Just over one hundred feet away, Ward said to Lawson, "Let's go."

THIRTY ONE

Mangrove Point - Miami

Dawes could clearly see the flashing lights of the police and paramedic vehicles half a mile away from the mainland. He eased back the throttle on the boat slightly, and Mosley instantly did the same behind him. He could see at least forty people standing by the quayside, and as he got closer, he could make out the lettering on the back of their jackets. Some read 'F.B.I.' and others 'D.E.A.'. Ward had given him strict instructions to keep the D.E.A. away from the hostages, and at the same time, to establish where a guy called Larry Stanyard was. The women and children on board continued to sob and hold onto each other, and the sobs intensified when they all caught sight of the people waiting to lift them safely back to land. Dawes smiled to himself; he had heard sobs of relief many times in his life but never from so many children. It made him feel good.

He had called Centrepoint immediately after he had told Ward the hostages were secured, and The Old Man had told him that an F.B.I. agent called Doobie would ensure that the hostages were transferred to hospital and that they would be looked after.

Two hundred yards away from the shore, as he backed the throttle off even further, he could see a heated discussion taking place between F.B.I. and D.E.A. agents, a discussion that had turned into jostling and pushing by the time he was a hundred yards away from docking.

He backed the throttle completely off so that the boat was just about cutting through the water at no more than walking pace, and Mosley pulled alongside him, just six feet apart.

"Remember," he shouted across to Mosley, Atkins and Rope in the other boat, "No D.E.A. agents are to even talk to any of these people. We hand them over to the Feds only. If the D.E.A. try to intervene, use maximum force, but stop short of firing shots," he added.

Twenty feet out he cut the engine and the boat bobbed towards the wooden jetty which was only about thirty feet long but had around twenty five guys crammed onto it.

As the nose of the boat touched the jetty, he jumped up onto the front of the boat and secured a thick rope to the mooring stud.

"OK. We'll take them from here," a guy said to Dawes as he stood upright on the nose of the boat. The guy had 'D.E.A.' emblazoned on the left breast of his jacket. Dawes ignored him and scanned along the jetty to the

313

F.B.I. agents who were by now, trying to jostle their way along to the boats.

"Who's in charge?" Dawes asked the D.E.A. agent.

"We are," he replied, "We need to question the hostages immediately," he added, as he raised his left leg to step onto the boat.

As soon as he had the sole of his left shoe planted flatly on the boat, Dawes raised his right foot and jerked it forward, the heel of his boot catching the guy full on the nose and he spun back and landed flat on his back on the jetty.

The arguing immediately stopped and everyone went quiet. A few agents moved their hands down towards their sides in the directions of their firearms, but no one drew their gun.

"We are Navy Seals operating under strict orders from people way above your pay grades," he shouted out to everyone on the jetty, his eyes scanning left to right as he spoke, "The next person who attempts to board either of our vessels will be considered as a hostile enemy and will be dealt with accordingly," he added, still scanning along the jetty, trying to establish who was going to be the most likely person to attempt to board their boats.

He could see that no one was that stupid.

"We have women and children here who need help, so tell me, who is in charge?" he shouted.

"I am," shouted a tall guy in a well cut suit.

"I am," shouted a guy in a dark blue F.B.I. jacket.

"Who are you?" Dawes said to the guy in the suit.

"My name is Larry Stanyard, I'm head of D.E.A. operations here in Florida."

Dawes smiled, finding Stanyard turned out to be much easier than he thought it would be.

"Who are you?" Dawes asked the F.B.I guy.

"My name is Paul Doobie, head of the F.B.I. Miami field office."

"Clear the jetty of all D.E.A. agents, you are responsible for these people Doobie, get the paramedics here now," Dawes said firmly.

"Stay where you are," Larry Stanyard shouted out to his men.

Dawes watched as every one of the D.E.A. agents adjusted their feet, like guys shifting their weight into sand, to indicate that they were in no mood to step away from the jetty.

"Target Stanyard," Dawes shouted out and Delaney, Case and Vic raised their guns and pointed them at Larry Stanyard from behind him. On the other boat, Mosley, Atkins and Rope aimed their guns at the D.E.A. agents on the jetty.

"We are authorised to shoot to kill," Dawes said, "I will talk to you, but you will remove your men now and let me put these people into the care of the F.B.I," he added, staring into Stanyard's eyes.

"Just then, a bright blue van pulled up with the letters 'U.S.B.C. NEWS' standing tall on the side, and a news crew jumped out of the van with their cameras already rolling. Stanyard caught sight of the camera's and said, "Everyone back off of the jetty," without moving his gaze from Dawes' eyes, "I need to talk to you, now."

"We will secure these people and then I will talk to you," Dawes replied.

Stanyard turned and walked back from the jetty to the quayside, his agents all following him, continuing to sneer at the F.B.I. agents as they passed them.

"Doobie," Dawes said, "I want these people taken to hospital immediately, I think they are all physically unharmed, but they have been through a pretty bad ordeal. When you transport them, I want you to put a man in each ambulance, and get the local PD to make sure that they are escorted all the way to hospital."

"Understood," Doobie replied, "I've already received the same instructions from up above," he added.

Dawes jumped onto the jetty and held out his hands to start lifting the hostages out of the boats. A woman lifted up a small child and he passed the child to a waiting paramedic.

Mosley started to assist the people on the other boat to step onto the jetty, into the waiting arms of paramedics, F.B.I. agents, and now the local police department were running down to the jetty carrying blankets and water bottles.

Dawes jumped onto the jetty and looked up at Stanyard. He had his agents huddled in a small group, like a sports team to prior to a match, and he was talking quickly to them. He started to walk towards the jetty stairs when a very pretty young woman tapped him on the shoulder.

"My name is Catherine Lambourne," she said, "I want to say thank you for saving my life. Please thank your men too," she added.

Dawes smiled at her. He noticed her eyes looked dead. She looked tortured and drained of emotion. He was going to ask what had happened, but thought better of it.

The psychologists would have their work cut out fixing her he thought to himself, he was sure of that.

He walked up the gangway, and when he reached the top, he turned right and walked the ten feet to where Stanyard was just breaking the huddle with his group.

"We were in the middle of a big D.E.A. operation that has been two years in the making and you have just messed that up," he spat at Dawes.

"All the Intel has been collected by the agents who discovered the hostages, and they will debrief you in an hour or so if you tell me where you can meet them?"

This seemed to pacify Stanyard immediately, so Dawes continued,

"You are the experts here, you know who is who and what they are doing, we are just the heroes who save people," he said, playing on the misconception that Seals were arrogant men.

Stanyard smiled, he was now convinced that Dawes and his team were simple killing machines, and that they didn't have a brain cell between them. It was exactly what Dawes wanted him to think.

"Our offices are hidden at the back of the Biscayne National Park Ranger Station, in a building marked 'Forest Control'" Stanyard replied, "Tell your agents that we expect them there within the next couple of hours with everything that they have, so we can try and salvage our operation," he added, before turning and saying, "Let's go," to his men who duly followed.

Dawes watched Stanyard walk off and then looked back down to the jetty. The boats were empty now and the hostages were slowly and unsteadily making their way up the gangway to the waiting vehicles. They were still all sobbing as the relief and realisation that they were now safe washed through all of their minds and bodies. The pretty girl who had thanked him looked over at him as she reached her ambulance, and as a paramedic took her hand, to help her onto the steps to climb into the ambulance, she smiled and mouthed, "Thank You," once again.

Dawes adjusted his earpiece and his microphone and spoke into it,

"Dawes calling," he said.

"Go ahead," Ward's voice said into his ear.

"The hostages are safe and delivered as instructed".

"Is the other thing done?"

"He wants to meet you in two hours."

"Where?"

"At the Biscayne National Park Ranger Station, in a building marked Forest Control."

"Great work. I want you to follow the hostages to make sure they all arrive safely at the hospital?"

"Understood," Dawes replied.

Adams Key – Upper Florida Keys- Block Five

Cardona and Franco had spent the last ten minutes watching events unfold outside. They had been watching through a slatted hole in the side of the building that Franco had insisted be built in so that he could keep an eye on their men outside, and to make sure that they were carrying out their duties effectively.

Franco did not suffer fools.

They had not moved for those ten minutes, and Franco was almost full of admiration for the way that whoever was coming had dropped his men like a bowling ball obliterates tenpins.

"You will have to make a call," Franco said to Cardona without moving his eyes away from the slit in the wall. "Then we can escape through the tunnel as planned," he added.

When they had chosen Adams Key as the perfect place to set up as a base for the hostages and the lab, Cardona had agreed everything perfectly with the D.E.A. about keeping people away from the island, and so meticulous was he in his planning, that he built the blocks around the escape route. He had built up his empire by never taking risks.

So before one frame for any of the buildings had been erected, he had his men work around the clock building an escape tunnel. There was a false wall at the back of block five that if you pushed in the bottom, it opened inwards to a set of stairs that led down, ten feet under the ground and into a tunnel which was four feet wide and six feet high. The tunnel ran for three hundred and twenty five yards under the ground, and came out the other side of the forest, where Cardona had a speedboat moored under cover. Only after the tunnel was completed and he had walked the route above ground at least eight times, and he was satisfied that it was impossible to establish that there was anything underground, did he give the go ahead for the blocks to be built.

He was never going to leave himself in a situation where he had no escape from the island.

Cardona took out his cell phone and dialled the number.

"You need to call off whoever is here," he said into the phone, as he still peered through the slit.

He was silent for a few moments and then he said,

"I have the man you are desperate for and the doctor. You think I was stupid enough to give you everything that you needed to know in one hit?"

He was silent again, this time for an even longer period, and then he said,

"You have ten minutes to get here with a chopper. If you fail me, the doctor and the prisoner will die. Now call them off," he shouted down the phone.

"Hello? Hello?" he then said before slowly putting his phone back into his pocket.

"They have tried crossing us Franco," he said, "They think we are stupid and that we have no escape plan, he just said the wrong thing,"

"What did he say?"

"He said that he has no control over the people out there, and that the best thing that we could do now is put a bullet in our heads to save the pain that these people are going to inflict upon us," Cardona replied.

Franco laughed,

"These Americans and their tough words, when it comes to it, they can never step over the line, they have no idea what real pain is. Columbian pain!" he said, without once moving his eyes away from the slit in the wall, and then laughing loudly in genuine amusement.

And then his laughing stopped.

Out into the clearing, about two hundred yards away, two men stepped forward and stood staring at the building where they were holed up.

One of the men was big, almost as big as he was, but he looked too handsome to be intimidating. But the other man looked different.

He stood about six feet tall, and even from two hundred yards away, there was something about him that caused Franco to move his face slightly back from the slit in the wall for the first time. They were both dressed in black battle fatigues, but the clothing seemed to sit better on the smaller one of the two. He looked menacing. He looked more than menacing in fact. Over the years, Franco had developed a sixth sense for identifying a dangerous opponent, by the way they stood, walked and looked, and this one man set every alarm bell off in his head as soon as he looked at him.

"I think we should go now," he said to Cardona without taking his eyes off the two men for a second.

"I agree Franco."

They both turned away from the slit at the same time and both stopped in their tracks immediately.

They looked at Dr Robert Anderton who was shaking his head at them.

Then they both looked at the false panel which was slightly ajar.

Then they looked at the chair that had been Gill Whymark's prison since they had arrived on the island. The chair was empty.

"Where is he?" Franco demanded.

"He just got up and went through there while you were looking through the wall," Anderton replied, pointing to the false panel.

"How?" Cardona asked.

And then three bullets smashed into the heavy door.

THIRTY TWO

Adams Key – Upper Florida Keys- Block Five

"They have just moved away from the hole in the wall,"
The Optician said down the phone to Ward.
"Take a few shots, let them know we are getting bored,"
he replied and hung up the phone.
They watched as the door splintered in three different
places and then he said,
"Let's go. If they lift one gun towards us, The Optician
will take them out before they can blink."
"Let's go?" Lawson enquired.
"Yes. We will be polite and knock on the door," he
replied without a hint of a smile.
Lawson rolled his eyes and shook his head.
He started walking, almost casually, towards the block,
accompanied by an unshakeable belief that The Optician
would ensure that not one shot would be fired towards

them, with Lawson strolling behind him, equally looking as though he didn't have a care in the world.

They crossed the clearing and got to within fifty yards of the block.

There were no shots or any movement.

They continued their approach and when they got about thirty feet away, they could hear raised voices coming from inside the building, raised voices that had a definite South American ring to them.

"Someone doesn't sound very happy," Lawson said.

Ward ignored him and listened carefully.

One of the voices sounded very deep and threatening while the other sounded very calm.

They continued walking and reached the door.

Ward raised his hand and knocked three times. There was no point in trying to use a friendly knock, the people inside would be in no doubt what they were there for.

The voices stopped immediately and the moment fell into complete silence.

He waited for five seconds and then knocked again.

Still silence.

He nodded at Lawson and they pulled their guns.

"There are two ways that we can do this Cardona," Ward shouted out.

They waited for ten seconds.

Still silence.

"Your one chance of getting out of this alive is to listen to me and respond. I have thirty Navy Seals surrounding you and crawling all over this island and they are getting impatient," he lied.

"We won't fall for that," the deep voice said.

He smiled to himself.

They had entered into dialogue, which told him that their self-preservation had kicked in, and that made this a whole lot easier.

A thought suddenly entered Ward's head.

Someone like Cardona would not leave anything to chance. His plan had been so complex and timed to perfection that there would be no way that he would not have come up with a contingency plan in the event that things went wrong, or the Key got stormed, and so Ward took a gamble.

"And your escape route is blocked. You can take your chances, but there are five Seals waiting for you to appear and they are on a shoot to kill order," he said as casually as he could.

The voices inside quietened to a mumble, he was tempted for a moment to put his ear to the door to listen but remembered the number of times that he had anticipated people doing just that, and had promptly fired through the door after gauging their height, and so he instinctively took a small step backwards.

After what seemed like a very long minute, the mumbling stopped.

"What do you suggest," the softer voice asked.

Ward smiled to himself yet again; Cardona was now taking charge and was preparing to negotiate.

"I suggest you open the door so that I can talk to you in a civilised manner," he replied, " If I wanted you dead, you would be dead by now, so clearly I have a different agenda,"

There was a pause for a few seconds and then Cardona said,

"If I open the door and you make one false move I will shoot you."

"If you open the door and you are even holding a gun we will kill you before you can even get a squeeze on your trigger," he replied assertively, "You are in an impossible situation, and your only way out of this is to not antagonise me," he added.

Silence from behind the door.

Five seconds later, the door started to open slowly.

The big guy was opening the door, and by the time that he had it fully opened, he was filling up most of the doorway.

He looked much bigger close up than he had looked from distance.

Ward's first thought was to shoot the guy in the face to get him out of the way, but he quickly concluded that would not be very sensible as he might need him if Cardona wouldn't give him what he wanted, so he decided to step forward and barged past him into the building.

The big guy, surprisingly, turned his body to the side to let Ward in.

Lawson followed two steps behind and stopped, square on to the big guy, and just stared into his eyes for a few seconds, before making a huffing noise in contempt of him. Ward noticed that the big guy and Lawson were of almost identical height and build, but he doubted very much that the big guy possessed Lawson's sexual prowess.

Cardona was standing about ten feet further inside the building, a fact that made Ward think how willing he was to sacrifice his own people to save himself. He was a typical coward.

Slightly behind him and to the right were two chairs. On one of them sat a guy that he instantly recognised as Dr Robert Anderton, and he was relieved that the doctor was still alive.

The chair next to him was empty.

Gill Whymark was not in the room.

"I'm looking for two people," he said, calmly, "The first one is there," he said pointing to Robert Anderton.

Anderton looked terrified.

"I'm here to take you home doctor," he said immediately as soon as he made eye contact with Anderton, "All of the hostages are safe," he added, knowing that the welfare of his family would matter more to him than his own life.

Anderton didn't reply, he didn't smile, he didn't move his hands in excitement or celebration, but instead, he just bowed his head and started to sob quietly.

"I'm looking for someone else," he said to Cardona.

"It looks like you have killed everyone else," Cardona replied.

Ward studied him.

He wasn't afraid, he could see that, but he wasn't resigned to dying either. It was almost as though he knew something that he didn't.

"Where's the other guy?" he asked, pointing to the empty chair next to Anderton.

"There was no one else," Cardona replied.

"Where's the other guy?" he asked Anderton.

He lifted his head and looked at Ward; he sniffed and wiped the tears away from his eyes. He then glanced at

Cardona, and Ward noted the complete fear that washed over his face.

He had seen that same look on lots of people just before he had killed them.

"He can't hurt you or anyone close to you ever again," he said quickly.

Anderton looked at Cardona again, and Cardona smiled. Ward was struggling to work out what Cardona knew that he didn't.

He walked across to Cardona, and without breaking stride, unleashed a lightning quick right hook that smashed into the bridge of Cardona's nose, breaking it instantly. Cardona stumbled back but didn't go down, much to Ward's displeasure.

Franco instinctively went to protect Cardona but Lawson pointed his gun at him and said,

"One more step and your dead."

Franco stopped moving.

Cardona cupped his left hand over his nose in an attempt to stem the flow of blood which by now, was gushing rapidly from his nostrils.

"What happened to the other guy?" he asked Anderton again.

"I can't tell you. I can't tell you anything," Anderton replied.

"Why not?"

"I just can't."

Only one thing could make Anderton so reluctant to talk Ward concluded, and so he instantly tried a different approach.

"If you don't tell me who he intends to harm really quickly, then it might be too late to stop it," he said softly, "You owe it to them to tell me immediately. I will have people there within ten minutes."

He instantly knew that he had guessed right. He watched as Anderton weighed up his faith in him against his fear of Cardona.

So he gave him a shove in the right direction.

"These people who have done this to you look at them now. They aren't so tough," he said pointing at Cardona, who was still fighting to stem the flow of blood from his nose.

Anderton looked at Cardona and then flicked his eyes across to Franco who was stood motionless with Lawson's gun pointing at him.

They didn't look so tough right then.

Anderton started to talk.

"That animal used a knife to dissect my friends and then forced us all to watch while he cut their eyes out," Anderton said.

Ward instantly thought of the picture of Harris.

"And then," he continued, "He forced us to feed drugs to our family members to prove that they would work and when they didn't......," his voice tailed off.

"Who is at risk now?" Ward asked, "It's really important that you tell me right now."

Anderton swallowed hard and then attempted to compose himself, so that he could get the exact information relayed properly,

"My daughter, Lucy," Anderton said as he struggled to hold back the tears, "She has three friends, Caiti, Jenny and Chelsea. His men have them held hostage with their parents, and he said that his men will rape the children and cut their eyes out when they have done, and force their parents to watch. Please help them, they are my friends," he added.

"Where are they?" Ward asked.

"At their homes."

"Where are their homes?"

"In Pinecrest. We are all neighbours. We live on the same street."

"Are you there Wallace?" Ward said into his microphone.

"I'm here." the voice came back into his ear.

"Cardona has three families held hostage in Pinecrest, I need you to call The Old Man and get teams around their immediately. No questions just kill whoever is holding them without hesitation."

"Names and location?" Wallace enquired.

Ward looked at Anderton.

"Give me the names and street?" Ward asked as he turned his microphone down for Anderton to speak towards.

"Caiti is Fuller, Jenny is Higuaín and Chelsea is Patten. They all live close to us on South West 70th Avenue," he replied.

"Did you get that?" Ward said into his mouthpiece.

"Loud and clear," Wallace replied, "I'm on it now."

"Who has the composition of the drug?" he asked Anderton.

"Only me and him," Anderton replied, pointing at Cardona who had now composed himself, the flow of blood now apparently stemmed.

"Wait!" Anderton suddenly said, "There was someone else, someone that he called and passed it over to."

"And no one else?"

"Only the man who was sitting here," he replied,
pointing to the empty chair.

"Where did he go to?"

"He went through that panel there."

Ward walked across to the panel and pulled it open. He
saw the steps and turned sharply towards Cardona.

"Where does it come out?" he demanded.

"The North East side of the Key. A thousand yards from
the water," Cardona replied, willingly giving Whymark
up to him.

"Mac," he said into his microphone.

"Here," came the reply.

"Get to the North East side of the Key. Whymark is
making a move to escape; you have to cut him off."

"We are moving now."

Ward turned to Cardona.

"Why did you have Whymark here?" he asked.

Cardona smiled at him and then laughed loudly.

Ward knew without doubt that he was missing
something completely, but he wasn't going to let on.

"I know why he is involved, but why go to the trouble of
keeping him here? Surely it would have been easier to
kill him on the mainland?" he asked.

"Who do you work for?" Cardona asked.

"I'm just the guy who hunts scum like you because I like
doing it. I work for no one."

"Well," Cardona said, "Whoever it is, he will be working
for the person who is helping me, whether he realises it
or not," he added smugly.

He wasn't in the mood for cryptic messages. He raised
his gun and pointed it at Cardona.

"You have three seconds to start talking or I will blow your face apart," he said casually.

"He first turned up about three months ago," Cardona said instantly, "Right at the start when this was only in the planning stages."

"Turned up how?"

"He tortured three of my men and killed them."

"Why?"

"Because he wanted to steal my idea obviously."

"So why didn't you just kill him?"

"Because the person helping us said that we had to keep him alive in case he had links to him."

"Who is this person?"

"I don't know."

"So how do you know he's this all powerful being then?" Ward asked sarcastically.

"Anyone who can get the D.E.A. to act as my courier, run my errands, and take out all of my competition has to be pretty important, don't you think?" Cardona replied.

"He's just a D.E.A. guy called Larry Stanyard," Ward said flippantly.

"Stanyard?!" Cardona said and then laughed, "He's right at the bottom of the food chain."

Franco joined in with the laughter at the same time.

"You have no idea what is going on. If you kill us, you'll never know either," Cardona said, and then continued to chuckle again.

"Give me your phone" Ward demanded.

Cardona put his hand into his pocket and pulled out his phone and tossed it to him.

He activated the screen; he was surprised to see that there was no lock on it, and scrolled through to the call directory. The last number dialled was an international number, no doubt an encrypted number that was untraceable and bounced around the world.

He pressed redial and waited five seconds.

The ringing tone rang three times.

Then it was answered but no one spoke.

"I'm going to find you," he said.

Still no one spoke.

"However important and powerful you think you are, the man behind me is at the very top of the tree, and I'm sure you have heard of him, and he's pissed because he doesn't like anyone being in control but him," he said firmly.

Still no one spoke.

"And guess what?" he asked, asking the open question to get a response which never came.

"The composition you've got. It's incomplete and I have the correct version," he lied.

The line went dead.

THIRTY THREE

Adams Key – Upper Florida Keys- Block Five

"He has the correct composition," Anderton said as he watched Ward toss Cardona's phone on the floor.

"But now he isn't so sure," he replied, "Where is it?"

"I wrote it down and gave it to him," he replied pointing to Cardona.

"Give it to me," he demanded of Cardona.

Cardona put his hand into his pants pocket and pulled out a piece of paper which looked like it had been torn from a notepad and held it out for Ward.

"Bring it here."

Cardona stepped forward and handed it to him, tilting his head back and stretching his arm out so that he was out of range from another right hook.

He took it and looked down at the piece of paper.

He was disappointed not to see any chemical symbols as he was looking forward to testing his memory of the periodic table. Instead, Anderton had just written each component in words with a numbered weight next to it.

He walked across to Anderton and handed him the paper, "Is this what you wrote?" he asked, needing to confirm that Cardona was not trying to attempt to dupe him with an alternative list.

Anderton studied the piece of paper and then held it out for him to take back,

"That's it. It is correct."

He folded the paper up and slid it into his jacket pocket and then he stepped towards Cardona,

"Now that I have......" he was interrupted by Wallace's voice in his ear.

"All three families are safe, six men have been eliminated," he said.

Ward smiled to himself.

Cardona looked at him blankly, not sure why he would suddenly stop in mid-sentence.

"Good work Wallace," he said into his microphone.

"Your neighbours are all safe doctor," he said to Anderton, "And you've just lost another six guys," he added, turning back to face Cardona.

"Mac calling," McDermott's voice came into Ward's ear.

"Go ahead."

"We've got to the North East side of the Key and there is no sign of him but we have found an entrance to a tunnel," McDermott said.

"Ignore it" he replied, "It only leads to us here. Scan the rest of the key towards the water, you have to try and find Whymark."

"OK."

"Where would Whymark go?" he asked Cardona.

"How would I know, he was my prisoner, not my friend," Cardona said, talking down to him like he was stupid.

So Ward raised his gun and shot Cardona in the left knee.

As the bullet smashed into his kneecap and obliterated the bone and cartilage, Cardona let out a high pitched scream as he collapsed to the floor, like a ragdoll.

Robert Anderton used his hands to cover his ears.

A second after Ward had fired his gun, Lawson spun towards Franco, and smashed a thunderous right hook into the centre of his face, and it landed with such ferocity and force, that Franco's head shot back and smashed against the door frame, and the sound of his skull cracking against the solid wood frame echoed around the room.

Franco hit the floor in a mirrored fashion to Cardona, and it was clear that he had lost the effective use of his senses and he was struggling to focus on anything, his hands lying limp by his side, unable to move them to protect his face.

Lawson then raised his right leg ninety degrees and stamped down hard with the heel of his boot onto the bridge of Franco's nose, and Franco immediately lost consciousness.

Lawson then moved to the side of Franco's head and swung his right foot back and then brought it forward with all of his weight and speed behind it. The steel toecap of his boot connected with Franco's temple with the force of a horse kicking a human being.

Franco was dead by the time Lawson had the sole of his right boot back on the floor.

"It's your fault that I am on a sex ban!" he shouted at Franco's lifeless body.

Ward laughed loudly and then Lawson said,

"I told you I would beat him to death."

Ward nodded.

"And note how my one punch put him on the floor, unlike your little slap."

Ward smiled again.

Robert Anderton looked bemused.

"Now shoot him so we can leave," Lawson said, pointing to Cardona, who was writhing around on the floor, totally unaware that his invincible bodyguard Franco, had just been beaten to death by Lawson.

"Shooting is too good for him, wouldn't you agree doctor?" Ward asked Anderton, who by now was lowering his hands from his ears.

"I just want to go home to see my family," Anderton replied, the tears running from his eyes again, but this time with sheer relief that he knew that he was no longer under any threat at all.

"Go and wait outside," Ward said to him.

Anderton stood up, walked towards the door, stepping over Franco's dead body on the way out of the door, and rushed outside and then slumped to the floor with his back against the building. He lifted his hands to his ears again and pressed tightly. He did not want to hear what was happening, however much he hated Cardona and wished him harm.

It was not remotely in his nature to be violent or vicious.

"It's all gone wrong for you, hasn't it?" Ward asked as he stepped over to Cardona.

Cardona was struggling to control his breathing; the pain was excruciating, and pulsating through him. It felt like someone was digging a hot poker into his knee and then pulling it out and then forcing it back in.

Ward could see a knife in a sheath hanging from Cardona's belt and so he leant down and pulled the knife out. He knew Cardona would have a sentimental attachment to his knife, guys like him always did.

He then pulled out his phone and ran his finger over the screen for a few seconds before lowering the screen for Cardona to see.

"Look at it," he demanded.

Cardona turned his head slowly.

He saw a picture of a man with his eyes cut out.

He then looked to his right and saw Franco's dead body on the floor.

For the first time in his adult life, he felt afraid.

"His name was Harris. He was my friend."

Cardona looked away from the screen.

Ward looked at the knife; the edges were serrated and very sharp. He was sure that Cardona had gotten someone to make it especially for him, the gaps between the points of the serrated tips and the next one identical. And it was also specifically designed to make removing people's eyes easier.

He moved his arm down and jabbed the tip of the blade into Cardona's side, around the kidney area, but making sure that he never pushed the blade too far in.

Cardona let out a piercing scream again.

He pictured Anderton outside with his hands covering his ears.

"What do you do with all of the eyes that you remove?" he asked.

Cardona did not respond, he was too busy moving his hands from his knee to his side, trying to stem the flow of blood.

So he plunged the knife deep into his left arm.

Cardona screamed again.

"I asked you a question," he said.

"What do you do with all of the eyes that you remove?" he repeated.

"I put them in a collection at my house," Cardona replied, in between short, sharp breaths.

He estimated that Cardona would bleed out in about twenty minutes.

He looked up at Lawson who touched his eyelid with a finger and he nodded.

He grabbed a handful of Cardona's hair and yanked his head back, exposing his throat fully.

"Look at me," he demanded, raising his voice for the first time.

Cardona moved his eyes to the left and looked into Ward's eyes.

Right then, he knew that he was going to die.

He saw an evil in Ward's eyes that even with the physical pain that he was experiencing, made him shudder.

He saw the end and he couldn't understand why this man suddenly looked seven feet tall.

"Look closer," he said to him.

Cardona moved his head slightly to look into Ward's eyes, when he suddenly felt a searing pain in his left eye. He had jabbed the tip of the knife into the direct centre of Cardona's eyeball.

He screamed and tried moving his one good arm up to his eye, but Ward quickly jerked the blade deep into the shoulder and it slumped back down by his side.

"I have one last question," he said.

Cardona turned his head, his one good eye barely open and Ward used all of his strength to push the knife deep into his right eye. The blade tore through the eyeball and went into his skull at least two inches. He then used all of his strength to push the blade in further and as it moved, he felt the blade burst through Cardona's brain and three seconds later, Cardona had stopped moving.

He looked down at his hands, they were covered in blood.

"Can I have sex now?" Lawson said, trying, as always, to lighten the mood.

"Go and check on Anderton. I'm going to clean myself up and then call The Old Man," he replied, completely ignoring Lawson's attempt at humour.

He didn't feel like laughing.

Gill Whymark had escaped, and he was involved with this, and Ward wanted him dead.

"Any sign of Whymark?" he said into his microphone.

"Negative. We think he has left the island somehow," Paul replied into his ear.

He stepped over to the sink and slowly washed his hands.

Everything had worked out apart from finding Whymark. He felt like he was chasing a ghost.

He dried his hands on a dirty towel next to the sink and took out his cell phone.

"Whymark has escaped," he said ten seconds later when The Optician answered.

"Escaped how?"

"He ran down a tunnel. He was gone by the time we got in the building. McDermott and the team are sweeping the Key at the moment."

"They won't find him," The Optician replied.

"Why?"

"Would they find you, if you were in his shoes?"

Ward thought about it and decided that even though he knew how good McDermott and the boys were, he would be confident of avoiding capture.

"You had better call The Old Man," The Optician said and hung up the phone.

Ward dialled Centrepoint's number. He answered on the second ring.

"Progress?" he demanded.

"The doctor is safe, Cardona and his boyfriend are dead, and I have the composition," Ward replied, somehow thinking if he didn't mention Gill Whymark then the subject would not be approached.

"And Whymark?" the old Man asked immediately.

"He wasn't there."

"What do you mean, he wasn't there?"

He ran through the events of what had happened, step by step, only omitting the fact that he had not put Cardona down with one punch.

"He can't have got far," The Old Man said, clearly displeased by the tone of his voice, "There will be a chopper there to collect you, Lawson and the doctor within five minutes; it's already on its way. You can still get him on the mainland. Dr Anderton will then continue on with his journey in the chopper, for a quick debrief and then a reunion with his family," he added.

"What about McDermott and the team?"

"A second chopper will be there in ten minutes to collect them. Do you have any leads?" The Old Man asked.

"A guy called Larry Stanyard."

"Do what you have to do, Whymark has to be found."

"Trust me," Ward replied, "I want him as much as you do."

"I doubt that," Centrepoint said, his voice sounding calmer now, "Do you have the composition on you?"

"Yes."

"Read it out to me, slowly and be exact."

Ward pulled out the piece of paper and started to read out the composition. He spelt every long word so there would be no mistakes. When he had finished, The Old Man said,

"Now destroy it. We can't let anyone ever get their hands on it."

"OK," Ward replied and hung up the phone.

"Can you head back to the clearing Mac," he said into his microphone, "A chopper will be here in ten to collect you and the boys."

"Understood," McDermott replied.

Ward pulled his earpiece out and walked out of the building.

Lawson was leaning against the wall of the block and Anderton was sat down, with his back against the wall.

"Did you take out his eyes?" Anderton asked.

Ward ignored the question.

"A chopper will be here in a couple of minutes. It will drop us off, and then take you to where your families are. It's over doctor."

Anderton started sobbing again,

"Thank you so much. I owe you everything."

Ward shot a warm smile back at Anderton.

"You ready to find Whymark?" he asked Lawson.

"I'm always ready," Lawson replied.

"And as soon as we have found him, you are free to have sex. OK?"

"Deal," Lawson eagerly replied, just as the chopper came into view, rising up from behind the trees of the thick forest.

THIRTY FOUR

Adams Key - Upper Florida Keys

"Captain Dawes is waiting for you on the mainland," the pilot said to Ward as Lawson grinned at Anderton struggling with the seatbelt, "And then we have to take him to the secure location where the hostages are being held," he added, using the thumb of his left hand to indicate that the 'We', meant he and the co-pilot. Ward completely ignored him and said to Lawson, "We have to see this Larry Stanyard first; he should be able to point us in the direction of Whymark."
"I'm not so sure," Lawson replied.
"Why?"
"Doctor, the other guy being held with you, what did Cardona say to him?" Lawson asked Anderton.
"About what?"
"About anything?"
"I got the impression that he was angry at him."
"Angry? In what way?"

"He was angry that the man had killed some of his people, but he was angrier in the fact that he was being forced to keep him alive," Anderton replied.

"How do you know that?" Lawson asked.

"Because the person who he was talking to on the phone told him that he could not kill him until he had ensured that the composition was correct."

"That must have been Stanyard." Lawson said to Ward. Ward didn't respond to either of them. Instead, he turned his head and looked out of the window at the vast mainland coming into view. He could now see the buildings clearly, and he noticed another chopper passing to their left, on its way to collect McDermott and the team he assumed.

He tried to visualise where Whymark would have gone, by picturing himself in his shoes and trying to establish what way he would go, but he was becoming more and more distracted by Anderton's comments.

"Doctor, can you tell me something?" he asked.

"Of course"

"Why did you say 'Person' and not 'Man' when you said that Cardona was instructed not to kill Whymark on the phone?"

"Did I?" Anderton replied, "I didn't realise I had."

"But was there any reason for it? Was there something that made you unsure if it was a man or not?"

"No reason other than the fact he kept quiet and listened I guess. Like all men have to do at home," Anderton replied, now feeling desperate to hear his wife's voice, giving him a list of jobs that needed doing around the house and doing exactly as he was told.

Ward smiled; Anderton was a nice guy, even though he was capable of creating a monster.

Mangrove Point – Miami

Ward saw Dawes and his men waiting by the quayside as the chopper touched down.

"Go and enjoy your family doctor," he said to Anderton as he slid the chopper door back.

"Thank you once again, for everything," Anderton replied, and extended his hand for him to shake. He took his hand and shook it firmly.

Lawson slid up from his seat and moved around Anderton to follow Ward,

"And now you are probably going to have sex," he said to Anderton, as he reached the door and jumped out.

A bemused look on Anderton's face was the last thing that Lawson saw before the chopper gracefully lifted up again and started heading back in the direction that they had just come from.

Ward approached Dawes and shook his hand.

"Great work Dawes."

"Thank those guys," he replied, pointing to his six men who were standing to his right. Ward approached the group and shook their hands individually. Dawes was clearly a very, very good leader who knew how to get the best out of his team. He gave the credit where it was due, and more importantly, he did it in front of them.

"Where do you want us now?" Dawes asked.

"You're done here. You've achieved your objective and we only have a little clearing up to do, and we are well covered for that."

A surprised look spread across Lawson's face.

"Understood," Dawes replied, and turned and headed across to his group and ten seconds later they were all heading up the gangway.

They passed a big guy who was wearing combat pants and a tee shirt walking in the opposite direction, the guy approached Ward.

"Are you Ward?" he asked, deliberately trying to sound casual in his question, but he was unable to hide the curiosity and excitement which was spreading across his face.

"He is," he said, pointing to Lawson.

The guy looked Lawson up and down, and then held his gaze on his eyes for a couple of seconds, almost transfixed.

"Here are the keys for the silver Sedan parked at the top there," he said, pointing up to the group of cars that were parked neatly in line in the quayside car park, "Is there anything else that I can do for you?" he asked.

"You've heard of me, haven't you?" Lawson asked the guy.

The guy nodded, way too enthusiastically Ward thought to himself.

"Well no doubt you are going to tell your buddies that we have met?"

"No. I won't say anything."

"I don't mind, I just want you to tell everyone that I haven't had sex for the past ten years," Lawson said as he took the keys from the guy and started heading up the gangway.

Ward just shrugged at the guy and then followed.

"Why didn't you want Dawes involved?" Lawson asked as they reached the car.

"Because we are hunting two people, Stanyard and Whymark, we don't need anyone else. McDermott and the two of us are plenty, and I never really trust any outsiders, you know that," he replied.

Lawson nodded. He understood Ward better than anyone, and he knew that control of any situation from timings of movement, to who was involved, were things that he always worked out way in advance of anyone else. He knew right then that he would have a plan, and had played it out in his mind exactly how things were going to turn out and invariably, he was always exactly right.

"I need to ring Nicole-Louise," Ward said, "You drive, head back to Doral, we'll meet Mac at his warehouse," he added, as he pulled his cell phone from his pocket and called Nicole-Louise.

"I thought you had forgotten about us," she answered.

"Never," he replied, "We've been a bit busy. Larry Stanyard, did you find out everything on him?"

"Of course I did. Actually, Tackler found where he is, so I can't take all the credit, although I've found most of the answers on this one, which is why he is glaring at me with a sour face."

"So what do you have on him?"

"He is as corrupt as they come in simple terms. In spite of all the deals that he had made with Cardona, which he notified Washington off to make himself look clean, he has been creaming a huge amount of money from a variety of different cartels. I've managed to find every last cent though," she replied in a matter of fact tone.

"How much money are we talking?"

"Three million dollars."

"And you know where it all came from?"

"Pretty much," she replied, "But that's not all," she added.

"So what else is there?"

"There is another three million dollars that I have found that has been split three ways."

"That makes sense," he replied, "He would have to have other agents close to him aware of what he was doing to carry out his instructions."

"Indeed he has. Three guys, Erik Swan, Shaun Keane and Robert Simon. All long term members of his elite unit."

"And that's it?"

"That's where all the money has gone. I can't guarantee that there aren't others, there have been some large cash withdrawals from the accounts of those three, maybe they are paying other agents in cash?"

"How big are the withdrawals?"

"They range from five thousand dollars to thirty thousand."

"How frequently are the payments made?"

"There is no pattern."

Ward thought about this. If other agents were on the payroll then the payments would be much more frequent and a definite pattern would be visible.

"I want you to steal all of their money."

"I already have," she replied.

"When?" Ward asked.

"Two hours ago."

"Do you think they will be aware of it?"

"I doubt it. They are accounts in the Cayman islands that have been bounced around the globe so I doubt they are checked every hour," Nicole-Louise replied.

"Can you find a way of getting the bank to contact them regarding the emptying of their accounts?" he asked.

"Of course I can. I just have to put some money in, make a few suspicious movements, and they will contact them for verification that they are the ones moving the money."

"Can you do it in about four hours' time?" he asked, looking at his watch, "That will give us plenty of time to prepare things."

"Of course I can. I will do it at five exactly."

"So where is Stanyard?"

"I'll let Tackler explain," she replied, and Ward could hear a crunching noise in his ear, obviously where Nicole-Louise had thrown the phone at Tackler.

"You know that I've let her have a bit of glory on this one, don't you?" he asked without making any attempt to greet Ward.

"Of course I do," he said, in a deliberate overly serious tone, "So where is Stanyard?"

"Don't you want to know how I found them?" Tackler enquired, eager to demonstrate the amount of work that he had been putting in.

"Not really, time is of the essence here."

"Well don't you want to know how I know that they are all together right now?"

He already knew how.

"You traced their cell phones, narrowed down hundreds of calls, probably confirmed each individual by tracing their records to a family member, and then hacked into the cell towers, and you are looking at your screen right now and seeing four red dots probably all pinging on top of each other?”

“Knowing how I did it and being able to do it yourself are two very different things Ryan,” Tackler replied sarcastically.

“I’m only joking. I appreciate everything you both do,” he replied, “But I need to know where they are now?”

“They are at 1328 South 20ᵗʰ Avenue in Hollywood, Miami.”

“Can you text me the address and their names please,” he replied, “And make sure that Stanyard gets a call at five from the bank,” he added, and hung up the phone.

“They have found him?” Lawson asked.

“Of course they have,” he replied, before he leant back into his seat and closed his eyes, visualising what he was going to do to Larry Stanyard before switching his thoughts to the demise of Gill Whymark.

30 Miles off of Adams Key - Upper Florida Keys

“This is where he wants it done,” the pilot said into the headphones of his co-pilot.

For only the second time since he had worked for The Old Man, The Optician was now following an order that he didn’t want to follow.

He had to kill Dr Robert Anderton.

Centrepoint had told him very forcefully that there was no way that they could let the doctor live with the knowledge that he had in his head. They could not be sure that other Cartels were completely unaware of his existence, or what he had created, and that in six months' time he could be creating the drug under duress for someone else.

They could not take that chance.

The Old Man had said that sometimes they had to do things that they didn't want to do for the bigger picture, and while he could see his view point, it still sat uncomfortably with him.

The only other time that he had followed an order that he was unhappy about was when he had to kill a woman who had been sleeping with a Senator's aide just to get information from him. While the act was deceitful, her reasons for doing so were to get her two kids through college and so he sympathised with her.

But he had never disobeyed an order in his life and he wasn't going to start now.

The Old man had told him that a chopper was on its way to collect Ward, and that he was to get to the other side of the island so that he could be collected first. He had covered almost two miles in fourteen minutes and reached the landing spot just as the chopper had touched down.

He had changed into clean clothing that the pilot had provided him with, and climbed into the empty seat at the front. He had no idea how to fly a chopper or a plane, but had taken up the role of co-pilot in the transportation of Ward and other Deniables more times than he could remember over the past few years.

When they had taken off and emerged from behind the trees, and headed towards the extraction point, he smiled to himself when he saw Ward and Lawson looking up to them in the sky.

Once again, they would be three feet away from him and they would never know. He estimated that Ward had looked at the back of his head at least forty times over the past few years. He liked being close to Ward; after all, Ward was probably the only true friend that he had in the world. He liked Lawson too. He liked how upbeat and cheerful he always was, and he had to admit to himself, he was very jealous of his good looks and stature. He wished that he could be Lawson, just for a week, because his was a lonely life, and he was envious of anyone who had people around them to share their lives with, and he had yet to see a female flight attendant on any flight that Lawson had taken, who didn't want to either date him or have sex with him.

He laughed when he heard Lawson mention sex to the doctor when he stepped out of the chopper at Mangrove Point.

The Old Man had said that the doctor was to be taken out over the sea, killed, and then dropped down into the ocean from nine thousand feet, a safe height to hoover before the air got too thin, and the sharks would take care of the rest.

He unbuckled his harness, without acknowledging the pilots comments, and pulled a Glock from under the seat. He wasn't keen on handguns, they were unpredictable and noisy, and killing people at close range with a gun always resulted in blood splatter. Through his scope, whenever he killed people, he almost felt as though he was playing a video game and not really killing people, and while he was happy to kill a bad guy at close quarters, killing a man for no other reason than he was smart, was something most people would struggle with.

But an order was an order.

He was incapable of disobeying any order; it was like he had a switch inside him that no matter how he felt, he could not disobey what his superiors demanded he do.

He turned around sharply and raised his gun.

Robert Anderton was gazing to his left out of the window, a quizzical look on his face, no doubt wondering where they were heading, and he slowly turned and made eye contact with the gun that was less than two feet away from his face.

"Please, don't," he screamed as he raised his hands to protect his face.

The Optician pulled the trigger.

The sound of the shot echoed around the inside of the chopper, and it veered slightly as the pilot shrunk his head into his shoulders as soon as the initial bang of the gun went off, a movement that he quickly corrected.

The bullet smashed into Anderton's throat and ripped his windpipe wide apart, the blood sprayed forward and covered The Opticians hand and the gun.

He was sure Anderton was dead immediately but to ensure that he endured no unnecessary suffering, he pumped three more shots into his heart.

The third shot making the pilot veer slightly to the left again before levelling up once again.

He then stepped into the rear of the chopper and slid the door wide open.

With one hand gripping the internal railing of the chopper, he used his other to drag Anderton off his seat by his collar, along the floor, and up to the doorway.

Without any further hesitation, and deliberately not looking at Anderton's face, he dragged his body with one big heave and tipped him head first out of the chopper.

As soon as his feet were out of sight, he slid the door shut and returned to the co-pilots seat.

"Get me back to Mangrove Point, quickly," he said to the pilot, "And you can tell The Old Man it's done."

THIRTY FIVE

NW 60th Street – Doral – Miami

They had all made their way back to McDermott's lock up within thirty minutes of landing at Mangrove Point. "We have a location for Stanyard," Ward said to McDermott as he stepped out of the Range Rover.
"So what are we waiting for?"
"He won't be going anywhere. There are four of them in on this. You think we can cope with four D.E.A. guys?" he asked in a mocking tone.
"So what's the plan?"
He pulled out his phone from his pocket and checked for text messages. There was the one from Tackler that he had been expecting. He opened it up and said,
"Wallace, write this down," and continued to read out the address and the name of the three other guys that were at the address with him.
"You have until five until we hit on them. If they move in the meantime, Tackler will let us know immediately."
"That place is pretty close so we have plenty of time for some recon work then," McDermott replied, "Paul, take

Wired and Fringe, and carry out a complete assessment of the address and be back here within the hour with a clear plan on how we are going to attack."

"Is anyone else hungry?" Fuller asked the room in general.

A resounding 'Yes' echoed around the room.

"Burgers and fries all round then," Fuller replied, and climbed back into the second Range Rover.

Ward felt his phone vibrate in his pocket. He pulled it out. The Old Man was calling.

He stepped out of the main warehouse and into the reception area and closed the door.

He pressed the answer button.

"Turn the television on," Centrepoint said as soon as he put the phone to his ear.

"We don't have one here" he replied bluntly, "What's so important?"

"There is a breaking news story on USBC News."

"About?"

"How a fun day arranged by Newton Pharmaceutical Limited for its staff, ended in tragedy when a boating trip went wrong, resulting in the deaths of four people," The Old Man replied, sounding incredibly pleased with himself.

"You think that vindicates your decision involving Ashurst-Stevens?" Ward asked, referring to an issue that divided their opinions deeply.

Centrepoint ignored the question.

"But there is something else," he said.

"There always is," he replied.

"Doctor Robert Anderton is unfortunately among the victims."

He was quiet for a moment while he worked out in his mind what had happened.

"You didn't take him to see his family?"

"How could I? If they saw him, they would know he was alive. There was no way that we could let what he had created ever get out. Now no one has the composition and so the drug will never exist."

"You have it, I gave it to you!" Ward replied.

The Old Man ignored him.

"It was easier to tell his family that he had been killed on the island with a bullet to the head, so it was quick and painless."

"Surely killing innocent people can't sit well with you. If it does, you are no better than the animals we hunt," Ward spat down the phone, anger clearly evident in his voice.

"I had no choice. I have to take into account the bigger picture. That creation had the potential to destroy millions of lives, and kill God knows how many people."

"I'm sure his wife will appreciate your bigger picture," he replied sarcastically.

"We will make him out to be a hero, and financially we will set her and her children up for life."

"That's very generous of you."

"With the six million dollars that you instructed Nicole-Louise to steal," he added.

He was now convinced that Nicole-Louise and Tackler's apartment must be bugged, he could not see how he could have got that information so quickly. He made a mental note to himself to tell them about that later.

"How did you have him killed?" he asked.

"Does it matter?"

"It matters to me."

"We had him taken back to Adams Key, shot in the head and directed the paramedics and clean-up crew to the body for a dignified extraction," Centrepoint lied.

Ward wasn't happy about this chain of events, but at least Centrepoint had done the right thing. Sometimes, The Old Man was human, he thought to himself. He would console himself with that and move on,

"Where would Whymark go?" he asked.

"I have everyone working on finding him. We have got our experts with the facial recognition programs hacked into every CCTV system in Miami, and lots of bodies on the street. There is a list of twenty or so possible places where he would go, and we are working through them right now. We will find him Ryan, and so be ready, as soon as we do; I want you to be the one who eliminates him once and for all."

While Ward was more than willing to be the one who wiped Whymark off the face of the earth, he was starting to wonder why The Old Man was so obsessed with him doing it.

"So why are you so adamant that it has to be me?" he asked.

Centrepoint was quiet for a few seconds and then said, "He was my protégé, the best I had ever seen until you came along. But he went bad, very bad, and I think it is only right that my new protégé, you, be the one to punish him accordingly."

"I'm not sure I like being called a protégé," Ward said, "It sounds like you own me," he added.

"You know what I meant. I respected him, as much as I do you, and he turned on me and he jeopardised all of the good that we do. It is only fitting that the one person who is good to the core takes him out so that he knows that nothing can break us," Centrepoint said, almost an air of resignation and sadness running through his voice.

"Careful," Ward said, "You almost sound as though you like me," he added, trying to lighten the moment. He understood what The Old Man was saying, he realised right then that he looked at his team of people as part of his family. He doubted that he even had his own family; he had probably devoted the whole of his life to the service of the U.S. and U.K. governments, and so it probably felt like one of his children had deserted him.

"Who do you think wanted Whymark kept alive and why?"

"I think it had to be Stanyard that he was in on it with then Whymark got greedy, and thought he would take the whole of the pie for himself," Centrepoint replied.

"So you think that Stanyard was the guy on the phone that Cardona gave the composition to?"

"It has to be. No one else could have known about it."

"Whymark was present when Cardona did that. What are the chances of him remembering every single component and measure?" Ward enquired.

"How much do you remember of the list you read out to me and the weights involved?" The Old Man asked.

Ward pictured the list and closed his eyes for a few seconds. He could see it all, very clearly.

"By your silence, you have just answered your own question," Centrepoint said.

Ward knew he was right.

"So, all he has to do now is take Stanyard out and he will be the only person capable of getting the drug into mass production," he said out loud, as opposed to directly to The Old Man, "McDermott has sent Paul, Wired and Fuller over to the place where Stanyard is hiding, if Whymark turns up, they will know. I need to let McDermott know."

"You need to get everything out of Stanyard that you can before you even think of killing him."

"I know, I intend to."

"I'll ring you immediately if there is any development on Whymark," The Old Man said, and hung up the phone. He walked back out into the main warehouse and approached Lawson and McDermott.

"There is a high chance that Whymark will be looking for Stanyard so make sure Paul lets us know immediately if he turns up," he said to McDermott, who nodded instantly, and walked across to Wallace who was sitting at the communication desk.

"What is it?" Lawson asked Ward.

"What do you mean?"

"I know that look. There is something missing. Like you've worked out the pieces of the puzzle but they are not fitting together."

"It adds up, almost perfectly it adds up, but I can't shake the feeling that we are still missing something."

"Me too," Lawson replied.

"You feel the same?"

"Yes. If I can shoot out for an hour and have sex with someone I might be able to see things more clearly," Lawson replied, with no hint of a smile.

Ward laughed loudly.

"Look," Lawson continued, "If you think that something isn't quite right, then I am with you one hundred per cent. You are never wrong, and I trust your judgement more than anyone else I have ever met in my life. So you work out what it is Ryan, and then you tell me what you want me to do. I'll back you unconditionally," he added. Ward patted him on the shoulder. Lawson had a knack of making him believe that he was right and that he would make the right call.

A few minutes later, the roller shutter doors opened Fuller rolled back in.

"The food is here. Let's eat," he said.

Lawson headed towards Fuller who was unloading four big carry bags of food from the Range Rover. 'Burger and Fries' actually meant three lots of burger and fries to fighting men. They didn't often have time to eat, so when they did eat, they ate well.

Ward ignored the food and stepped out into the reception area again.

He called The Optician.

"Did you kill Dr Anderton?" he asked as soon as the ringing tone stopped.

"I was just following orders. It's what I do. You know that," he replied.

"You aren't getting any judgement here," Ward said, "I just wondered how that sat with you, truthfully, just between us,"

There was a pause on the line for a few moments.

"Not very well, but I understand why."

"So do I, but I sometimes think that we are all too trigger happy and with our resources, there must be other ways that we can remove people from harm's way," he replied, "Anyway, I just wanted you to know that I know it can't have been easy."

"The call is appreciated my friend," The Optician replied and the line went dead.

Next he called Eloisa. He wasn't expecting her to answer and he was surprised when her soft voice said, "Hello?" on the third ring.

"Hey. How are you?" he asked.

"I'm all the better from hearing from you. Are you finished whatever you were doing?"

"Almost."

"What's wrong Ryan? You only ever call when you are halfway through something if you need a distraction to clear your mind, so what is it?" she gently asked.

"The usual, I just need to hear your voice to remind me that I have a normal life away from the evil, death and greed that consumes my days when I am working."

"When are you likely to be back in New York?"

"Tomorrow at the latest, maybe tonight even," he replied.

"Make it tonight, we can spend the night together, and I will give you a massage to soothe all of your worries away. I'll remind you how it feels to be loved again."

Ward smiled to himself. There it was; he felt better instantly.

"How's work?" he asked.

"It's good. We have achieved extra funding today, and I definitely seem to be a very popular girl with the chief's at the moment," she replied, and laughed her sweet chuckle that always made his heart feel like it was melting.

"You have anything good lined up for me?"

"Yes, but that can wait, I just want to talk about you."

"Listening to your voice is all I need to make me feel better so give me a little clue. Who are we after now?"

"Just a taste then," she replied, "There is a monster called The Reverend Solomon Tower."

"Where is he?"

"He is from Oregon."

"What is he involved in?"

"He has a commune, one that our leaders in their politically correct wisdom have effectively declared an independent zone on the basis of religious grounds," she replied with a sigh.

"But it's not that?"

"No."

"So what is going on there?"

"He is forcing girls as young as ten to marry men and have a child with them on the basis that the Lord demands it."

"But it's really a paedophile ring?" he asked.

"It's more than that; we believe that they are responsible for the kidnapping of young girls throughout the states to act as child bearers for the lord. There have been fifteen girls around the age of ten go missing in the past two months."

"You will have everything ready for me when I get back?"

"It's ready already. But let's make tonight about us, no talk of work. And that means either of our jobs, just about us. Let's be normal, OK?"

"You make me so happy," he said.

"Why?"

"Just by being you," he replied.

"I love you Ryan. Hurry home."

"I love you too," he said, and the line went dead.

He walked back into the main warehouse and looked at everyone tucking into their burgers. Lawson was holding court again, everyone was listening to him talk, no doubt about his sexual conquests again, and he smiled to himself.

While he was standing back and looking at them he understood what The Old Man felt about Whymark turning. These men were his people, his family and the people that he trusted more than anyone else in the world. McDermott sat in the tatty armchair, not speaking but overseeing proceedings, while Lawson continued to tell his tales, McDermott sat looking at them, content in the fact that they were being normal, switching off from being the ruthless killing machines that they were, and for the first time, he wished that The Optician could be there with them, being part of the family, belonging with someone. Eloisa made him feel that he belonged somewhere, McDermott's men belonged to each other and Lawson belonged to the female race. But The Optician belonged to no one, and Ward knew for sure that right then, he would be feeling very lonely.

THIRTY SIX

NW 60th Street – Doral – Miami

Exactly fourteen minutes after Ward had last spoken to Centrepoint, his phone vibrated in his pocket. The Old Man was calling back.

"We have him," he said as soon as Ward put the phone to his ear.

"Whymark?"

"Yes."

"Where?"

"He is in one of the CIA safe houses," The Old Man said eagerly.

"How do you know it's him?" he asked.

"Because it hasn't been used for over two years, and there is an activation alert switch on the windows and doors, and it was activated five minutes ago."

"It's definitely him?"

"The CIA has just confirmed that none of their operatives are using it. It has to be him because he used it four years ago, and he knows exactly what it is."

"We are waiting for Stanyard to move. I need Lawson on that," he said.

"The Optician is on route to the house already; he will provide all the protection that you need."

Ward felt a rush of adrenalin surge through his body. He had been after Whymark longer than he had ever been after anyone, and now he had found him.

"Send me the address."

"Just be careful Ryan, you have not come up against anyone as good as him yet," Centrepoint replied.

"I'll win," he replied, "I always do," he added, and then hung up the phone.

"They've found him?" Lawson asked.

"Yes."

"Then let's go."

"You have to stay here," he replied.

"No way am I leaving you to go there alone," Lawson said, standing to his feet as he spoke.

"I won't be alone, The Optician is coming with me, and he's already there. I need you here with Mac to be ready to go immediately if Stanyard moves."

"I don't like it. I should be there to back you up," Lawson protested.

"And I need you to get all the information out of Stanyard. We can't let him slip through our fingers Mike. If we lose him then we are back to square one, and if he gets that drug produced all of this has been for nothing," he replied firmly.

"I still don't like it," Lawson reiterated.

"And I will probably be back way before five, so then we can get to Stanyard and then all go home," he replied, "Now give me your car keys."

Lawson tossed his keys to Ward.

"I still don't like it."

"So much sexual tension inside of you," he replied and everyone in the warehouse laughed.

"I'll be back shortly Mac, draw up the plan and fill me in when I return," he said to McDermott.

McDermott nodded at him, and Ward walked out of the warehouse.

As soon as he stepped outside, he felt his phone vibrate in his pocket. He pulled it out and the text from an international number simply said,

'6477 SW 10th St West Miami'

He climbed into the car and put the zip code into the sat nav. It said that he would be there in sixteen minutes.

6477 SW 10th Street – West Miami

As it turned out, it only took thirteen minutes to get to the safe house, the traffic on the roads was light, as it was a couple of hours before the rush hour traffic would start.

He drove down the street to get a feel for the area, he passed number 6477 and it looked like a completely uneventful building. The movies always portrayed CIA safe houses as fancy buildings or complex locations, but the truth was, with budgetary constraints, and the ever growing need to not overspend, the houses were always totally unremarkable and never that well-hidden. The best way to hide something was always in full view of everyone.

The house itself wasn't actually a house at all. It was more a chalet.

It looked like a small beige box with a tiled roof. There was a small, neat lawn, at the front of the building with a very neat, but small again, semi-circular paved driveway. Three white awnings were down above the windows, and this gave the building some much needed colour.

It was an unremarkable building in every way possible. The drive was empty and the building looked quiet. He turned around at the end of the road, waited three minutes, and drove past again. The three minute gap enough time to convince Whymark, if he was watching that he was delivering or collecting something from the neighbouring houses. He would not risk driving past a third time.

He reached the end of the road where there was a crossing marked out, and turned right, and then parked the car thirty yards down the road, after he had turned the car around facing back in the direction of the chalet. If Whymark made a move now, he was sure he would see him.

He slowly and firmly screwed the silencer onto his Glock and tucked it inside his jacket, then he pulled out his phone and called The Optician.

"I'm here," The Optician answered.

"Where are you?" he asked.

"There are some trees behind the house opposite. I have a clear view of the front of the house, but I am blind as far as the rear goes, be careful," he replied.

Ward hung up the phone.

He got out of the car and walked up to the crossing and turned the corner towards the chalet. He passed the house on the corner of the street, and in less than thirty strides he was outside number 6477. He stepped onto the driveway and confidently walked up to the dark mahogany coloured door, and knocked four times, on the fourth knock, he slipped his hand into his jacket and pulled out his Glock.

Then he waited.

No one answered the door.

He waited ten seconds and knocked on the door again, four knocks, light and close together.

No one answered the door.

He counted to fifteen and then knocked again, the same deliberate four knocks, and he waited once again.

No one answered the door.

He reached out and turned the door handle.

The locking mechanism clicked and the door opened.

He stepped inside quietly, closing the door behind him, and as he did so, he raised his Glock directly in front of him, shoulder high, with both hands gripping it tightly.

The Hallway was tight. The walls were painted in a cheap looking magnolia, and there was a wheat coloured carpet on the floor, the type you see in office blocks rather than houses, and there was no furniture.

The hallway ran down the centre of the chalet, and there were a total of five doors, all painted in white gloss paint, all fitted with the same cheap looking gold coloured handles, and all closed.

He stopped for a minute and tried to use his senses to feel if there was anyone else in the house. There was no sound and he didn't get the feeling that there was any movement anywhere either.

He stepped slowly and deliberately forward, checking the sound of his feet to make sure that he wasn't walking across any creaking floorboards. The floor felt firm under his weight and by the third step, he had established that he was walking on a concrete screed, and not floorboards.

The first door he came to was on his left, he used his left hand to push down lightly on the door handle and it moved effortlessly. He paused for a moment.

The Old Man had said Whymark had not used the house for the past four years, and he suddenly thought to himself that if no one else had used it, the handle would have been much stiffer. He cursed himself for not asking The Old Man the last time that the CIA had used it.

He pushed the door with his fingertips, and it slowly swung open without making any sound. He moved back behind the wall to the left of the doorway and then realised how stupid that was. If Whymark was in there he would just shoot through the flimsy partition walls, and he would be dead by now, and so he stepped through the doorway and into the room.

To the left, there was a cheap looking, round wooden table with three chairs around it, all tucked neatly underneath, to the right, a sofa, big enough to seat four people, opposite a television set. That was all there was in room. He walked into the room and checked the window. It had a security latch on the inside and he turned it and noticed that it was very stiff.

Whymark had not come in through this window.

He walked back to the doorway and let his Glock lead him out of the room and back into the hallway, cautious and alert at all times.

The hallway was still empty.

The next door he came to was on the right. He went through the same routine of trying the handle, again it moved down effortlessly, the door swung open after he had given it a light push with his fingertips.

He peered inside.

There was a bed and a set of drawers. That was it. No cupboards or closets, not even a bedside lamp. He tried the security latch on the window and it was the same, very stiff and not easy to move.

Whymark had not come in through this window.

He stepped back into the hallway and walked towards the next door, which was also on the right, with care and attention.

He leant on the handle. This handle felt much stiffer. He was not sure if that was because it had not been used recently or if it was just poorly fitted. Either way, it was enough to put him on high alert. He pushed against the door and it slowly swung open. He stepped inside. The room was the bathroom, fitted out in the most basic way, with just a bath, with a shower head attached on the wall, and a flimsy shower curtain, the type that always made him think of Hitchcock's Psycho film, and a toilet and sink which were virtually on top of each other. He ran his fingers across the sink to see if it had been used and looked inside the toilet. Everything looked bone dry. He then stepped across to the window and tried the security latch. It didn't move at all.

Whymark had not come in through this window.

He stepped back into the hallway and for a moment, he felt his heart beating in his chest more than it should be been beating, and so he inhaled a big breath and exhaled slowly and quietly to get his heart rate back under control.

The next door was about twelve feet away on the left. He leant on the handle and it moved easily. He pushed the door slowly open and stepped inside.

There was a large double bed against the far wall to the left and an open doorway which led to a bathroom on the right, he walked across to the bathroom and ran his fingers across the sink again. It was also bone dry.

Then he checked the security latch on the window. It was so stiff that he couldn't move it at all.

Whymark had not come in through this window.

He stepped back into the hallway and stood staring at the last door which was directly in front of him at the end of the hallway. He already knew that the kitchen had to be through the door, it couldn't be anything else, and he approached it cautiously. If Whymark was here, he would be on the other side of the door.

He moved forward and reached the door. He pushed down on the handle and the lock made a loud click as the mechanism kicked in. For a moment he was in two minds to either step back or lay on the floor so that any shots fired would go over his head, but then he decided against it, and pushed firmly on the door, and then threw his body behind the wall to the right of the door. No shots rang out.

He peered around the corner and then stepped through the doorway.

There was a table to the left with three chairs placed unevenly around it, a small refrigerator, an equally small stove with three rings, and three cupboards above a sink and a back door. He walked across to the sink and ran his fingers across it. It was dry. He then tried the security latch and it was solid.

Whymark had not come in through this window.

Next he tried the back door, it was locked.

He stepped across to the table and pulled out one of the chairs and sat down.

He knew what had happened and why.

Whymark had simply used a key to walk through the front door. He was now convinced that he had just unlocked the door, opened it and then closed it, leaving it unlocked.

This was all a diversion, he would by now be on the other side of Miami, maybe even further away, and The Old Man would have got all of his resources focussed on this side of Miami allowing Whymark to disappear without trace.

He had played them all and won. He smiled to himself; he was as good as Centrepoint had said.

He took out his phone and dialled The Optician.

"Was he there?" he answered.

"He never was, he played us," Ward replied, "He got all of our eyes focussed this way, and he has gone the other way."

"I'll let The Old Man know," The Optician replied and the line went dead.

He stepped up from the chair, walked out of the kitchen, back along the hallway and out of the front door.

By the time he had got back to the car and started the engine, he was still smiling to himself, because he had concluded that he would have done exactly the same thing in Whymark's position. But he still had Stanyard to get to, and as he drove up the road he was more sure than ever that Larry Stanyard would know something about where Whymark would go, and so he let his mind wander, visualising on how he would get Stanyard to tell him what he needed to know.

The image of Stanyard begging for mercy and telling him where to find Whymark was shattered after a few minutes, when he felt the barrel of a gun against the bottom of his skull and a voice said,

"You've been looking for me. If you make one sudden move you are dead."

THIRTY SEVEN

West Miami

"Gill Whymark I assume?" Ward calmly asked.
"That includes talking," Whymark said, "Just drive, I'll tell you where to stop."
He looked in his rear view mirror and caught his first glimpse of Whymark in the flesh. He looked badly beaten. There was a big cut above his left eye, and dried blood down the side of his neck.
Whymark stared straight back into his eyes.
For the first time ever, he knew what people saw when they looked into his own eyes.
He knew right at that moment that he was going to die.
He had recently asked himself how he would feel just before he died. He wondered if he would be overrun

with fear, and if he would have a sick feeling in the pit of his stomach.

He concluded that he would never really know until that day came.

And now he had his answer.

He felt sad and full of regret, but he was not scared. He had always accepted that living the life he led and swimming in the pool of evil that he regularly swam in, came with the possibility of him being killed in the line of duty highly likely, almost a certainty, he now told himself, and so he wasn't afraid.

He felt sad, sadder than he had ever felt in his life.

The first person that he thought of was his mother. He thought how she had worked so hard to make him everything he was today. He thought about how she had worked four jobs to get the money to support him through university in England, and how she had devoted her whole life to making sure that he had everything he needed to make him a success. She had installed a solid moral compass in him, along with a sense of knowing that right from wrong made you a good person, but putting the wrongs of the world right, made you even better. He felt sad because he had a feeling consuming him that he had let her down.

But he wasn't scared.

His mind went back to when he was a young boy at school, and how his mother would patiently sit down at the table with him and work through his homework with him, and once he had finished, work through it again to make sure that he had clearly understood everything that he had just finished. A vision of him as a young boy, walking home from school, without a care in the world, fixed itself firmly in his mind.

And that vision of him as a young boy brought his thoughts firmly to Eloisa.

He saw her beautiful face, specifically her beautiful smile looking at him, and he felt his heart sink.

He had spent so many hours over the past couple of years daydreaming about the two of them leading a normal life, and he was desperate to be a father. He often thought of the two of them running away and living in a cottage, away from everyone, surrounded by vast mountains and fields. It was his favourite daydream. But he wasn't scared.

For a reason that he couldn't explain, and much to his surprise, he thought about Sean Gilligan, his friend and colleague who was the type of father that he wanted to be, and then his thoughts switched immediately to McDermott and his son Paul and how, while they probably had the most unconventional working father and son relationship that he had ever known, the pride that McDermott had in his son was something that he could never hide, no matter how hard he tried. It was a feeling that he would never live long enough to experience, and that is why he felt sad. He regretted the path that he had taken, but decided that he would do the same thing again if he had the same choices.

But he wasn't scared.

He snapped himself out of the sadness and self-pity that was consuming him, and reminded his self that his greatest asset was his ability to problem solve.

And right then he had a very big problem.

Behind him, holding a loaded gun pressed into the back of his skull, was a killer as ruthless as he was, maybe more so, if he listened to The Opticians appraisal of him, and it was highly unlikely that he was going to make a mistake.

He knew without any doubt that if the tables were turned, Whymark would have no chance of wrestling back control of the situation.

This fact was confirmed when he looked in the rear-view mirror and saw Whymark fasten himself in with the rear seatbelt and then extend his knees into the back of the passenger seat so that he was braced if Ward decided to crash the car.

He was only slightly reassured by the fact that Whymark had not killed him yet, that clearly meant that he wanted some information from him, but as he had done himself, more times than he could remember, once Whymark had what he wanted, he would kill him anyway.

His only chance was to try and delay, or add something into the mix that Whymark might consider important enough to keep him alive a little longer

"Take a left at the lights and then first right," Whymark said, pushing the barrel of the gun a little harder into the base of his skull as he spoke.

The lights were red and so he slowly pulled the car to a stop. For a split second he contemplated opening the door and making a run for it, but he quickly dismissed that idea when he weighed up the fact that even if Whymark's reflexes were slower than his, that would still give him enough reaction time to pump three bullets into the back of his head.

He pulled away as the lights turned green, and swung the car slowly left, he then took an almost immediate right turn up a tight road which had high brick buildings on either side; he drove forward and came to a concreted area which accessed the service doors of the surrounding shops.

The whole place was deserted.

"Stop here and cut the engine," Whymark demanded.

He pulled to a stop, engaged the hand brake and cut the engine.

"Now throw the keys out of the window, and do it slowly," Whymark instructed.

His voice was calm, as he expected it to be, he knew that Whymark had killed without any thought or doubt many times, and that at that moment, he knew that he was completely in control and nothing could alter that fact.

He had felt that same sense of power many times himself.

He lowered the window about eight inches then pulled the keys out of the ignition and tossed them through the gap a good eight feet, making sure that they landed firmly in the middle of a pile of old boxes and trash bags that were piled up outside a service door. He didn't want any kids turning up, seeing keys on the floor and then dumping his body like an animal before stealing the car.

"What do you know about me?" Whymark asked, lowering his knees from against the back of the front seat and releasing the seat belt as he spoke.

He figured that there was no point in lying to him so he told the truth.

"I think you are dumb," he replied calmly.

"I was hoping for a more informed reply, considering that you are meant to be the smartest of all of The Old Man's monkeys," Whymark replied, equally as calmly, "Can you specify why?" he asked.

"You are dumb because you didn't need to do all the crap you have done for money, there are easier ways of getting it," he said, offering a smile into the rear view mirror as he spoke, a smile that was promptly returned by Whymark.

"Elaborate on that point?"

"Just take it," he replied, "I've taken millions of dollars, and decided to keep it for myself, and The Old Man has known all about it but chose to ignore it. You get to a point where you have enough money. That's what makes you dumb, you could have just carried on doing the right thing, and no one would have cared what you took from the bad guys."

Ward maintained eye contact with Whymark in the mirror as he spoke, searching for a reaction, or the smallest sign of what he was thinking, but he saw nothing. No emotion, no agreement or disagreement with what he was saying, nothing.

"So, I'm just a guy who got greedy?"

"No. You are more than that."

"Such as?"

"Where do I start?" he asked with a smile, "You let a terrorist under your watch run loose and set off bombs everywhere, you tried creaming off of the sex trafficking industry, and now you are trying to develop a drug which would cause social destruction across The States. That's pretty much a full house. You are only missing political conspiracy and the oil trade and you would have a complete set," he added.

"You forgot the guns," Whymark said, raising his eyebrows as he spoke.

Ward ignored him.

"When you found me, what were you meant to get from me?" Whymark asked.

"Nothing"

"Nothing?"

"Yes. Exactly what it means. Nothing."

"You weren't told to get a list of names, places, events or people?" Whymark asked, a slight frown appearing on his face for the first time. It was only just noticeable but enough for Ward to seize on it.

"I guess you aren't considered important enough. I was told what you are I've actually been coming behind you clearing up the mess you have created, so why would I want to talk to you."

"You weren't told to ask me anything at all?" Whymark asked again.

"I was told quite the opposite to be honest. I was asked to find you, kill you, and specifically told not to engage into any conversation with you. It seems that everyone wants you gone. You are quite the irritant it seems," he replied.

"But you couldn't find me, could you? I found you. I think you are the dumb one to fall for such a poor trick. I saw The Optician turn up ten minutes before you. He's got an admirable sense of loyalty and devotion to rank, so he can be excused for being dumb. But you Ryan Ward, you are meant to be the main man, the number one, and here you are with a gun pressed against your head after falling for a schoolboy trick. How does that make you feel?" Whymark asked, an even bigger smile spreading across his face now, "And you are meant to be the best of ten, and you'll be dead within a few minutes. Am I that good, or are you just dumb?" he asked.

That was actually a good question, Ward thought to himself. But he felt it needed rephrasing.

"Are you that good or are we both that dumb?" he asked.

"Probably both," Whymark replied.

"Tell me something. Why were you so obsessed with The Deniables?"

"What do you mean?"

"I know that when you were Asif Fulken's handler, you had pictures of us all on your wall, like you were hunting us. Obsession is not a healthy trait."

"Maybe I was sizing up the competition?" Whymark replied sarcastically.

"No. It was something else. You weren't worried about competition. But I am curious to know how you knew who we all were?"

"Does that bother you that much? Is it because you were meant to be the smartest ever and you couldn't find out?" Whymark asked, sarcasm running through his voice.

"I was never actually that bothered. I was more than happy working on my own. Inadequacy has never been one of my traits," he replied, equally as sarcastically, "But if you weren't hunting us, why did you go to so much trouble to find out who we all are?" he asked.

"You really have no idea what is going on, do you?" Whymark asked.

Ward ignored him,

"Another question," Ward continued, "One of the people in the photos was a woman, who is she?"

Whymark smiled an even bigger smile. He could feel the anger building up inside of him. Ward was angry that he was sitting there like a lame duck, he had no control over the situation and he was angry that this man had beaten him.

"I want to talk about you Ryan Ward," Whymark replied, "All indicators say that you are a good guy, someone who wins at all costs and someone who The Old Man struggles to control, but because you are so good he lets you roll how you see fit. I'm going to kill you within the next minute or so because you were always the prize scalp. With you out of the way, I will achieve my main objective."

"Which is?" Ward asked.

"You really don't have any idea what is going on," Whymark replied.

The sadness that Ward had felt had now been firmly replaced with anger and frustration.

But he wasn't scared.

Death was always one of those things that he wondered how he would react to. He looked in the mirror and he saw a normal guy holding a gun to his head. No seven foot giant, no evil eyes, just someone who had beaten him fair and square.

"You win Whymark," he said, and he released his hands from the steering wheel and leant back into the driver seat and exhaled loudly.

"You have given up just like that?" Whymark asked.

"I gave up the day I killed for the first time," Ward replied.

"I know that feeling," Whymark replied, "I have to say, I like you. There is something endearing and honest about you. You are a little raw and naïve, but you seem like a fundamentally good guy," he added.

"Then you could always choose not to kill me and we can shake hands and go our separate ways?" Ward said, and then laughed.

"And you promise not to tell anyone that you found me and you will never come looking for me again?"

Ward laughed and at the same time, he felt a calm consume his whole body.

"I've done a lot of good things; I just had to do the bad things well to do those good things. That sits OK with me Whymark. But at least everything I have done has been for other people. What have you got to console yourself with? Because I'll tell you one thing I never knew, when it comes to the end, what path you took on your journey, if you did it for the right or wrong reasons, matters a lot. So I guess I should thank you for teaching me that. The Old Man was right; you turned because you were greedy."

"Do you not find it strange that The Old Man wanted you to kill me without engaging in any dialogue with me first? I mean after all, I'm the bad guy here who has committed a million and one different sins," Whymark asked.

Before Ward could reply, a 7.62mm bullet smashed through the rear driver's side window and then everything went black.

THIRTY EIGHT

West Miami

Nine minutes later, Ward felt a vibration against his upper thigh and opened his eyes. His cell phone was vibrating in his pocket. He closed his eyes tightly and opened them wide again, trying desperately to regain clarity in his vision, which thankfully, returned a few seconds later. He could feel a searing pain in the top of his skull, and he raised his right hand to feel for any injury. His hair was matted with blood, and he lightly ran his finger along his skull where he felt a shallow gauge which ran for about two inches, he quickly worked out that it was a cut that was caused by the base of the gun handle being smashed hard down against his skull. As his senses all came back to normal, he quickly spun around to check the back seat of the car.
It was empty.

He had lost all track of time and had no idea how long he had been unconscious for. He pulled out his phone and saw eight missed calls, six from The Optician, one from The Old Man and one from Eloisa.

He scrolled down the calls and dialled The Optician.

"Finally woken up have you?" he asked as he answered.

"What happened?" Ward asked.

"I saved your ass again, that's what happened"

"Whymark?"

"He got away."

"How?" he asked.

"I only had one shot, I didn't have time to position myself properly, and as soon as I saw your predicament, I had to take it. Those surrounding buildings are too high I couldn't get to an elevated position quickly enough."

"You should have taken him out and not worried about me."

"I may well have hit him; I only had a partial line and could only see his left arm. Check the back seat, is there any blood there?"

Ward turned around and looked at the back seat for signs of blood. All he could see was shattered glass lying across the length of the seat, but no blood.

"No blood," he said, "How long was I out?"

"Ten minutes. Are you injured?"

He raised his hand to the wound on his head. The blood was thickening and starting to congeal, and so he ran his fingers down his neck and wiped the blood, it was starting to dry out.

"I'm OK," he replied.

"That was stupid Ryan. You should know better than to get into a vehicle and not check the back seats. It's a basic error. Have you any idea how lucky you are?" The Optician asked. He heard annoyance in The Optician's voice for the first time ever.

"Where would he go? We have to find him," he said, as he suddenly remembered where he had tossed the keys, and so he opened the door and stepped out of the car and headed towards the pile of old boxes and trash bags.

"He's gone, let it go. We won't find him."

"I'm not letting it go. I want Whymark. He had his chance and he blew it. He lost," he replied, annoyance clearly evident in his own voice now.

"You have no idea how lucky you are. I only checked your GPS on my phone when I stopped for gas. I saw where you were and it didn't make sense, so I came back. I can't believe that you would make such a basic error," The Optician said again.

Ward knew he was right. It was stupid. Worse than stupid, actually it was negligent and inept. He remembered that he was so distracted of thoughts of what he was going to do to Larry Stanyard and Whymark, that he lost sight of the here and now. He would never make the same mistake again, he swore that to himself right there and then.

He found the keys after thirty seconds of sorting through the boxes and trash bags; they had dropped through the litter and onto the floor.

"I guess I should thank you my friend," he said softly as he climbed back into the car, and the enormity of what had just happened, that he had escaped death just because someone needed gas, started to sink in.

"It's my job. You can just make it so much easier in future," The Optician said, the usual calm now fully returned to his voice.

Ward started to recall the conversation that he had with Whymark and so he said,

"Has Whymark ever met you, face to face?"

"No. Why?"

"Because he told me that when he saw you turn up at South 20th Avenue, he knew we had taken the bait. So he knows who you are and what you look like," he replied.

There was silence on the end of the line for a few seconds.

The Optician had in fact been in very close proximity to Whymark over the years, under the guise of being a co-pilot, or run of the mill operative, but he had never given any indication that he knew who he was. This unnerved him, anonymity was his deadliest weapon, and The Old Man had always sworn that no one would know who he was, and even though Tackler had recently been instructed by Ward to establish his name and siblings, he knew that his physical appearance had remained a mystery.

He didn't like anyone knowing what he looked like, it would make his job impossible.

"I don't know how he could know what I look like," he replied.

"He seems to know a lot of stuff that he shouldn't know. How close was he to The Old Man?"

"Not overly. Sure, he was good, maybe the best, but he was different to you."

"What do you mean different?"

"You do what you want, when you want and you get results your way. That means The Old Man trusts you more than any other operative. Whymark was different. He would ask permission from The Old man before taking the step. If he was told no, then he wouldn't do it. I don't think that they had anything but a working relationship at all."

"I need to call The Old Man. I'll make the call and then head back to Mac's warehouse. We still have Stanyard to take down."

"Just don't ever make such a stupid mistake again, OK?" The Optician asked.

"I won't, I guarantee it," he replied, and then the line promptly went dead.

He then dialled Centrepoint.

"Awake at last are you?" he answered.

"You didn't seem that concerned, only one missed call?" he replied.

"The Optician said that you were still alive."

"And he knew that from a partially covered position did he?"

"No. He called me while he was checking your pulse actually," Centrepoint replied, "What did Whymark say?"

"He spent most of the time telling me how great he was and how useless I am to be honest."

"In all fairness, after you had made such a stupid mistake, you probably deserved to hear that. What else?"

"He kept telling me that I had no idea what was really happening."

"What did that mean?"

"No idea. He was probably trying to justify why he turned into a scumbag. People like him are always the same, it's everyone else's fault but their own," he replied, "I want you to use your resources to find him. And when you do, I want you to pass that information over to me because I am going to kill him."

"Based on your last attempt, maybe I should just leave it to The Optician."

"How does Whymark know who he is and what he looks like?"

There was silence on the line for a good few seconds. Ward didn't like it when The Old Man went quiet. It meant he was either receiving bad news, or he had a dilemma that he was trying to calculate the best way to deal with it.

In the end, he simply ignored the question.

"You have to find out what Larry Stanyard knows and what he can tell you, and then finish this Cardona business. Then have a few days off to recover, and I mean days off, not running around everywhere for your lady, then we will talk about Whymark again," he replied.

He suddenly remembered that he had told Eloisa he would be back in New York tonight, and he would hunt some bad guy in Oregon for her and right at that moment, he had an overwhelming urge to call her and hear her voice.

"What I do in my own downtime to relax is my business only," he curtly replied.

"Not really," Centrepoint said, "It's my resources and people that you use when you are on your downtime. Get

Stanyard sorted and then report back to me so that we can put this one to bed."

"OK," was the only reply that he could muster.

"And Ryan?"

"Yes?"

"I'm angry because we came so close to losing you today, and you know what I think of you. I'm annoyed that you were so careless. Don't ever take your eye off the ball again. Understood?"

"Loud and clear," Ward replied and then hung up the phone.

His next call was to Eloisa, but her phone went straight to voicemail, so he hung up without leaving a message. He put the keys in the ignition and started the engine. He carefully turned the car around and drove down between the two high buildings and back onto the main road heading towards the warehouse. He had been driving for five minutes and out of all the things that Whymark had said, one thing kept springing back up in his mind. And so he called Tackler.

"I thought Nicole-Louise was your main woman?" he said sarcastically as he answered the phone.

He still felt a little hazy, and he wasn't in the mood for the usual verbal sparring that took place between them both, but he quickly told himself that none of this was Tackler's fault, and so he played along.

"I'm not after number crunching, I'm after the real smart opinion of someone I trust," he replied.

That did the trick.

"What do you need Ryan?" Tackler asked.

"You remember when I asked you to find out who The Optician was and who his siblings were and you found them for me?"

"You promised me that we would never speak about that again. You know that guy frightens the life out of me," Tackler replied, an urgent tone in his voice.

"Don't worry; I'm not going to ask for the information, just a couple of simple questions."

"OK. I remember."

"Did you find him through his military records?" he asked.

"No. they were wiped clean. I mean completely clean. The Pentagon does not have one record of him," Tackler replied.

"So how?"

"I traced him back through his siblings. Once you told me their birthplace, and I knew how many family members there were, and that they had been placed into the social care system, I worked it back to him," Tackler replied, completely forgetting his genuine fear of The Optician, and revelling in his deductive genius once again.

"And when you found him, did you find a picture of him?"

"No. That was the one weird thing."

"Why weird?"

"Because after I had established who he was, curiosity got the better of me, and I wanted to know what he looked like. So I went back through public records, social system records and school records to find a picture,"

"But you found nothing?"

"No. I found everything."

"I don't understand?"

"I found that someone had gone to great lengths to remove all photographic traces of him. The social care system had no file on him, and his siblings had huge files, they had been moved frequently between foster carers, and at one time there were a number of family pictures included in those files but any reference to him had been removed," Tackler said, clearly happy at how thorough he had been.

"People can do that electronically?"

"No. That was done physically at some point. I hacked into the main server for the Social Care system, and sent an urgent e-mail from the top brass requesting that all data and information included in the siblings files was sent urgently. I then re-routed the e-mails to me. There were lots of pictures, but not one of him."

"And the schools had nothing either?" Ward asked.

"It was the same story. At some point they did, but all the yearbooks and sporting achievement pictures have all gone."

"But there must be hard copies?"

"No doubt there is," Tackler replied, "But I wasn't going to start knocking on doors asking who had a copy of an old yearbook."

"So you are telling me that there were no pictures of him to be found, anywhere?"

"That's exactly what I am telling you. And if I can't find anything, no one else will be able to," Tackler replied. Ward believed him.

"Eloisa has a problem that needs my attention tomorrow. Are you and Nicole-Louise available to help?" he asked.

"Aren't we always?" he replied.
"Yes you are. You are the best Tackler but don't tell Nicole-Louise," he said and hung up the phone.

He wasn't sure why out of all the things that Whymark had said, that his statement that he knew what The Optician looked like bothered him the most, perhaps it was simply that he didn't like not knowing what he looked like himself, and so he decided to put it to the back of his mind for now. He was back outside the warehouse fifteen minutes later, and he parked the car and leant back into the seat and inhaled and exhaled deeply and slowly. Whymark was gone and he had now accepted that. He was sure that The Old Man would find him soon, and then he could show Whymark what a big mistake it was in letting him live. He now re-focussed back on Larry Stanyard. He would know who Whymark was, and what his part in all of this was, and he would torture it out of him until he was convinced that he had told him every single piece of information that he knew. He suddenly felt re-energised and invigorated. He stepped out of the car and walked into the reception area. He was back, focussed and ready to destroy these corrupt drug runners once and for all.

THIRTY NINE

NW 60th Street – Doral – Miami

He walked into the main warehouse and saw McDermott and Lawson loading up the Range Rover.

"Christ, what happened to you?" McDermott asked.

Lawson immediately turned around and looked at Ward and then laughed,

"That's what happens when you put people on sex bans," he said, and then turned back to slide a big black duffel back into the trunk of the car.

Ward laughed,

"Whymark wasn't there," he said.

"So what happened?" Lawson asked, walking towards him, and using his five inches in extra height to look down at the top of Ward's head.

"Whymark played the old rope-a-dope. He conned us."

"How?" Lawson asked.

Ward went onto explain what had happened, not leaving any detail out, recalling the conversation that they had shared in complete detail.

395

"I'm amazed you were that stupid," Lawson said, a comment that had McDermott nodding furiously in agreement.

"I think I get that part now," he replied.

"So how come he knows what The Optician looks like?" McDermott asked.

He found reassurance in the fact that it was not only him that found that the strangest part. If McDermott found it out of place, there was definitely something not sitting right.

"I don't know. That bothered me," he replied.

"What did he mean that you have no idea what is going on?" Lawson asked.

"I assume by that he meant that we were two steps behind him all the time. I'll ask him for clarification just before I kill him the next time that we meet," he replied, "Where are we with Stanyard?"

"Paul and the boys say that the four of them are definitely in the house, and that no one else is coming or going apart from three hookers who have been in there since they arrived there. Access is pretty straightforward, and they won't be able to escape once we have them surrounded," McDermott replied.

"I'm not happy about the hookers, I don't want any more collateral damage on this one, because we've had enough already," Ward said.

"Don't worry, we will keep them well out of harm's way," McDermott replied.

"Go over the plan with me."

"Paul has established that there are two of them in the lounge right at this moment watching sports on TV, and the two others are in the bedrooms. One guy is with one hooker, but they have been doing coke all afternoon and so he won't be much use, and the other guy is in the other room with two hookers," McDermott said.

Ward looked at Lawson and smiled.

"Look as smug as you like Ryan, my ban will be lifted soon and I will be sharing my bed with four women, and more than that, I might even get them to pay me for the pleasure," Lawson said, without a hint of humour in his voice.

"He's serious, isn't he?" McDermott asked.

"Probably," Ward replied.

"We can access the house through the back door," McDermott continued, "Leaving you the front door; no doubt you will be knocking asking for permission to come in as usual. We will secure the men, and separate the women from them, and then once we have established which one is Stanyard, we can kill the other vermin."

"Are the boys looking at all of them right now?" Ward asked.

"I can check, hang on," McDermott replied as he clipped his earpiece back into his ear and mumbled into his microphone.

"They are now," he said, twenty seconds later.

Ward pulled out his phone and called Tackler.

"I've told you all I know," Tackler said as he answered.

"It's nothing to do with that. The four phones you have a lock on, can you call Larry Stanyard's right now please?" he asked.

"OK," Tackler replied and Ward hung up the phone.

"Tackler is going to call Stanyard, tell Paul and the boys whoever answers the phone is Stanyard," he said to McDermott.
After speaking into his microphone, McDermott said, "Just waiting for Tackler."
Twenty seconds after that, he said,
"He's the guy with the two hookers in his bed."
Lawson rolled his eyes, and they both laughed. He looked at his watch; it was just after 4:00pm.
"How long will it take to get there?" he asked McDermott.
"Forty minutes tops," McDermott replied.
"Let's go now then and take a leisurely drive, tell Paul we are on our way."
McDermott nodded.
"Here put this on," Lawson said to Ward, tossing him a clean black tee shirt. Ward caught it in his right hand and peeled off the blood stained shirt he was wearing.
"Fringe, Walsh, you two come with us. Wallace, you stay here and keep an eye on the satellite to make sure we don't get any unwanted visitors turning up," McDermott shouted across the warehouse floor and one minute later, they were driving out of the warehouse.

1328 South 20th Avenue – Hollywood – Miami

The drive took exactly fifty minutes, as the evening rush hour traffic was just starting to build up, and they arrived at their destination at one minute to five. They drove down South 20th Avenue and passed the house.

398

Like the CIA safe house on Southwest 10th Street West, it wasn't a house, it was more a chalet. Only this one wasn't as well kept. It had two small lawns about ten feet wide, either side of a grey pathway that led to the front door. There were a couple of sparse trees that were meant to be a garden feature at the front of the lawn, and the awning over the front entrance was skewed, giving the whole chalet an unkempt and uncared for look. It looked exactly like you would expect a building being used by corrupt D.E.A. agents for their deviant pleasure to look.

They parked thirty yards up the road, there was no need to do another drive past the chalet, Paul was already there doing the recon work, and both Ward and Lawson screwed their silencers onto their handguns. McDermott, Fringe & Walsh stepped to the back of the vehicle, and each took out a silenced machine gun from the black duffel bag.

Ward looked at his watch.

It was now one minute past five.

"Let's go," he said and headed back up the street towards the chalet.

"Move on my go," McDermott said into his microphone.

"Understood," Paul replied.

They reached the front lawn Ward and Lawson headed down the pathway towards the front door with McDermott three steps behind them. Fringe jogged to the left hand side of the chalet and jumped over the flimsy brown fencing adjacent to the side of the house, while Walsh walked through the gap in the fencing on the right.

With Paul and the team at the rear of the chalet, the whole building was now completely covered.
They reached the front door and Ward said to McDermott,
"As soon as that door opens, go."
McDermott nodded.
"Can I knock for once?" Lawson asked in a deliberately childish voice, "Four knocks, right?"
Ward smiled.
Humour was a crucial part of managing the world that they lived in, and Lawson understood that better than anyone.
"Go for it," he replied.
Lawson stepped up to the door and knocked four times, each knock close to the last.
They waited for ten seconds and then they heard someone removing a security chain from behind the door and the moment that the door started to open, McDermott said into his microphone,
"Go!"

At the rear of the house, Paul heard the order in his ear and raised his right foot and smashed the heel of his boot just below the handle of the flimsy back door. The wood splintered and the door flew open. As soon as his right foot had touched the ground again, his left leg was stepping forward and he strode into the kitchen with his silenced machine gun held firmly into his midriff. Wired and Walsh followed him, no more than three steps behind, and Paul crossed the kitchen and came to the door. He grabbed the handle and swung the door open, following the arch to the left as the door opened, moving out of the way so that Walsh had a clear view of the hallway.

"Clear," Walsh said, and Wired stepped through into the hallway with the other two no more than three steps behind.

In three seconds, the line of entry had gone from Paul, Walsh and Wired, to Wired, Walsh and Paul. They headed towards the lounge as it was the nearest door to them on the right.

The door was open.

Wired spun around into the opening and saw a guy in the process of pulling himself up from the sofa, reaching for a handgun that was on the table in front of him. The guys' eyes widened as he looked at him, and he stopped immediately in mid-movement as Walsh appeared in the doorway with his gun pointing directly at his head. In almost slow motion, the guy sat back down and put his hands on top of his head. Paul tapped Walsh on the shoulder, and they moved up the hallway to the next door, which was on the left, and was the room where Stanyard was with the two hookers, leaving Wired to guard the guy in the lounge.

When they reached the door, without any hesitation, Paul yanked on the door handle and swung it inwards, allowing Walsh to fill the doorway, the barrel of his machine gun being the only object that entered the room.

Larry Stanyard was a very effective agent in his prime. But his prime had long gone. He was overweight, and his reactions had been dulled a long time ago due to his liking for drugs and women. At one time, he had the reflexes of a panther and his speed of movement had reflected that.

But all he was capable of now was trying to clamber across the bed and over a small, thin woman, to reach for his gun on the bedside table. As soon as Paul stepped into view behind Walsh, Stanyard shouted,

"OK!" and moved his bulk back against the headboard and put his hands on his head.

Paul immediately stepped up to the next door, which was on the right hand side of the hallway and burst through the door with his finger primed on the trigger of his machine gun.

There was a guy and a woman lying naked on the bed and they were just coming around, having been woken from their drug induced sleep by the noise of the teams' entry.

The woman screamed and Paul said,

"One more noise and you are dead," the woman clasped her hand over her mouth.

Paul simply said,

"Three targets secure," just as Lawson, Ward and McDermott were stepping over the body of the guy who had opened the front door.

The guy who had opened the front door was alert. When he heard the knock on the door, he noted that it sounded like a non-threatening knock, but he knew that they weren't due any visitors. His name was Robert Simon and he had worked for the D.E.A. for eleven years. He had originally wanted a career in the Special Forces, but a knee injury had scuppered that dream, although in his mind, he was kind of a Special Forces operative through the work he did.

The reality is there is a very big difference between operatives of most government agencies, and the men who make up the Special Forces.

He had picked up his handgun as he went to answer the door and clicked the safety off as he removed the security chain, holding the gun in his left hand so that he could fire if he saw a threatening situation.

Lawson on the other side of the door wasn't waiting to see 'If' he saw a threatening situation, he was expecting it.

That was the very big difference between a D.E.A operative and an ex SAS soldier.

As Simon opened the door about eight inches, Lawson delivered a kick to the area just above the door handle that had all of his two hundred and forty pounds of muscle behind it.

The door shot open, and the edge smashed into Simon's face, and the force of the impact sent him falling backwards, as the door swung fully open, Lawson fired two shots into Simon's chest he was dead before he hit the floor. Lawson stepped forwards, Ward and McDermott followed him in, stepping over Simon's body and McDermott closed the door.

Ward saw McDermott listening to his earpiece and he then said,

"They have everyone secure," and then he said, "Fringe, Walsh, guard the front of the house and watch for any visitors."

Ward looked along the hallway and he saw, Walsh, Wired and Paul standing outside the doorways with their machine guns pointing through the openings. He walked down the hallway and looked inside without speaking and then after he had looked over Wired's shoulder, who was standing in the doorway at the end of the hallway, he walked back and said to Paul,

"Get the women dressed and bring the men to the lounge and make sure they bring their wallets and phones. Then get the women moved to one of the bedrooms until we have done, they don't need to be witness to anything."

He watched as instructions were given, and a minute later, two women came out of a room and walked up to where Paul was standing and walked into the room. Ten seconds after that, two guys came out of the two bedrooms. Ward knew instantly that Stanyard was the overweight looking guy.

Stanyard glanced along the hallway and made eye contact with Ward, he then stepped into the lounge. The other guy looked like he was struggling to wake up and compute what was happening and Ward instantly had another idea.

These guys had no idea who the people who had burst into their house were.

So he decided to let them tell him who they thought they were.

FORTY

1328 South 20ᵗʰ Avenue – Hollywood – Miami

The three guys were forced to sit on the sofa after they had placed their wallets and phones on the table in the centre of the room.

Stanyard sat in the middle and the other two guys sat either side of him.

"They look like naughty boys who've just been caught stealing to me," Lawson said.

"Which they have," Ward replied.

The three men stared at them, and then glanced at each other. Ward could see that they were confused by the British accents, and so he picked that moment to create as much uncertainty in their minds as he could.

"We are mercenaries," he said to no one in particular, a comment that was technically mostly true with McDermott's team present.

"Who is the dead guy in the hall? Stanyard, Swan, Keane or Simon?" he asked.

None of the guys spoke.

He raised his gun and pointed it at the guy to Stanyard's right, and fired a shot into his right foot. The guy screamed as the bullet smashed through the fragile bones, and he lunged forward, grabbing his foot with both hands.

Lawson stepped into him and shoved him hard on the shoulder so that he was leaning against the back of the sofa,

"It's only a scratch," he said with contempt in his voice.

"Who's the dead guy in the hall?" Ward asked again, ensuring he had a deliberate and calm tone to his voice.

"His name's Rob Simon," the guy with the shattered foot replied through gritted teeth.

Before he could respond, one of the cell phones on the table started vibrating. Ward picked the phone up.

"Whose phone is this?" he asked calmly.

"It's mine," Stanyard said.

Ward tossed it to him,

"Answer it," he demanded.

Stanyard pressed answer and put the phone to his ear.

"I didn't authorise that," Stanyard said, a frown creeping over his face, "No, that shouldn't have happened. You have to get that back," he said, his voice sounding panicked and slightly desperate.

"Hang up," Ward demanded as he pointed his gun directly at Stanyard's face.

Stanyard hung up.

"That was the bank I take it," he asked.

Stanyard didn't reply but Ward could see him visibly trying to piece everything together but not finding the answer.

"You must be Stanyard?" he asked.

Stanyard nodded.

"Who's he?" he asked, pointing to the guy with the shattered foot.

"He's Swan," Stanyard replied.

Ward raised his gun, aimed it at Swan and fired three shots into his face.

The bullets smashed into Swan, and ripped his face clean off, the bone with attached flesh spraying forward, and the force of the bullets knocked him sideways, and he fell off of the sofa and onto the floor.

Stanyard momentarily frozen, then shifted all of his bodyweight to his left, almost leaning on top of the guy next to him.

"So you must be Keane?" Ward asked the guy that was now pushing Stanyard's weight off of him.

The guy nodded.

"We are going to play a game, OK?" he asked them both.

They both nodded.

"You are going to tell me who we are," he said, "You first," he added, pointing to Keane.

"Are you Cardona's men?" Keane said eagerly.

Ward shook his head.

"I'm really disappointed in you Keane," he said, "He is milking you boys and you are doing all the work and still you are trying to cover his ass," he added, raising his gun and pointing it at Keane's face as he spoke.

"Then you are Willard's men?" Keane said, even more eagerly this time.

"Now we are getting somewhere," Lawson interrupted, even though he had no idea who Willard was.

"Tell me from the beginning and you might live, you will be penniless, but you might live," he said to Keane. "I've never dealt with Willard, only he has," Keane said, using his thumb to point at Stanyard.

"I want your version," he demanded.

"I don't know much."

"You don't even know what he does?"

"Well of course I do. Everyone knows that he is the Chief Intelligence Research Specialist in Miami, but I don't know how he organises and moves things for us, that comes through him." Keane replied, thumb pointing at Stanyard again.

"That's all you have to offer in an attempt to save your life?" Ward asked calmly.

"I know that he gives him the money to share out," Keane replied desperately, by now, trying to distance himself from what they had been doing, and attempting to place the blame firmly at Stanyard's feet.

"SHUT UP SHAUN! Not another word," Stanyard shouted.

Ward now understood. Stanyard was the second in command, the feet on the ground, the guy who did all the dirty work, and right then he was pretty convinced that Keane was giving up their one bargaining chip. He moved over to Lawson and whispered in his ear,

"Go outside and call Tackler. Ask him to find out who this Willard guy is, where he is now, and to get Nicole-Louise to go through his bank accounts and take whatever he has. And tell them to be quick, I want this ended today."

Lawson looked at Stanyard and smiled,

"That's a good idea," he said, "My favourite form of torture," he added, and then turned and left the room. The fear washed over the faces of both Stanyard and Keane.

"One last question for you Keane," Ward said, trying to offer a reassuring smile as he spoke, "Cardona is dead, so there will be no come back on you, but the guy he was holding, the CIA guy, what is his part in it?" he asked.

Keane looked completely blank.

And worryingly, so did Stanyard.

"I don't know about any CIA guy," Keane replied, "We gathered the intelligence for Willard, we built up the relationship with Cardona, and then he took the credit for all the busts that Cardona was tipping us off on. Everyone knew that Cardona was our snitch, it is all logged and recorded officially," he added, his thumb going into overdrive by now.

"Who collected all of the information about the chemists, their families and so on?" Ward asked.

"Swan did," Keane replied, glancing at the dead body of his former colleague on the floor.

Ward raised his gun and shot Keane three times in the chest. He preferred the face shot, but he had already noticed that he had blood on his boots and he didn't fancy getting covered in any more.

Keane's body slumped back, the force of the bullets jerking his head back and he slumped to the side of the sofa but remained in the seated position.

"I will testify," Stanyard said quickly, "I have other information that will be worth its weight in gold to both Willard or Cardona or whoever you work for," he added urgently.

"What I don't get," Ward said, "Is how an Intelligence Researcher can be the one who gives you orders. You are the big chief down here, the big boss and you way out rank him, so how did that happen?"

"Four years ago we were involved in an operation and temptation got in the way. We creamed some cash off, Willard had set up cameras that we were unaware of and he had us over a barrel. We had no choice after that. Prior to that, I had given sixteen years unblemished service. It's not easy doing undercover work like we do, it's impossible not to get hooked up in the greed and high living of it," Stanyard replied.

"Everyone has a choice," Ward replied.

"Not always."

"It's fine that you stitch up the bad guys, it's even fine that you steal from them in my eyes, but you crossed a line when you put innocent people at risk," he said, pulling a chair up from the table where the phones and wallets were and sat down, two feet away from Stanyard, "Those chemists have lost family members. They had to watch while Cardona did unspeakable things to the people they loved. Do you think that is fair?"

Stanyard did not reply.

"And what impact do you think that the creation of that drug would have on the country? You must have cared about stopping those types of people from producing narcotics at some point, because you said yourself that you had sixteen years of honest service. So you got greedy and you made the choice to look after yourself before anyone else."

"It wasn't like that. It just sort of happened," Stanyard protested.

"It's always like that. With people like you, it always comes down to greed and resentment."

"Resentment?"

"Sure. You look at people like Cardona with their mansions and their millions, and you see the wealth and women that they accumulate, and you resent it. You resent the fact that they have everything that you want but you can't get it. But that always comes at a price. You sacrifice your own morals and decency to become like them. Not only have four innocent people died today, how many deaths do you think that you are directly responsible for over the time that you have been covering Cardona's ass?" he asked.

Stanyard said nothing.

"Do you have a family?"

Stanyard still said nothing.

"Well if you aren't going to converse with me and give me anything else to help me with, then I may as well kill you now," he said as he raised his gun.

"No, wait!" Stanyard said, raising his hands to protect his face, "There is something. Something Willard said to me."

"What did he say?"

"He said that even if this thing with Cardona went south, there were people who would be able to protect us, people much higher than us."

"What people?"

"I don't know. But I sometimes got the feeling that Willard was in the pocket of someone else too," Stanyard replied.

Ward thought about this for a moment. He was probably telling the truth. Such was the corruption that ran

411

through the government from top to bottom, that everyone was in it for themselves and taking what they could. The smart people did it legally though, and tended to be at the very top of the Senate.

He didn't want to keep chasing after the man at the top, mainly because he knew that it would take forever, as there was always someone higher up in government who had someone below them doing the dirty work, but also because he wanted to get home to New York to see Eloisa, and now he was pissed because Stanyard had told him about Willard, and he would have to take care of him before he could wrap this whole saga up.

"For the innocent people," he said, and he raised his gun and fired three shots into Stanyard's chest from close range.

The bullets ripped through his flimsy tee shirt and a hole the size of a golf ball appeared instantly. Stanyard slumped back and then forwards, and then he fell face first onto the floor.

Ward stood up and looked at McDermott.

"Can you call The Old Man and get a clean-up crew here, and I'll see where Lawson is with this Willard guy. Get one of the boys to give the hookers all the money from the wallets, the men won't need it, and then meet me outside in five."

McDermott nodded.

Ward walked out of the house and down the pathway and headed towards the car, where Lawson was leaning against the side of the hood.

"Willard?"

"Tackler is sending me the address now, but he says finding the money will take a little longer. He says his first name is Roy and here is his address," Lawson replied, turning his phone for Ward to see an address, "I've checked it against my GPS and it is only twenty minutes away," he added.

"Who do you think is pulling Willard's strings?" Ward asked.

"Does it matter?" Lawson replied, "Because there will be someone pulling his strings, and then we find who that person is, and there will be someone pulling his strings, and it goes on and on. Sometimes we have to deal with what is in front of us and then go home to celebrate."

"That's exactly what I was thinking," Ward replied.

"But you aren't on a sex ban, are you?" Lawson said with a smile.

Ward smiled back.

"One more visit and then I will get us back to New York and you can do what you need to do," he said.

"This Whymark guy," Lawson said, apparently becoming bored with the sex ban jokes now, "I still don't get where he fits in. I mean, no one seems to know, and I know that you are a big fan of making speeches before you kill people, but why didn't he just shoot you when he had you in an isolated place?"

"I guess that he is much more similar to me than I realise. To some of us it's important to explain to someone the error of their ways."

Lawson shrugged,

"If you say so," he said.

McDermott came walking towards the car, followed by Paul and the rest of the team.

"We are parked around the corner," Paul said, "Are we meeting back at the warehouse?"

"You take Wired, Fuller, Fringe and Walsh back. The rest of us will go and visit this Willard guy and end this now," Ward replied.

"Where is he?" McDermott asked.

"He's over in Davie, on Southwest 42nd," Lawson replied.

The three of them climbed into the Range Rover.

"How are we going to play this one?" McDermott asked.

"We are literally going to walk in, kill him, and then walk out and then we can all go home," Ward replied.

McDermott put the address into the cars GPS system and then pulled away.

Ward looked out of the window as the sun was starting to set, and he couldn't wait to get back to New York to see Eloisa.

He felt tired, the last couple of days had been relentless, and he just wanted to switch off and be normal, if only for a few hours.

Being Ryan Ward was becoming more and more exhausting with each passing day.

FORTY ONE

7591 Southwest 42nd CT – Davie – Miami

The evening traffic was heavy, and they seemed to spend as much time stationary as they did moving. Lawson had received an e-mail from Tackler with a picture of Willard's driving licence, and he leant across the passenger seat to show Ward the picture.

"He looks like a weasel," Ward said.

"Lucky him," Lawson replied, "Do you know, weasel's can have sex for seven hours at a time?"

"Really?" McDermott asked.

"No, not really," Lawson replied, "But I bet they have it more than I have lately," he added.

They all laughed loudly.

As the traffic ground to a halt yet again, Ward said, "Can either of you remember the last time you had a vacation?"

"What, you mean an actual organised vacation or a few days off from killing people?" McDermott asked in all seriousness.

"An organised vacation?"

"When Paul was four," McDermott said, "Me and his mum took him to Rio. It was our belated honeymoon."

"Mike?" Ward asked Lawson.

"Sure I can. Eight months ago I hired a yacht of the coast of Ibiza, and just relaxed for ten whole days," Lawson replied.

"Were you on your own?" McDermott enquired.

"No. I had Chloe, Giselle and Annabel with me."

"How does that work?" McDermott asked, "I mean, don't these women ever get jealous of each other?"

Lawson laughed,

"God Mac, for one of the best killing machines that I have ever seen, you know nothing about women at all," he said.

"Do you want to enlighten us?" Ward asked sarcastically.

"Do you want to pay me to?" Lawson quipped, and they all laughed again.

They finally broke free of the extensive traffic and they were turning onto Southwest 42nd CT a few minutes later.

"Thirty seven minutes that took," McDermott said with a sigh.

They drove down 42nd, and slowed down for the junction as they reached number 7591, glancing casually to the right as they stopped.

7591 was a reasonably well presented bungalow, it was more than a chalet, and it was situated on the corner, adjacent to Kirkland Road.

The walls of the bungalow were painted beige and they looked clean. A recently renovated grey, tiled roof gave the bungalow a just purchased look to it. There were neatly trimmed lawns to the front and side of the bungalow, and a neatly paved driveway, in grey pavers, matching the new roof. A black SUV was parked on the drive.

Ward pulled out his phone and dialled Centrepoint.

"Stanyard is being removed as we speak," he said as he answered.

"I need another crew in ten minutes time and for you to smooth things over with the D.E.A." Ward said.

"Already done, I've just got off the phone to their senior director explaining about Stanyard and his team. I warned him against the bad press that he was likely to receive if he didn't bury it," The Old Man replied, sounding rather pleased with himself.

"I meant you will need to smooth things over with them after I kill their Senior Intelligence Researcher here in Miami."

"What's his name?" The Old Man asked, not remotely fazed by the latest news.

"Roy Willard."

"Where are you?"

"At his house."

"His address?" Centrepoint asked.

"7591 Southwest 42nd, Davie."

"How is he involved?"

"He was the one pulling Stanyard's strings. There's probably someone above him, but I doubt you are too concerned about that. No doubt you will do your own digging and find whoever it is, and put them firmly in your pocket for use at a later date," Ward replied bluntly.

"It's how it works Ryan. I have never corrupted the government, they do that all off their own back, I just use it for our bigger picture and greater good."

Ward was not in the mood today for one of his long discussions on corruption and the unfairness of it all, he genuinely felt too tired.

"I know you do and today, that sits OK with me," he replied.

"That's it? No lecture?"

"Not today," he said, "But as soon as we are done here I want the jet ready to take me and Lawson back to New York in an hours' time."

"It will be ready and waiting."

He hung up the phone.

"Let's get this over and done with. Park a little up from his house" he said to McDermott as they turned off of Kirkland Road and back onto Southwest 42nd.

McDermott pulled the car to a stop and all three of them climbed out.

"We are doing this for the chemists and their families not forgetting Harris, OK?" he said, as he headed towards Willard's bungalow.

Both Lawson and McDermott nodded but didn't speak. They followed the driveway until it thinned and turned into a pathway that led directly to the front door.

"You can knock again Mike, you do it so gracefully," Ward said, as he pulled his Glock out, the silencer still securely fixed to the barrel.

"Is that like a promotion?" Lawson asked, attempting to look really pleased with his self.

Both Ward and McDermott smiled broadly.

He knocked on the door five times.

Ward looked at him and frowned.

"I'm pushing myself," Lawson protested.

A few seconds later the door opened and a tall, muscular South American looking guy wearing shorts and a tee shirt, stood back when he saw the gun that Ward was holding.

Without any hesitation, Lawson stepped forward and planted a solid right handed jab into the centre of the guys face, and he collapsed to the floor, his brain depriving his body of the signals required to keep a person upright.

"Who the hell is he?" McDermott asked, as he stepped into the house after Lawson and Ward and shut the front door.

"Maybe he's one of Cardona's men?" Ward said.

Just then, a tall wiry guy appeared from a room on the right.

All three of them swung their guns around and pointed them at the guy.

It was Roy Willard.

He instantly raised his hands above his head.

"Please, don't hurt me," he said.

"Who's he?" Ward said, pointing to the guy who was now unconscious on the floor.

"That's Chico," Willard replied.

"But who is he?"

"He's my partner and housekeeper."

"Ooops!" Lawson said.

McDermott smiled.

"Well he is still alive so don't panic," Lawson said, trying his best to reassure himself rather than anyone else.

"Who are you? I haven't done anything. Take what you want but please, don't hurt me," Willard pleaded, and his eyes started to fill with tears.

"Are you crying?" Lawson asked, highly amused by how feeble, pathetic and weak Willard really was.

"Please, don't hurt me," he pleaded.

"Stanyard and his team are dead," Ward said.

"How?" Willard said.

"We killed him you douche. Obviously we are here to kill you," he replied in a bemused tone, "That's why we have guns," he added.

"Please. Don't hurt me, I'll tell you everything."

"We know everything already," Ward replied.

"You don't know who my boss is. Please, I beg you, I won't say anything," Willard pleaded.

The three of them stood there looking at him as he lowered one hand and squeezed his groin area. They watched as a large damp patch appeared on his pants.

"Seriously, what's wrong with you?" Lawson asked

"I don't care who your boss is. You were responsible for the deaths that the employee's and the families of Newton Pharmaceuticals suffered, and nothing you can say will justify or excuse that," Ward said calmly, "There is one thing that might help you though," he added.

"What? I'll give you money," Willard begged.

"We are going to take your money anyway."

"I'll tell you anything."

"I just want to know one thing," Ward said, "What was Gill Whymark's role in this?" he asked.

"Who's Gill Whymark?" Willard asked, looking totally confused.

Ward raised his gun and shot Willard in the stomach. He screamed and fell to the floor, his hand pawing at the wound. He stepped forward and leant over him.

"Four people died because of your greed," he said, and then proceeded to fire three further shots into Willard. The first two bullets hitting him in the chest, and the last one into his face as he fell backwards onto the floor. By the time he had hit the floor, he was unrecognisable.

"I hope Chico is alright," Lawson said, as he stepped over him and opened the door, "I'm sure the clean-up crew will convince him that none of this ever happened."

The three of them walked slowly back up the driveway and turned back onto the street, all without speaking. Ward pulled out his phone and called The Old Man.

"Problem?" he asked as he answered.

"There is some guy called Chico in Willard's house who is an innocent party in this. He has seen us all so you need to make sure that he is OK, and then somehow convince him that none of this ever happened."

"Is this Chico alive?"

"Yes. Lawson punched him that was all."

"OK. I'll fix it," Centrepoint replied, "And Ryan?"

"What?"

"You've done a great job here, stopping the production of that drug was a massive thing and not to be underestimated. Try not to run around for your good lady too much and try and rest," he said.

"There's one thing that I want."

"Name it."

"We have a few million dollars that we took from Stanyard. Can we use it to buy Lawson a place in New

York, because I can't stand the thought of him having to share with three women that he doesn't really like," he said.

"It was more than a few million, it was just over six, and because you asked nicely, he can keep it, but only to buy a property," The Old Man replied

"Make sure the jet is ready," Ward said, and hung up the phone.

"Wow!" Lawson said from the back seat, "My very own bachelor pad paid for by the U.S. government. Six million dollars will buy a lot of floor space."

"It's two million, not six. The other four will be going to the families who have lost someone because of Cardona," Ward replied.

"You are forgetting the money that Tackler was going to find and take from Willard," Lawson said, "Can that go to my real estate fund as well?" he added and nudged Ward on the shoulder.

"You'd best let him have it Ryan, just to shut him up," McDermott said.

"Perhaps you are right," Ward replied.

"My lips are now sealed," Lawson said as he mimed zipping his mouth up, before he leant back into his seat.

"Thank god for that," both Ward and McDermott said at the same time.

They drove slowly back to the warehouse in Doral. The traffic was even worse on the way back than it had been coming over to Willard's place but now, there was calm, and a feeling of satisfaction that washed over the three of them. Yet another mission had been completed with resounding success. The collateral damage that was suffered was the only downside to the events, but they all knew that was something out of their control as it had occurred before they had established where Cardona was holed up. The killing of Dr Robert Anderton was something that Ward wasn't happy with, but he had decided to keep it from Lawson and McDermott because they didn't need to know. The downside to everything was that he knew without doubt that another Cartel would already be stepping into Cardona's shoes, so the real issue, the supply of narcotics and the corruption within the D.E.A. would continue as normal. The biggest enemy that the U.S. and U.K governments faced was the greed and corruption of the people that had been elected into power. Until the day came when the people at the top were held to account or eliminated, then it will continue as it was. Sure, Ward and people like McDermott and Lawson could stem the tide for a while, but the tide always turned back. A part of him wished that people knew how the world really operated, rather than just spoke of conspiracies and corruption, without actually having any proof, and it suddenly dawned on him that he was not helping the common man by burying this corruption and deceit under a pile of bodies. He was as guilty as hiding the truth as the criminals who controlled everything that made the world go around. He looked across at McDermott who was focussing on the road with the steely look that he applied to everything he did, and then he turned and looked at Lawson who was leant back into the comfortable seats at the rear of the Range Rover with his eyes shut. No doubt he was dreaming about God knows how many women Ward thought to himself and he smiled.

They had done the best that they could have done with the information that they had, and even if it was only temporary, they had put a dent in the evil machine that rolled on.

He closed his eyes himself and thought of Eloisa and then opened them quickly. He pulled out his phone and wrote, 'I'll be home by eleven' and pressed send. Just thirty seconds later he got a reply saying, 'I'll be waiting. I can't wait to see you. I love you'.

He closed his eyes again.

Far from being bad, things were very, very good in his world.

FORTY TWO

NW 60th Street – Doral – Miami

They arrived back at the warehouse fifty minutes after leaving Willard's place. Paul and the others were already packing up.

"Where are you planning on taking them to relax?" Ward asked McDermott.

"Perhaps it would be easier for you to tell me where The Old Man will have you running around next, so I have a rough idea where to be?" McDermott replied, "And maybe you need to sound him out about the crooks who live in The Bahamas or some other exotic place," he added.

He watched as McDermott's team scurried around the warehouse, packing weapons into cases before placing them back behind the fake partition wall, disconnecting communications equipment and securing the building.

Each one of them had a clear task, probably the same task that they had at every single warehouse that McDermott owned, and as he stood watching them, he smiled at just how incredibly organised they were.

"Do you ever get tired Mac?" he asked McDermott.

McDermott studied him for a few moments and then said, "Follow me," and he headed off towards the reception area.

He followed him through the door that led into the empty reception area and McDermott closed the door.

"What's wrong?" he asked.

"What do you mean?" Ward replied.

McDermott looked at him, up and down for a few moments and then said,

"It's Whymark, isn't it?"

Ward was unsure what he meant and so he just shrugged.

"You aren't tired Ryan, you came close to death for the first time in your life, and now you are blaming it on tiredness, rather than facing up to the fact that you were scared," McDermott continued.

"I wasn't scared Mac. I felt more sadness."

"Trust me, you were scared," McDermott replied, "Fear manifests itself in a number of ways, just because you never felt the sickness in the pit of your stomach, or you never started shaking in a physical show of fear, it doesn't not mean that you were not scared."

"But I genuinely didn't feel scared," he declared again.

"Really?" he asked, "So you can't see that all of this talk of tiredness, and the impatience that you have displayed since you got back from your confrontation with Whymark, particularly how impatient and unprofessional you were with Willard, is actually you just trying to run away from that fear and get home where you feel safe?"

"Unprofessional?"

"Two days ago, you would not have just settled at putting him out of action. I know you Ryan, better than you think I do, and you are normally like a dog with a bone. You wouldn't just step away when something was half finished," McDermott replied.

"So you are saying I have got some sort of PTSD?"

"No."

"Then what are you saying?"

"I'm saying that if you can't admit to yourself that you were scared then you are dumb," McDermott replied.

"It's not a macho thing Mac. I specifically looked for what I was feeling when he had that gun to my head, and all I thought about was my mom, and Eloisa, and how I felt sad that I would never see them again."

McDermott smiled at him.

"I've been scared only twice in my life, both times with a gun pointing at me, and a twitchy finger on the trigger. I wasn't scared about the pain of the bullet hitting me or slowly bleeding to death, I was scared that I would never hold Paul in my arms again, and that his mom would struggle raising him alone. I was scared that I would never see Paul to grow up to be a man, and most of all; I was scared that I would never hear his voice again. It was the most scared that I had ever felt in my life, and I never, ever want to feel like that again. That's why I am so thorough and alert all of the time. I never want to feel that I am losing the one thing that matters to me more than anything ever again," he said, putting his hand on Ward's shoulder as he spoke.

Ward looked at the floor.

"And yes, when the realisation of how close I came to never seeing him again hit me, I did cry. I needed to cry when I was alone. I had to get it out of my system," McDermott said.

Ward forced a smile at him,

"So, how do I pick myself up?" he asked.

"Easy. You go home and see Eloisa and then you call your mom. Then you tell yourself that you aren't invincible after all. You remind yourself that behind every door you kick down, and every car you get into, someone will be waiting to kill you. Then you will increase your chances of living longer at least tenfold," McDermott replied.

It was like someone had hit a light switch. Everything that McDermott said had been right, and he immediately felt more energetic and aware and he cursed himself for being so flippant and arrogant with Willard. But he also felt like the weight of the world had been removed from his shoulders and back to how he always felt.

"You are one of the few true friends that I have in this world Mac," he said, and he leant in and wrapped his arms around McDermott's granite-like frame and hugged him.

"I'm more your big brother and I have to look after you because if anything ever happens to me, you will have to be Paul's big brother," he said, "And for God's sake, don't ever put Lawson on a sex ban again."

Ward laughed,

"I guess I had better formally lift his sex ban now then."

"Can you just wait until you are away from me and the boys, there's no saying what he will do once you release him from his chastity," McDermott said.

They both laughed and McDermott led the way back into the warehouse.

"Ryan, can you do something with Mike," Paul said as they walked over towards them all, "He's hitting on us all, and Fuller is getting worried."

Fuller looked over at them both, jumped up onto the battered old armchair and said,

"Mikey will take whatever he can, he can't escape his imposed sex ban, he's overrun with sexual frustration, it's time to remove this cruel limitation. New York awaits, the women are calling, but Ryan is cruel, he's deliberately stalling, so do the right thing and set him free and remove his lust away from me."

Everyone in the warehouse burst out laughing, loudly. Fuller jumped from the armchair and exchanged immediate high fives with Wired and Wallace. Lawson fell to his knees and assumed the preying position and all eyes turned to Ward.

"Mike Lawson, I hereby set you free," Ward said and everyone cheered.

Ward and Lawson spent the next couple of minutes saying their individual goodbyes, shaking hands and hugging each of the team individually. There was a trust between them all that was never spoken about, but defined them as a group and sealed them as an unbreakable team. Then they walked out of the warehouse and got into the Ford Taurus that was outside. It was the same car that Harris had collected them in when they had first turned up in Miami. The Old Man had it collected from Hilary Whelan's place after the clean-up.

"Harris seemed like a good guy," Lawson said as he put the car in drive and started the short journey to the airport.

"He was," Ward replied.

Lawson was quiet for a moment and then said.

"If I say something, don't take it the wrong way."

Ward looked at him, he looked serious. Lawson never looked serious.

"I'll try not to."

"You've threatened to shoot me before, only in jest I know but all the same, I know you are capable of it. Agreed?" Lawson asked.

"What's your point Mike?"

"My point is, if you ever do anything as stupid as get in a car without checking behind you ever again, I will beat the shit out of you until you beg me to stop. Understood?"

Ward was briefly taken aback by Lawson's tone. But then he realised that it was said because he cared for him so deeply. They had a bond that most men can't understand. Trusting someone with your life created that bond. He knew that Lawson was saying it to remind him that nothing can be left to chance, but also because Lawson was terrified of anything happening to Ward as a friend. He also knew without a doubt that in a fist fight against Lawson, he would have no chance. He was actually the toughest guy that he had ever known in his life.

"Understood," he said and drew a finishing line under the discussion with his response.

Lawson nodded.

Miami International Airport – Florida

Fifteen minutes later they were pulling the car to a stop on the tarmac, fifty feet away from the Lear Jet. The engines were warming up and everything looked good to go.

In just over three hours he would be back in New York. He took out his cell phone and called Eloisa but there was no answer and it went straight to voicemail. He typed out a text that said, 'Home by 11' and pressed send. He felt good. He had learned a lot from the events of the last two days, and he felt he was a better operative and a better person for it. He was still annoyed about the way he handled Willard, but he knew that he now had three hours to wash it all from his mind.

They stepped out of the car and headed towards the steps of the plane.

They reached the bottom of the steps and Lawson stopped dead in his tracks,

"You've got to be kidding me," he said.

Ward looked up, and waiting to greet them at the entrance to the jet was a smartly dressed flight attendant, immaculately presented and wearing a smile that was excessively forced.

He was male.

They climbed up the steps and the attendant said,

"Good evening gentlemen, I'm Adam and I am here to look after you until we land at JFK."

Ward shook his hand warmly, and felt a big smile spreading across his face.

Adam shook Ward's hand warmly and then extended it to Lawson.

"Whatever," Lawson said as he stepped past him and walked onto the plane.

"You did that on purpose, didn't you?" he said to Ward, who by now was laughing.

"Honestly, I didn't. It never even entered my head. I wish it had, but it must just be the way the rota's work," he replied in between laughs.

Lawson slumped down into the chair, clearly sulking and Ward sat opposite him.

He looked up the hull of the plane and could see the pilot and co-pilot carrying out their last minute checks and then watched Adam eloquently close the door.

Lawson pulled out his cell phone and started messaging someone. Ward thought it was best not to tease him anymore, he looked genuinely angry.

"I am going to need your help over the next couple of days," he said to Lawson, "Eloisa has all the information about this guy in Oregon who….."

"I'm not talking to you," Lawson replied, "Do your mind wash thing and leave me in peace."

Ward laughed again.

"And tomorrow I will be unavailable, period. I have things to do."

"Understood" Ward replied, trying his best to look appropriately scolded.

Three minutes later they were in the air. Ward leant back into his chair and closed his eyes and then started to inhale and exhale slowly and deeply. He pictured Newton, the innocent victim in everything, and then

Hilary Whelan and he cleared them from his mind. Then he thought of Cardona and Franco, and how they thought they were untouchable and the meanest of the bad guys until they had crossed paths with them, and McDermott's team. He thought about Stanyard and Willard, and how their greed had caused their demise, and he thought about the corruption that was rife within the D.E.A.

He cleared all of them from his mind.

He thought about Whymark, and how McDermott was right when he said that it was OK to be scared, and he told himself that he had been scared, and that he would never forget that feeling, but he would waste no more time thinking of Whymark as the one who got away.

He cleared Whymark well and truly from his mind.

He then thought of the good things in his life.

He thought of Lawson, McDermott and his team, and The Optician. He appreciated how rich he was to be part of something so strong and reliable.

He thought of his mother, and how much he had realised he appreciated the sacrifices that he had made when he was growing up, and he told himself that he would call her tomorrow and tell her that he did appreciate her.

And then he thought of Eloisa.

He thought of how excited he was feeling to see her, and she inspired these teenage emotions in him without ever trying. He thought of how lucky he was that such an amazing beautiful woman loved him as much as he loved her.

And then he gently and quickly fell into a deep sleep surrounded by an immense feeling of contentment.

He woke up just as they were descending into JFK airport.

He looked across at Lawson who was now smiling. He was going to ask why he looked so pleased with himself, but then he realised that he had no doubt arranged to meet with at least one woman as soon as they were back in New York and so he just smiled back.

Five minutes later they were sitting in the car that Lawson had left there what seemed like only an hour ago.

"Home please driver," he said to Lawson.

"Of course sir," Lawson replied, "Everything is very good in my world right now."

Ward ignored him. Just to irritate him.

They drove a mile before Lawson spoke again.

"Tackler has found me an apartment and will have it purchased by tomorrow," he said.

"Already?"

"Yes. While you were sleeping like a baby I was delving into the realms of real estate purchase," he replied.

"Where is it?"

"I don't know."

"How many rooms does it have?"

"I don't know."

"How much was it?"

"I don't know."

"What do you know about it?" Ward asked.

"I know that it is unfurnished, and at 9:00am tomorrow morning Tackler has set up a meeting with a girl called Jenna who will collect me and take me there," he replied.

"Where are you staying tonight?"

"You want the details?"

"No," Ward replied.

They drove the rest of the way in silence.

Lawson was clearly happy thinking about whatever he was going to be doing after he had dropped him off, and Ward was enjoying the silence and calm after the last couple of days.

He brought the car to a stop just down from Ward's apartment block.

"Thanks for everything Mike. Enjoy your time off and I'll call you as soon as I am ready to go to Oregon," Ward said as he extended his hand.

Lawson shook it firmly.

"You enjoy your downtime too Ryan. And just remember, check the back seat," he said, as he watched Ward step out of the car, and then pulled quickly away heading towards the latest lucky lady.

Ward breathed in deeply and took in the smell of New York. The air was warm and the smells were still thick in the air. He could smell the car engines and restaurants and it really did smell of the city that never slept. It was his favourite smell in the world.

It was the smell of home to Ryan Ward.

FORTY THREE

DUMBO – New York

Ward turned his key in the lock, opened the door and walked into his apartment.

Eloisa was standing next to the worktop and as she saw him, she shrieked and threw down the towel she was holding before running across to him and jumping up, into his arms.

He caught her, and she wrapped her arms tightly around his neck, and he instantly dropped his grab bag that he had been carrying. Over her shoulder he could see the dining table set for two and four tall candles flickering gently.

"I've missed you so much," she whispered in his ears, before kissing him slowly and passionately.

He savoured the taste of her, and he instantly fell under her spell, like he always did whenever he was in her company.

"I've missed you too," he whispered, in between kissing her back equally as passionately, "More than you realise."

She uncrossed her legs, which were wrapped tightly around his back, and dropped to the floor.

"Dinner will be ready in fifteen minutes," she said, "Time for you to grab a shower," she added, gently pulling at his tee shirt in mock disgust.

He kissed her again and then said,

"I want to know all about your last few days"

"I'll tell you over dinner but first, clean up and put on one of your crisp, white shirts for me."

He smiled at her and kissed her on the cheek before heading for the bathroom.

He turned on the shower and then stripped his clothes off slowly, item by item.

It was a symbolic gesture that he carried out whenever he returned home from a mission. He saw it as stripping away the layers of violence, deceit and hate that he subjected himself every time he went into the field, and once he was naked, he felt normal again.

Ryan Ward the assassin, the warrior and the killer was now just a pile of clothes on the bathroom floor. In his nudity, and laid completely bare, he was just a normal guy, who had a different skillset to the majority of the men on the planet.

He stepped into the shower and stretched his arms out and put his hands against the cubicle wall and he let the hot water consume his neck and his back. It felt soothing and it felt calming.

He lifted his head slightly and the water bore down on top of his head. He felt a dull sensation as the high pressured water made contact with the cut that Whymark had put in his head, but he quickly told himself that what had happened had now gone and everything was about looking forward. He decided right then to never, ever give Gill Whymark another thought.

He used shower gel and a flannel to wash himself vigorously from head to toe, and five minutes after stepping into the shower, he turned the tap off and felt like a new man as he stepped out.

He dried himself off and selected a pair of dark blue jeans from his wardrobe, and slid them on without feeling the need to put underwear on first. He then dried his hair roughly with the towel and styled it with his fingers, nodding at himself in the mirror that he was happy with it after he had done. He selected the right cologne, Eloisa had a preference for one specific type of aftershave from one of the French fashion houses, and he covered his whole torso and neck with a light spray. Finally, he took a brand new white shirt from his cupboard and put it on, leaving the last three buttons undone.

Then he walked back into the living area.

Eloisa was already sitting at the dining table, with an expensive looking piece of steak, and a sprinkling of roasted vegetables, expertly laid out on the plate in front of her. On the plate opposite, there was twice as much food displayed equally as fancily.

She poured some red wine slowly into his glass as he approached the table, unable to take her eyes off of him for one second.

"God, you are gorgeous," she said to him softly.

He reached the table, leant down and kissed her softly on the neck. She groaned with pleasure for a moment and he took his lips away from her and went and sat down opposite her.

"All good things come to her who waits," he said, and smiled at her, "But I swear you get more beautiful and more desirable every single time I see you," he added, and tilted his wine glass towards her before taking a sip.

"Did everything work out for you in Florida?" she asked as they began eating.

He spent the next ten minutes giving her a brief overview of what had happened, and the majority of that time was spent explaining about the incident with Whymark, and how the only people he thought of when he thought the end had arrived was her and his mom.

"Do you think it's sad that I'm only really loved by two people?" he asked her.

"It depends how you look at it I guess," she replied.

"Is there any other way to look at it?"

"Of course there is."

"How should I look at it then?"

"I work with so many people who are unhappy," she started, "Sure, they are married, and some of them have kids, but they all look miserable most of the time. They have the love of their partners or kids, but that love doesn't seem to inspire them or consume them," she added, gazing into space for a moment before continuing,

"So maybe you should look at it this way. What is that love worth?" she asked.

"I doubt any love is equal to a child's love for their parents," Ward replied.

"Really?" Eloisa responded, "Every day in my job I see children that are abused by parents, sold by parents or killed by parents, because they have become a hindrance. Love can be destroyed Ryan. Let me ask that another way."

"I'm listening."

"You might only have unconditional and deep lying love for me and your mom, but would you swap that love for the love of fifty other people?"

"Of course I wouldn't, that's a silly question," he replied, almost dismissively.

"But it's not silly, is it? The unhappy people at work would probably swap the love they have, for a love where they feel appreciated, valued, respected, desired and important. So you actually have the love of fifty people rolled into just two," she said.

"But when it came to it, they wouldn't really swap it, would they?" he asked, trying to find fault in what he could already see was a pretty flawless argument from her.

"Well as over fifty per cent of them are having affairs and cheating on their partners, I would say that they would swap it in a heartbeat," she added with a smile.

He knew she was right. To continue trying to find a weak link in her argument was a pointless exercise. If he did so, he would just be being petty.

"I really am lucky, aren't I?" he asked, "If I ever do see Whymark again, I'll shake his hand and thank him for making me see how rich I am."

"A woman is always right Ryan, it's how the world works," she said, and stuck her tongue out to tease him.

"Agreed and understood," Ward replied, "Now tell me about your work."

"The last two days I have spent looking into this Reverend Solomon Tower animal," she said and then went quiet for a few moments.

"The guy in Oregon He's that bad?"

"I don't know if it's him, or the stupid liberal society that we have become, where we allow people to set up effectively a completely self-sufficient town under the sign of religion, and then people are terrified of upsetting the liberal apple cart, and so the local authorities hear the whispers yet chose to ignore them, so they can't be accused of not valuing diversity or religious beliefs. It gets me down. If I didn't have you to put right this stupid world we have created, I think I would go mad," she replied.

He clearly understood how she felt. He was in a unique position where he didn't have to adhere to the stupid liberal rules. He respected everyone for their beliefs and culture, but the moment people did something bad, they became the bad guys against his good guy, and that was a totally non-discriminatory fight. His world was simple.

"I have everything you need to know about him in this file here," she said, pushing her chair back and moving to stand up.

He put his hand on hers.

"Not now Eloisa. I'll get on it tomorrow; if everything is in the file then I have everything that I need. I'll deal with it, as I always do, and I will fix that problem. Do you believe me?" he softly asked.

"You know I do Ryan," she replied, sitting down and pulling her chair back under the table, "I love you so much. You are right, we both need to switch off and enjoy this brief window we have together."

They spent the next couple of hours talking about the future. After some lengthy discussion they agreed that in three years' time they would both walk away from their respective worlds and buy a family house in the Mediterranean. Eloisa spoke of the need to save to prepare for their future and Ward agreed, declining to mention that he had enough property and money stored away to last not only their lifetimes, but that of their great grandchildren. He thought she looked so incredibly excited and beautiful as she explained to him how, if they made the right investments, they could live comfortably in their new life; he didn't want to spoil the moment.

After they had eaten and drunk two whole bottles of wine between them, they cleaned the table and loaded the dishwasher. This was one of Ward's favourite things to do with her; it was normality in one of its most simple forms.

"That's everything," she said to him as she wiped the last crumb of food from the kitchen worktop and she slowly put her arms around his neck and kissed him slowly and deeply.

He took her hand and led her into the bedroom.

She started to unbutton his shirt, one button at a time, kissing his chest as she did so, and she let it drop to the floor when the last of the buttons was undone. She then slowly undid his jeans and dropped them to the floor she pulled him forward, so that he stepped out of them, he was completely naked. She then took his hand, walked him over to the bed, and pulled out a pair of handcuffs from her bag.

"Turn around," she whispered in his ear.

He turned around slowly, and she put the cuffs on him, and then walked him to the end of the bed.

"Sit!" she demanded, and he sat on the bed.

She took his legs by the ankles and swung them around so that he was sitting in the middle of the bed with his back hard against the headboard.

She then stood before him and started to undress herself, very slowly and very deliberately, stopping only to tease him by leaning down to kiss him hard and stroking him lightly between his legs.

When she was completely naked, she climbed onto the bed and straddled him, and they slowly joined to become one person. She moved against him slowly to begin with, and then faster to get him close to climax and then she slowed right down again. Her perfect breasts brushed over his face as she moved slowly against him, and all of his senses were heightened to the point that every light touch that her fingertips made on his skin, felt like a small but pleasurable electrical charge running through his body. She kept this up for over an hour, and after they had both climaxed, she undid his cuffs and they made slow, intense love with their bodies entwined and sliding against each other in the pool of sweat that they were creating.

When they had finished, Eloisa placed her head on his chest and he stroked her hair until she fell into a deep and satisfied sleep.

He watched her sleeping and he felt so complete and lost in her, that he knew right then, he was going to spend the rest of his life with her.

He couldn't remember falling asleep when he woke up in the morning, and he couldn't remember her getting up to leave, but she was gone.

He looked at the clock on the bedside table and saw it was 9:45 am. It had been the longest he had slept in a long time.

He got up did his daily workout of sit ups, press ups and squat thrusts, and then he showered.

He felt so alive and energetic that as he washed himself, he drew up a list of things that he had to do.

He came up with three things that were very important and needed doing before he could focus on the guy in Oregon.

As he ate some toast and drank a cup of coffee, he read through the file of the Reverend Solomon Tower and he then read it again.

After finishing the file for the second time, he knew that he was going to kill him.

FORTY FOUR

DUMBO – New York

The first thing he had decided to do was call his mother in Ireland.

He walked out of his apartment building and walked a couple of blocks to a payphone on a quiet street. He slid his fully loaded call card into the slot and dialled her number.

"Hello?"

"Hi, it's me."

"Hello son. Everything OK?" she asked.

"Everything's fine. I just wanted to talk to you," he replied.

"Are you sure everything is OK?" she asked again, concern in her voice.

"I promise it is."

"So, what have you been up to?"

"Just the usual really, work and more work," he replied, "Something happened at work that made me think of you, and I just wanted to tell you that I appreciate everything you have ever done for me."

"What happened?" she asked with concern in her voice.

"It was just a guy at work. He lost his mum recently and he was telling me that he regrets not telling her how much he loved her and appreciated her enough," he lied.

"Poor boy," she said, "You need to be a good friend and be there for him and listen to him. That will be what he needs right now."

"I am mum. It just made me realise that I don't tell you often enough. You worked so hard to get me through school and college, and you must have been drained all of the time, but you found the strength to go out and work more, and it was all for me. I would do anything for you and give you anything, you know that right?" he asked, trying to stem the emotion that he could feel rising up in his throat.

"But you give me everything son," she replied.

"Do I? Do I really?" he asked, "I spend most of my time thousands of miles away, and I call you when work isn't in the way, but I don't spend enough time with you. Even the visit I had a couple of weeks ago was brief," he added, referring to an overnight visit he had recently paid when he had gone to Dublin to take out a child trafficker.

"It doesn't work like that son. You give me a smile every morning when I wake up. You might think that I let you go, but I never have really. You will always be my baby boy. I did what I had to do to give you the best chance of succeeding in this life; no one gives you anything for free."

"But you did more than could be expected."

"And I got more back than I could ever have hoped for," she replied, "Every test you took at school and passed, I was so proud, every exam you took and passed I was even more proud of you, and then when you went to one of the best universities in the world, I was so proud I could have burst. You motivated me son. Nothing I ever did felt like a chore or hard work. It always felt like a purpose. Do you think I could have done that if you were like a lot of the other kids, little ragamuffins who were always getting in trouble? No, of course I couldn't," she added, answering her own question.

"But I don't tell you often enough."

"You tell me every day. I see the life that you have created for yourself and I am so proud. Everyone around here knows that you have some big computer job with the American government, and they always ask me how you are getting on. So I brag about you every day, and I know that you love me and appreciate me as much as any son loves his mum in the world, so don't you worry about that," she replied.

Ward felt so happy. She did know, he knew that now, and while he didn't say it very often, he realised that he didn't need to say it. He just needed to make her proud.

"But there is one thing that I want from you," she said

"Name it?"

"When are you going to find a pretty young girl and start giving me some grandchildren? I won't be this young and sprightly forever, I want to enjoy them while I can still move."

"I have someone," he replied, a comment that caught him off-guard as much as it did his mother.

"Who is she? How long? Tell me about her?" she said excitedly.

He spent the next few minutes telling his mum all about Eloisa, leaving out the part about him effectively being her own private assassin, although he knew, with almost certainty that his mother would approve of it. She listened carefully, asking questions mainly about her leaning towards wanting children or not, and when he had finished talking about her she said,

"I expect to see her over here with you in Ireland within the month. No excuses or arguing. Do you understand?"

"I promise mum, we will be there within a month," he replied.

"I have to go, I have to ring Mags to tell her, speak soon son, I love you," she said and the line went dead.

He stood in the phone booth holding the phone in his hand and he smiled to himself.

He knew how lucky he was to be her son, and he was happy that she would now be running around Fermoy in County Cork, telling anyone who would listen about her son and his woman.

He put the phone back and walked out into the morning sunlight feeling ten feet tall.

Park Avenue – New York

The next thing on the 'to do' list was to head over to Nicole-Louise and Tacklers to get them to look at the

Reverend Solomon Tower's file, and to start setting things up so that he could meet him face to face. He jumped in a cab and he was knocking on their apartment door twenty minutes later.

Nicole-Louise opened the door.

"Hello Stranger."

"Have you missed me?"

She ignored him.

He walked into the apartment and Tackler was at his desk, tapping away on his keyboard as usual,

"You look busy," he said.

"I'm just sorting the payments for our friends' new apartment," Tackler replied, "He's not very domesticated, is he?"

"You could say that," Ward replied, and they both smirked, "Where have you set him up?" he asked.

"Three blocks away," Tackler replied.

Ward smiled. He thought back to when Tackler had initially met Lawson, and the jealousy that he had towards him, and now he was setting him up to live three blocks away.

Lawson's ability to charm knew no limit.

"I take it you are here about this thing in Oregon that you mentioned?" Nicole-Louise asked.

"I am indeed."

Nicole-Louise stood there staring at him, as she always did when he returned after being away.

"Happy with how I am feeling?" he asked her.

She studied him carefully for a further thirty seconds without speaking and eventually said,

"I've seen you worse," holding a tone that he could not establish was sarcastic or serious.

"Can you both read through this and start setting the wheels in motion for me to start moving on it later today. He's a nasty character, stopping him needs to be done quickly."

"Let me look at it first," Tackler said, "Then I can allocate her the easy parts," he added.

Nicole-Louise rolled her eyes.

"Good idea," Ward replied, and pulled the file from under her arm and walked the few steps over to his workstation and placed the file down.

"Is that his place?" he asked, looking at the interior of an apartment that was on his screen.

"Yes. Three bedrooms and he insisted on a utility room that was soundproofed," Tackler replied.

Ward raised his eyebrows.

"I can't say I am surprised knowing Mike, but I'm impressed that you found somewhere that already had one."

"I was spoilt for choice," Tackler replied, "The whole of New York seems to be into kinky stuff. Except me," he added.

"Maybe if you knew what romance was I would let you beat me and punish me," Nicole-Louise said from behind them.

"Really?" Tackler asked excitedly.

"No, not really you idiot," she replied.

Ward laughed out loud, and Tackler sank back into his chair.

"I'll be back this afternoon if that's OK to make a plan for getting to meet that scumbag in Oregon," he said as he headed towards the door.

"See you then," Nicole-Louise said.

Tackler just grunted something inaudible.

Harlem – New York

The last thing he had to do was to face something that he had been putting off for longer than he should have. He hailed a cab and headed over to Harlem. The cab pulled up in a nice street and all the houses were well presented and cared for. The house he wanted had a Stars and Stripes flag flying proudly on the front lawn.

He walked up the pathway to the house and knocked on the door three times and slowly. He wasn't sure of the welcome that he was going to receive here.
The door was opened after about ten seconds by a pretty woman in her late-thirties, who was of African American heritage. She had a slim figure, and she had thick, black, shoulder length hair that complemented her features perfectly.
"Can I help you?" she asked politely.
"My name is Ryan, is your husband there?" he asked tentatively.
She studied him for a moment and looked him up and down.
"Are you one of them?" she asked.
He had no idea what she meant but replied anyway,
"No I'm not," he said.
A man's voice came from inside the house,
"Who is it?"
It was a voice that Ward recognised immediately.

"Just Ryan?" she asked, looking at him even more suspiciously.

"No Mrs Gilligan," he replied, "My name is Ryan Ward."

Her eyes instantly lit up, and she flung her arms wide and hugged him, so Ward hugged her back,

"Come in, please Ryan," she said, beckoning him into the hallway.

He walked in and closed the door. He followed her ten feet down the hallway, and through a doorway that was open, and into a lounge.

Where Sean Gilligan was sitting on a sofa, feet up, watching the Yankee's on TV.

Gilligan looked up at him and smiled.

"How's it going Marvin?" Ward asked, in reference to the fact that Gilligan was the spitting image of former boxing champion Marvin Hagler.

Gilligan stood up and opened his arms.

"I'm not hugging you," Ward said, and smiled at him.

"That was for my wife," he replied.

Ward stepped forward and shook his hand.

Gilligan looked remarkably well for someone who had died, and then been resuscitated just two weeks ago. But then again, he was as strong as an ox, and built like one too, so if any guy could survive being shot, it would be him.

"Can I get you boys a beer?" his wife asked.

"That would be nice thank you," Ward replied.

"Yes please," Gilligan replied.

She walked out of the room.

"I'm sorry I haven't been here before now, I've been busy. You know how it is," he said.

"I understand. You are here now, that's all that matters," Gilligan replied.

"She looked pleased to see me?" he asked, before suddenly realising why, "You got the money I take it?"

"It's not the money," Gilligan replied.

"Must be my good looks then?"

"You saved my life, do you know that?"

"You were dead when I left you."

"I was, but they used the defibrillator and got my heart going again. They said that the time you spent putting pressure on my wound was the difference between me living and dying," Gilligan replied, "I'm alive because of you," he added.

Ward smiled and he felt a sense of pride rush through his body.

"Which is ironic really because you spend most of your day killing people," Gilligan said, and laughed loudly.

"I was sure that I couldn't save you."

"Want to know the weird thing about all of that?" Gilligan asked.

"Not really, but I came to visit you so may as well listen," he replied with a smile.

"I remember everything. As I was laying there on the cold floor, begging you to take care of my boys, I looked into your eyes, and I knew you would. I felt a safety and calm consume me, and I knew that you would do the right thing. I died happy and all because of you," Gilligan said, his eyes almost glazing over as he recalled the moment.

"But you shouldn't have told your wife about me Sean. You know the rules."

"I didn't."

"Well she seemed pretty pleased to see me and seemed to know who I was."

"When I came round in hospital, I was a little delirious due to all the drugs they had given me. All I kept saying was tell Ward I am OK, tell Ward I am OK. When she asked who you were I told her. She's my wife, she should know the man who saved her husband's life," Gilligan argued.

He was right. Ward knew that, she had every right to know.

Mrs Gilligan walked back in carrying two bottles of beer.

She sat down next to her husband and said,

"He's explained to me that you are emotionless and don't do dramatic, but I want you to know that me and the boys are so incredibly grateful to you Mr Ward."

Ward genuinely didn't know what to say. So in the end, he just said,

"No worries."

"See. Man of many words," Gilligan said to his wife, and she smiled a reassuring smile at Ward to let him know that it was fine for him to say as much or as little as he wanted to say.

"You are more understanding than your husband," he replied, and smiled back at her, "So, desk job or out for good?"

"Can you see me at a desk?"

"Not really. So, you are out for good. Have you any idea what you want to do?" Ward asked.

"I'm not out at all," Gilligan replied, "I only know how to do one thing, and we have spoken about this at length, and we've both agreed that I will start to ease myself back in a few weeks when I pass the physical tests," he added.

Ward wasn't surprised with Gilligan's decision; he even expected it sitting opposite him, seeing how well he had recovered.

"You didn't even pass the physical on selection, so how are you going to do it now?" he asked, holding a deadpan expression on his face.

Mrs Gilligan burst out laughing.

"I told him that," she said.

"And I am available to work with you as soon as I am fit," Gilligan said.

Ward stood up and put his half-drunk bottle down.

"One step at a time Sean," he said, "We'll discuss it when you are back in the field."

Sean Gilligan stood up and hugged Ward and whispered in his ear,

"Thank you. I mean it. I owe you my life, and I will be there when you need me. And you will need me, we both know that," he said.

"It was lovely to meet you Mrs Gilligan" Ward said, "I'll see myself out," he added, and he walked out of the room before the emotion of the moment could hit him.

As he walked out of Gilligan's door, he thought about the mistakes that he had made in Miami, and that he would never make them again. He thought about how lucky he was to have the love that he had, and he thought about Gilligan and how good it felt seeing him again. But most of all he thought about the Reverend Solomon Tower, and how he was going to inflict the pain on him

that he deserved, before he killed him. He felt good and he felt focussed.
He no longer felt tired, he felt alive, strong and ready to take on the world.

Ryan Ward felt invincible.

Part Four

Gun

The first person to die was his math teacher, Mr Harper. He slowly walked the halls of the school with tears in his eyes, armed with the intention of walking proudly into the gymnasium to kill all of the jocks who had made his life so miserable for the past two years. As he passed Harper's class, he caught a glimpse of the teacher through the glass panel on the door, and he immediately remembered the ridicule that he had exposed him to in front of his classmates just last week, when he had flunked his test, and he felt a rage surge through his body.

He placed the holdall that he was carrying on the floor, before carefully unzipping it with two hands, and taking out the AK-47,and the two hand guns that she had provided him with, and he took a deep breath. He swung the strap of the machine gun over his shoulder and tucked one of the handguns into the waistband of his pants. Clutching the other handgun in his hand, he opened the door to the classroom, walked in, and stood in front of Harper's desk, his knuckles white through the tightness with which he was gripping the handle. Harper looked up at him and went white.

Then he squeezed the trigger of the gun three times.

The bullets smashed into Harper's chest and he died instantly, the impact of the bullets knocked him forcibly off of his chair. As he spun round, the kids sitting at their desks behind him screamed, and a number of them fell to the floor, desperately attempting to become invisible to his eyes which scanned quickly left to right.

But they were not invisible. He saw them all.

He tucked the handgun into his waistband and then gripped the AK-47 tightly in both hands. Without any hesitation, and with no particular aim, he lowered the short barrel slightly and squeezed the trigger. The burst of automatic gunfire could be heard throughout the school. Four of his classmates died instantly, two others who were hit in that first burst, would die later that day.

He walked out of the classroom and into the hallway with the intention of heading towards the gym. To his right, he saw two teachers running towards him. He knew Miss Bloom and Mr Keeting well, they had both taught him, and they had both been sympathetic to his inability to mix with other kids. As they got to within twenty feet of him, he squeezed the trigger hard and the volley of bullets stopped them both in their tracks immediately, ripping through them like a knife through butter. He noticed Miss Bloom's white blouse turning a deep crimson red, as she fell to her left and smashed into the lockers that lined the hallway, before Keeting fell forwards, their lives terminated by him just, because they were in the wrong place at the wrong time.

He started to move forward along the hallway, stepping over the two bodies of the more likeable teachers, and as he passed over them, he noticed that Keeting was still moving, and so he squeezed the trigger hard once again and emptied out the magazine into his torso. He then suddenly remembered that he had left the spare magazines in the holdall, and so he turned and walked back towards Harper's classroom. A security guard appeared at the end of the hallway heading towards him, desperately screaming into his radio, and holding a handgun in his right hand. He threw the machine gun to the floor and grabbed the two hand guns from his waistband.

And then stepped back into Harper's class and closed the door.

The kids inside were crying and screaming at him. He could hear some of them calling his name, begging him to stop, but he ignored them.

She told him that this would happen, and that everyone would suddenly want to be his friend.

He turned and scanned the room.

Josh Gallagher was hiding at the back of the room, using two girls and a boy as a human shield. This was the same Josh Gallagher who hadn't been hiding when he and three other kids had forced his head down the toilet and flushed it last month. He raised both guns and pointed them at the terrified huddle and fired both of them at the same time. The bullets from the gun in his left hand hit the two girls in the chest, and because his right hand was raised slightly higher, the two bullets fired from that gun blew the boys head apart. All three of them collapsed like a house of cards in front of him, and Gallagher's human shield had vanished. He then lowered the gun in his right hand slightly and fired four shots into Josh Gallagher's stomach. He died instantly.

Out of the corner of his eye, he caught a glimpse of the security guard peering through the pane of glass in the door, and so he fired both guns towards him, counting as he pulled the trigger. The gun in his left hand ran out of bullets first, and so he dropped it to the floor and clasped both hands around the remaining weapon, and fired five more shots into the door and then stopped firing. Two seconds later, the guards head appeared through the glass for a brief moment and then ducked out of sight again.

He knew he only had one bullet left.

He lifted the gun to his head, pressed it hard against his temple, closed his eyes and pulled the trigger. Russel Collyfield, just sixteen years old, died instantly.

In Washington D.C., the woman monitoring the police radios in Missouri State heard the news five minutes later. She picked up the phone and dialled a New York number.
'The Missouri Kid came through' she said, before listening to the person on the end of the line and saying, 'I will keep you informed about the other two.'

She then looked across her desk at her colleague sitting opposite and said, 'How close is the kid in Dallas?'

'Just a day or two at most,' he replied.

Printed in Great Britain
by Amazon